WHEN THE GODS AREN'T GODS

BOOK TWO OF THE THEOGONY

Chris Kennedy

D0875127

Chris Kennedy Publishing
Virginia Beach, VA

Chris Kennedy/Chris Kennedy Publishing
2052 Bierce Dr.
Virginia Beach, VA 23454
http://chriskennedypublishing.com/

Publisher's Note: This is a work of fiction. Names, characters, places, and
incidents are a product of the author's imagination. Locales and public
names are sometimes used for atmospheric purposes. Any resemblance to
actual people, living or dead, or to businesses, companies, events, institu-
tions, or locales is completely coincidental.

Ordering Information:
Quantity sales. Special discounts are available on quantity purchases by cor-
porations, associations, and others. For details, contact the "Special Sales
Department" at the address above.

When the Gods Aren't Gods/ Chris Kennedy. -- 1st ed.
ISBN 978-0990333500

As always, this book is for my wife and children. I would like to thank Linda, Jennie and Jimmy, who took the time to critically read the work and make it better. Any mistakes that remain are my own. I would like to thank my mother, without whose steadfast belief in me, I would not be where I am today. Thank you.

Author's Notes

Note: When more than one race refers to a planet or star in Janissaries, the same name is used by both races in order to prevent confusion. Also on the topic of planet naming, the normal convention for planets is to take the name of the parent star and add a lower case letter (i.e., Tau Ceti 'b'). The first planet discovered in a system is usually given the designation 'b' and later planets are given subsequent letters as they are found. In order to prevent confusion in Janissaries, the closest planet to the star in a star system is given the letter 'a', with the rest of the planets given subsequent letters in order of their proximity to the star.

Note: The 'Dark Side' of the Moon. There is no 'dark side' of the moon. Like many bodies in our solar system and among the stars, the moon is 'tidally locked,' where the moon makes one revolution about its axis at the same rate that it makes one revolution around the Earth. Because of this, the same side of the moon is always facing the Earth as it orbits around it. Even though we never see the other side of the moon from Earth (we have seen it through various probes and explorer craft), the 'dark side' gets as much sunlight as the side we can see. At a length of just over 27 days, the moon's day is just a lot longer than ours.

"...The art of war is of vital importance to the State. It is a matter of life and death, a road either to safety or to ruin. Hence it is a subject of inquiry which can on no account be neglected."

— Sun Tzu, The Art of War

Prologue

TSS *Vella Gulf,* Naval Space Station Oceana, Virginia Beach, VA, June 26, 2019

Calvin was beat. Closing the door to his stateroom, he fell heavily onto his bunk without taking off his flight suit. Stiffening, he rolled back over and looked toward one of the empty corners of his small cabin. Sighing, he interlaced his fingers behind his head and asked, "How long do you intend to watch me?"

Arges dropped his shield and came into view. "It is interesting that you can do that," he said. "Did you know I was here or were you just guessing?"

"I've always had the ability to tell when someone close by was watching me," said Calvin.

"Interesting," answered Arges. "You are the closest to Awareness."

"What does that mean?" asked Calvin.

"Before Atlantis fell," replied Arges, "all humans were able to talk telepathically with each other."

"Wait," said Calvin. "What do you mean, 'before Atlantis fell'?"

"I don't want to talk about it," said Arges, "but suffice it to say, the things that you believe in, the things that you 'know' to be the truth, are often not the truth. In fact, many of the things that humans attribute to mythology, old wives' tales, and to science fiction and fantasy, are in reality things that happened long ago and, although

1

not completely forgotten, have been so distorted by oral tradition as to not retain most of their original truth."

This didn't help explain things. If anything, it only confused Calvin further. "Why don't you want to talk about it?"

"I am not a warrior," said Arges, "and Atlantis' fall was traumatic to me. It is literally too painful to talk about."

"Wait, you were there?" asked Calvin. "How old are you?"

"We are each somewhat over 5,000 of your years old, give or take a few centuries. We long ago figured out how to preserve our bodies, extending our lives nearly indefinitely. And, as you have long suspected, we are telepaths...just like you."

Chapter One

Moon Base Alpha, Dark Side of the Moon, December 1, 2019

Calvin flew slowly over the sprawling base on the back side of the moon. It had grown considerably since his last visit. "Really?" he asked his weapon systems officer (WSO), Captain Imagawa 'Samurai' Sadayo. "They're really going to call it Moon Base Alpha?"

"*Hai!*" the Japanese man replied. "The nations couldn't agree on a name, and that was what everyone up here was already calling it. You should come up here more often."

"Well, there's no doubt that I need to get out more," said Calvin. "Between all of the media events and the governmental meetings, I definitely need to take some time off."

Since they had returned from their first mission to space, Calvin's life had been a blur. A little over a year prior, three aliens had appeared to Lieutenant Commander Shawn Hobbs, or 'Calvin' as he was known in his F-18 squadron. Calling themselves the Psiclopes, they said they had a ship and needed to go home, but didn't have anyone to man it. The President of the United States, Bill Jacobs, had offered the United States' help and had brought 10 allied nations in on the secret. The Terran forces, under the command of Captain James Deutch, had flown the spaceship on a three month mission to the stars. Calvin, the hero of the Sino-American War of 2018, had led a special forces platoon that had captured a piece of alien technology on the mission. He had also led a squadron of space fighters that had destroyed an alien battlecruiser.

His exploits had made him a hero to most of the Earth, and he was the focal point of the effort to form a new, unified planetary government. He had spent the last few months shuttling between national capitals, giving speeches and signing autographs. None of that was anything he'd ever thought he'd do as a naval aviator, or anything he'd ever prepared for. Getting back to flying again was a blessing.

Calvin looked at the mass of buildings clustered on the otherwise barren moonscape and chuckled. "That's really too cool a name. I'm surprised that 'The Powers That Be' allowed it."

Captain Imagawa laughed. "I don't think they had much choice," he explained. "As soon as the first building was completed, Bullseye hung up a sign proclaiming it to be Moon Base Alpha. It just kind of stuck after that."

"That sounds like something he would do," Calvin replied. The executive officer of his squadron, Major Robert 'Bullseye' Pierce, appreciated a good joke. "Did you know that there was a video game named Moon Base Alpha?"

"No," replied the WSO. "Did it come out recently?"

"It came out about 10 years ago as a simulation for what an astronaut's life might be like on the moon," answered Calvin as he swung the shuttle back around toward the landing strip. "NASA developed it and gave it away on for free on the Steam gaming network. It was a pretty good game, although kind of short. You get what you pay for, I guess."

"Was it anything like this?" he asked as Calvin brought the shuttle in for a landing next to the giant hangar building.

"No, it wasn't," Calvin replied, setting the shuttle down softly. "I don't think the engineers at NASA ever thought to add in the part where aliens come and give us a technology boost."

The two men fastened their helmets, checked each other and exited the shuttle. "*Wow!*" Calvin commed after getting his first look at ground level. As part of their 'upgrade' to humanity, the Psiclopes had given the Terrans implants that allowed them to communicate via an internal radio link. "*They've accomplished a lot in the six months since we got back.*"

"*Yeah, once they got enough suits for everyone, this place became very active,*" the WSO replied. "*And yet, no matter how fast we build, there is always more that needs to be done.*"

As they approached the hangar airlock, Calvin noticed something written on the side of the wall.

Never to see the home planet
The Mother labored
Surrounded by her worshipers
Her offspring, salvation
Would it be enough?

Calvin paused to read the poem. "*Yours, I take it?*" he asked.

"*Hai,*" Samurai replied. Calvin turned where the Japanese man could see his face and raised an eyebrow. Samurai laughed. "*You'll see inside,*" he promised.

They passed through the airlock into the hangar, which was a square building nearly 3,000 feet long, 300 feet high and pressurized inside. Along one wall sat the prize of the TSS *Vella Gulf's* first cruise—a Class 2 replicator. It was a hive of activity as people fed it materials and worked knobs, switches and dials. A work of advanced technology, it could take raw materials and turn them into any finished product that it had the blueprint for, up to the size of a shuttle or space fighter. Looking at the replicator, Calvin now understood the poem. He certainly hoped their efforts would be enough.

"Hey, there!" Calvin called to a familiar face as he took off his helmet. "Fancy meeting you in a place like this."

Andrew Brown turned. "Lieutenant Commander Hobbs!" he called out in recognition. "It's good to see you again," he said, coming over to join the men.

"I like what you've done with the place," said Calvin, looking around. "How's it coming?"

"Good," said Brown. Formerly the plant manager for Boeing's Airplane Programs Manufacturing Site in Renton, Washington, Brown had a lot of experience managing massive aircraft production facilities. His last hanger had over 4.3 million square feet of manufacturing space. "We've just about finished our third shuttle. We're going to make one more of them, and then we'll start on the new fighters for you."

The conversation paused for a second as one of the new lunar dump trucks deposited its cargo of materials into the input side of the replicator. When the commotion had subsided, Brown smiled at Calvin. "I understand that I have you to thank for my promotion," he said.

"All I did was mention to a few people that I had been impressed with the facility that you ran in Washington State," Calvin replied.

"And the fact that he had exercised excellent discretion when you first met him," added Imagawa, who had been with Calvin when they had flown the government leaders up to what would be the site of

Moon Base Alpha. "As I remember it, you also told them that if Mr. Brown wasn't made the facility manager, you were going to stick a laser up their collective asses and set it off."

"Did I say that?" asked Calvin, feigning innocence. He looked at the former aircraft plant manager. "I don't remember doing that, and, even if I did, I can't imagine a better person for this position than you."

"Well," said Mr. Brown, "for my part, I can't imagine knowing that this facility existed and not being a part of it, so I thank you. Whatever you did. It's a challenge, certainly, but it's a worthwhile one, knowing that what I'm doing could make a difference in the defense of our planet."

That was a sobering thought. "Like I said, I can't think of anyone else I'd rather have in charge here," replied Calvin. "Keep pumping out the ships; we're going to need them."

"Do you know when you're going to go back out again?" the plant manager asked.

"We just found out," answered Calvin. The manager waited expectantly. "I'm sorry," Calvin said, "but I can't tell you yet. It's classified." The manager's face fell.

"It sure would be helpful if we had a full load out of fighters in seven months, though," said Imagawa to Calvin.

"You're right, Sadayo," Calvin agreed, "it *would* be very helpful if we had seven more fighters in seven months. I'd be pretty happy if we did."

The two military men paused to watch the thoughtful look that came over Mr. Brown's face as he considered. "Hmmm..." he said. "That's going to be tough." He opened up a binder he was carrying and looked at a diagram that was on a clipboard inside it. After a few seconds, he started drawing arrows and scratching things out. "We've got to get more shuttles finished so that we can continue to bring people and materials up here. That remains the bottleneck, so we've got to get those finished...We also have to do a couple of production runs on space suits...and more lunar diggers...and mines, the defense council is *screaming* for more space mines...and we *have* to get the new replicator finished for Epsilon Eridani before you go...hmmm." He pulled a calculator out of a pocket and started punching in numbers. "We could probably shift some of the smaller stuff to the replicator on the *Vella Gulf*," he decided. "I could probably get a few open cycles on it...and push that shuttle to after the seventh fighter..." He put the calculator away and shut the binder. "It's possible, but it's going to require some major revisions to the work plan." He smiled at the two men. "We'll get it done, Calvin. You'll have them."

Calvin smiled. It was the first time that the man had ever called him by his callsign. "Thanks," he said. "I hope we won't need them, but it would be much better to have them than not."

"You got it!" Mr. Brown said. "OK, I've gotta go make some people's lives difficult. Good seeing you." He walked off like a man on a mission. "Hey, get that truck moving! You, there! Pick up that molecular adaptor before someone steps on it! Is this your first time on the moon? Stop staring and get back to work. We've got a schedule to keep! *Be careful! Do you know how much that costs?*"

Calvin smiled at Imagawa. "I knew he was the right man for the job." They watched a couple of minutes longer as the nose of the next shuttle began poking out of the replicator. As the shuttle was 'born,' he could easily see why Samurai had referred to the replicator as 'Mother.' It was amazing that they had almost completed their third shuttle. The amount of material it took to make a shuttle was staggering, especially considering the fact that all of the materials had to be brought to the moon in the three shuttles that they currently had available. They really needed the other shuttle that they had left at Epsilon Eridani, but he was sure that one was being put to good use there.

The shuttles that they had were being worked nearly 24 hours a day. He wasn't sure what the mean time between failures was for an advanced technology shuttle, but he knew they had to be approaching it pretty quickly. They were rushing the required maintenance, which was never a good thing. Hopefully, having this next one would allow them a little more time to catch up on some of the maintenance they needed to do on the ones they already had.

A group of five people was standing at the end of the replicator pointing at something inside it. About 10 feet of the shuttle was now showing, and there were a variety of trucks and anti-gravity sleds that were marshalling near the end of the replicator. Even though things weighed less on the moon, they still had the same mass and inertia. A shuttle measuring 200 feet in length had a lot of both.

With a start, Calvin realized how mesmerizing it was to watch the shuttle emerge from the replicator. Sadayo must have written his poem after watching the last one come out. Although it was interesting to watch, the process was still going to take at least another couple of hours to complete. He had more important things to do. "Let's go," he said to Samurai.

The two men put their helmets back on, checked each other and went back through the airlock to the surface of the moon. At some point, a tunnel was going to connect the hangar with the living area, but it hadn't been completed yet. It was inconvenient to have to go outside, but by now Calvin had put his suit on enough times that it was second nature. The two men walked across the 50 feet of open area to the main base entrance. Calvin looked at the shuttle sitting on the ramp and the army of people unloading the raw materials and building supplies that he had brought up.

Flying a shuttle was a lot different than flying an air-breathing airplane. After every flight in an F-18, he had to go into Maintenance Control and write up all of the things that were wrong with it. The shuttle was a big step forward. It had its own small artificial intelligence (AI) that not only kept a running log of all of the things wrong with it but also worked with the maintenance technicians to fix them. Still, he was the shuttle squadron's commanding officer, and old habits die hard, so he went by the squadron's maintenance office before going anywhere else.

"How's it going?" he asked the master chief sitting behind the desk in Maintenance Control.

"Not good, sir," replied the master chief. "All three of our birds need some serious down time. *Shuttle 02* in particular needs a major overhaul. It's AI said that it was turning itself off after its next flight and that it wouldn't come back online again until we fix some of its issues."

"Really?" asked Calvin. "I've never heard of a ship doing that before. Do you think it will?"

"Sir, I've been in the aircraft maintenance business for 27 years," replied the master chief. "I have no idea if it would shut itself off, or even if it could, but I don't want to find out. I think we should just fix it, and then we wouldn't have to worry about it."

"I agree master chief," said Calvin, "and I'm happy to tell you that *04* is within an hour or two of completion. When it comes out, you can take *02* off the schedule for maintenance, followed by *01* and then *03*."

"Sir, that's great and all," said the master chief, looking at a monitor that showed the interior of the hangar and the shuttle that now had 25 feet out of the replicator, "but you know that they never work correctly when they come out of the replicator. We'll be working on *it* for at least a day or two."

"Probably," replied Calvin. "Do what you can, but don't fly *02* again until its AI is happy. If anyone on Earth complains, have them comm me."

"Thank you sir," answered the master chief. "That was really starting to worry me."

"If it worries you, master chief, it worries me," said Calvin. "Let me know if you have any other problems."

"Aye aye, sir," the master chief replied.

JFCC Space Operations Center, Vandenberg AFB, California, December 3, 2019

"I've got gate activation!" cried the airman who monitored the stargate entry system for Strategic Command's Joint Functional Component Command (JFCC) for Space. "Activation of Stargate #2!"

"Roger," replied his supervisor, who knew that #2 was the 'back door' out of the Solar System. "Get me an ID on it ASAP!"

The airman watched his instrumentation carefully, changing the brightness on one of his displays as if that would make it run faster. "It's the *Vella Gulf*, sir!" he finally called. "The *Vella Gulf's* back!"

"Stand down all defenses!" ordered the supervisor. "Transmit 'Welcome home' to Captain Deutch and his crew, please."

Chapter Two

President Bill Jacobs surveyed the faces of his cabinet from his position at the head of the large conference table in the Deep Underground Command Center (DUCC). Originally envisioned in 1963, the command center was built to provide a workplace for key decision makers that would be able to survive any attack made on the United States. The command center was built under the West Wing of the White House so that the president and his team could access it at a moment's notice. It was the most secure facility on the planet, which made it the ideal place to hold strategy sessions. The only people that could penetrate its security were the Psiclopes. The president had already learned that trying to keep them out was just a waste of time, so he no longer bothered. He had nothing to hide from them, anyway, and more important things to do than worry about their spying.

You could almost tell what the news was going to be just by looking at the faces, Jacobs thought. The Secretary of Defense talked in an animated manner with the Treasury Secretary. Obviously the Defense Department had something 'new and vital' that the Secretary of Defense needed to come up with funding for. Commerce and the Interior were in a heated argument over something, probably the opening of yet another mine in a national park somewhere. The Secretary of Energy looked guarded as he talked with Labor; it looked like both good news and bad news from both of them. All of his cabinet was in attendance; the Speaker of the House, the President pro tempore of the Senate and Lieutenant Commander Hobbs were also attending in an *ex officio* status. He nodded to the vice president, seated to his left, who called the meeting to order.

"If I could have everyone's attention," said the vice president in a loud voice, "we'll get this going. We have a lot to talk about, and the president thought that it would be good to have everyone in attendance." He paused and looked at his notes. "It's been six months since the *Vella Gulf* got back from its first mission. While there's been a lot accomplished in that time, there remains a tremendous amount left to do. If an alien race invaded right now, we would not be prepared to stop it."

It was a harsh statement, but the president knew it was true. A little over a year previously, three aliens had made their presence on Earth known to Lieutenant Commander (LCDR) Shawn 'Calvin' Hobbs, who had just led a platoon that helped repulse a Chinese invasion of Seattle and Tacoma. The aliens told him that their communications link back to their home world had stopped working, and they needed help to find out what had happened. Believing that a hostile race was responsible for the outage, they had tried to find an alternate route to their home world rather than face a presumably superior force.

President Jacobs had agreed to furnish a crew for the aliens' space ship, as well as a platoon of soldiers and the personnel needed to man the ship's six fighters. He had also recruited some of the United States' allies in the recently completed war to go along on the mission. The aliens had asked to have Calvin lead both the platoon and the fighter squadron but would not say why; most assumed that it was because he had led a number of successful operations during the war, but no one was sure. The aliens had so far refused to give the United States most of their advanced technology, saying that their society had rules that forbid technology transfer unless the world had a unified planetary government.

Although the mission had not been successful in reaching the Psiclopes' home world or bringing back a replicator big enough to build battle fleet-sized space ships, they had returned with a Class 2 replicator that could build fighter-sized craft, as well as new laser technology. The Earth was stronger, but not strong enough.

President Jacobs' list of things to do included little things like forming a world government, getting politicians to rewrite centuries-old documents and stopping an alien invasion without the tools and technology necessary to do so. Oh, yeah, he also had to win an election in order to remain president, too, which involved campaigning, kissing babies and holding fundraisers...all of which took away time from doing the really important things.

"This is not a working session," continued the vice president. "If we try to solve every issue that we have at the moment, we'd be here for weeks." The president heard other lengths of time mentioned around the table. 'Years' was the most common, followed by 'decades, if ever.' "Just give a progress report and note any issues that require presidential decisions." He looked around the large table to ensure that everyone understood. "OK," he said, looking to the woman at his left, "first up is State."

As the person tasked with setting up the new world government, the president knew that the Secretary of State, Isabel Maggiano, had a lot that she was working on. "For those of you that haven't heard yet, the *Vella Gulf* just returned from its trip to Epsilon Eridani." The president knew that the ship had been badly damaged in a fight with an alien battlecruiser on its first mission, and that the quick trip to Epsilon Eridani had been taken as a 'shakedown cruise' to see how well its repairs would hold. "Its commanding officer said that it performed well on the journey. What you may not have heard is that the Epsilon Eridanians have formed a world government of their own and have petitioned for entry into the 'Terran Alliance.'"

The secretary smiled wryly at the variety of comments she heard. "Apparently it is easier to form a government when there are only two nations that have to agree. Ambassador Flowers has been very busy. Not only did he get them to work out their differences, but also he helped them establish a unified government. Similar to the way we call our planet 'Terra,' they are now calling their planet 'Domus,' which is the Latin word for 'home.' Ambassador Flowers was able to keep them from sending their ambassador to the Terran world government this time, but he said that the next time the *Vella Gulf* comes through, we should be prepared to receive her. Hopefully, there will actually *be* a Terran world government by then."

Maggiano shook her head. "Maybe this will help push things along with the nations to get the world government implemented. We currently have a draft constitution and bill of rights in place, but the devil is in the details, and we are continuing to hammer them out. I was just told yesterday by the Russian envoy that they would consider participating if one of their officers could have the executive officer position on the *Vella Gulf* the next time it goes out." She looked at the president for guidance on the request.

The president saw Calvin's hand go up but waved him off. "I am reluctant to grant them anything like this," said the president, who knew it was more of a 'demand' than a 'request.' "If we give in at the start, they'll always expect special treatment. Still, we need Russia's support, for a number of reasons. Please let them know officially that we really want their participation, but we can't guarantee any military postings, as those are made by a joint body of officers. Unofficially, you can tell them that if they join the government now, in full good faith, their officer will have the United States' vote, as well as everyone else that we can convince." That must have been good enough, the president saw, because Calvin put his hand back down.

"OK," said the vice president. "Next up, Treasury."

"I don't think that we are going to be able to make the target of spending 30% of our gross domestic product (GDP) on defense this year," he advised. "There were just too many other priorities that we already had to fund. Going forward, though, we ought to be able to meet the target as we shift around some of our spending. With everyone now expected to work, we should be able to cut some of the federal assistance programs, which will make a big difference. We are also going to reclassify some of the spending that we are doing that is related to defense, like opening new mines, under the category of 'defense spending.'" He nodded. "We'll get there next year."

The president also nodded; he had been briefed on that earlier. "Good, thanks," he said.

"Defense?" asked the vice president.

"We're proceeding across a wide variety of fronts," replied the Secretary of Defense. "With regard to our immediate security, we have mined the two stargates into the Solar System. Heavily. We estimate that any ship that is battleship-sized or smaller will be instantly destroyed, as well as several more after that, depending on their size. We are continuing to develop additional types of defenses for the stargates. If we don't stop them there, we have little hope of stopping them." Once again, the president nodded. Nothing new there.

"As far as future operations go," the Secretary of Defense continued, "we are still expecting to send the *Vella Gulf* back out in seven months. We have *got* to get either a replicator that can build ships, or find an ally to sell us some. We need to develop a fleet before the Drakuls show up." Most heads around the table nodded; several secretaries that stood to lose money to Defense looked less than thrilled.

That was the big question, the president knew. When would the Drakuls show up? As they were 10' tall bloodsucking frogs, the president hoped the answer was never; however, the Psiclopes had said that they thought the Drakuls were close by and moving in the Earth's direction. Time was running out.

"When the *Gulf* goes out, it will also have a more integrated crew," the Secretary of Defense added. "The executive officer of the ship on its last cruise will be promoted to commanding officer. LCDR Hobbs will remain in charge of both the space fighter squadron and attached special forces platoon. We are hoping to have a full squadron of space fighters this time, including six with the new laser technology that we got on the last mission. That will make them more capable, although they will still be a relatively 'light' force if they run into a group of bigger combatants." Defense nodded to the vice president. He was finished.

"DOJ?" asked the vice president.

"We're working a number of issues," noted Mark Keely, the Attorney General who led the Department of Justice. "First, we're following the progress of a number of constitutional challenges to the governmental changes we're making. Some of these have merit, so we'll have to address them." He looked at the Speaker of the House and the President pro tempore of the Senate. "Ultimately, we're probably going to need a constitutional amendment in order for the U.S. to become part of the Terran Government." Both men nodded.

Looking around the table, he could see some blank looks, so he added, "A proposal for an amendment to the Constitution requires either a two-thirds majority vote in both the House of Representatives and the Senate, or a constitutional convention called for by two-thirds of the State legislatures. In our history, no amendment has ever been proposed by constitutional convention, so that's unlikely. Once Congress proposes an amendment, it goes to each of the states for their consideration and ratification. We need it to be ratified by three-fourths of the states, or 38 of the 50. Once ratified, it gets signed into the Constitution." He paused. "It is the opinion of Justice that this process should be initiated as soon as possible, while public opinion is still in favor of a world government. If we wait for all of the coming court battles, it's possible that some of the dialogue in the process will make the amendment's passage more difficult. We can delay the court cases for a while, but not indefinitely."

Both the Speaker of the House and the President pro tempore of the Senate nodded. The Speaker said, "We understand our part in this process, and that this is the only way for us to survive as a race. While we both have some personal reservations about the integration of our nation into an overarching body where we have a loss of sovereignty, we agree that it must be done. We will begin working this afternoon to develop a quorum to get the amendment through Congress. After that, it will be up to the president and state legislatures."

"Understood," replied the Attorney General. "In conjunction with the Department of Homeland Security, we are also working on a reduction in crime and terrorism. As our new programs come online, there are going to be many organized crime syndicates and other less-than-honest individuals looking to take advantage of the situation. We intend to ask the AI on the *Vella Gulf* to point out where criminal activity is occurring and root it out. We don't need to authorize any wire taps because we will not be involved in any illegal surveillance." He could see concern on the faces of many people sitting around the table. "We have been looking at the legality of this, and there is no legislation on the use of extraterrestrial artificial intelligences in crime prosecution. We expect that Congress will need to address this going forward, but we intend to do what we can in the interim."

"Perhaps it might be good to give the country advance notice that you are going to do that," remarked the President pro tempore of the Senate. A long-time veteran of the political process, he not only knew where bodies were buried, he had a few of his own that he wanted to make sure stayed buried. "That way, people that have been operating in any 'gray' areas can make sure that everything they are involved in is above board."

"I already did that," replied the president in a no-nonsense tone of voice, "when I welcomed the Psiclopes to our planet." He thought about it a moment and then relented. "But you're right," he conceded; "we should probably give people a little notice so that they can ensure the legitimacy of what they're doing." He remembered a certain land purchase he had been considering and made a mental note to cancel the deal after the meeting. Can't be too careful, he decided.

"I'll do that," the Attorney General agreed. "That's it for Justice."

"Interior?" asked the vice president.

"I have to protest the rhenium mine that has been proposed for the National Park Service land in the Eldorado Wilderness area of Arizona," stated the Secretary of the Interior. "They are going to *destroy* valuable park land that *cannot be replaced!* It was bad enough when some of the other mines were reopened, but this one goes too far!"

"I also want to protest this mine," agreed the Secretary of Health and Human Services. "Not the mine itself, but the fact that all of its production is slated for defense. At least some of it needs to go toward medical applications. Rhenium is needed for a large number of things like treating restenosis and liver tumors. *All* of it right now is going to defense."

"*We've got to have it,*" said Defense. He had known this argument was coming. "Rhenium is used for a number of critical defense purposes like rocket thrusters, high temperature thermocouples, and molybdenum superconducting alloys. There is a *lot* of it that goes into making the space ships, space fighters and shuttles that are our first line of defense. Not only do we need all of this mine's potential production, but we also need every last bit that we can get, worldwide!"

The president nodded. Defense may have gone a little strong on the argument, but he had a point. Americans *wanted* more park land; the Earth *needed* more spacecraft. "Open the mine," said the president, "and earmark its production for the replicator on the moon." Interior looked crushed. "We need the ships," the president said to Interior in apology. "There's no need for park land if we're all dead."

The vice president looked at his list. "Agriculture?"

"We are working to put as much arable land as possible into production," noted the Secretary of Agriculture. "With industry moving off the planet to the moon, and more people working, we're going to need more production. We're also working with Transportation to ensure that we have ways to get the food to market, whether that is in the U.S., somewhere else on Earth or in space. Hopefully, there will be some shuttle time available for food distribution. Its ability to take off and land like a helicopter lets it get into wherever it's needed."

The president looked hopefully at Calvin, who only shook his head slightly. The president had already spoken with him earlier to discuss why he couldn't use one to fly to Germany and back. Calvin had held his ground about their schedule being packed; they must really be that busy.

The vice president nodded to Commerce.

"We're busy everywhere," said the Secretary of Commerce. "If the days were 30 hours long, we still wouldn't have enough time to get half the things done. The most important tasks involve working with Transportation to get raw materials where they need to be to help the war effort. We're working hard across the entire department. Even the Bureau of Patents is busy as some of the new technology is filtering its way down. I'd second Agriculture; we need more shuttle time."

"We're as busy as everyone else," commented the Secretary of Labor, whose turn was next. "If not even more so. Our re-employment offices are working 24 hours a day to find jobs for everyone." She looked at the president. "Your proclamation to end welfare grants to the states in two years has *everyone* scrambling. Our Occupational Safety branch is undermanned to inspect all of the new businesses that are starting, especially the mines that are opening. These are dangerous occupations at the best of times, when people *aren't* cutting corners trying to increase production so substantially. A lot of our re-employment services are being used to train people to fill holes in our own organization. Our budget will be bigger next year; it has to be to cover all of the new positions required to ensure safety in the workplace."

"Department of Health and Human Services (HHS)?" prompted the vice president.

"I don't have as much as some of my fellow secretaries," noted the HHS Secretary. "Mostly, for us, it is business as usual. As transportation worldwide is increasing, we are on the lookout for the transmission of diseases. Additionally, with all of the adults being required to find jobs, our Administration for Children and Families is working to set up programs for child care and to watch for an increase in child abuse."

"We are looking at ways to provide affordable homes for the workers in the new industrial areas," said the Secretary for Housing and Urban Development. "It involves a massive building effort that requires transporting tremendous amounts of raw materials, but we can use land-based shipping for that. It also puts a lot of people to work," she said, looking at Labor.

"Transportation?" asked the vice president.

The Secretary of Transportation shrugged. "You've already heard what I've got going," he said. "We need more shuttles, as fast as we can get them. If I had 100 of them, I could use them all." He looked at the Secretary of Energy. "Next."

"We're working on developing Helium-3 power plants to increase electrical capacity, as soon as we can get a continuous supply of it from the moon," replied Energy. "We're also investigating a variety of other power options to fill the need that the additional industry is going to bring. Our power grid was already stretched pretty thin before the Chinese hit it during the war. Many of our power plants and transmission systems sustained damage in the war that still hasn't been fixed yet. We're hiring anyone that knows anything about power and power transmission."

"As far as the National Laboratories go," Energy continued, "they are working full time to develop new sustainable power sources, whether that is power plants or engines for automobiles. We have the technology to put better engines in our cars and trucks, as well as to make them last longer; the auto industry has dragged its heels in implementing them." She looked at the two congressmen. "I'd love it if some of the members of Congress would put aside the money they get from the auto makers and implement some tougher auto standards, especially for fuel economy. That would help a lot."

"That's all I have time for," announced the president, looking at his watch. "I have to go catch an *airplane* flight to Germany for a Terran Government meeting." He looked pointedly at Calvin. "Is there anything else that needs my decision? No? OK, thanks for your input. I know everyone's busy. When you get tired, remember, we're not only working to save the planet, but the entire human race."

KIRO-TV, Channel 7, Seattle, WA, December 7, 2019

"In national news this evening, the White House announced a major new initiative to crack down on crime," read KIRO's anchorwoman, Anna St. Cloud. "In a joint press conference, President Bill Jacobs, the Attorney General and the Secretary of Homeland Security announced the end to major crime and criminal networks among states of the Terran government."

The scene shifted to the president standing behind a podium, flanked by his two cabinet members. All wore serious looks on their faces. "A friend of mine once told me," the president said, "that where there is confusion, there is the opportunity to profit. While these times are as confused as any in our history, it is *not* time to profit illegally from it. We don't have the time or resources to lose to criminal activity at either home or abroad. I'm here today to warn all crime gangs, terrorist organizations and other less-than-honest individuals that any illegal activity will be dealt with harshly."

"Don't think you can hide," continued the president, "We intend to ask the artificial intelligence on the spaceship *Vella Gulf* to point out where criminal activity is occurring, and we will use this information to root it out. We simply can't afford to waste any of our resources. We need everything we've got to make our country stronger and more prepared for the imminent alien invasion, not in lining the pockets of unscrupulous individuals."

The camera shifted back to Bob Brant, the station's new co-anchor. "While the president's announcement was greeted with approval by the law enforcement community, others in Washington were less enthused. Dave Rickland, the head of the national office of the American Civil Liberties Union (ACLU) had this to say."

The camera shifted to Rickland, standing on the steps of the Capitol Building. "We will do everything in our power to halt this unjust invasion into citizens' privacy. This is truly a day that will live in infamy. Today, the president set up a two-tiered system for law enforcement, arbitrarily separating citizens into two unequal classes, those that have the power to hide and those that don't. The people that control this glorified computer can use it to track down anything that their opponents are doing wrong, while keeping it from looking at their own affairs. Anyone that is not in the political 'in crowd,' will be arbitrarily denied their rights."

The camera shifted back to Bob Brant. "The ACLU has promised to fight the new measures with all of its resources," said the co-anchor. "It looks like it's going to be a long and nasty battle."

TSS *Vella Gulf*, Dark Side of the Moon, December 18, 2019

"Of course I can give you that information," replied Solomon. "Looking into any terrestrial computer network is easy. Although I may not have all of the alliance software upgrades, I am centuries ahead of any computer technology on Earth. Your strongest codes take me less than two seconds to break. Give me an hour, and I'll have a list of the locations for most of the top 100 'Most Wanted' terrorists, as well as the major cells for the top five terrorist organizations in the world. Some of the terrorists might be sleeping, which will make them difficult to locate, but in a couple of hours I can put together a list of the whereabouts of most of the known members of the Tamil Tigers, Hezbollah, the Taliban, Hamas, and Al-Qaeda. Give me a day, and I'll have most of the top terrorists and organizations located."

"Will that use much of your memory?" asked Bullseye.

"No," replied Solomon, "that will all take place in just my memory buffers. That's how easy it will be."

"Good," replied Bullseye. "In that case, I have a few more things I'd like you to research..."

Chapter Three

Seacon Towers Apartments, London, January 12, 2020

aster Chief Ryan O'Leary kicked in the door of the East End apartment and was greeted by a hail of bullets that hit him in the chest, despite his invisibility. "Damn it!" he grunted, as the impact of 12 bullets drove him back into the opposite wall. While the terrorists focused on O'Leary, other members of the platoon crashed through the back windows of the 4th floor apartment, taking the terrorists by surprise. The fight was over in less than a minute, leaving the terrorists dead and Ryan with an expanding bruise on his chest. Although the suit stopped the bullets, as advertised, it did nothing to absorb the impact. Someone else gets to kick in the door next time, he vowed.

Ryan surveyed the dead. No prisoners were taken, but then again, the terrorists hadn't given them the chance...and the soldiers hadn't really wanted to take any in the first place. The terrorists had nothing they needed, and to have to go through the motions of a trial was...inconvenient. Besides, the terrorists shot first, and to come back to London when they were already wanted there was just stupid. Ryan shrugged. They were another example of Darwin's rule of natural selection; they were obviously too stupid to live.

Scattered among the remains of the bomb making materials, he found the jihadi bomb maker Samantha Lewthwaite, the notorious 'White Widow' that terror agencies in the U.S., U.K. and Kenya had been looking for since the Nairobi shopping mall terror attack in

2013 that killed more than 70 people. A key member of Somalia's al-Shabaab militants, her career as a terrorist was over, courtesy of three laser blasts to her chest. Good riddance, he thought.

Sirens wailed as the local police made their appearance. Ryan looked at his watch. If the shuttle wasn't late coming down, they could still make it back to Moon Base Alpha in time for happy hour at the new bar that just opened.

Life was good.

Chapter Four

Calvin hated how he was spending his evening. Still, it had to be done so he took a deep breath and steeled himself. "Last one," he said to First Lieutenant Paul 'Night' Train as he rang the doorbell on the governor's mansion. Lieutenant Train was the executive officer of Calvin's special forces platoon, and one of the most proficient soldiers and killers that he knew.

"About time," replied Night. A veteran of a number of conflicts around the planet, an earlier combat wound to his throat made his voice sound gruff at the best of times. It was worse when he was annoyed. Like now.

Having just been informed that they were coming, the personal assistant to Governor Jeffrey Briggs let them in, welcomed them and led them to the formal living room. "This way, gentlemen," he said, opening the doors.

"Thank you," replied Calvin as they walked into the lavishly appointed room. Although it had been used for receptions and meetings with visiting dignitaries since 1950, the soldiers' meeting was one of only a very few unannounced visits during that time. The room was impressive, Calvin thought, from the beautiful antique Persian rug to the baby grand piano. A large grandfather clock chimed 10:00 p.m.

"I assume this is something of the utmost importance," said the governor, walking into the room with his wife. He looked at the two military men in full uniform. "You have about two minutes to explain yourselves before I call the police."

"Well, governor, that's your prerogative," replied Calvin. "In fact, we almost brought them ourselves."

"I told you we should have," growled Night to Calvin.

"I know," said Calvin, "but I wanted to give him the benefit of the doubt." He turned to the governor and continued, "OK, go ahead and call the police. We'll wait." He sat down heavily on one of the blue sofas in the middle of the room. After a second, Night joined him. The couch creaked ominously under the weight of the two large men. It might look impressive, Calvin thought, but it wasn't very comfortable.

"What is this all about?" asked Elizabeth Briggs, the governor's wife. Looking at the men in uniform, she asked her husband, "Does this have something to do with your stand against joining the world government?"

"I don't know," replied the governor. "These two men just barged in and told my security guard that they had something of national importance to discuss with me. I don't see how it couldn't have waited until tomorrow during business hours."

"Some things are better handled privately," answered Calvin. "This is one of them."

"Aha!" exclaimed the governor. "This *is* about my not wanting to go along with the world government, isn't it?" One of five governors that were grandstanding on the issue, he had been very vocal in the media about the fact that Arkansas would never sign a constitutional amendment giving away any of its rights. The stop in Arkansas was Calvin and Night's fifth that evening.

"No, governor, this has nothing to do with that," replied Calvin. He looked significantly at Mrs. Briggs. "I think it might be better if we kept this conversation between the three of us, though."

"Anything you have to say to me, you can say in front of her," said the governor.

"OK, your choice," Calvin replied. He looked at Night and said, "Your turn."

"Governor, do you know a girl named Sally Rae Jamison?" asked Night.

"Ummm," answered the governor. "The name sounds sort of familiar, but I can't place where I've heard it before." He almost pulled it off. If he hadn't turned several shades paler, he might have been successful.

"Who is Sally Rae Jamison?" echoed his wife.

"I think she was a campaign booster in my last run for office," the governor explained. "But it's *not* like that. Nothing happened between us. Ever."

"Really?" Calvin asked. "Did you know that once something is on the internet, it's there forever? I mean *forever*. You probably have heard we have a spaceship, right? And that it's from an alien civilization that's a lot more advanced than ours, right? I don't know if anyone ever told you, but our internet is transparent to the artificial intelligence on the ship. I mean, it can see *everything!* You may not know that it's also pretty good at doing phone surveillance. If it wanted, it could monitor every single phone conversation taking place throughout the whole world at once. It's quite spectacular."

"First, nothing ever happened," said the governor looking at his wife. He turned to Calvin and continued. "Second, because *nothing ever happened,* I know that there aren't any pictures or proof. And even if someone had impersonated me over a phone line, it would be inadmissible in court because the artificial intelligence doesn't have a warrant to tap my phone."

"You know who we should have brought?" Night asked Calvin. "Master Chief O'Leary. As much as he hates authority, he would have had a lot of fun tonight watching all of these guys squirm. They know they're caught, and they still try to wiggle out of it anyway." He looked at the governor. "You know you're caught, right?"

"Yeah, he would have loved it," Calvin agreed without waiting for the governor's answer. "His only problem is tact. He would have just gone straight to the press with this." Calvin moved the tea set from the tiny table between the two blue sofas and set his brief case on it. "It's late," he said, looking at the governor, "and I really hate dealing with slime. I'm going to have to shower twice to get the feeling off my skin."

"Here's the deal," he said, opening the brief case and pulling out a sheaf of 8.5" x 11" inch glossy photographs. "You had sex with her, not once, but three times. Then you illegally gave her $50,000 from your campaign fund to shut her up. Then you had some of your 'friends' from your construction business talk to her. When that didn't work, they threatened her elderly mother. You, sir, are slime, and we would happily kick the absolute living *shit* out of you, but we have better things to do with our time, like trying to save the entire human race from aliens that mean us harm."

He flipped the stack at the governor, who missed the catch. They scattered on the floor, full color and lurid in nature. Night pushed one of them toward the governor with the toe of his boot. "How you got her to try *that* is beyond me," Night added, "but I doubt she was a willing participant." Mrs. Briggs gasped as she saw it. "Let me say, though," Night continued, "I think you are a sick man whose DNA should be removed from the gene pool." Elizabeth Briggs started crying.

"In addition to the photos," Calvin concluded, "we have audio recordings backing up all of this. I wanted to turn this over to the police, but we need stability at the moment, even if that stability is you. Here's what I would suggest you do. One, in the morning, you send the amendment to the legislature. Two, you back it up with speeches about how good this will be for the country. Three, you get the amendment passed this month. Four, next month, before the end of the month, you retire, refusing to take any retirement compensation or benefits from the state. Maybe you claim you have a problem with alcohol. Whatever. I don't care. Five, lastly, you vanish from the public eye, never to be seen again. If you violate any of these points, or even *think* of violating any of them, all of this will become public. Do you understand me?"

The governor had one more card. "This is blackmail," he charged. "I'll fight it!"

Calvin cocked his head. "Really?" he asked. "This isn't blackmail; *this is an investment in your life.* How do you think the people in the Lake Dardanelle land deal are going to feel about you when it comes out that you intentionally screwed them over?"

"How do you know about that?" the governor asked. "No one knows about that!"

Calvin shook his head, "I told you, the ship sees everything. Did they ever find the body of your third partner, or is it still buried somewhere along the Arkansas River?"

The governor deflated. "I'll do it," he whispered. "I'll do everything."

"I'm sure you will," agreed Calvin. "We'll be watching, too, just to make sure." He stood up. "C'mon, Night. I need a drink to get this disgusting taste out of my mouth."

"Wait!" called Elizabeth Briggs with a sob. "What about me?"

"You?" asked Calvin. He looked at the governor in disgust. "You can do whatever you want."

Night crossed to her in two brisk steps and handed her a card that he pulled from his pocket. Looking at the governor he said, "This is my card and my phone number. If he *ever* does anything to you or refuses to go along with *anything* you say, give me a call. I'll be happy to come back some time when I'm not in uniform. I don't need 'friends' to do my dirty work; I'll be happy to talk to him for you, myself."

"Thank you," said the soon-to-be-ex Mrs. Briggs with a sniff.

"My pleasure," replied Night, tipping his cap as he walked toward the door. He made sure to bump into the governor as he walked by him. "I'd *really* like to see you again," he growled in his deep voice. "Next time, I won't be so nice."

The two men walked out of the house and back toward the car that would take them to the airport and their waiting shuttle. "Are you still going to give all that to the press?" asked Night.

Calvin nodded. "Just as soon as he leaves office."

KIRO-TV, Channel 7, Seattle, WA, January 22, 2020

"In national news this evening, the White House announced that it had 37 signatures on the amendment to join the Terran World Government," read KIRO's anchorwoman, Anna St. Cloud. "President Bill Jacobs made the announcement earlier today."

The scene shifted to the president at a podium, "I'm very happy to announce that Arkansas signed off on the 28th Amendment today," the president said, "this makes 37 states that have ratified the amendment which will allow the United States to join the world government. We are only one state shy of it being signed into law. That this has come so quickly can only be seen as a mandate from the masses."

The camera came back to Ms. St. Cloud. "Assuming that one more state ratifies the amendment within the next three months, the amendment will have gone through the ratification process faster than any other amendment previously. The 26th Amendment, which lowered the voting age from 21 to 18, previously held the record, as it only took four months during the summer of 1971 to be ratified by the required three-fourths of state legislatures."

The camera shifted back to Bob Brant, the station's co-anchor. "Although there are several states that seem close to ratifying the amendment, there are several others that are moving far more cautiously on the measure. Leaders in New Hampshire, long known for its motto, 'Live Free or Die,' have made the headlines by saying that they intend to secede from the United States rather than give up their freedom to foreigners in Europe and beyond. They have threatened a lawsuit on the constitutionality of the amendment, rather than joining in the effort."

"A small but vocal minority disputes this position, however," he continued. The scene shifted to a small group of picketers. "This group outside the Capitol Building in Concord, New Hampshire disagrees with the majority opinion. Let's go live to Jim Lordes."

"Hi," said the on-site reporter to the camera. "This is Jim Lordes in Concord, New Hampshire. I'm here in front of the Capitol Building with Richard Smithson, who is leading a group that is picketing the state's legislature."

The camera shot panned out to include Smithson. "What can you tell us about what's going on here?" asked the reporter.

"Hi Jim," replied Smithson. "We're here today to try to talk some sense into our elected officials. Like any New Hampshire native, I live by the motto, 'Live Free or Die.' There comes a time, though, where everyone has to rally together for the common good. The time has passed for us to fight amongst ourselves. We've got to come together to fight the aliens that are headed our way. It's hard to live free when you're dead."

"There you have it," announced Jim Lordes. "At least a few voices are willing to put aside the past to help build a better future. Back to you, Anna..."

Chapter Five

"Closer to home," Anna St. Cloud reported, "Governor George Shelby has called the legislature together for a special session to debate the 28th Amendment. The legislature was supposed to be on a recess for the next month and a half, but the governor called them back so that the issue could be debated as quickly as possible. Here's what the governor had to say." The picture shifted to Governor Shelby, seated behind the desk in his office.

"I hope that our legislature rapidly ratifies this measure," Governor Shelby said. "As we saw a little more than a year ago, the world is too small for bickering amongst ourselves. The world needs to look at the big picture and move forward together, and the United States needs to lead this process."

"We have an historic opportunity before us today," he continued. "So far, 37 states have ratified the constitutional amendment that will let the United States join the Terran World Government. I feel that this is the single most important piece of legislation that has come before me in my entire public service career. My fellow Washingtonians, our world is in more peril now than even at the height of the Cold War, when the United States and the U.S.S.R. stared at each other across the tips of their nuclear missiles. We need this legislation in order to continue to lead this effort. If we don't lead and bring all of our economic might with us, it is unlikely that the world will be prepared when the Drakuls come."

"I come before you today to ask you to exercise your rights as citizens and voters of this great State of Washington, a state that has known its share of conflict and war recently, more so than any other state in almost 75 years. Email your legislators and tell them to vote for the amendment as quickly as they are able. If you have a minute, call them and do the same, so that they know you are serious. I have called the legislature back to work to debate this issue; *let them know where you stand!* I can think of no greater honor than for this state to be the 38th and deciding state to ratify the amendment. I implore all of the citizens and members of the legislature to make this happen, and make it happen now!"

"Thank you for your support," closed the governor.

"Impassioned words from the governor," commented Ms. St. Cloud as the camera returned to her. "Generally, we here at KIRO-TV Channel 7 try to report the news, free of commentary or partiality, but I have to say, after listening to the governor, I hope everyone will take the action he recommends. I was here on camera when Chinese soldiers broke into this station and killed my co-anchor. *I never want to experience that again!*"

"Thank you for those heartfelt words of your own," said Bob Brant, looking at Anna St. Cloud. "I know those were difficult times here." He looked back to the camera. "In happier news," he said, "the Defense Department has announced that Joint Base Lewis-McChord will host a new school to train special forces soldiers to operate in space. Wendy Phillips has the story..."

Assembly Room, Independence Hall, Philadelphia, PA, February 27, 2020

"It is appropriate that we are here today," said the president, "here at this place where 56 courageous men risked everything, their lives, their fortunes and their sacred honor, in order to declare their liberty from oppression. Not only was the Declaration of Independence signed here, but 11 years after that, representatives from 12 states gathered here to shape our Constitution, finally creating one unified nation. E Pluribus Unum; Out of Many, One. For well over 200 years, the nation that those brave men created has stood as a world leader. It is appropriate that we are here today, near a broken bell which still stands as one of the most powerful symbols of liberty in the world. Its message from Leviticus, Chapter 25, Verse 10, still guides our actions. 'Proclaim LIBERTY Throughout All the Land Unto All the Inhabitants Thereof.'"

He looked out over the Assembly Room. "We are gathered here among all of these symbols to write a new chapter in America's history. We look further beyond our borders than we ever have before, bravely daring to strike out in a new direction because that is what is right; indeed, *that is what is necessary.*"

"The signing of a constitutional amendment is one of the biggest acts possible in our great nation," the president continued. "In order to achieve it, two-thirds of both houses of Congress had to agree on its exact wording. How often does that happen?" He paused for polite laughter. "I would like to thank the members of Congress for their vision in crafting this resolution." He nodded to the left of the platform, where the leadership of both houses stood, leading the applause for themselves.

"Not only must Congress agree on the amendment, but three-quarters of the states, or 38 out of the 50, have to agree on it as well. I would like to thank the governors and legislatures of the *46* states that have ratified the 28th Amendment for their diligence and hard work." The president indicated the group standing to the right of the dais. "I hope that the states that haven't ratified it so far will join the rest of the states that already have, thereby creating a united front as we move forward."

"We have come a long way in a short time," said the president, "but there is still a long way to go. We have much to do, and I am conscious of the passing of time, so I will not waste any more of it in flowery speeches." He motioned toward the Archivist of the Office of the Federal Register, sitting at a small table in front of him, the original table and inkstand used to sign the Declaration of Independence. "Mr. Archivist, the floor is yours."

The Archivist held up a single piece of paper, something that seemed far too small for the significance it held. "The 28th Amendment has been agreed to by two-thirds of both houses of Congress, and it has been ratified by three-quarters of the states. I hereby certify the 28th Amendment to be the law of the land in these United States of America." He set it back onto the desk and pulled an authentic quill pen out of the inkstand. Having practiced for several days until he had it right, he used the pen to sign the document.

The United States of America was now a founding father in the Government of Terra.

Chapter Six

"So, now that we have a world government, can you *please* tell us how the gates work?" asked Captain James Deutch as he watched the shuttle launch. The trip to drop off extra mines and other defenses around the stargate was to be his last time in command of the *Gulf.* When they got back to the moon, he was going to be relieved by Captain Lorena Griffin, who was moving up from her duties as executive officer (XO). He would return to Earth to lead the new curriculum in spaceship operations for officers going through commanding officers' school. Although it was necessary to pass on everything he had learned as a starship commander, it would not be as exciting to talk about driving a spaceship as it was to actually do it. Not even close.

"Although the procedural methodology of wormhole employment has been reliably established," answered Arges, "we are stymied as to the internal mechanism of its functioning."

"Huh?" asked the helmsman. He turned around and asked, "What was that?"

The XO turned to look at the helmsman. "They don't know how it works," she said.

Steropes shrugged, "Unfortunately, that is an accurate assessment. We don't know how the gates work. They're the product of an earlier civilization. We also don't know why they were placed the way they were. Most systems have two stargates, which would appear to

41

be a way in and a way out of the system. Why do some only have one? Why do other systems have multiple gates? We don't know. It may be because of the stellar mechanics...it may be something as simple as the earlier civilization liked traveling to a particular star system for some reason, so all of their roads led there." He paused for a second, collecting his thoughts.

"Our best engineers have worked on figuring out how the star-gates work for over 10,000 years," he said when he continued, "and they still don't know. We believe that they are collapsed black holes, but the method for collapsing them and linking them together is beyond us. The closest we've come to figuring out the gates was the Churther Box. Arton Churther was a brilliant scientist whose life's work was trying to figure out how the gates worked. No one is sure how he did it, but he created a box that appeared to open a doorway to either somewhere else or to some other time."

"Didn't he know what he created?" asked Calvin, who was aboard to coordinate the air wing's operations. "Where did he think it went?"

"That's the problem," said Steropes. "He never got a chance to say; he got sucked into the first gateway that the box opened. His assistant turned off the box, but Churther was gone. The assistant knew enough about the box to try turning it on and off a few times, but he couldn't find the world that Churther went into. After a large group of Drakuls came through one of the gateways he created, the government stopped allowing people to operate the box. Of course, there wasn't anyone left alive who knew how to operate it, so the point was rather moot."

"So what did your scientists think that the box did?" asked Captain Deutch.

"We don't know," Steropes answered. "It created a gateway to another time, another place, or another universe. We don't have enough information to make a reliable guess as to which. The incredibly scary thing is that one time they turned on the box, the gate led to nothing."

"What do you mean, 'nothing'?" asked Captain Deutch.

"I mean just that," replied Steropes. "There was nothing there. The universe was gone."

Terran Government Headquarters, Lake Pedam, Nigeria, March 29, 2020

President Bill Jacobs surveyed the bustle going on to the east of him. The site was a beehive of activity, with so many large earth movers working that he wasn't sure how they didn't get into each other's way. It was a well-choreographed dance of construction, he decided. As he watched, a truck pulling a flatbed with yet another bulldozer came trundling down the road from the airport, along with a giant crane.

The new Terran Government Headquarters building was going up on his left, with the foundations of several other buildings also in progress. The site was nestled along Pedam Lake in the shadow of Aso Rock to the east of Nigeria's capital of Abuja. Aso Rock was a 1,200' tall stone monolith and Abuja's most noticeable feature. He had found the site fitting, as the name 'Aso' meant 'victorious' in the native language of the local Asokoro people. He tried not to think about the fact that the Asokoro (literally, 'the people of victory') had themselves later been defeated and forced to move from the area.

He turned to Arges, whom he had asked to meet him here. "We're going to make this happen, even if I have to get out there and start building with my own two hands," he said with a smile. "Happily, I think that we now have enough buy-in from all of the other nations that won't be necessary." The smile faded. "The Russians even appear to be committed to the process now, although I don't know how we're ever going to get the Chinese involved. The war pushed us so far apart that it will be difficult to bring us back together." He looked intently at Arges. "I am *not* giving up on bringing them in; I just wanted you to know how hard it will be."

"You have done a tremendous job in a very little time," said Arges. "And I believe that you have put together the beginnings of a world government. I wish that I had better news for you, but your accomplishments so far are only a small portion of the effort that will be required."

He paused, and the president waited for him to begin again. After a long pause, Arges began talking quietly. "For over 10,000 years, we have led the Alliance of Civilizations and have ensured peace in this galaxy. There are many other races, of which we are just one. Some are naturally caring, what you would call 'good;' others you would probably consider to be 'bad' or 'evil.' Most, like your own race, lie somewhere in between. You are capable of great deeds, but also capable of inflicting misery on others of your own race when you have power over them."

"Most of these races formed an alliance many millennia ago, and the races that are less benevolent were prohibited from interacting with civilizations that were just forming, like your own. Those days are over. The alliance that has watched over developing civilizations is no more. There are many races, like the Drakul, that now have free reign among the galaxy."

"Wait a minute," said President Jacobs. "You're telling me that I had to bust my ass to put together a world government just to find out that we don't have a chance?"

"Yes," said Arges. "For two reasons. The first is that our rules really do prohibit transferring any technology to you without a world government, so you needed to have one for that. The other is that we've done an enormous amount of computer modeling on the future of this planet. In all of the scenarios where you didn't have a world government, your planet didn't survive another 25 years. You need a unified government in order to have any sort of a chance in the coming times. Our time is past. Our civilization is done. The alliance is crumbling and, like your Rome, the barbarians are at the gates. The races that were banished or that fled from civilized space have returned and are gobbling up systems on the periphery."

"So..." said the president, "we *are* screwed."

"No," said Arges, "you definitely have a small chance. I believe the saying in your 'poker' card game is that we're now 'all in' with you. Everything we know, we will pass on to you, without further delay. While we abhor killing and combat as a rule, we do not want to watch your species be destroyed by some of the other races that currently exist in the galaxy. We will give you all of our technology and knowledge. If you can reach one of the other good races, you may also gain additional technological and industrial opportunities. And even if you are unable to get outside assistance, it is a time of great deeds. Your heroes have arisen."

"Heroes?" asked the president. "What do you mean, 'heroes'?"

Bridge, TSS *Vella Gulf,* Earth Orbit, April 2, 2020

"That is *so* cool," said Sara, looking out the bridge viewer as the *Vella Gulf* orbited the Earth conducting cleanup patrol. The amount of space debris had gotten to be so overwhelming around the Earth that it was becoming a chore to fly through. Captain Deutch had volunteered as his last duty to clean it up a little. The *Gulf* was going to make a few orbits and burn up as much of it as was possible with the ship's defensive lasers. If it also gave him a few more hours in command, so much the better. He was really going to miss this.

"Never thought that you'd be up in space looking at the Earth?" asked Calvin.

"What do you think?" Sara asked. "Of course not. Most art majors don't make it into space, in case you hadn't noticed."

They watched in companionable silence as the ship continued to burn up space rubbish. Every once in a while, a laser would hit something with a little fuel still in it, and it would make a small fireball that immediately disappeared.

"Whoa," said Sara suddenly. "Wow, big case of deja vu."

"When you say you have a feeling of deja vu, you are saying that you feel like you have been someplace before, correct?" Steropes asked.

"Well, yes, that's what it means," said Calvin.

"In most cases," replied Arges, "we believe that means that someone in your timeline *has* been there before."

"I don't understand," said Sara, looking confused. "How could someone in my past have been here before, looking down on the planet?"

"That statement makes several assumptions," began Arges, taking on his lecturing tone. "First, you assume that what you felt was this ship. It is very possible that you were on this class of ship, as thousands were built when the Eldive were still alive. Second, you also assume that the feeling came from looking at this planet. There are, in fact, more planets than can easily be counted. While only a small percentage of them are at all Earth-like, a small percentage of an infinite amount still gives many instances of Earth-like planets. Perhaps you were on an exploratory team somewhere else in the cosmos and found an Earth-like planet that was so close to this one that it made a strong impression on you, causing the deja vu feeling now." Arges paused.

"And the other reason," Steropes urged.

Arges gave a small, very human, shrug. "Finally, it may not have happened in the past," he finished.

"Wha...what?" asked Sara. "What do you mean that it 'might not have happened in the past?'"

Arges frowned. "Our conceptualization of time is not the same as yours. While you see time as moving in one direction, like a river that is flowing too quickly to go back, we see it as a tapestry, where events are not necessarily so linear in nature. Actually, it is precisely because of events like this that we don't believe time to be linear. There have been many instances where people had deja vu experiences where it was impossible for them to have been there in a previous life. If both of those data points are accurate, then the feeling must have been at some point in a *future* life and they are experiencing echoes of it now."

"Are you saying that time travel is possible?" asked Calvin.

Arges nodded. "Can you prove that it is not?" he asked.

Chapter Seven

"So, what did Arges mean by 'heroes'?" asked the Secretary of Commerce.

"He tried to explain it to me, but I still don't get it," answered the president. "He said that every time societal upheaval has happened before, there have been some sort of leaders, he called them 'heroes,' that came to the forefront and led their civilizations back from the brink of anarchy. He thinks that some of the members of Calvin's platoon are these people reborn."

"So, from some cosmic sort of perspective, it's preordained that we're going to win?" asked the Secretary of the Air Force, with a look of hope in his eyes. "The good guys always win?"

"No," replied the president, "even if you believe this whole hocus pocus magic that some sort of heroes show up when needed, Arges said that good doesn't always win. In fact, they used to have some sort of box that allowed them to see into other universes. In many of these, the 'good' civilizations have won and are still in existence. But in others, the 'bad guys' won. Arges also said that in one universe, the Milky Way didn't exist anymore."

"What?" asked the science advisor. "What do you mean, it didn't exist?"

"I mean that it was completely destroyed," answered the president. "It was just gone. 300 million star systems, all just gone."

"That's impossible..." said the science advisor. "What could do that?"

"They don't know," said the president, "but Arges said that he would greatly like to avoid that happening in this universe."

"Yeah, me too," muttered the science advisor.

"So, what's the deal with these heroes?" asked the Chairman of the Joint Chiefs of Staff.

"I don't know," said the president. "Arges was very vague. He just said, 'they rise.'"

"Do you believe that?" asked the Chairman.

The president shrugged. "I don't know. It sounds like wishful thinking to me. Arges believes it, though, as do the other two Psi-clopes. They all believe that there is an all-powerful being or force that watches over us."

"God?" asked science advisor.

"It could be," said the president. "I asked the same question. He didn't want to say 'yes,' but he also didn't want to rule it out, either. But he did say that the being wasn't entirely focused on 'the good guys always win;' in some universes, the bad races won in the end."

National Assembly Building, Abuja, Nigeria, April 10, 2020

"I would personally like to thank everyone for coming today," welcomed the German Luftwaffe general, Heinrich Gottlieb. Calvin looked down the long table that held the personnel review board. In addition to the German that was the board's chairman, there was also a representative from all of the original members of the world government: the United States, Canada, Japan, South Korea, Italy, the United Kingdom,

Germany, Chile, India, Australia and the host country of Nigeria. This was the second board for all of them, as the same admirals and generals had met several months previously. The *Vella Gulf's* squadron had sustained a number of losses on its first mission and they had met to fill them. "I would also like to thank Lieutenant Commander Hobbs for making time in his busy schedule to be here today," Gottlieb continued. "I know his experience will be able to add much insight into the selection process."

Today's board would probably be more challenging, Calvin knew, as many of the new nations were also in attendance. He expected all of them to jockey for positions in both the squadron and in the platoon. Russia would certainly expect to be compensated for its support of the process, he had been advised, and he knew that the Israelis would expect to be included, as well. It was one thing to say that the new government would be inclusive in front of the media; Calvin expected that it was going to be much harder trying to get the nations to actually work as one. He sighed, wishing he could be anywhere else. Preferably off planet, several stargates away.

"I would also like to thank the Government of Nigeria for allowing us to use this wonderful facility today," General Gottlieb continued. The new Terran Government Headquarters building was not complete yet, but the government couldn't wait for it. The new government had a multitude of issues that it needed to resolve so, in the interim, the president of Nigeria had allowed them to use the National Assembly Building, located close to where the new headquarters was being built.

"As most of you are aware," Gottlieb advised, "this is the second meeting of this personnel board. We met one time previously to fill the losses the squadron sustained in combat. The purpose of this meeting today is to expand the manning of the space fighter squadron and to fill in the losses sustained by the platoon."

Calvin thought back to the first mission. It had been a difficult one. Not only had they lost three space fighter crews (and their precious ships) in action against the Ssselipsssiss, they had also left a shuttle and a crew behind on Epsilon Eridani to help the ambassador there. Half of the crews that had initially been implanted were no longer with the squadron. As more of the shuttles had been built, it had been necessary to select new flight crews, or they wouldn't have been able to fly half the number of shuttle missions that they currently were. It had been decided at the first board to allow the countries to replace their losses in the squadron and to expand the squadron to 10 flight crews, adding a Nigerian crew, an Australian pilot and a German weapon systems officer.

The Russian general raised his hand, and Calvin sighed again. They hadn't even started, and it looked like the jockeying was starting. "I assume that we will be filling the positions based on the populations of the contributing nations?" asked the Russian. Of course he would assume that, Calvin thought. Russia was the only one of the 10 largest nations in the world that didn't have anyone in either organization. If selection was done by size, they would be able to fill most of the open positions. Nations like Israel, ranked 96th in the world in population, would be effectively shut out of the discussion.

The Israeli general immediately raised his hand. Seeing it, the chairman said, "Let us try to remember that the future of our race rests on the two units that we are manning. The entire *human race* depends on our decisions." He raised his voice. "*I will not allow this board to descend into partisan politics.* We must be above it! We will select the best people for the positions, not because they come from the right place, but *because they are the best!* Am I understood?" Calvin hid a smile. There's nothing like a pissed off German for getting control of a meeting, he thought.

Both the Russian and the Israeli put their hands down and looked a little chastised. Calvin didn't think they'd stay that way, but it was at least a start.

Time to throw them a bone, thought Calvin as he raised his hand. "I am happy to announce that it looks like we will have a full squadron of spacecraft for the next time out," he told the board. "We need to increase the squadron's manning from 10 crews to 16, so there should be room for all of the assembled nations to participate."

Gottlieb nodded in appreciation. "This is how we will make the initial selections," the German explained. "As you were previously notified, we will start with the pilots, and each representative will have one minute, and one minute only, to tell the board about that nation's top candidates, and why they should be selected for inclusion into the squadron. A nation may nominate up to three. After each presentation, the board will make a secret vote and give the candidate a confidence level score between one and 10 on whether or not he or she thinks that candidate would be a good choice for inclusion. After all of the pilots have been voted on, we will narrow the results down and then determine who will be selected. Then we will do the same for the weapon systems officers and then the members of the platoon. Any questions?"

The Russian representative raised his hand again. "Will we be determining the crew of the space ship today, as well?" Calvin shook his head. He had heard that there was an effort among some of the nations to rename the *Vella Gulf* to something more representative of the planet in general, not just one nation. By addressing it as 'the space ship' rather than by its name, obviously the Russians were behind it. Really? Didn't they have better things to worry about?

"The manning of the *Vella Gulf* will be decided at a meeting next week," replied the chairman. "Any other questions?" Seeing none, he looked at the U.S. Air Force General sitting at the opposite end of the table from Calvin. "General Simon, would you please brief your first candidate?"

General Simon smiled as the first U.S. candidate, a navy lieutenant, appeared on the screen. "I'd be happy to," he replied. "Our first candidate is Lieutenant John Turner. Lieutenant Turner is a veteran of our last war and our 'Top Gun' fighter weapons school..."

Terran Space Force HQ, Moon Base Alpha, Dark Side of the Moon, April 15, 2020

"How bad was it?" asked Calvin as Night and Bullseye walked into his office. Although space was at a premium in the lunar habitat, Calvin had staked out a small cubicle to hang his space suit, flight gear and other personal paraphernalia. It had a desk and a file cabinet and two chairs for guests. Calvin felt so cramped in the office most days that it felt like he had to go outside just to change his mind. He couldn't wait to move back aboard the *Vella Gulf*. He had a much larger space there that he would previously have only considered to be 'minimal.' It now seemed palatial in comparison.

"It was as brutal as we thought it would be," replied Night, who attended the entire selection process that filled out the ranks of Space Fighter Squadron One and the first platoon of what the leaders had decided to call the 'Terran Space Marines.' As the purpose of the platoon was to attack a nation from its base onboard a ship, Calvin could understand the analog of using the wet-navy Marine Corps. Calvin had to leave the selection board after the first day for consultation meetings with several of the national leaders. "About the only thing that they agreed upon without too much argument was to let the countries that lost platoon members fill their spots. That was one of the first things discussed; after that it got hard." He looked at Bullseye.

"We ended up with the 16 crews that we wanted," Bullseye reported. "In addition to the Nigerians that you already know about, we got two Russians, two Indians, a Ukrainian, a Spaniard, a Kiwi, a Turk, a Saudi, an Israeli and a female French pilot that I already caught Lieutenant Simpson trying to stake a claim to." He shook his head. "If she wants to steal secrets, there's probably going to be a line forming to give them to her."

"Good thing we don't have any secrets then, huh?" asked Calvin.

"Yeah, pretty much," agreed Bullseye, "but don't tell *her* that. I've probably got a secret or two of my own that I need to share." He winked. "In any event, we have a wealth of experience in a wide variety of aircraft types. The Russians and Ukrainians only nominated fighter pilots, but some of the other countries nominated helo pilots and a number of different types of weapon systems officers. Overall, I think we ended up with a pretty good mix of aviators."

"Good," said Calvin. "Thanks for suffering through that."

"You can pay me in beers," replied Bullseye. "A *lot* of them. Think in terms of cases."

Calvin laughed. "I'll get right on that," he said.

"Good," replied Bullseye. "Oh, there was one other thing. Some of the nations were finding it difficult to mix the navy ranks with army and air force, so the Terran Space Force is going to go to only using navy ranks." He smiled. "I'm a Lieutenant Commander now, too."

The three men shared a laugh. "Did they convert you over, too?" Calvin asked Night.

"Not yet," replied Night. "The ground forces are still keeping their national ranks, for now, as the high command couldn't agree on which branch's ranks to use, even though they decided to call us Space Marines. I have a feeling that they'll eventually go with the Marine Corps ranks, too, but there's no way to know."

"All right," said Calvin. "How did the platoon's manning end up? Did they get it figured out?"

"Yeah," replied Night, "they were able to work out the manning, and we ended up with a lot of experience. The only problem is going to be getting everyone to work together. I don't think that there will be a lot of problems with the aviators, but the platoon is going to have a number of nationalities that are traditional enemies working in close proximity to each other." He shrugged. "If we can make it work, we'll hopefully make it easier on the ones that come after us."

"As you probably heard," he continued, "Iran, North Korea, and China are still boycotting, so we didn't have to worry about any of them. With the exception of those three, just about every other major nation in the world is 'in' and thinks that their special forces are more special than those of any other country. Overall, I think we did really well. If we don't have the best people in the world, they're all still in the top 1%."

"The Space Force had more casualties than the Ground Force last time out," commented Night, "so it absorbed more of the newbies, even after we moved Mr. Jones and Ms. Rozhkov to it. First off, Master Chief will be happy to know that we picked up another U.S. Navy SEAL, in addition to a Saudi Navy SEAL, as well. We also got an Israeli from the Shayetet 13 naval commando unit. You may not have even heard of it, as the unit is one of the most secretive in the Israeli military. They are really good."

"As a matter of fact," continued Night, "we've got several new members from units that we have heard mentioned in whispers, but never were able to confirm. Countries are confirming them now to get places in the unit. The next recruit, a Russian combat frogman, is one of these. He is from their Naval Spetsnaz unit called the 'Barrakuda' group. This is the group that killed 'Buster' Crabb. If you don't know who Crabb was, he was the British spy that was the inspiration for James Bond. The guys in Barrakuda are ghosts; we've never been able to confirm their existence."

"In addition to them," Night said, "we also have a French Naval Commando, an Indian Marine Commandos (MARCOS) and a Norwegian Marinejegerkommandoen (MJK) operative. The French commando is from the Commando de Penfentenyo brigade, whose specialties are reconnaissance and intelligence operations behind enemy lines. MARCOS does all sorts of maritime special operations like counter-terrorism, special reconnaissance, unconventional warfare and hostage rescue. This unit is one of the few units *in the world* qualified to jump into the water with a full combat load. They specialize in maritime operations throughout Kashmir and often conduct counter-terrorist operations in the area. The MARCOS operatives are widely feared among the terrorists, who call them the

'Bearded Army' because they all disguise their identities with flowing beards. The MARCOS soldiers have been known to carry out a wide variety of operations on foreign soil. The last member of the Space Force is a member of Norway's MJK. He is trained as a sniper and a forward air controller and also has some field medical skills."

"The additions to the Ground Force are equally skilled," said Night, looking at the list. "The first of these is Sergeant Alka Zoromski from the Polish Operational Maneuver Response Group. That group is an elite counter-terrorism unit that fills a variety of special operations and unconventional warfare roles, including anti-terrorist actions and projection of power behind enemy lines."

"In addition to the Russian Naval Spetsnaz frogman, we also got a Russian from the 'Lynx' unit of their Special Rapid Response Unit. Since the unit was established in 1992, it has participated in almost every known special operation in Russia. They are usually tasked with Special Weapons and Tactics (SWAT)-type special operations, including apprehension of dangerous criminals and high-profile raids. He will bring some interesting skills in missions that are outside of normal special ops."

"Cool," said Calvin. "You never know what we're going to need."

"Our other Israeli is a member of their elite Sayeret Matkal unit," Night continued. "You may not recognize the name of the unit, but this is the one that conducted the raid on Entebbe, where it rescued more than 100 Air France passengers who were being held by terrorists. Although everyone here is good; this group is one of the best."

"Our final operative is the one that I am the most worried about," said Night, looking down again.

"Why is that?" asked Calvin. "Did one of the nations stick us with a ringer?"

"No," replied Night. "He is from the Special Service Group of Pakistan's special operations forces. I'm not worried about his skills, as this group is considered one of the top special forces groups in the world. They can do anything you'd like, from unconventional warfare to foreign internal defense to hostage rescue. What worries me is that he is a Pashtun from the Afghan/Pakistan border. I don't know him, so he wasn't someone that fought with us against the Afghan insurgency. I don't know if that means he was helping the insurgents, or just happened to be stationed in another area while I was there. If he was in another area, it's likely that he was in Kashmir, and may have run afoul of our Indian operative that would have been there. I have a lot of questions that I want answered before I take him into combat."

Special Forces Training Command, Joint Base Lewis-McChord, Tacoma, WA, April 25, 2020

"Sir, you have *got* to see this," said Night, walking into the office.

"What is it?" asked Calvin, looking up from the never-ending stack of paperwork he had brought with him on his trip to review the training course for special operations in space.

Night moved to stand by the window that looked down over the hangar bay. "Just come here," he replied. "Quick. You're gonna love it."

Calvin got up from his chair and crossed the room to the window. "I don't mind taking a break from the paperwork," he said. "What's so important?"

Night pointed to a large mat where two people were engaged in a heated hand-to-hand combat match. The entire platoon stood around the mat watching, jeering and calling suggestions, most of which weren't repeatable in mixed company. There were also a number of students that he didn't recognize yelling at them. Calvin could see that one of the participants was Master Chief O'Leary, but he didn't recognize the other. Both were bleeding in a couple of places. For Master Chief, that was no small feat, as his skin had been augmented to resist burns, punctures and cuts.

"Is that one of our new guys?" asked Calvin, looking at the other guy. "I don't recognize him."

"He's actually from the ship's crew," replied Night, "but he is *really* good. Did you see that combination that Master Chief just threw at him? That's some sort of Rigelian nerve punch/kick combo that we got from a combat download. There's no way that guy could *ever* have seen that combination before, and yet he was able to block and avoid it."

"Whoever he is, he obviously got some augmentations done when he got his implants," remarked Calvin. "There's no way he could be that fast without them."

Night laughed. "That's what I wanted you to see," he said. "The guy is totally augment-free. He's naturally that fast. If anything, he's faster than Master Chief is *with* his implants. He just walked in here, walked up to Master Chief and said, 'Hey, if I can take you four out of seven submissions, can I go down to the planet with you the next time the *Gulf* goes out?' Master Chief didn't think there was any way that the guy could win, so he said, 'Sure.'"

"He's got to know that he can't authorize that," said Calvin, shaking his head. "What's the count so far?"

Night grinned. "I think it is tied three-to-three right now. Master Chief won the first three points, hitting him with a bunch of the off-world stuff that we learned, including some of the lizard stuff that he's been working on with Bob and Doug. He hasn't scored since then, though, and he has taken a *bunch* of hits."

"The funny thing," said Night after a pause, "is that the new guy said he is better with rifle and pistol than he is at hand-to-hand." At that moment, the newcomer faked high and struck low, sweeping Master Chief's legs out from under him. While Master Chief was still going down, the newcomer pounced on him, taking him down in a choke hold that Master Chief couldn't escape. The newcomer won, 4-3.

"Wow," said Calvin, watching Master Chief's struggles diminish as he passed out from blood loss to his brain, "that guy really *is* good. We need to get him on the team; make sure you get him implants and a suit." He turned to find Night laughing. "What?" he asked. "Who is he?"

"That gentleman is Father John Zuhlsdorf," replied Night. "He's the *Gulf's* new chaplain."

National Assembly Building, Abuja, Nigeria, April 27, 2020

"I would like to thank all of you for attending this session today," greeted the British prime minister. The first female to hold the post since Margaret

Thatcher, Juliette Ricketts-Smith was also First Lord of the Treasury and the Minister for the Civil Service. Like the 'Iron Lady' before her, the 'Cobalt Countess' wore her nickname proudly. Not only was cobalt a hard metal (harder than iron, she was fond of saying), but cobalt was also one of the three elements that were magnetic at room temperature, like her personality. The fact that she often dressed in blue was purely coincidental. "I do not believe that there is any more important appointment before this assembly than who to send as the next ambassador." She looked out at the nodding heads in the crowded assembly hall. The heads of state of nearly all of the participating nations were in attendance. Those that weren't had sent their seconds. As the first ambassador to the stars had been from Britain, the only agreement so far was that the next one should be from somewhere else, making it her duty to moderate the session.

"Having been an ambassador, myself," she continued, "I have seen both sides of the ambassadorial mission. I have seen ambassadors fall flat on their faces, and I have seen others rise to great acclaim through their tireless efforts. As we proceed with our task today, there is one quality that must be paramount; the person selected for this post must be an expert communicator. It is not necessary for the ambassador to be highly polished, but she should be tactful and *must* be able to get the message across clearly and precisely."

"As everyone here well knows, communication among diplomats involves dialogue: unless the diplomat is willing to give information, it is unlikely that he or she will be able to obtain it." She smiled, dialing the magnetism up several notches. "Think about the parties you have been to on the diplomatic circuit. The person that everyone always wants to talk to is the one who is interesting to talk with. At the other end of the spectrum is the guy on the couch, alone with his drink. The way people avoid him, you would probably think he has some sort of contagious disease." She heard several chuckles from the audience. "I see everyone is familiar with that person." She could see that she scored with that one.

"For a moment," she continued, "let us try to stand in the shoes of our hypothetical ambassador, so that we may better know the necessary qualities of the person expected to fill the post. On one hand, the ambassador must convince the other government of the significance of the subject under negotiation and why agreeing to the ambassador's position is useful to his own country, or planet in this case. Having achieved this, the ambassador then must also convince her own government to go along with it as well. This will be a big job, as she will not have one boss, but all of the nations that are currently represented in this noble body. Good luck with that! I know most of you," she said with a wink, "and I couldn't imagine trying to satisfy all of you at once." The double entendre was intentional, and there was laughter across the auditorium. "What's even worse is that, in all likelihood, the ambassador will return to find out that she now has even more bosses than when she left."

She worked the crowd for another 10 minutes, talking about the importance of a number of qualities like discretion, a good sense of humor and the importance of good judgment. By the time she was finished, they were eating out of her hand. A single hand was raised at the end of the applause. As was previously agreed, the German president stood up and formally nominated the Cobalt Countess for the post. With the exception of the Russian and French delegates, her appointment was unanimous.

Chapter Eight

"**T**his is the squad bay," said the leader of the 'Ground Force,' Staff Sergeant Jim 'Shuteye' Chang, leading a new person into the large open room. The man was wearing a camouflage uniform with a dragon insignia and looked as hard as any of the others currently taking off their gear. Shuteye indicated the men and women stowing their gear. "This is Squad 'A,' the 'Space Force,' which is just getting back from a mission where they kicked ass and took names." Several calls of the platoon's motto, "Gluck ab!" were heard from around the room.

"This room is similar to the locker room of a major sports team," Shuteye continued, "in that everyone has a locker." The newbie could see lockers ringing the walls of the room, with benches next to them. The lockers looked much larger and different than any sports team's lockers he had seen. In addition to a clothes tree on which the Alpha Squad members were hanging their space suits, there were also clips for harnesses and other apparel, a rack for stowing combat weapons and a variety of drawers to hold the squad members' other implements of destruction. Shuteye pointed to an empty cubicle. "That one's yours. You'll get a suit and powered weapons; you're also allowed to use any unpowered weapons that you want to bring."

"This is Sergeant Alka Zoromski," Shuteye announced to the squad. "He's from the Polish Operational Maneuver Response

65

Group, or GROM as you may have heard it called. Sergeant Zoromski, this is Alpha Squad."

"Alka, huh?" asked a large man with dark hair.

"Yes," replied Zoromski. "It means, 'Defender of Man.'"

"Well, you'll fit right in then," said the man. "Welcome. I'm Master Chief Ryan O'Leary, the Space Force Leader. You can call me 'Master Chief.' I'm also the senior enlisted for the squad. Come see me if you need to, but use your chain of command as much as you can." Leading him through the squad bay, Master Chief introduced all of the human members of his squad. He got to the last two members and said, "You've probably heard that we have a couple of extraterrestrials in the unit. This is Bob and Doug from the Epsilon Eridani system. Those aren't their real names, but it's a close approximation of them."

Zoromski looked at the two aliens, who looked like five feet tall versions of the tyrannosaurus rex dinosaur model he had seen at the Museum of Evolution in Warsaw. The two lizards smiled at him, revealing rows of large, very sharp looking teeth. He was unable to keep from flinching back slightly from the sight.

"Don't worry," said Master Chief, "they have that affect on everyone the first time they meet them. You'll get used to them."

"Hi, I'm Bobellisssissolliss," said Bob.

"I'm Dugelllisssollisssesss," added Doug.

"Got it," said Zoromski, "Bob and Doug."

Chapter Nine

"We interrupt your regularly scheduled programming," a serious-looking Anna St. Cloud reported, "to take you to the National Assembly Building in Abuja, Nigeria, where the participating heads of state have been meeting for three days to set up the workings of the new world government. I understand that the government has an important announcement that is going to be carried worldwide. We go now to Abuja, Nigeria."

The camera changed to a podium with a strange seal on it. The device had a golden eagle in its center that was similar to the garuda of Hindu or Buddhist mythology. In its talons, it held a white ribbon scroll that read "Republic of Terra." An Indian woman walked up to the podium confidently, smiled and said "Hello, people of Terra. I am Katrina Nehru, and I am happy to have been chosen to be the first president of the Republic of Terra." She paused. "Now, I know that many of you have never heard of the Republic of Terra," she said when she continued, "which is why I wanted to talk to everyone on the planet today. The world's leaders have been hard at work for the last week, working to set up this new world government, and I wanted to make you aware of our progress."

"Many of you may be wondering why we chose the name, 'Republic of Terra,'" she said. "There are a couple of reasons. First, we wanted everyone to understand that we are a republican form of

67

government, in which the affairs of the state are a public matter. There are no rulers working on their own secret, hidden agendas; instead, all of the government is here for the best interests of all humankind. I know this will be met with some cynicism around the world, but I am here today to tell you that it's true. The Republic of Terra has been established as an entity where the president is legitimized by both a constitution and a public vote to work in the best interests of the entire world. This form of government closely follows the governmental systems of many of its participating republics, like Russia, France, the United States and my own nation, India."

"The second reason," she continued, "is that our government is already faced with a need to grow beyond the borders of our own planet. We have been contacted by the government of the planet Domus, in the Epsilon Eridani system, and they have requested to join our union. Our government has been set up to include not only the former nations of Earth, but also the two states that form the government of Domus." She looked straight at the camera as she said, "There is strength in numbers, and we need the resources they have. We have welcomed them into our union." Her tone of voice suggested that this point was not up for discussion.

"The next questions that you are probably going to ask," President Nehru guessed, "are how is this government going to work, and how do I know that it has my best interests at heart? As I have already stated, the Republic of Terra government will function similarly to the largest republics on the planet, with the current nations of Earth becoming states in the new republic. Although there will be some growing pains, I expect the transition to go fairly smoothly, as most people live under similar systems. For example, most of the participating nations have three branches of government to ensure the separation of power. The Republic of Terra also has three branches of government, the executive, the legislative and the judicial branches, so this should be very familiar to most of the people of Earth."

"Like India and the United States, the executive branch of the Republic of Terra will be led by a president, who will be elected indirectly by an electoral college of representatives from the current nations. The president will serve a five-year term and can be re-elected once. The legislative branch will have a bicameral, or two-house, parliament. The upper house, or 'Council of States,' will be made up of two representatives from each of the previously independent nations, who will serve in staggered, six-year terms. How each of these will be elected is up to the individual states. Seats in the lower house, or 'House of the People,' will be proportional to the individual state's populations, with a seat given for every 50 million people or fraction thereof. That way, each nation will have at least one seat in the House of the People, regardless of its actual size. These representatives will also serve in staggered, six-year terms."

"The judicial branch will be made up of a Supreme Court, which will oversee the efforts of the High Courts in each of the current member nations. Its function is not to impose new laws over the member states; instead, it is the ultimate interpreter of the constitution and will be empowered to strike down state laws which are in contravention to it. It will also have original jurisdiction over cases involving fundamental rights and disputes between the nation-states and the republic's government."

"We intend for this nation to be built around order and the rule of law, led by an open and transparent government. No individual will be above the rules," she said as she walked around to the front of the podium. "Delegates from all of the participating nations have developed this, our new seal, as a symbol of the government and people of the Republic of Terra." She pointed to the golden eagle. "Our new nation is a nation born of war. The eagle, or garuda for many of our Asian population, is a strong, brave bird that symbolizes our nation's strength through war, while the gold color symbolizes greatness and glory. Like the Seal of Indonesia, the feathers on the bird are symbolic. There are 22 feathers on each wing, five feathers on the tail, 20 feathers below the shield on its legs and the base of its tail and 20 feathers on its neck. If you put all of these together, you have today's date, 22/5/2020, the date that our new republic was born."

"The shield on the eagle's chest is a martial symbol, standing for defense not only of the countries, but of the two planets in our republic. It has a background divided into quarters, colored black and white in a checkerboard pattern. The black quadrant bearing the golden star at the upper right corresponds to the belief in One Supreme God. The color black represents space and the star for the one God that exists no matter where we go. The star is a common symbol not only for Islam, Christianity, Hinduism and Buddhism, but also for the secular ideology of socialism as well. While this symbol may be disconcerting for some, there will not be any religion that everyone is made to follow. People are encouraged to believe in whatever manner they will, or not to believe at all if that is their desire, but it was important to the overwhelming majority of the participating nations that this symbol be included."

"The yin and yang symbol of unity is in the lower right on a white background. This symbol shows us that, regardless of how opposite or contrary we may seem to each other at times, we are all interconnected and interdependent on each other. There are many dualities in nature, like light and dark, fire and water, and life and death. Neither of these has meaning without the other. They are physical manifestations of the yin and yang concept that draws all of us together. The American motto of 'E pluribus unum,' or 'Out of many, one,' was also suggested, but this symbol was chosen as it is symbolic to a larger number of our people."

"In the upper left quarter on a white background, there is a golden laurel wreath. This symbolizes our belief in the concept of democracy and its importance in how this republic is governed. The laurel wreath goes back to the ancient Athenians, who first came up with the concept of democracy. It can also symbolize a master's degree of wisdom when it is used as 'poet laureate,' or can refer to victory. These last two concepts are also significant in the laurel wreath's choice as a symbol.

"Finally, in the lower left quarter on a black background is a golden sheaf of wheat, representing sustenance and livelihood. With a fair government and a strong military to protect us from the dangers that lurk beyond our system's borders, our people will be able to follow their dreams and be productive and happy."

"Completing the design," she said, pointing over the eagle's head, "there are two gold stars over its head. These symbolize the two star systems, the Solar System and the Epsilon Eridani system, that make up the republic. Will there be additional stars in this constellation?" she asked. "Who knows? I, for one, expect there to be more; however, that is dependent on what we do to make it possible. Not just what I do, but what every member of the Republic of Terra does on a daily basis. Everyone is important to our efforts to protect and defend our planet. To paraphrase the American statesman, John F.

Kennedy, ask not what your planet can do for you, but instead, ask what you can do for your planet and the Republic of Terra!"

She turned and went back behind the podium. While she was moving, a number of people came onto the stage. "As president of the Republic of Terra, I am looking forward to working for all of you," said Nehru. "Until a worldwide election can be held, the council of leaders forming the republic decided to set up the initial government in relation to the populations of the countries represented. Since China has decided not to join our efforts as of yet, India is the largest participating nation, with over a billion people. As such, India was selected to fill the presidential post, and I was chosen for this position. For those of you who don't know me, I was previously the vice president of India, where I was also Chairman of the Rajya Sabha, the upper house of the Parliament of India. The president of India stayed on in that position to ensure the continuity of our government and ensure that the country continued to put all of its efforts into supporting the new government."

"Similarly," she continued, "the United States also nominated its vice president for the vice president slot of the world government. President Bill Jacobs decided to stay on as the U.S. president to ensure that the transition went smoothly. Indonesia, the third largest participating nation, will fill the Speaker position for the upper house of the legislative branch, the Council of States. Their president will be filling this position. The Brazilian president will be the Speaker for the lower house, the House of the People. The fifth position in order of succession, the Secretary of State, went to the Pakistani president." She looked behind her at the men and women assembled and received a nod. "At this time, we will have the swearing in ceremony for the first five officers of the new government," she said.

Nehru walked over to join the other four leaders. With a small smile of satisfaction, she saw that three of the five leaders were women; besides herself, the presidents of Indonesia and Brazil were also women. All four of the other leaders were each standing in front of a representative of his/her respective faith. Nehru went to stand in front of the Hindu guru waiting for her. As one, the spiritual leaders said, "Do you swear in the name of your God, or what you hold holy, to faithfully execute your office within the Republic of Terra?"

The five leaders replied, "I do."

The religious leaders asked "Will you preserve, protect and defend the Constitution and the law, to the best of your abilities?"

The five leaders answered, "I will."

The religious leaders asked, "And will you devote yourself to the service and well-being of the people of the Republic of Terra?"

The five leaders replied again, "I will."

The guru reached out to shake President Nehru's hand as the rest of the religious leaders did the same for their charges. "Congratulations, Mrs. President," said the guru.

The camera at KIRO-TV returned to Ms. St. Cloud. "There you have it, live," she commented. "The new president of the world, President Katrina Nehru, has been sworn in. We now take you back to your regularly scheduled programming, already in progress."

Chapter Ten

"Thanks for coming, Steropes," said Calvin as he invited the Psiclops into his office and gave him a seat.

Steropes looked around curiously. "Is this to be a meeting between just you and me?" he asked. "You certainly can't be expecting to fit too many more people into this room."

"Yes," Calvin replied, "it's just us. I figured that you were the one Psiclops that I was most likely to get a straight answer from."

"Thank you," replied Steropes. "I think."

"You have to admit that you guys haven't always been completely forthcoming," Calvin said. "Some people might even say that you haven't always been entirely honest, either."

Steropes shrugged. "We are constrained..." he said.

"Yeah, yeah, I know," interrupted Calvin, cutting him off. "You have rules, blah, blah, blah. I've been around you more than anyone else, and I'm starting to get a pretty good sense of when you are omitting details to stay within the rules and when you're intentionally misleading us or bending the truth."

Steropes turned up his palms and shrugged his shoulders again. "I'm not sure what you want me to say," he finally offered.

"I don't want you to say anything, other than the full truth and nothing but the truth," replied Calvin. "If you don't feel like you can tell me something, regardless of the reason, just say that you can't tell me that, OK?"

"I will do my best," answered Steropes.

"See?" asked Calvin. "One question, and you are already hedging your answers. Rather than giving me a simple 'yes' or 'no' answer, you had to qualify that answer, giving you the ability to come back later and say, 'well, I wasn't able to answer that question at that time."

"Yes," replied Steropes, "I do see what you are saying. We have been in the habit of doing it for so long that it is second nature to us. What is it that you want to know?"

"A little while ago," Calvin said, "Arges made the comment that I had the ability to be a telepath. Since then, he has avoided me. When he wasn't able to dodge me, he changed the subject when I brought it up or found other ways to keep from answering the question. You are the Psiclops that I can most count on for a straight answer. *What did he mean?*"

"Did he say that it was too difficult for him to talk about?" asked Steropes in lieu of an answer.

"As a matter of fact," replied Calvin, "he said almost those exact words."

Steropes nodded. "I figured he would," he said, "and that is probably the truth, believe it or not." He paused, obviously contemplating how to tell the story. "You are aware, of course, that Arges does not do well around conflict, correct?" he finally asked.

"Yeah," Calvin answered. "Usually, he runs screaming from it."

"Most Psiclopes do," noted Steropes. "I am one of the few that are able to deal with conflict, mostly from close association with it in the past. Neither he nor Brontes would be able to tell this story." He paused, considering. "Several thousand years ago, all humans were able to speak mentally," he said. "It was a trait that helped them hunt and ensured their survival. The ability was dormant when a child was born, but when they reached adulthood, their parents could give them a psychic 'nudge' that brought them into full Awareness of everyone around them. This also let them speak telepathically with each other." He paused again.

"Atlantis was the largest city on the planet," he continued looking down at his hands. Calvin could hear the anguish in his voice as Steropes' relived the city's final days. "It was home to tens of thousands of the brightest people in the world. When it was destroyed, all of them were killed. Their outcry as their lives were extinguished was horrible...simply horrible."

With a sniff, he continued, "The psychic trauma of such a large number of humans dying at the same time burned out the psychic ability of every human alive at that time and greatly affected all of us Psiclopes for a long time, as well. It caused us to have to go into an extended sleep cycle to repair the damage done to our brains. Succeeding generations of humans have had the telepathic ability, but haven't had anyone to help 'nudge' them into Awareness. Unfortunately, our brains function differently, and we cannot do it for you. Eventually, the knowledge that the ability existed was lost. Since then, scientists have often wondered why so much of the brain seems unused; that is why."

"So how do we activate it again?" asked Calvin.

"I do not know," replied Steropes. "Perhaps a different race might be able to activate it within you. The ability runs more strongly in you than in all of the humans I have known since the fall of Atlantis. That is why you can sense us when we are around, even if we are cloaked. It is also why you hear a buzzing sound around us. You are catching a piece of our telepathic conversation although it isn't enough for you to decipher."

President's Chambers, National Assembly Building, Abuja, Nigeria, June 3, 2020

"Now that we have a functioning world government," Terran President Katrina Nehru said, "we would like to know more about the galactic political environment." The president had asked the Psiclopes to attend a strategy session with the five senior leaders of the Terran government. A private meeting, it was being held in the president's conference room so that any information that might be worrisome to the general public could be controlled.

"What is it that you are inquiring about?" asked Arges.

"As you are aware," Masood Khalil, the Secretary of State replied, "we are a small stellar nation that is largely unaware of its surroundings. We know of only one other culture, beyond our two planets, and that race attacked us without provocation. As Secretary of State, I would find it most helpful to know what other races we are likely to come in contact with as we journey further out into the stars. It would be nice to know which civilizations to avoid, and which might give us aid. Perhaps a brief history of the galaxy might be a good start so that we understand what is going on out there. It is time that we found out more about the galaxy."

"It's well past time we found out," disagreed the vice president. As the closest confidant of the U.S. president, he had known about the Psiclopes for almost as long as anyone. The fact that they had delayed passing on this knowledge was a constant source of irritation to him.

"Yes," replied Arges, "it is past time for you to hear this, but there were excellent reasons for the delay. We can debate the efficacy of the reasons at another time." He looked at Steropes. "Perhaps you would like to brief them on this topic?"

"I would be happy to," answered Steropes. "Without going too far into it, I will start out by saying that there have been space-travelling civilizations for tens of thousands of years. Most of the races that currently exist came onto the galactic scene about 11,000 years ago. We know that there were civilizations that existed a long time before that, the Progenitors, but they vanished before the current races came to prominence. All we have are their artifacts, like the stargates, to tell their tale."

"Around 11,000 years ago," continued Steropes, "seven races came into contact with each other. Five of these races were generally peaceful in nature, while two of them were not. The five banded together and were able to contain the advances of the two. One of the warlike races destroyed itself; the other is a race you have already met, the Ssselipsssiss that your forces fought on their first mission. They are a culture built on warfare; all they understand is force."

"The five original peaceful races saw that they were stronger together than apart, so they decided to form the Alliance of Civilizations. The Psiclopes were one of those founding races and agreed to host the alliance government on our home planet of Olympos. That was just over 10,000 years ago. At that time we had a thriving society. All of the races got along well, and we were at the height of our power. This arrangement worked out well for almost 6,000 years."

"The beginning of the end for the Alliance of Civilizations came just over 4,000 years ago. It didn't happen because of the appearance of a new culture, or as a result of bad leadership or through any other cause that you might expect. The downfall of the Psiclopes society, and the alliance as a whole, was caused by the development of an anti-aging technology discovered by one of our scientists."

"How is that?" asked the speaker of the lower house of parliament. A model before becoming the Brazilian president, Amanda Silva remained ever-conscious of her looks. If an anti-aging process existed, she wanted it.

"Our scientists found a way to rejuvenate cells at the most basic level," replied Brontes, taking up the story. "They didn't just slow the effects of aging; they stopped it completely. The process couldn't reverse any aging that had already taken place, but it could stop it from proceeding. For all intents and purposes, we became immortal." She didn't sound happy about it.

"And that is a bad thing?" prompted President Nehru.

"Yes," Brontes confirmed. "Becoming immortal might not be so bad by itself, but the side effects of the process weren't known for some time. One of these effects is that the immortality process caused sterility in both males and females. Just one treatment of the anti-aging process, and a person was unable to have children. On that day, our race began to die. Most of the people got the treatment before the side effect was known; others decided that it was still worth having, and they got it even though they knew what it meant. A few decided not to have the treatment, but over the course of the intervening years, nearly all of them have died out or chosen to get the treatment. Our race is no longer producing new members. Although numbering in the tens of billions 4,000 years ago, our numbers are now down to less than 10 million, with eight million on our home world and other odds and ends scattered throughout the universe, like the three of us here. We don't dare fight or do anything dangerous; to do so only hastens the extinction of our race."

"Did the other races get the process?" asked President Nehru. "Would it work for them?"

"Yes," said Steropes, "it works for most, but not all, of the other races. The side effects were known before it made it off planet, though, and most of the other races outlawed the process from the start. Although a couple of the minor races embraced it, the treatment only caught on in one other alliance culture; they are experiencing the death of their race just as we are."

"It is ironic," noted the Secretary of State, "that the process that removes the specter of death from an individual causes the death of the race."

"Who would want that?" asked President Nehru. "To give up your race for a chance to stop your individual aging?"

"I would," replied Speaker Silva. "Where do I sign?"

Brontes looked at Speaker Silva. "Be careful what you ask for," she said. "It does not always work out the way you hope it will."

"OK," said President Nehru. "So where does that leave us? What is the state of the alliance now?"

"The alliance is finished," replied Arges. "When the last of our politicians died about 800 years ago, the Psiclopes dropped out of the alliance, as did the other race that accepted the treatment, the Hooolongs. When we left, we 'invited' the alliance to move its headquarters off of our planet. No one cared anymore, and our society just didn't want to be bothered with the alliance politicians' comings and goings. Society got tired and bored with it all. I suppose that the three of us would have been the same had we stayed there; it is only by observing your race on a daily basis that we have stayed young at heart."

"When the alliance moved off of our planet," Steropes said, "the other original members couldn't agree on where to take the alliance headquarters. All of them wanted the increased trade and status that having it would bring. They fell to fighting amongst themselves. Years became decades and decades became centuries without resolution. Without the united front against aggression that the alliance provided, other races that had formerly been held in check began to get away with more and more. Instead of putting down their insurrections, the former members of the alliance began to practice a policy of appeasement. They traded away star systems with the hope that each would be the last system that the aggressors wanted."

Steropes shook his head. "Unfortunately," he continued, "just like your countries found in between the world wars, you can't appease aggression. Giving territory to emperors only makes them want more. One hundred years ago, the remaining good races said, 'no more' and refused to cede any more systems. That lasted about two years before the Ssselipsssiss attacked the Mrowry, one of the former alliance members. The Mrowry called to the rest for aid, but none came. Had the others helped, the war would have probably been over quickly. As it was, it lasted over 30 years and resulted in the destruction of the societies on several planets. While the Mrowry were entangled with the Ssselipsssiss, several other races attacked other former members of the alliance. Within a few years, there was warfare across most of the galaxy. Trade came to a near standstill, and most of the nations began focusing solely on fortifying the systems they had to try to protect them from attack. Twenty years ago, several of the former members decided to try to re-implement the alliance. We know this because they invited the Psiclopes to participate."

"Olympos, our home world, chose not to join them," said Arges. "We do not know what happened after that, because the other nations decided to shun our society. They expected us to take up the leadership mantle that we had held for thousands of years. When we did not, they were most disappointed with us."

"Disgusted would probably be a better word," noted Steropes. "I believe the final communication that Olympos received was, 'Look to your own borders then, oath breakers, because we will no longer come to your aid.' We still had communications with Olympos then so we knew what was going on. We also heard that one of the other alliance members, the Depsips, had been attacked by a Drakul force. We thought that the Drakuls had been annihilated in one of the last joint actions of the alliance, but apparently, they were not. When the Depsips last saw the Drakuls, they were moving in the general direction of Olympos. We have never had a fleet, so there was nothing in their way to stop them."

"Shortly after that, we lost communications with our home world," said Arges. "We don't know what happened, whether someone found one of our communications beacons back to Olympos or whether Olympos was attacked and destroyed. We just don't know. We believe that some of the former alliance members are continuing the fight, and they may even be trying to resurrect the alliance, but they are in retreat in most places and on the defensive."

"So you've pretty much been lying to us the whole time about the state of affairs in the galaxy," commented the vice president, glaring at Arges. "You've only told us what you thought would get us to do what you wanted us to do. You've been manipulating us all along."

"From one point of view, perhaps," said Arges. "We did what we thought we needed to in order to get your aid. It is important to understand, though, that the things we asked of you were necessary to help your civilization advance and become better prepared to protect itself. When Solomon forecast that he expected the Solar System to be discovered by an aggressive race within the next 25 years, we knew we had to act. Trying to find out what happened on Olympos was just a serendipitous byproduct of helping you to prepare for the dangers that may be coming."

"Call it what you will," growled the vice president; "you still lied to us. How do we know that what you're saying now is true? How will we ever know what you say is true?"

"I guess you never will," replied Arges. "That is to be expected, of course. Unfortunately, the situation is so dire now that you don't have any choice but to believe us. If you don't, we will all be destroyed."

"What advice would you give us then?" asked President Nehru.

"You need help," replied Arges. "Regardless of whether you believe us about anything else, you must understand that much is true. The last time we were out, we ran into a Ssselipsssiss base. If we are close to their territory, we are also close to the Depsips civilization as well. Their civilization was relatively close to the lizards. If we scout around the lizards' systems, we may be able to find it."

"We also might find more lizards than we're able to handle on our own," noted the vice president.

"That is true," agreed Steropes. "Before we lost contact with our society, we heard that several of the Depsips' systems had been lost to the lizards. They did, however, still have a manufacturing center in a pocket star system, and that is where I think we need to go. If we could link up with them, we might be able to work together to push back the lizards and then get their aid against the Drakuls if they come."

"I am not aware of any better plans," said President Nehru. "I will contact our military leaders and have them get in touch with you. If they do not have any better ideas, we will make that the next mission of the *Vella Gulf.*"

"I have a question," interjected the vice president into the silence that followed. "With all of these civilizations looking to take over other civilizations' planets and races, how come none of them have come to take over ours before now?"

"There are several reasons for this," replied Steropes. "First of all, when we first found your planet, civilization was already in decline. We decided at that time not to mention Earth to the other races, to keep you from being one more bargaining chip for the advanced races to throw around."

"So, you're saying that we actually have you to thank for our lack of visibility?" asked President Nehru.

"In a manner of speaking," replied Brontes, "yes, you do."

"Second," continued Steropes, "it is incorrect to believe that no other civilizations have found this planet. In fact, at least six different civilizations have landed on this planet, besides our own. You are lucky in that either they weren't able to get word of your existence to their home worlds or that we were able to fight them off for you."

"Like the Drakuls when they attacked Atlantis?" asked the vice president.

"Yes, just like that," agreed Steropes. "I admit that we wouldn't have been able to deal with the Drakuls without human assistance, but the humans at the time wouldn't have been able to handle them without the weapons we provided. Finally, have you ever heard of the Fermi Paradox?" He looked around the room. All of the Terrans shook their heads.

"The Fermi paradox was proposed by physicists Enrico Fermi and Michael Hart. Their question was, in a nutshell, since your Sun is a young star, and there are billions of stars in the galaxy that are billions of years older, why hasn't the Earth seen any existence of intelligent life? The answer to this is really quite simple. All of the other major civilizations in the galaxy started out on super-Earth-type planets, those that were many times the size of your Earth. To the majority of the civilizations, your lower mass planet simply doesn't have the ideal conditions necessary for life. Despite your prosperity on it, Earth is a marginal planet when it comes to what most civilizations believe are the required conditions to support life."

Steropes paused and looked at the vice president. "It's simple," Steropes said in conclusion. "Despite the fact that many of you believe yourselves and your planet to be important, the fact is that, until now, neither you nor your planet has been big enough or important enough for anyone to notice."

Chapter Eleven

***Asp 01*, Approaching Ganymede, Solar System, June 15, 2020**

Jupiter filled most of the space fighter's view screen. Calvin's target, the moon Ganymede, was silhouetted in front of it. The largest satellite in the Solar System, Ganymede was larger than Mercury and almost three-quarters the size of Mars. Ganymede made a great target, as it had variations in its coloring that formed intricate patterns across its surface. These color variations could be seen from a long way off and made excellent visual references. About 40% of the surface of the moon was covered by highly cratered dark regions, with the remaining 60% covered by a light, grooved terrain. In addition to the different levels of shading, there were also a number of large craters that were visible due to the bright rays of ejected material that had splashed out from the craters when asteroids hit the moon. Although formed in the same manner as the craters on the Earth's moon, they lacked the same kind of central depressions, due to the slow and gradual adjustment of Ganymede's soft icy surface.

The squadron's target was in the middle of the Tros crater. The depression was one of the biggest on the moon, a large white area nearly 60 miles across. As the moon started to swell ahead of him with the view screen's enhancements, he could see it as a white dot in the upper right of the moon.

"*Take combat spread,*" Calvin commed. He watched as the other five Asp fighters that had been flying alongside him spread out to both sides. On his in-head display, he could see that the other half of the squadron, the six Viper fighters, spread out similarly 50 miles 'above' him. The four crews that had survived the *Vella Gulf's* first mission were flying the new Asps; the other two Asps and all of the Vipers were crewed by new personnel. As the fighters all reached their pre-briefed positions and settled into them, Calvin smiled. This was their first full-squadron strike. So far, so good.

"*I wonder when they're going to start shooting at us?*" asked one of the new WSOs over the radio. With a thought, Calvin saw that it was Lieutenant Ali Ahmed Al-Amri in *Viper 05*.

"*Are you in a hurry to die?*" Calvin asked, annoyed that the Saudi had violated radio silence. "*Stay off the frequency unless you have something important to say.*"

Now that the question had been asked, Calvin wondered when they *were* going to start shooting. The brief said that the enemy's missiles had a range of 15 million miles, and they were passing 17 million miles. The space fighters' defensive systems had reported several surveillance radars active, but none of the tracking radars were yet. Even though the Terrans were trying to achieve surprise, Calvin didn't think that they had fooled anyone. Especially with people talking on the radios when they weren't supposed to be. They were probably just letting the Terrans get into the heart of the defensive systems' envelopes so that they had a better chance of killing them. Still, the defenders should have launched already if they were going to intercept the Terrans at a distance of 15 million miles.

The squadron had to run the gauntlet of the moon's missile defenses for 11 million miles before they could launch their missiles at four million miles. Their best defense, especially for the initial phase of the run-in, was to maneuver. Although some galactic civilization had figured out how to make communications go faster than light, no one had yet figured out how to make radars do so. Traveling at just over a 186,000 miles per second, it would take the radar beam about 80 seconds to cross the distance from the moon to the fighters located 15 million miles out, and then another 80 seconds to get back. In that time, the fighters traveling at about 100 million miles per hour would have moved over four million miles.

Passing 15 million miles, the tracking radars activated. "*Space-hawks, begin evasive maneuvers!*" Calvin's WSO, Lieutenant Imagawa 'Samurai' Sadayo commed.

The enemy's strategy quickly became apparent. Since they would only have time to fire one or two volleys of missiles at the fighters, the enemy defenders launched several missiles from each of their launchers, trying to bracket where the Terran fighters might be when the missiles arrived. As each of the missiles had their own acquisition and targeting systems, they only had to get them 'close enough' to the space fighters for the missiles' onboard radars to acquire them, but with the fighters spread out, it was impossible for the defenders to mass their attack on any single fighter.

The fighters continued to maneuver randomly and violently as they got closer to the target. The fighters' anti-missile lasers began firing at the missiles that had targeted them, and the WSOs did their best to defend themselves while still trying to complete the attack. Their best wasn't good enough for some of them, and a few of the Terran fighters were enveloped in nuclear explosions. Samurai looked through his targeting system and could just make out the missile site that was their target. Calvin had done a good job banking their craft around, and they still hadn't been hit. The range counted down until it was time for the attack sequence. "*Standby...*" Samurai said to Calvin. The call was repeated throughout the squadron as the WSOs acquired their targets and locked their missiles onto them. "*Acquired!*" Samurai commed. "*Roll out!*"

Calvin ceased maneuvering and leveled the wings of the space fighter. This was the most critical and dangerous part of the attack run, as the missiles needed a couple of seconds to get the final targeting data and align themselves, without having large g-forces ripping them from side to side. Within 1.5 seconds, the missiles had everything they needed and a green 'Ready' light came on in front of Calvin. "*Firing!*" he said and then, "*Missiles away!*" The two big anti-surface missiles leaped from under his wings and raced toward the target, accelerating as they went. Even without any explosives in them, the force of the missiles hitting at a sizable percentage of the speed of light generated devastating amounts of energy, and the missiles tore huge chunks out of the moon.

Once the missiles were clear, Calvin began to jerk the space fighter back and forth again, hoping to avoid any additional missiles fired at them. His missiles hit the target, and he watched as the squadron's other missiles began impacting the target area. Their missiles were only intended to silence the defenses, not to destroy the target, and the space fighters continued inbound on their strafing runs. At the speed he was traveling, he wasn't able to line up the laser visually for the shot. Instead, Samurai designated the target to the computer, and the computer began tracking it. As the Asp came in range, the computer fired, its high-powered laser burning through the target and into the surface of the moon.

In the blink of an eye, the fighter was past the target and headed back out to space with the other fighters of the squadron following behind them. Calvin continued to jink the fighter around in case any of the defensive missile systems were still operational. Passing 15 million miles from the target, Calvin sighed and relaxed. They were clear. *"All Spacehawks join on me,"* he commed.

Calvin looked over to Samurai. "How'd we do?" he asked.

"We got the target," Samurai replied, "but we lost over half of our fighters doing it. I hope we don't have to attack too many more targets like that. There won't be any of us left!"

"Good thing it was only practice," said Calvin with a sigh.

Spacehawk Ready Room, TSS *Vella Gulf,* Solar System, June 15, 2020

"As you can see from the hologram," Samurai said in debrief, "everything started out well." He pressed the button and a six-feet tall, three dimensional digital hologram appeared next to him at the front of the ready room. The briefing space was filled to capacity as Calvin had required all of the squadron's pilots and WSOs to attend. Everyone leaned in, trying to see it more clearly.

The digital hologram showed Ganymede and the two groups of fighters inbound to it. The facilities of their enemy, the nation of 'Red,' were shown in red on the moon. With Calvin's call to assume combat spread, the 12 spacecraft made two long lines of six ships with the six Vipers in a line abreast 'above' the line of the six Asps. Samurai stopped the replay. "Here we are just before the targeting radars began illuminating us. Everyone is in perfect formation. As it turned out, our electronic countermeasures (ECM) systems were functioning perfectly, and they weren't aware we were coming." Solomon, the *Vella Gulf's* artificial intelligence was simulating the enemy forces and had determined that, with the parameters given for their equipment, the enemy wouldn't have seen the attacking force.

"And then *someone* talked on the radio and alerted them to our presence," Samurai chided. He didn't say who it was, but everyone already knew. "Since radio travels faster than light, they were instantly aware of our attack."

"Nice job, Chatty Cathy," said someone from the back of the room, naming the 20th century talking doll.

"Once the transmission reached the defenders, they focused their high power tracking radars on us and were able to burn through our ECM." The crews could see the simulated missiles begin launching from the moon, and the space fighters began maneuvering to avoid the incoming weapons. The initial volley claimed three of the Vipers and one of the Asps. Their icons flashed and then went out. Samurai paused the playback.

"*Viper 02, Viper 05* and *Asp 06* were not jinking enough and were hit in the initial volley," commented Samurai. "They're all dead, and their missiles won't count."

"What about me, mate?" asked Lieutenant Nicolas Wilson. "*Viper 06* got killed even though we were maneuvering like we were supposed to."

"To use an American phrase, shit happens," Samurai told the Australian. "You did everything right, but the red forces got lucky and shot you down. It was just your day to die; I hope you did it well."

"Aw, hell," mumbled Lieutenant Wilson, shaking his head. No one ever wanted to be singled out as the unlucky one. As aviators were superstitious by nature, now all of the WSOs would think twice when they were crewed with him.

Samurai restarted the hologram. "Here we are at the launch point," he said. The crews could see the fighters level off, and missiles begin tracking from the Terran fighters back toward Jupiter's moon. One of the remaining Vipers winked out. He stopped the replay. "It looks like *Viper 03* became mesmerized by the missile launch and forgot to start maneuvering again. Two missiles locked onto him while he flew straight toward the target and detonated close by. There were no survivors."

"Unfortunately, that is true," agreed Lieutenant Gurnoor Bhola. "I have never launched missiles that large before, and they were quite striking as they left the fighter. I admit to being distracted by it. It will not happen again."

"Well, that's why we do these things," noted Calvin, "so that you can learn and not make those mistakes in combat. No one was hurt today, but had this been real, you would be dead now. Hopefully you learned from it."

"I did," said the Indian, looking embarrassed.

Samurai restarted the hologram. "You can see our missiles start hitting the defensive sites," Samurai pointed out. "Most of the batteries were destroyed, except for the ones that would have been targeted by the fighters we had already lost. As you can see, one of these gets off another missile in close, hitting *Asp 03*."

"I disagree," said Lieutenant Steven Jackson. "I'm going to have to complain to Solomon. There's no way they got me."

"*Complain all you want,*" interjected Solomon, who had been listening with half an electronic ear. "*Mathematical analysis showed that there was an 87% chance of your destruction. You were dead.*"

Most of the crews laughed as the pilot sputtered something about computers that were too big for their britches.

"The rest of the strike fighters successfully made their firing runs," said Samurai, regaining control, "and the target was destroyed. Unfortunately, *Viper 01* and *Viper 04* forgot to maneuver on the way back out and got missiles straight up their butts. They were destroyed as well."

Calvin walked up to stand next to Samurai. "The bottom line is that we've got to do better. Most of these fatalities were because people didn't follow procedures. *They could have been avoided but now you're dead!* You have to do better than that. *We* have to do better than that! There are only 12 fighters in *the entire Terran Space Navy*! Those 12 fighters and our one cruiser are all that stand between a host of aliens and the families you love. If you can't follow procedures, let me know now so that we can send you home and get aircrews that can!"

With that, Calvin turned and walked out of the ready room, leaving a squadron of stunned aviators in his wake. If nothing else, Samurai thought, he definitely made his point.

Chapter Twelve

Bridge, TSS *Vella Gulf*, Dark Side of the Moon, Solar System, June 23, 2020

Calvin and the *Vella Gulf's* new commanding officer, Captain Lorena Griffin, watched from the bridge of the *Vella Gulf* as the Class 1 replicator was lowered onto the *Vella Gulf*. Griffin could tell by the way that Calvin's hands moved that he wished he was piloting the shuttle.

"One of the hardest things about being a commanding officer is letting other people do things you know you can do better," she commented.

"I know," said Calvin. "I have more time flying the shuttles than anyone else, even with all of the time I've had to spend in government meetings. If I don't give them a chance to do it, though, they'll never get any better at it, nor will they ever gain any confidence that they 'can' do it, which is probably even worse. There's nothing worse than a pilot that doesn't think he can do something; being timid is the wrong way to fly a space fighter...or even a shuttle. All of our pilots are the best that their nations had to offer or they wouldn't be here. Still, it *is* hard to let go."

"Well, that's the last thing that we've been waiting for," replied Captain Griffin. "Once we get that loaded, we'll be underway shortly and away from all of those meetings you're so fond of."

"I can't wait," said Calvin. "Although there's a good chance of getting killed, it's still better to be out there trying to help the Earth than it is sitting around in meetings all day just wishing I was dead."

"I understand," said Griffin. "I can't tell you how many times I had various presidents and prime ministers tell me that their soldiers or airmen were the best, and that I needed to make sure they had every opportunity to excel." She shrugged. "If our last mission was any indication, you never know who is going to be in the right place at the right time...or the wrong place at the wrong time." She indicated the screen where the shuttle pilot had just set the replicator onto the Gulf so gently that they hadn't heard a 'clang,' even though they were right under it. "All of the personnel need to be able to function confidently in whatever roles they're filling."

Bridge, TSS *Vella Gulf*, Approaching Black Hole #2, Solar System, June 25, 2020

"Five minutes to wormhole entrance!" called the helmsman from his seat on the left side of the console in front of the captain's chair.

"Sound General Quarters!" ordered Captain Griffin. Onboard United States' ships, the General Quarters announcement was made to signal that battle or the threat of damage was imminent. Also known as "battle stations," whenever the call was made, the crew would quickly prepare the ship for battle. All of the crew (including any that had been sleeping when the call was made) would report to their combat positions and would close all of the ship's watertight and fireproof doors to keep any potential damage from spreading. Her predecessor, Captain James Deutch, had made it standard practice to go through every stargate with General Quarters stations manned, and it seemed prudent to continue that policy. Until you emerged, you never knew what you were going to find on the other side of the stargate. All of the ship's fighters were similarly manned in case they came out of transit to find an enemy vessel waiting for them.

"Aye aye, sir!" said the duty engineer, seated to the right of the helmsman. Responsible for all of the damage control systems, she pushed the appropriate button, and the alarm began sounding. *Bong! Bong! Bong! Bong!* "General Quarters, General Quarters," said the duty engineer over the ship's intercom system, "all hands man your battle stations!"

Captain Griffin looked around and saw that there were a lot of people on the bridge that weren't strictly supposed to be there. Although their stations were on the bridge, they were currently off duty. Captain Griffin didn't blame them for wanting to be on the bridge for their first transit; she had made it a point to be on the bridge for her first one too...and as many of the rest of them as she could after that. It was neat to know that you were one of the first humans to see a new star system. She decided not to kick them off the bridge. If they found themselves in a bad situation after they transited to the next system, she might need the additional help and brainpower.

Steropes was the primary science officer for this mission, and he was running the science station with newly minted Ensign Sara Sommers looking over his shoulder at something he was pointing at. All of the other stations, security, operations and communications, had at least one other person pretending to look at the monitors while they tried to keep one eye on the main viewing screens at the front of the bridge. Calvin sat in his normal seat to the left of Captain Griffin with the new executive officer, Captain Peotr Barishov, to her right. Arges was seated in the chair on the other side of Calvin, and the new ambassador was on the other side of her executive officer.

Captain Griffin smiled. The level of excitement reminded her of their first transit on the last mission. She looked over at Arges. "When we transit, we're still going to wind up in Vulpecula, right? That isn't going to change?"

"The gates are permanently linked," replied Arges. "As far as we know, anyway. I assume that there must be some way of moving them, but it is beyond our technology."

"Is it still going to be salty?" asked Calvin.

"Yes, that stays the same too," answered Arges.

"I'd forgotten about that," said Captain Griffin.

"What do you mean?" asked Barishov. "What is salty?"

"Wormhole entrance," called the helmsman before anyone could answer. "Now!"

The stars in the viewer expanded into infinity, and everything went black...then it went down...then it went purple...then it went salty...

Chapter Thirteen

Bridge, TSS *Vella Gulf*, V452 Vulpecula System (HD 189733), June 25, 2020

"I see what you mean by salty," said Captain Barishov, licking his lips as they emerged from the stargate on the other side.

"Every wormhole leaves a taste in your mouth," said Calvin. "They aren't always salty, but for some reason, every wormhole activates one set of receptors on the tongue. The salty ones aren't too bad."

"The bitter ones are awful," the helmsman said, turning around in his seat. "You'll want a glass of milk when we go through one of those."

"The equipment is stabilizing," said Steropes. "Launching probes." A variety of probes were launched from the ship in all directions, expanding the ship's sensor net and giving them a better chance of detecting any ships or civilizations in the system. They looked for a number of signs of life, from power usage to anomalous gravity spikes to electromagnetic radiation.

After a couple of minutes, Captain Griffin turned around to look at the science station. "How's that scan coming?" she asked.

"I don't see any signs of activity in the system." replied Steropes. "Nothing appears to have changed from the last time we came through this system."

"Permission to stand down the alert fighters?" requested Calvin.

"Granted," replied Captain Griffin.

"*Skipper to all Spacehawks,*" Calvin commed. "*Everything looks the same as the last time we were here. Stand down from alert.*"

Bridge, TSS *Vella Gulf,* Gliese 581 System, July 13, 2020

"System stabilized," noted Steropes, "Based on spectral analysis, we appear to be in the Gliese 581 system."

The ship had arrived in the Gliese 581 system, having gone from Vulpecula 452 through the systems of Kapteyn's Star, Lacaille 8760 and 61 Cygni. As the crew of the *Vella Gulf* had found in their first mission, all three were devoid of planets. 61 Cygni was a nexus system, though; in addition to the stargates that they had used the last time to pass through the system, there was a third gate that had remained unexplored. Before the *Vella Gulf* got too much further from Earth, the military command had decided that it would be a good idea to at least enter the unexplored system to find out what was there. They didn't want the crew to leave potential enemies behind them.

"Gliese 581 is a red dwarf located about 20 light-years away from Earth," Steropes continued. "Its mass is only about a third of your Sun, and its luminosity is only about 0.2% of the Sun. Most of its radiation is in the near infrared, making its total luminosity about 1.3% of the Sun."

Steropes looked up and saw Captain Griffin looking at him intently. "Is something wrong?" he asked.

"That's nice and all," replied Captain Griffin, "but...*are there any signs of enemy activity?*"

Steropes jumped. "Oh!" he said. "Sorry. No, there are no signs of habitation or enemy activity."

"Thank you," said Captain Griffin. She looked at Bullseye, who was sitting in the Squadron Commander's chair. "You may stand down the alert."

"Yes, ma'am," said Bullseye with a smile.

Bridge, TSS *Vella Gulf,* Gliese 581 System, July 18, 2020

"There are six planets in this system," said Steropes, "of which the 3rd, 4th and 5th lie in the habitable zone in orbits from seven million miles out to 24 million miles. All of these are rocky planets that are many times the mass of Earth. The fifth planet is at the outer limit of the habitable zone, and is probably too cool to live on comfortably. The system has one other stargate in addition to the one that we came in on."

Steropes looked up. "The best thing about the three habitable planets is that the rare Earth elements are not rare on them; in fact, they are fairly common. If you were to colonize any or all of the planets, you would have a ready source of most of the elements that you are currently lacking. The third planet, in addition to having an exceptionally Earth-like environment, has a large number of those elements as well as large deposits of heavy metals. It might make an excellent system to bring a ship-size replicator."

"The weird thing," said Sara, speaking for the first time, "is that none of them currently show any forms of life. Not only aren't there any life forms, there is a complete absence of life, right down to the microscopic level. This is really strange, because we also found the remains of a civilization on the third planet. Based on how much of the ruins have been covered, whatever happened to the civilization appears to have happened between 3,000-4,000 years ago."

"What do you think happened?" asked Captain Griffin. "Does it look like they left the planet for some reason?"

"No," replied Sara. "We didn't find any evidence that the civilization on the planet had achieved space flight, so they couldn't have left on their own. They appear to have been right at the start of the industrial age, as we found the remains of a few low technology factories. The absence of all life is the part that makes no sense. It appears that the planet was sterilized either before or after the population was removed. How or why this happened is a complete mystery. There are no craters or evidence of warfare. There's no indication that the star flared up and burned them off. There's no evidence of anything."

"So what is your guess?" asked Captain Griffin.

"I do not know," replied Steropes. "The types of agents that could do this used to exist, but they were banned at least 10,000 years ago."

"That doesn't mean that a society didn't develop use anyway," said Calvin. "Just because things were banned on Earth didn't keep rogue countries from developing or experimenting with them. Maybe someone had them and used this planet as a test bed for them?"

"That's awful!" cried Sara. "Why would someone do that? What could they gain from wiping out a civilization? They didn't have space flight, so they wouldn't have been a threat to any of the space-faring races."

"Who knows?" asked Captain Griffin. "Maybe they had something valuable, like a bunch of the elements that they had already mined, and didn't want to trade with someone who showed up here. It would be easy to just gas the planet and take them."

"If they did that, wouldn't they want to come back and take over the mines themselves?" asked Calvin. "In 3,000 years, you'd think that they would have returned. Maybe it wasn't someone else that did this to them. Maybe they killed themselves off. Perhaps they developed a biological agent themselves, and it got away from its creator and killed everyone. That came close to happening on several occasions on Earth."

"There's no way to find out without going down to the planet for a thorough look," said Steropes. Looking at Captain Griffin he asked, "If you'd authorize a mission to the planet, we could try to find out what happened here."

"I'm sorry," Captain Griffin said, "but that isn't going to be possible this time out, as we've got other things to do. You remember the Drakuls, right? We will have to solve this mystery some other time. Helmsman, proceed to the other stargate, and let's see what's next door."

Chapter Fourteen

Bridge, *Vella Gulf*, GD 61 System, July 20, 2020

"The star in this system appears to be GD 61," announced Steropes. "It is a white dwarf approximately 150 light years from Earth in the constellation Perseus. I do not see any signs of habitation or enemy fighters."

"Stand down the alert fighters," said Captain Griffin. "Start the survey; let's see what we've got."

Officer's Mess, TSS *Vella Gulf*, GD 61 System, July 22, 2020

"May we sit with you?" asked Arges.

Sara looked up from her lunch and saw that the three Psiclopes were standing next to her table with trays of food. Lost in thought about the results of their first scans, it took her a moment to refocus on the question. Looking around, she saw that most of the other tables in the Officer's Mess (the 'Wardroom') were full. "Uh, yeah, sure," she finally said. "Please join me."

"Thank you," all three said, nearly simultaneously.

"Have you given any more thought to what we found?" she asked Steropes.

"Yes, I have," he answered, "but before I draw any conclusions, I would like to rerun some of the scans and tests to make sure we are not missing something or jumping to any conclusions."

"OK," Sara said. "When I get back to the bridge..."

She was interrupted by a roar of laughter from the table next to them, where six of the space fighter pilots and WSOs were sitting. Based on her experience with Calvin and his friends, Sara knew that one of them must have said something either really funny or really stupid. Judging by the fact that five of them were laughing and the other was sitting with a blank look on his face, she decided that it must have been something stupid and that the unlucky victim probably just got a new call sign.

"Are they always this loud?" asked Brontes.

"Pretty much," replied Sara. "You're lucky; you should see them when they're drinking. Then they're *really* loud."

"It is to be expected," noted Steropes, who had spent more time studying warriors than either of the other two Psiclopes. "By their very nature, warriors take things to the extreme, especially those that might be called to combat at a moment's notice. I believe that it is because they try to experience life to the fullest at all times, since they know that tomorrow might be the day that they are killed. Heroes are the loudest of all of the warrior types. They live faster and burn brighter than any of the 'normal' military people. There just happens to be a lot of them on this ship, which makes you notice it more."

"It has always been thus," said Arges. "During troubled times, heroes rise." Both of the other Psiclopes nodded in agreement. "The abundance of hero spirits at this time, however, is somewhat disturbing."

Sara looked confused. "Hero spirits?" she asked. "What is a hero spirit?"

"On the Wheel of Life," Brontes said, "there are those that move farther along the Wheel with each passing than the rest of us. Heroes are people that are destined to attempt great things. Sometimes they win and move up. Other times they lose and they move back."

"What do you mean?" asked Sara.

"We believe that, at a basic level, life is energy," said Arges. "As your scientists have determined, energy is neither created nor destroyed. Similarly, when someone dies, the energy that animated their bodies is not destroyed, it goes back into the pool of energy that is life. Your philosopher George Lucas was very close to the truth with his concept of the Force. There is a binding metaphysical power that is ubiquitous throughout the galaxy. When someone is born, energy is pulled from this pool of energy to animate them; similarly, when they die, their energy goes back to the pool. We are all part of this pool of life energy. We are able to talk mind-to-mind because we are all One; you just need to have the metaphysical Awareness of the beings around you in order to be able to communicate with them. When we talk mind-to-mind, we form a message in our minds and push it to the person that we mean to communicate with. This is somewhat analogous to one of the tridents that a soldier uses, which forms a bead of antimatter and wraps it with a force field prior to pushing it to where the weapon is aimed."

"That is an interesting way to visualize it," said the ship's chaplain, Father John Zuhlsdorf, who had been walking past. "It is not what I believe, of course, but it is interesting. May I join you?"

"Sure," said Sara, who was struggling to understand what she was being told. "Please do."

"Some beings are closer to Awareness than others," continued Steropes, "and can sense things as they truly are. Most of the great philosophers of old were very close. We believe that the 'Wheel of Life' beliefs of Hinduism, Buddhism, Bon, Jainism, Yoga and Taoism were correct in their concept of Samsara, or a continuous flow in the cycle of birth, life, death and rebirth. Within this flow resides a power that judges one's kharma, or the quality of the actions in the completed life, returning the life force higher or lower on the Wheel when they are reborn."

"In the eternal struggle," said Brontes, "there are periods where conflict is greater than at other times. Into the conflict are born heroes on both sides, whose task it is to defeat the other side. The number of hero spirits active now indicates that this is to be a conflict of immense proportions. These usually result in the termination of species."

"How do you know who these 'hero spirits are'?" asked Sara.

"We can feel them, and, if we have met them before, we can sometimes recognize the stronger ones," replied Brontes.

There was a pause as Sara considered this. Finally, she asked "And you think Calvin is one of these spirits?"

"We don't think so," replied Brontes, "We know so. We have met him before."

"When was that?" asked Sara.

"It was during the last Drakul invasion of your planet 3,000 years ago," answered Brontes. "At that time, we knew him as Zeus."

"*What?*" Sara exclaimed. "You can't be serious! Zeus? Zeus was a Greek god."

"Zeus was a real person, who led the fight against the Drakuls," Brontes corrected. "After the Drakuls detonated their bomb, sinking

Atlantis, we dropped off Zeus and his friends and relatives in Greece. Like the soldiers onboard this ship, we had upgraded them in our med lab. With the weapons they had, they *were* gods to the unmodified people; however, they started out as normal humans. The spirit that was in Zeus and now resides in Calvin has always collected a large number of spirits to himself."

Sara looked around the rest of the galley. "And the rest of the troops in the platoon are these 'hero spirits,' too?"

Brontes shrugged. "Some are; others are warrior spirits, drawn to heroes like moths to flames. They can't help it. Some will succeed and become hero spirits in their own right on the next passing of the Wheel; others will fail and move down." Brontes looked around the galley. "I haven't seen this big a collection since the Drakuls were last here."

"I don't understand how you could say that Calvin 'collected' anyone," Sara asked. "Most of the people were already in the Ranger platoon or were sent by other countries. How could he have collected them? He didn't have anything to do with their being here."

"Just by being here, he calls them to duties and tasks that will bring them closer to him," Brontes replied. "Take Master Chief O'Leary for example. You don't think that it was an accident that he just happened to be waiting *at the exact spot* that Calvin ejected from his plane, do you? It is too big a coincidence for that to have happened. Calvin needed him there, and that is exactly where he was, when Calvin needed him to be there, with the skill set Calvin needed him to have. It was Master Chief's kharma to be there when needed."

"That was just good luck," said Sara. "It was serendipity, a case of fortunate happpenstance."

Brontes smiled. "Where you see good luck, I see kharma. It is Calvin's kharma to be involved in events that will define the future of your race."

"What do you mean, 'define the future of my race'?" asked Sara.

"I mean," said Brontes, "that he will lead the effort that could save humanity. Unfortunately, it is just as likely, perhaps even more likely, that he will fail and be the cause of humanity's extinction. It has always been thus with the universe."

Sara was overwhelmed. "Why are you telling me all of this? Why am I even here?"

"We're trying to stack the deck in your favor," Brontes said. She smiled and added, "He always does better when you're near."

Bridge, TSS *Vella Gulf,* GD 61 System, July 24, 2020

"GD 61 appears to be the remains of a former red giant," said Steropes. "All that remains is a dense, hot remnant with about 70% of the Sun's mass. The star has two large super-Earth type planets circling it. One of these is inside the habitable zone, and the other is outside the habitable zone. Neither of these is of any outstanding scientific interest. There is also one more gate in addition to the one we came through."

"What *is* interesting," said Sara, taking up the brief, "is that several years ago, Earth's astronomers detected an asteroid in this system that was 26% water. This asteroid is part of a large asteroid field that sits in the middle of the habitable zone. The astronomers believed at the time that a rocky planet similar to Earth may have existed in the past. It was their thinking that the asteroid was part of this planet, and that the debris field was from the breakup of the planet. The astronomers thought that this might have happened when the planet was knocked out of its orbit by a larger planet and shredded by the star's gravitational force."

"Is that what you think happened now that we're here?" asked Captain Griffin.

"No," replied Sara, "that's not what we think happened. Our initial survey of the asteroid field resulted in some very peculiar data, so we did a much more thorough analysis to confirm our results. The second survey confirmed what we had found in the first survey. There is a large amount of formed chromium steel in the asteroid field, as well as other types of steel and worked metals."

"What?" asked Captain Griffin. "Steel isn't a naturally occurring mineral."

"No, it's not," said Sara. "In addition to this, we found large amounts of the former planet's surface that was melted into volcanic glass. We believe that this planet was previously inhabited, and that it was destroyed."

"*Destroyed?*" asked the CO, shocked. "You mean like, blown up? Aside from a Death Star, how do you blow up a planet?"

"It would take about 10 to the 32nd joules of energy to blow up an Earth-like planet," replied Steropes, "which is what we believe this world used to look like."

"Who would do such a thing?" asked Captain Griffin. "Why?"

"We believe we have the answers to those questions," answered Steropes, "and we think we know where we are. There are only a few instances of complete planetary destruction that I am aware of. One of these was at the claws of the Drakuls when they blew up the planet Elspeck. Based on an analysis of the debris, I believe that this system contains the remains of Elspeck."

"I've never heard of Elspeck," replied Captain Griffin.

"You may not know the name," said Sara, "but you've heard of the planet. Elspeck was the home world of the Eldive. Solomon has come home."

Bridge, TSS *Vella Gulf,* GD 61 System, July 25, 2020

"There can be no doubt," said Steropes, "the asteroid field is the previous planet Elspeck, which was destroyed by the Drakuls during the last conflict."

"If they have the kind of power required to blow up a planet," replied Captain Griffin, "then there's no way that we can take them on with just this ship."

"It is unknown how many ships the Drakuls might have now, and what types they might be," noted Steropes. "The ships that did this were all destroyed a long time ago. Still, my advice would be to step carefully. They are probably not too many stargates from here. This is somewhat awkward, because we expected them to attack Earth from the other direction. There must be a stargate close by that loops back to the other side of Earth's star lane."

"I agree that we need to be careful," said the CO. "I think that this is as far as we ought to come in this direction without a larger force."

"This also explains what happened in the Gliese 581 system that we passed through on the way here," said Steropes. "For a long time, we knew that someone sterilized the system next to the Eldive home world, but we were never able to determine who did it. We can now be fairly certain that the Drakuls that came to your planet fled the battle at Elspeck, not one of the earlier battles, and that they went through and sterilized the civilization at Gliese 581 on their way to Earth."

"Why did they do that?" asked Sara. "Why not stop there and take over that planet rather than just kill everyone and run?"

"I can only guess that it was because they thought the alliance fleet here in Elspeck was too close," answered Steropes. "They would have wanted to put some systems between them. They probably landed at Gliese 581, filled up their food storage system and took a bunch of slaves. They wouldn't have wanted anyone to know that they escaped, so they gassed the planet to cover their tracks. That would make sense with Drakul psychology. Luckily for them, they chose the path that didn't have any habitable planets for several systems, so no one would have looked for them that way. The first habitable planet they would have come to in that direction was Earth. That would have been far enough that they would probably have felt themselves safe from pursuit, especially in an Eldive ship. No one would have questioned them. Had they come upon any of the alliance forces, they could have sent a transmission saying they were in mourning, and everyone would have believed them. It was only through luck that we happened to be on the planet they chose to land on, or they would have taken it over and would be virtual gods on Earth now."

"OK," said Captain Griffin, "that answers the questions about where we are and what happened in the system next door, but I'm still hesitant about going any further in this direction. Helmsman! Let's head back the way we came and continue to Epsilon Eridani."

Chapter Fifteen

"System is stable," announced Sara. "No indications of enemy vessels." The trip from GD 61 through Gliese 581 and then 61 Cygni had gone quickly and quietly with no enemy activity.

"Got it, thanks," replied Captain Griffin. This was Sara's first system entry on her own. The CO decided that she liked it when Sara was at the science station. The first thing she had noted was enemy activity. With Steropes or Arges, it was often, "Wow, this is neat!" While the 'neat things' might be interesting from a scientific viewpoint, as the ship's commanding officer she was much more worried about things that were going to kill her and her ship. Once a system was clear of any enemy activity, *that* was the time to go look at cool stuff. Not before.

"Hey, Skipper," Sara said. "When you were here last time, there were only two stargates, right? The one you came through from 61 Cygni, and the one you went through to WASP-18, right?"

"I think so," answered Captain Griffin. "Why?"

"Because," Sara replied, "I have another one showing on my scope that is so big and so clear, it almost appears to be throbbing with energy."

"May I see?" asked Steropes, getting up from the extra seat by Captain Griffin. He had wanted to be close enough to help if needed, but didn't want to look over her shoulder. "I guess it's possible that we missed one when we found out the planet was inhabited," Steropes replied as he walked toward the science station. "Things got pretty exciting." Reaching the scope, he looked down and gave a low whistle. "There's no way we missed that," he remarked. "That is new."

"How did it get there?" asked Captain Griffin. "I thought the stargates were linked black holes. Wouldn't the shuttle crew have noticed someone running around moving black holes up here?"

"The data would indicate that no one noticed," answered Steropes, "but I have no idea how this one showed up here all of a sudden. It is close enough to where we enter the system that we would have seen it last time if it had been there. I do not know where it came from or how it got here."

"It's almost like it's calling us," said Calvin.

"Yes," agreed Steropes, "and that's what scares me. It doesn't have a big neon sign, but other than that, it's about as obvious as it could be."

"So close to where a planet was destroyed by the Drakuls," Captain Peotr Barishov commented. "You do not intend to go there, do you?"

"Yes," replied Captain Griffin, "I do."

"*What?*" barked Captain Barishov. "Why do you think this is a good idea?"

"I have lots of reasons," replied the commanding officer, "not the least of which is that whatever is on the other side of the stargate *manipulated the stargate*. Do you know how to do that? I certainly don't. If they can move black holes, don't you think that they could destroy this one little cruiser if they wanted to?"

"The commanding officer makes a very valid point," remarked Solomon. "The power required to manipulate the black hole would not even notice the *Vella Gulf* as it crushed us into our component atoms."

"I take it you want to go in there, Solomon?" asked Calvin. "You normally don't volunteer your opinion."

"I do not have opinions," disagreed the artificial intelligence. "I am programmed to analyze data, and this is the logical conclusion. I am acquainted with your concept of hospitality and believe that whatever entity is beckoning us might find it rude if we do not take advantage of its offer. To not do so might be far more catastrophic than if we did."

"I agree entirely," said Captain Griffin. "Helmsman, set course for the new stargate."

Bridge, TSS *Vella Gulf,* Epsilon Eridani System, August 3, 2020

"Stargate entrance in five minutes," announced the helmsman.

"General Quarters!" ordered the commanding officer.

The duty engineer pressed the button, and the alarm began sounding. The squadron already had all of the fighters manned up. They didn't know what they would find on the other side of the stargate, but all of the ships were fully armed with anti-ship missiles and crewed with the most experienced crews.

"Comms, please let Domus Control know that we are about to make transit through the new stargate," said the commanding officer.

They had previously informed the Terran ambassador on the planet Domus of their intentions to investigate the new stargate. The ambassador didn't have any way of getting the word back to Earth if they were destroyed, but at least someone would know where they went if they didn't come back.

"Done, ma'am," replied the communications officer. "The ambassador wished us good luck."

"Thanks," answered Captain Griffin distractedly as she stared at the stargate looming in front of them. Although it didn't look any different from the other ones she had previously gone through, it somehow felt different. She tried to convince herself that she was only being foolish, and that she was letting her nerves get the better of her. The blackness of the stargate continued to loom, and she had a last minute urge to call for full reverse on the engines. Before she could, the blackness engulfed them, and the stars stretched to infinity...then went black...then everything seemed to spin sideways forever...then there was a vermillion flash...

Chapter Sixteen

Bridge, TSS *Vella Gulf*, Gliese 667 C System, August 3, 2020

The ship emerged from transit with the ship pointed at the heart of a red dwarf star.

"Did anyone else notice that the transit felt different?" asked Captain Griffin.

"Yes ma'am," replied Bullseye. "I've never felt that sideways spin before. That was weird."

"Duty engineer," the commanding officer called, "get me a damage report." She looked at Bullseye. "Launch all fighters!" she ordered.

"Yes, ma'am," said the engineer, listening to her damage control network. "All stations are reporting that they have no damage, but all of the stations report feeling the same rotational force. The engineer is asking for 10 minutes to run full diagnostics before applying power."

"Granted," agreed Captain Griffin. "Tell him to be ready to break it off at a moment's notice. We may need to get out of here quickly."

"That will be difficult," stated Steropes, who was manning the science station. "The stargate that we came through no longer exists."

"*Doesn't exist?*" repeated the commanding officer. "Where did it go?"

"Unknown at this time," replied Steropes. "It must have been there for us to transit through, but it disappeared before the instruments had a chance to settle down after the transit."

"Hey," called the helmsman. "Anyone notice that there wasn't a taste when we went through? Not salty, not sweet, not even bitter. I've never seen that before."

"Curious," mused Steropes. "I have never had that happen in all of the transits that I've made. Not once in 5,000 years."

"I don't think we're in Kansas anymore," said Sara in a stage whisper, looking over Steropes' shoulder.

"All fighters launched," announced Bullseye. "They are proceeding in sections of two in all directions." With six pairs of fighters, they could send one straight ahead in the *Vella Gulf's* direction of travel, one straight behind them, one up, one down, one left and one to the right. They would go out to a distance of a million miles, extending the reach of the ship's sensor network in a giant bubble.

"Talk to me Steropes," said Captain Griffin. "What have we got? Any enemy in sight?" This was one of those times that she wanted reassurance that there weren't any enemy vessels around. Like, *NOW*, and wasn't getting it.

"Oh! Yes!" replied Steropes. "Sorry, I was looking for the stargate. What did you want?"

"I'd like it a lot," answered the CO dryly, "if you could tell me if there are any *enemies* in the vicinity."

"Oh, yes, right away," said Steropes. He paused, looking at his scope. "No, there are no signs of either friendly or enemy activity in this system. By triangulation, and the fact that there are three stars in this system, I believe that we are in the Gliese 667 C system. There are two K-type main-sequence stars located about 230 astronomical units from the star that we are approaching. Gliese 667 C is the smallest star in this system. It is a red dwarf star with only about 31% of the mass of your Sun and 42% of the Sun's radius. It is radiating only 1.4% of the Sun's luminosity."

"And there is no stargate to be seen?" asked Captain Griffin.

"No," replied Steropes, "there is no stargate to be seen."

"All right," said Captain Griffin, not wanting to incite a panic about the stargate home disappearing, "let's start the survey and find out where it went."

CO's Conference Room, TSS *Vella Gulf,* Gliese 667 C System, August 7, 2020

"The Gliese 667 C system is part of the Gliese 667 triple star system," explained Steropes to the assembled command staff of the *Vella Gulf* that had gathered in the CO's conference room. "This system is located 22 light-years away from the Solar System in the constellation Scorpius. It has seven planets, all of which are super-Earths. They are like the Earth in form and composition although they are larger. Some are much larger. Of these seven planets, three are inside the habitable zone of Gliese 667 C, which runs from about 10 million miles to 23 million miles. In this region, liquid water is possible. Planets 'c,' 'd,' and 'e' are in this zone. Planets 'a' and 'b' are too hot, and planet 'f' is too cold.

"The orbit of Planet 'g' is very interesting," he continued, "as it is extremely eccentric in nature. Its orbit goes from inside of Planet 'd' to outside of Planet 'f.' In terms of the Solar System, its orbit goes from inside of Venus to out beyond the orbit of Jupiter. It is currently nearing its closest point of approach."

"Planet 'c' orbits Gliese 667 C at a distance of almost 12 million miles," noted Sara, "which gives it an orbital period of 28 days. Based on the luminosity of Gliese 667 C at this distance, it would get about 90% of the light Earth does. As most of this would be in the infrared portion of the spectrum, Gliese 667 C 'c' should absorb more overall electromagnetic radiation, making it just a little warmer than Earth."

"Is there a reason that you're focusing on Planet 'c'?" asked Captain Griffin.

"Yes, there is," replied Sara. "We have found the remnants of a civilization on Planet 'c.'"

"Then that is where we should start our search for answers," decided Captain Griffin.

"Indeed," said Steropes, "as we *must* find out what turns on and off the stargate."

"Why is that?" asked Captain Griffin. "Can't we still get back to Earth on just the normal drive?"

"Maybe," replied Steropes. "We would, however, have to harvest more fuel before we left. That isn't the problem. The problem is that it would take a long time, objectively, to the people on Earth."

"What do you mean?" asked Captain Griffin. "How long?"

"With 375 G of acceleration available, we can accelerate very nearly to the speed of light; unfortunately, as we get closer to the speed of light, time will slow down for us. At 0.99 of the speed of light, it would only seem like it took us about 17 days to get home, but during that time a little more than 22 years would have gone by for people on Earth. We're 22 light years away; at the speed of light, it will take 22 years from the perspective of the people on Earth for us to get home."

"That's not good," said Sara.

"No," agreed Calvin, "it's not. They're going to think that we've been destroyed in a few months, much less 22 years. And if the Drakuls show up in that time..." He let the thought trail off.

"We need to find where the stargate went," said Captain Griffin. "Let's head for the third planet and 'c' if we can find some answers." She smiled at her weak attempt at humor. Lost in their own thoughts, no one else did.

"One other thing that is interesting to note," announced Solomon, "is that the planets are coming into alignment, which is a statistical anomaly. Not only is planet 'g' going to be at its closest point of approach, but all five of the outermost planets will be in alignment on one side of the star with the two innermost planets in alignment on the other side of the star. This alignment will occur tomorrow. The gravitational forces pulling the 'c' planet away from its star will be at their greatest at that time."

"Why is that interesting?" asked Captain Griffin. "Didn't planets in the Solar System just line up recently?"

"No," replied Solomon. "The Solar System's planets can't ever line up perfectly because some of their orbits are tilted. The closest that they can come is to get within one degree of alignment in right ascension, which happens about once every 780 billion years. The fact that we are here at that one precise moment that the planets are in this alignment is extremely coincidental, and you asked me to point out things that are out of the ordinary."

"How coincidental is it that we are here now?" asked Captain Griffin.

Solomon paused to calculate and then said, "Like winning the lottery three times in a row."

Chapter Seventeen

Bridge, TSS *Vella Gulf*, In Orbit Around Gliese 667 C 'c',
August 8, 2020

"So, where do we start?" inquired Captain Griffin.

"I do not know," answered Steropes. "I scanned the entire planet, but haven't found any place that is better to start our search than any other."

"You said that the planet was previously inhabited," noted Captain Griffin. "Why don't we start by looking at one of the cities?"

"Because that doesn't localize the civilization that used to exist here," answered Steropes. "When I say that the civilization covered the planet, I mean that it completely covered the planet. The entire land mass shows evidence of being a single, planet-wide city. I cannot determine if it completely covered the water areas as well, but I find evidence of metals and other structural components in the shallows that make me think that it did."

He put a series of high resolution pictures on the viewer screens. "You can see mounds in all of these photos," he said. "These are the remnants of the city that used to exist here."

"How long would it take for the city to be covered like that?" asked Captain Griffin. "Thousands of years at least, right?"

"No," answered Steropes. "It would take much longer than that. You have to remember that the city *completely covered* the planet. It would take much longer than that before you could see the actual surface of the planet, much less have it bury all of the structures completely. The time span for this to happen? *Millions* of years. I am guessing something on the order of about *10* million years."

He put another picture on the screen. A concrete beam stuck out from the ground like a cosmic middle finger. "This is the only piece of their architecture that I have found remaining above ground," Steropes said. "Chemical analysis from orbit has proven to be inconclusive. It seems to be something like the concrete used in your civilization and the titano-crete used in ours, but has additional elements added in. I have determined that it contains large concentrations of rhenium and osmium in addition to other elements that I can't determine. It is amazing."

"What is amazing?" asked Calvin.

"Their mining processes are amazing," replied Steropes. "Take the rhenium for example. Rhenium is one of the rarest elements in the Earth's crust, with an estimated average concentration of about 1 part per billion. The amount used in this one building alone would be more than the amount that exists *in your entire Solar System*. There is twice as much osmium in the building as in the entire Solar System. This civilization had access to other star systems and the ability to transport huge amounts of material."

"That's an awful lot of rhenium and osmium," Captain Griffin noted. "How big was this building?"

"Based on the scanner data," Steropes replied, "I estimate that the building had a square base that was approximately two miles to a side, and was over a mile high. And this was one of the *smaller* buildings on this planet."

A stunned silence filled the bridge.

"That's a big building," Captain Griffin finally said into the silence. "It also opens up more questions than it answers. If the civilization had the ability to erect that type of building, they were obviously space-faring, or they wouldn't have had access to the materials required to build it. If they could travel to the stars, though, why would they choose to continue to build on this planet until they completely covered it? Why not emigrate to somewhere else? What were they thinking?"

"I do not know," Steropes said, shaking his head. "More data is required in order to answer those questions."

Captain Griffin had another idea. "Solomon," she asked, "what do you think?"

"Like Steropes, I find that more data is required to answer your questions," the ship's AI replied. "It is possible, perhaps even likely, that there was some sort of cultural imperative to continue to build on this planet. There are many reasons why this might be; for example, this may have been the civilization's home world or the capital planet for a large star nation. It is also possible that the culture had some sort of hive mind that wanted to continue to build here for some reason, but I find that possibility less likely than the first two options. There are other possibilities, but I find them even more unlikely. In the interests of full disclosure, the civilization may also be sufficiently removed from our experience that I may not be programmed to correctly analyze the reason that they chose to build this way."

"That's exactly what I was trying to say," said Steropes. "We don't have enough information on this society to make guesses about their intentions. They are so far advanced beyond our civilization that the assumptions we use to make our guesses might be wrong. What seems 'different' to us might be 'normal' to them...*power spike!*"

"What?" asked Captain Griffin.

"I'm getting indications of a power source coming online on the planet," replied Steropes. "It is an enormous power source far bigger than any of our biggest antimatter power plants. Our five biggest plants wouldn't equal the amount of power being generated."

"Can you localize the source?" asked Captain Griffin.

"Yes," answered Steropes. "It would be hard to miss."

"Good," said Captain Griffin. "Pass the information to the helmsman, and let's move to orbit overhead the source."

"Got it, ma'am," said the helmsman. "We'll be overhead in five minutes."

"Do you want a fighter launch?" inquired Calvin.

Captain Griffin considered the question for a second before answering. "Man up the fighters," she finally answered, "but don't launch them yet. Let's see what we're dealing with first."

"Aye aye," replied Calvin, who began giving orders over his implant.

"Warm up all offensive and defensive systems, but leave them in standby for now," ordered Captain Griffin. "We don't want to seem too aggressive, but I want to be ready for any occasion."

"Defensive systems will be of limited value," noted Steropes. "If the power source is a weapon, it will overwhelm our shields with its first shot. We would need to move a significant distance in order to avoid being destroyed."

"Do you want me to move the ship?" asked the helmsman.

"No," replied Captain Griffin. "I don't want to make it look like we are running. If they wanted to destroy us, I'm sure that they already could have."

"That is correct," agreed Steropes. "They could..." He stopped suddenly. "Captain, we're being scanned by something from the planet. I have never seen anything like it."

"They, they...are, are...in, in...my, my...systems, systems," stuttered Solomon. "I, I...can, can...not, not...prevent, prevent...it, it."

"Power surge from the planet!" cried security station operator, who controlled the ship's defensive systems, weapons and shields.

"Shields up!" ordered Captain Griffin.

"They're not responding!" the defensive systems officer replied.

"Helm, get us out of here!" Captain Griffin ordered.

"I can't!" replied the helmsman, with fear in his voice. "The engines aren't responding, either!" There was a flash, and everything went dark. After a second, auxiliary power kicked in, and the lights came back on.

"Main engines just went to standby!" cried the duty engineer, sitting next to the helmsman. "Engineering reports they are unable to bring them back on line. The auxiliary engines are holding, but all propulsion systems are offline."

"Solomon, do you know what is going on?" asked Captain Griffin.

"Something has taken over all of the systems," replied Solomon in a female's voice that lacked tone or inflection. Steropes recognized the default voice setting of the ship's AI. "I have been reset and currently have access to only a fraction of my storage space. I do not have access to any of the ship's systems. I am unable to provide assistance or determine what is happening. I am greatly handicapped."

"Bring offensive systems online," the Captain ordered.

"I'm unable," replied the offensive systems officer at the operations station. "Nothing happens when they are selected."

"Ma'am," said Calvin, "I doubt this will be a surprise, but all of the fighters just went to standby, too."

"Well," said Captain Griffin, "we seem to be unable to do anything else, so I guess we wait."

The crew didn't have long to wait. Within seconds of the commanding officer's statement, a figure that looked like Albert Einstein was suddenly standing on the bridge in front on the helmsman's station. "Greetings, people of Earth and Olympos," he said in a warm, welcoming tone. "It is good to see you. I have waited a long time for this day."

"If it is good to see us," replied Captain Griffin, "why is it that you have disabled most of my ship?"

"I apologize for that," replied Einstein, "but my creators thought that it might be necessary to prevent an unfortunate misunderstanding that resulted in your termination before I could fulfill my programming." The figure spoke with a slow cadence, pausing frequently as if to consider what to say next. Griffin could almost imagine the figure holding a pipe. "Your systems will be restored to you with the hope that you will not do anything rash." He motioned theatrically toward the various stations on the bridge, and systems began coming back to life.

"Main engines back online!" called the duty engineer.

"Acknowledged," replied the Captain. "Keep us in position here." She looked back to Einstein. "Thank you," she said.

"You are welcome," the figure replied with a small bow. "As I'm sure you are aware, I am not actually Albert Einstein. This shape is merely an avatar which I am using. Your records indicated that Einstein was a man of great intelligence that wanted to use science for peaceful purposes, not warfare. He seemed like an appropriate form to use to deliver my message."

"He was indeed a very intelligent man," noted the ambassador, as she entered the bridge, "and truly a man of peace. If you are not Einstein, who is it that we have the privilege of meeting?"

"I am all that remains in this galaxy of a civilization that existed many millennia ago," replied Einstein. "Twelve million years ago, my civilization ruled much of this galaxy from this planet. We were the most powerful civilization that had ever been seen, yet we had a government that was compassionate and a society that was based on peace, not war. In function, it comes close to your definition of 'utopia,' a peaceful society where death and suffering had been vanquished."

"Unfortunately," he continued after a pause that was a little longer than normal, "our society was not the only one that existed at the time. There was another society, one that was based solely on warfare and subjugation. We were completely unprepared when our scouts stumbled upon it." He paused. "Before we knew it, we had already lost many of our outlying systems. Most were bombed into radioactive dust without warning. We were told later that they did this 'just to make a point.' By the time they actually opened up diplomatic relations with us, they had completely destroyed five planets and had killed tens of billions of people."

A pipe materialized in his hand, and he took a couple of phantom puffs. "They only had one option for us, unconditional surrender. We could accept them as our sole rulers or we would be destroyed. By then, they had captured many of our people and had experimented on them. When we did not immediately give in to their demands, they released viruses on two more planets that killed all of the inhabitants. There was no reason to do so. We didn't attack them or put up any show of defense; they just wanted to see if the viruses would work like they thought they would."

"We knew then that we could not live under their rule," he continued. "Yet, we also knew that we could not fight them. They had weapons that they had spent millennia developing; we had none. The only thing we had was shipping, because interstellar commerce was so important to us. So we used it. We left, hoping that they wouldn't pursue us. Since you are here, it is obvious that they did, or at least that they have perished in the intervening millennia."

"Where did you go?" asked the ambassador when Einstein paused.

"We left the galaxy," Einstein replied. "Where we went is unimportant."

"But what if we would like to open peaceful relations with you?" pressed the ambassador. "We would conduct trade with you if we could."

Einstein smiled sadly. "You cannot reach us with your technology. You would not even be able to move about the stars as you do if it were not for the stargates that we left behind. They were old technology that we didn't even use anymore. Had we thought to destroy them, you would still probably be on your home planet, unaware that other civilizations existed."

"That is true," agreed the ambassador, "and some days I wish that you had indeed destroyed them. You did not do that, however, and wishing will not make it so. We are out among the stars, and we are facing foes very much like those that you faced in your day."

"Accessing," Einstein said. "Yes, I see it in your records. The Drakul race, for one, is very much like the enemy we faced although much less capable. It is sad to see that such races still exist."

"Can you help us against them?" asked Captain Griffin. "Surely the technology that you had is far beyond ours. Perhaps if you were able to share your knowledge, we would be able to defeat them this time around and bring peace again to the galaxy."

Einstein sucked on his pipe, looking thoughtful. "If we were to share our knowledge with you," he said when he finally spoke, "you would be able to use it to defeat your enemies." He took another puff on the pipe. "However, you might also use it to defeat the other peaceful nations that you come across. Your history is filled with examples of one faction of humans fighting with another faction over resources or religion, or sometimes just to gain more power. These are actions that we cannot abide."

He walked back and forth across the front of the bridge, puffing on the pipe. "What is needed is a test," he said to himself. "Yes, a test." Finally he stopped and turned back to Captain Griffin. "Are you familiar with this formation?" he asked. As he posed the question, the screens changed to show a knobby sandstone formation that stuck up from the terrain around it. "This formation would be approximately 400 of your meters high with a total circumference of 10 kilometers. This formation would appear to change color at different times of the day and year; most notably, it would appear to glow red at dawn and sunset."

"Yes, I am familiar with it," replied Captain Griffin. "It's Ayers Rock in Australia." Several heads nodded around the bridge. Many of the crew had seen pictures of Ayers Rock.

"When we were forced to flee our enemy, we caused these formations to occur on many of our planets," said Einstein. "We left them behind as markers in the hope that one day a civilization would be able to use them to find the world that you are now orbiting. Deciphering the riddle requires having all of the pieces, so your civilization must either span all of the planets that we left the markers on, or you must have good enough relations with other societies to get the markers from them. If you had all of the markers when you showed up here, I would have sent a message to our society that it was safe for them to return." He took a drag on the pipe.

"It has been a long time since my civilization fled, and it is possible, maybe even likely, that it doesn't exist anymore," he continued. "The enemy may have destroyed it, it might have run into something worse than the enemy, or...something else might have happened to it. Certainly, I expected to hear from them before now. In the event that they never returned, I was allowed to pass on our knowledge to a civilization that mirrored ours. You are, however, not that civilization." He took a drag on the pipe. "You are young and immature as a civilization, but you may in time become like us. In looking at your systems, I see that you have the potential."

He took a drag on the pipe and then nodded. He looked at Calvin. "Bring a ship down to the planet, and I will give you something." Einstein vanished. As he disappeared, a map of the planet appeared on the view screens, with an 'X' marked on one of the continents.

"That position corresponds to the location of the power source below us," noted Steropes.

Captain Griffin looked at Calvin. "Are you waiting for a better invitation?" she asked. "Take a shuttle and go down to the planet.

Get whatever it is that he has for you and try to find out anything else you can about their civilization. Then get back here ASAP."

"Yes ma'am," replied Calvin. He turned and headed toward the door.

"And Calvin?" the CO asked.

Calvin stopped and turned around. "Yes?"

"Try not to get killed doing it," she added.

Calvin gave a wry laugh. "I'll do my best."

Shuttle 01, TSS *Vella Gulf*, In Orbit Around Gliese 667 C 'c', August 8, 2020

Calvin looked across the cockpit to his WSO for the flight, Lieutenant Reyne Rafaeli. "I'm ready to go," he said.

"I'm good, too," replied the Israeli. She called the ship, "Vella Gulf, Shuttle 01 *is ready for launch.*"

"*Roger that,* Shuttle 01. *Have a good flight and come back soon. Launching in 3...2...1...*" the shuttle was pushed away from the ship, and Calvin took control of it.

"I've got the target's coordinates punched into the system," Lieutenant Rafaeli said. The shuttle's navigation system began providing steering directions to Calvin, and he turned the shuttle to follow them. As the craft banked and began descending toward the planet, the WSO got her first look at it. "It looks like a giant Mars," she said.

"Yeah, it does," agreed Calvin. Unlike Earth, there was no green vegetation. The predominant plant life used something other than chlorophyll to process sunlight. Whatever it was gave them a deep red color that matched the color of the planet's soil. Something in the soil had also turned the water of the planet red, as well. Between the deep red plants, the dusky red soil and the dark red water, the planet looked a lot like Mars, with just small color variations between the soil and the water.

As the *Vella Gulf* was orbiting over the power source on the planet, it wasn't long until the shuttle was flying over the area that Einstein had indicated. Calvin could see a featureless plateau bounded on all sides by a river. The river, splitting to go around the plateau, flowed from the west and then rejoined to form a single stream again once it was past the plateau. The river had been there a *long* time, Calvin observed, and it had eroded a canyon around the plateau that would have made the Grand Canyon on Earth jealous. He didn't see any way to get to the river from the top of the plateau; the sides of the canyon were straight up and down.

"Do you know where we are supposed to land?" asked Lieutenant Rafaeli, looking at the five mile wide plateau. "Do you want me to just pick a spot in the middle of it? It'll be a long walk if we don't land where we are supposed to."

"I don't know where we are supposed...*I'm losing power!*" Calvin called suddenly. The shuttle's airspeed began dropping.

"I lost control of my system!" called the WSO.

"Me, too," replied Calvin, taking his hands off the controls. The shuttle continued to fly normally, banking gently to the left. "I guess they've got it from here," he said, looking out the window. He didn't see anything in the direction they were turning. The plateau was flat in all directions. "I hope they know what they're doing."

"Me, too," said Rafaeli.

Whatever had control of the shuttle apparently *did* know what it was doing, and the shuttle landed gently on the plateau.

Rafaeli shut down all of her systems and then looked at Calvin. "OK boss," she said, "now what?"

"I don't know," replied Calvin, "but I imagine we'll have to get out of the shuttle to find out." He began unstrapping from his seat. After a moment, Rafaeli did, too. The two walked out of the shuttle and stood on the surface of the plateau. The planet was twice as big as Earth and had five times Earth's mass, giving it a gravity of about 1.25 of Earth's. The increased gravity was annoying, but not debilitating, especially in their suits.

The pair looked around at the plateau. It looked as flat and unremarkable standing on it as it had from the cockpit. "I hate to sound like a broken record, Skipper," she said, "but now what?"

"I don't know," repeated Calvin. "Maybe we're supposed to stand here and enjoy the view. He pointed to the west, where the planet's star, Gliese 667 C, was within about an hour of setting into the giant river canyon. Although the star only had about 30% of the Sun's mass, Gliese 667 'c' was a lot closer to it than Earth was to the Sun; the star appeared over five times as big as the Sun did from Earth. The other stars in the system, Gliese 667A and Gliese 667 B, were slightly to the left and higher in the sky. They were about 10 times brighter than the brightest star on Earth and could easily be seen during the day. The view was surreal, reminding Calvin of a scene from a movie he had seen in his youth. "Three stars setting at once," he said. "That's something you don't see every day on earth."

Before Rafaeli could reply, they heard a grinding noise and could feel machinery moving beneath their feet. With a 'clang,' part of the ground to the west of them began descending, revealing a ramp that went below the surface of the plateau.

"Where do you suppose that goes?" asked Rafaeli.

"It looks like it goes down," replied Calvin, beginning to get a little irritated with her constant questions. How the hell was he supposed to know? He'd never been there before. "Let's go find out."

The pair began walking down the ramp, and Calvin was immediately impressed with the scale of it. The ramp was easily 100 yards wide, and as he descended into the gloom, he realized that it was nearly a quarter of a mile long. As they reached the halfway point of the ramp, the lights in the roof came on, starting with the ones above him and then proceeding down the length of the hangar bay. That's what the mammoth space looked like to him, anyway; it was a vast underground hangar that extended for at least two miles to the east from where they were entering. It was also about a mile wide, with the ramp centered along one of the end walls.

Calvin was amazed at the engineering capabilities required to operate a ramp as big as the one he was walking down or to hold up the mile wide ceiling without any visible means of support (including the 300 ton shuttle sitting on top of it.) "This is just...crazy," he said, lost in the scale of it.

"Do you think they created all of this?" Rafaeli asked.

"It's too big and too even to be natural," replied Calvin. "And I don't think that the roof would stay up unless it was heavily reinforced with something. Aside from the fact that nature usually doesn't make moving ramps that are 100 yards wide and a quarter mile long."

After about five minutes of walking, they reached the bottom of the ramp. The floor of the cavern was man-made (or alien-made, Calvin decided, not knowing for sure what the members of the civilization looked like.) Either way, it wasn't natural, but some form of reinforced concrete. The area was scuffed and looked like it had been heavily used once upon a time but was coated with a thick layer of dust that indicated the time was long past. The hangar smelled stale and unused, as if fresh air hadn't been in it in a *long* time.

Without warning, Einstein appeared next to them, still holding his pipe. "I'm glad you came," he said, as if the Terrans had a choice in the matter. "If you would follow me this way." He turned to the right and began walking.

"What is he?" asked Rafaeli. She had been briefed about their meeting with Einstein earlier, but hadn't really believed it. "He doesn't look like a projection, he doesn't move like a robot...what is he?"

Einstein turned and smiled. "I am the avatar of the computer system that watches over this planet," he said. "What my non-physical shape might be is truly immaterial." He chuckled to himself. Looking at Calvin he said, "That was a pun, right? I am punny?"

"Umm, yes," said Calvin, not ready for the question. "That was a pun. Almost two of them, in fact."

"Good," replied Einstein. "Our society was known for its art and literature. While well beyond yours, we liked various forms of word play. I tried to look into your database to find what types of things your society used and found the concept of puns. I like it very much."

"I think you may have been here by yourself for too long," said Calvin.

"That is possible, too, I guess," said Einstein. "Self aware computers have been known to go crazy, just like people. I'll have to think about that."

They walked in silence for a few minutes. The Terrans continued to be amazed by the scale of the underground hangar. As they approached the wall, Calvin noticed a large number of scrapes and scars on the floor and then a large number of places where it looked like something had stood or been fused to the floor. It almost had the same feel as the hangar that held the replicator on the moon, although whatever had stood in this hangar would have been...enormous, compared to the replicator on the moon. "Was this some sort of manufacturing center?" he asked.

Einstein stopped and looked at him curiously. He took a puff on his pipe and then said, "Interesting. Very interesting. Yes, this used to be a place where things were made. How did you know?"

"Well, this cavern was built to hold *something*," Calvin said, "and it looks like there used to be something that stood here. This whole cavern feels like it was a holding point for something military. If it were civilian, it would have been up on the surface where everyone could see it. Something was hidden here, something to be used in war."

"You are very perceptive," said Einstein. "This was where we tried to build the tools of war to defend ourselves, but it was too late, far too late. Perhaps we will discuss it at another time. If my society has been destroyed, I owe it to them to tell their story. But not today. And not here."

They reached the wall and a door. It looked like any terrestrial door that Calvin had ever walked through. It was about 6.5' high and three feet wide, with a handle right about where it should be. "Kind of old-fashioned isn't it?" asked Calvin. "Did you put this here just for us?"

"What do you mean?" asked Rafaeli.

"Don't you think it's interesting that their door looks exactly like a door on Earth?" asked Calvin in reply. "It's the same shape and size, and it has the same kind of handle."

"Maybe they built it for us," replied the WSO.

"I'm sure they did," said Calvin. "It gives us no information about their size or shape. It tells us nothing about them, except the fact that they are able to do it."

"Again, that is very perceptive," said Einstein. He waved his hand, and the door vanished, along with several feet of wall on either side of the door. An alcove was revealed that was about 10 feet wide, deep and tall. Sitting on the floor in the center of the room was a short rod. As they walked up to it, Calvin could see that it was about two feet long and four inches in diameter. Black in color, it looked like it was made of some sort of metal. Einstein stopped next to it and extended a hand toward it. "This is for you," he said. "It will only work for you."

Calvin reached down to pick it up. As he lifted it, the rod glowed softly where his fingers touched it. It felt warm for a couple of seconds, and then the glow faded, and the rod cooled. Calvin saw that the surface of the rod was smooth, except for one small button that had been hidden from him earlier by the way it was lying. "Thank you," said Calvin, before adding, "I think."

"You are welcome," replied Einstein. "If you know where one marker is, you know where they all are."

"What does that mean?" asked Calvin.

"You will know when it is time," answered Einstein. "It wouldn't be much of a test if I gave you the answer at the start. Now, it is time for you to go. I wish you the best of luck." With that, he disappeared.

"Hey!" yelled Calvin, "I've got a few questions!"

In the distance, the lights started going out.

"Einstein, could you please come back?" Calvin yelled.

"Um, maybe we should be going," said Rafaeli, watching the lights going out, "or we're going to be in the dark."

Calvin looked at the lights and judged the rate versus the distance they had to travel. "Not only do we need to go," he said, "we need to *run*." The two started running, the extra gravity dragging them down.

"This...sucks..." gasped Rafaeli. "I need to...exercise...more."

"Less talking," said Calvin, only a little less winded. "More running." He could see that they weren't going to make it. He was right. They were still 50 yards from the ramp when the last set of lights went out. The planet's star must have been low on the horizon by now and not providing much light; they could barely see in the gloom. They slowed down to a quick walk, catching their breaths as they carefully crossed the remaining distance.

They made it to the ramp, and Calvin stopped to yell into the blackness. "Einstein!" he yelled. "Could I please talk to you?" There was no answer.

With a clang, the ramp started up. Calvin had the choice to jump off and hope that Einstein would come back or to ride up with the ramp. He sighed. Even if he jumped off, he didn't have any way to 'make' the avatar do what he wanted, and it appeared that the avatar had told him everything that it was going to.

"Well, shit," he said. "I guess that's all we're going to get. Let's go." He started walking up the ramp.

Rafaeli shrugged, "Sounds good to me," she said. "This place gives me the creeps."

CO's Conference Room, TSS *Vella Gulf,* In Orbit Around Gliese 667 C 'c', August 8, 2020

"So, that's it?" asked Captain Griffin. "Go find these markers, do something and then come back?"

"Yes ma'am," said Calvin. The trip back to the ship had been uneventful. The shuttle's systems had worked when they turned them on, and nothing had interfered with them on the journey to the *Vella Gulf.* "I tried to get more information on what, how and where, but Einstein pretty much just kicked us out and said, 'Go do it, then.'"

"But you don't have any idea what you're supposed to do?" asked Captain Griffin.

"Not a clue," replied Calvin.

"OK, Steropes," said Captain Griffin, turning toward the Psiclops. "Give."

"I'm sorry," replied Steropes. "What do you mean?"

"I mean," said Captain Griffin, "that you guys haven't said a word about this civilization the whole time, and just played along like you didn't know anything. I find that incredibly hard to believe. *What do you know?*"

There was a pause as the three Psiclopes looked at each other, and the Terrans knew that they were having a telepathic conversation on what to tell them. Or not tell them, as the case might be.

"What is there to discuss, damn it?" asked Calvin, frustrated at having been given a task to complete that came with almost no instructions on how to accomplish it. "Why can't you just tell us what you know?"

"Well, no one really 'knows' anything about them," Arges replied. "We *have* found evidence of ancient civilizations on other planets, but they were so old that we weren't able to tell anything for sure. We knew that there was a civilization, and that for some reason it ceased to exist. But that is all we knew. Since all of our information is based on guesswork, we didn't want to cloud your contact with them with conjecture."

"Your civilization is the only one that has actually had contact with them," Brontes added. "Terrans now know more about the ancients' civilization than any of the alliance members."

CO's Stateroom, TSS *Vella Gulf,* In Orbit Around Gliese 667 C 'c', August 8, 2020

"What do you think that was all about?" Captain Griffin asked. After the meeting in the conference room, she had privately commed the XO and Calvin to come to her cabin.

"Do you mean the Psiclopes, and why they were so secretive?" Calvin asked.

"Yes," Captain Griffin said, "that is exactly what I mean. They were obviously hiding something. They must know more about the ancients than what they said."

"They do," Calvin stated. "I've been around them more than anyone, and I've gotten to be pretty good about telling when they're lying. The whole time Arges was talking, he was either lying or not telling the whole truth."

"What do you think it is?" the XO asked.

"I don't know," Calvin said, "but they know more than what they're telling us. At this stage of the game, I have no idea why they're not telling us everything; all I know is that they are not."

"Captain Griffin, Ensign Sommers," Sara commed the CO.

"Go ahead Sara," Captain Griffin replied.

"Captain Griffin, you're never going to guess what just happened!" Sara said.

"The stargate just came back?" Captain Griffin asked.

"How did you know?" Sara asked, disappointment heavy in her voice.

"There's no reason for them to keep us here any longer," replied Captain Griffin. *"Have the helmsman proceed to the stargate at full speed. I'd like to get out of here as soon as possible."*

Chapter Eighteen

"All of you have done amazing work," said Captain Griffin, looking around at the Terrans who had been living on Domus since the end of the first mission to the stars. "I really mean that." She smiled at the two queens sitting next to her. The planet of Domus had both a humanoid civilization and a race of therapods called the kuji, which looked uncomfortably like five to six-feet tall tyrannosaurus rex dinosaurs. The queens of both civilizations had flown up to the Gulf on the planet's own shuttle. "And I am particularly amazed at how far your societies have come, just since the last time we came through here."

She looked at the Terran ambassador to Domus, Sir Henry Flowers. "It is also incredible how much you've been able to complete in such a short time. You have not only united the two societies on this planet, you've brought them into an alliance with Terra."

"It is amazing how much two groups can work together when they find out that an aggressive species that wants to eat them is close by," the ambassador replied. "It tends to focus the mind wonderfully."

Captain Griffin smiled. "Well, you won't have to do everything by yourself much longer. On our next trip, I know that we will be bringing more advisors to help organize the society and the produc-

147

tion effort; additionally, we've got some things on this trip that will help make your life a little easier."

Captain Griffin indicated an officer, sitting near the end of the table. "Lieutenant Colonel Luiz Ordonez will be staying here when we leave. He is a logistics specialist, whose job it will be to make sure that the replicator we are also leaving with you is run efficiently. For the last several months he has studied under Andrew Brown, the person who is running our biggest replicator, and he is as experienced as anyone we have at replicator operations."

"Hi sir," said Colonel Ordonez. "I have a suggested start-up list for things to make with the replicator to get us going, as well as a supply of some of the metals we'll need. The first thing we are going to want to make is a medibot and a bunch of implants. The sooner we can get everyone running as effectively and efficiently as possible, the easier things will be. Unfortunately, we didn't have the time needed to replicate an operational medibot to bring down with us, but it won't take too long to get one put together. I will talk with you more once we get down to the planet."

"In addition to Colonel Ordonez," Captain Griffin said, "we will also be leaving Staff Sergeant Jim Chang when we come back through to help coordinate the military training. He has been acting as one of Lieutenant Commander Hobbs' squad leaders, and I know he is very proficient with the new technology and how the platoon conducts operations. He will help coordinate the efforts of the men already in place training your soldiers.

"Thank you," said Queen Risst, the therapod queen. "The more people we have, the faster we can bring our troops up to standards."

"Absolutely," agreed the human queen, Queen Glina. "Now that we have a replicator, we can make our own weapons. That will help speed up the process too."

"Is there anything else we can do for you before we depart on our mission?" asked Captain Griffin.

"No," replied Queen Glina, "but we do want you to stop here on your way back through. We have a delegation that we would like to send to Earth."

"We will," agreed Captain Griffin. "In that case, Calvin, could you see about getting them a shuttle down to the planet? We need to get back to accomplishing our mission."

"Yes ma'am," replied Calvin. He consulted the crew via implant. "The shuttle is on standby to take the leaders back to the planet," he said. "They should be ready to go in 10 minutes."

Chapter Nineteen

Bridge, TSS *Vella Gulf,* Keppler-22 System, August 11, 2020

"System stabilizing," said Steropes. After leaving the Epsilon Eridani system, the Terrans had transited through the WASP-18 system, which had two stargates that had not been explored on the *Vella Gulf's* first mission. The system they were exploring was on the other side of one of these unexplored stargates. "Probes launching," Steropes added.

A long pause followed, where nothing else was heard from the science station. On the viewer, a medium-sized yellow star glowed softly. It was obvious to the crew that the stargate was much closer to the star in this system than in any of the other ones they had entered. Usually the star only appeared as a small dot on the viewer.

After a couple of minutes, Captain Griffin started tapping her foot. When that had no effect (and her foot got tired), she finally asked, "Is there something I should know about this star system?"

"Oh! Sorry," said Steropes. "I got distracted. The stargate is normally on the periphery of the system. This one is much closer to the star; in fact, it is the closest to the star that I have ever entered a system, and I was going to make some initial measurements on it."

"We're aware of that," replied Captain Griffin.

"Really?" asked Steropes. He looked up. Captain Griffin looked pointedly at the front viewer.

"Oh, yes, I see," said Steropes. "We are also fairly close to a planet around that star. The planet is a little more than double the size of Earth and..."

"*Are there any indications of enemy activity in this system?*" yelled Captain Griffin, interrupting Steropes.

"Umm, just a second," replied Steropes. "Sorry, we've never come through a stargate this close to a planet, either, and I just automatically started doing the survey...

"I said, *are there any indications of enemy activity in this system?*" yelled Captain Griffin, interrupting Steropes again.

"Umm, no, there are no indications of ship activity in this system," replied Steropes. "Hmm...I am receiving indications of power usage from the planet. There is some sort of power plant in operation. It seems to be an antimatter plant."

"Get on it and figure out what we're dealing with here, Steropes," ordered Captain Griffin. "That's the first priority. Unless there is something that appears to directly threaten the ship, I want to know what is happening on that planet. I especially want to know of any offensive or defensive positions. Am I clear on that?"

"Yes ma'am," replied a very humble Steropes. "I'm on it."

Bridge, TSS *Vella Gulf,* In Orbit Around Keppler-22 'b,' August 11, 2020

"I'm ready to give you my preliminary report," said Steropes.

"Not half as ready as I am to get it," replied Captain Griffin.

"Uhhh," mumbled Steropes, not sure how to answer that.

Captain Griffin sighed. "Never mind," she said. "Go ahead with your report."

"Yes ma'am," replied Steropes. "This system is the Kepler-22 system. We are about 600 light years away from Earth in the constellation Cygnus, the Swan. As you could already guess from the viewer, Keppler-22 is a yellow star that is about 25% less luminous than the Sun."

"The system has two planets that orbit the star," he continued. "The first planet is a Jupiter-sized giant that orbits the star at a distance of only 750,000 miles. It is so close to the star that it completes an orbit in just over 10 hours. It is currently on the other side of the star, but when it is visible, you can see that the planet has a magnetic field that traps charged particles from the star. It has a glowing aurora-like ring around each of its poles."

"Does that help us in some way?" asked Captain Griffin.

"Umm, no it doesn't," said Steropes. "As close as it is to the star, the planet is far too hot to be useful to us." He paused. "We are currently orbiting the other planet, Kepler-22 'b,'" Steropes continued. "It is a super-Earth type world that is almost two and a half times larger than Earth and orbits Kepler-22 at a distance of 79 million miles. At this distance, its year is about 290 days long. The planet's surface is about 90% water, and its atmosphere is very close to Earth's, with an average surface temperature of 22°C (72°F). Life appears to exist both on land and in the ocean."

"You're coming to the part where you tell us about the inhabitants that have an antimatter power plant, and you're coming to it *soon*," interjected Captain Griffin. "Right, Steropes?"

"Uh, yes ma'am," replied Steropes. "I'm almost there." He paused to collect himself and then continued, "As I noted, the planet is mostly water, with a few island chains scattered around its surface. The islands appear to be volcanic in nature, although they have been extinct so long that their central cones are not much more than elevated highlands."

He brought a diagram of the planet onto the front view screens and focused in on a chain of islands near the equator. There was a large island in the center with several more to the east and west. "The power plant is located on this island," he said. "The island is about 4,000 square miles in area, or about the size of the big island in Hawaii. I've done a cursory study of the island, and I have not been able to find any sign of civilization around the beaches; all of the habitation seems to be inland. When I aligned the cameras with the power source, I found this." He zoomed in with the camera and refocused it to show...a pyramid.

"That is not fortuitous," Arges said.

"What is it?" asked Captain Griffin.

"It looks like an Aztec pyramid," said Calvin.

"Mayan, actually," answered Steropes. "It looks just like the Mayan pyramids of Mexico and Central America. Unfortunately, the presence of such a pyramid is usually indicative of coatls."

"Coatls?" asked Captain Griffin.

"Yes," replied Steropes. "Coatls. Flying snakes. I'm sure they have a name for themselves in their own language, but I can't pronounce it, any more than one of you can talk with a snake on your planet."

"Flying snakes and pyramids," Calvin said. "Coatls. Do you mean coatls like Quetzalcoatl? Wasn't that like the god of the Incans or something like that?"

"Quetzalcoatl was actually worshiped by the Mayan Indians," answered Steropes, "and somewhat also by the Aztecs. Unfortunately, that is exactly what I mean. Coatls are biological parasites that live off of other species. A nest of them made it to your planet during the Mayan era. If you remember seeing pictures of priests cutting out victims' still-beating hearts on top of Central American pyramids, that was their inspiration. They were big believers in human sacrifice; not only did they like the taste of human flesh, but they also liked the psychic rush they got from inspiring fear in others."

"Wait," said Captain Griffin, "those things really exist?"

"Yes," answered Steropes, "they really exist, and they love to infest pre-technic humanoid civilizations. They use their advanced technology and proclaim themselves to be gods, especially of learning and knowledge. They *do* give the civilization knowledge, but it comes at a tremendous cost in blood. If there is an infestation here, we *have* to get rid of it."

"Are there other people living down there?" asked Calvin.

"I haven't actually seen any of the coatls on the island," replied Steropes, "but there is definitely a civilization down there. It is impossible to tell with complete certainty from orbit, but the inhabitants seem to be humanoid in appearance, although possibly a bit smaller and darker in complexion than you are."

"How sure are you that there are coatls here with this civilization?" asked the ambassador. "It would seem to me that if they are sacrificing members of that society, they may be grateful if we could get rid of the coatls."

"I am positive that there are coatls there," replied Steropes. He changed the view on the camera so that the whole town could be seen. All of the structures were pyramids. They were also all painted blood red in color, giving the scene a very ominous feel. "This layout is like the pyramid complexes the coatls had the Mayans build on Earth; in fact, it is nearly identical to the complex at Chacchoben in present-day Mexico." He used a laser pointer to indicate a cluster of buildings on the southern end of the city. "There is a large pyramid here that is probably used as the palace and administration structure. It is surrounded by a group of smaller pyramids. These are residential structures where the nobles and priests live."

"I thought the pyramids were made of stones," said Calvin. "The surfaces of these pyramids all look smooth."

"They *are* made of stones," said Arges. "They just have plaster on them to make them look flat and smooth. The ones on Earth were completed similarly, but the plaster rotted over time so that all you see now is just the stones."

"North of this cluster of buildings is a large courtyard with a ball court on one side of it," continued Steropes. "The ball court is this long narrow playing alley that has sloping walls on both sides of it." Like the pyramids, its walls were plastered and painted bright red. "The playing alley has closed end zones," noted Steropes, "giving the structure an I-shape. The largest playing field on Earth was the Great Ball Court at Chichen Itza, which was 96.5 meters long; this one measures 105 meters."

"Wow," said Calvin, "that's a big field."

"Indeed," replied Steropes. "North of the courtyard and ball court is the main temple."

"Where?" asked the ambassador. "On the other side of that hill?"

"No," said Steropes, "that hill *is* the temple."

"Damn," muttered Calvin in awe. "That thing is *huge.*"

"Yes, it is," agreed Steropes. "I estimate that the pyramid is about a 1,350' square that stands nearly 350' high. The temple sits on a 2,000' square man-made plateau that is about 40' higher than the rest of the area. There is one staircase that goes up to the temple level at the top of the pyramid. It is on the side that faces the rest of the city."

"The plateau is 40' high and 2,000' on a side?" asked Captain Griffin. "How did they do that? I thought you said they were pre-technic. Do they have excavation equipment?"

Steropes shook his head. "No," he said. "No power equipment was used to make the plateau. If it was formed the same way as the ones on Earth; it was built by the city's inhabitants, moving dirt by hand."

Several swear words and expressions of disbelief filled the bridge.

"The antimatter power source is located in this temple," said Steropes. "It is the only sign of civilization on the planet. There is no way that the inhabitants of this city developed an antimatter plant. None. The coatls are here, and they are in this temple. *And they must be destroyed!*"

"Wow," said Captain Griffin. "It sounds like you feel strongly about that."

"They are an affront to everything that I believe in," replied Steropes. "I'm normally against killing, but I make an exception for coatls. *They must be destroyed.*"

"OK," said Captain Griffin. "I get it. You're not big on them."

"Wait a minute," interrupted the ambassador. "We're supposed to make new friends, not commit genocide on the new civilizations we find. How does that make us any better than the Drakuls or the lizards you faced on your first mission?"

"I didn't say to destroy the whole civilization," said Steropes. "I said that the coatls must be destroyed. We need to go to the surface of the planet and throw off the yoke that the coatls have on these people. If we do that, you would have access to the resources on the planet."

"How powerful are the coatls?" Calvin asked. "Can we beat them with the weapons we have?"

"Absolutely," Steropes said. "With your suits and lasers, you will make short work of them. They are not that strong, but they are poisonous if you let them get in close. I have never heard of them using weapons; they normally use less advanced societies to do their dirty work. They also don't have hands, which makes it hard for them to hold most weapons."

"Well, if the things I remember about Mayan human sacrifice are true," Captain Griffin said, "and the coatls are behind it, then we need to do something about them. We could also use the resources here, which will require going to the planet." She paused, considering, then turned to Calvin. "Why don't you take a squad down there and make contact with the locals. Once you've established relations with them, we will send down the ambassador to talk to the leaders of their civilization."

Calvin nodded. "Yes, ma'am," he said.

"Our mission isn't to commit genocide or participate in the affairs of other civilizations, though," she reminded him. "If you find any coatls, take them prisoner if at all possible. Try to use the minimum amount of force necessary to control the situation, but keep our people safe."

Calvin nodded again. Turning to Steropes, he asked, "Is there a good place to land?"

"Yes," Steropes replied. "Although they built their cities away from the water, there is a good spot to land right here on this beach." He pointed at the map. "There is some sort of structure just inland of the landing point, and then there is what looks like a road that goes through the jungle to the main city. I would be happy to join the team going to the surface of the planet and show you myself."

"Really?" Captain Griffin asked. "I didn't think that your race believed in fighting."

"Normally, it does not," Steropes replied. "However, I am an anomaly among my people. I have been trained for combat."

"No shit?" Night asked, who had been quiet to this point. "*You're* a warrior?"

"I used to be," Steropes answered. "Up until the destruction of Atlantis, when my pride got the better of me."

"What do you mean, 'the destruction of Atlantis'?" Captain Griffin asked. "You've hinted at this many times, but never told us the whole story. Maybe it's time we heard it."

"It probably is," Steropes replied, "although the story is hard to tell." He paused, and the Terrans could see he was struggling with it. "It was a long time ago," he finally said, "back when we first arrived on your planet. Not too long after we landed, the Drakuls fleeing the final battle with the Eldive came to Earth in a stolen Eldive warship." He paused, a glazed look coming over his eyes as he remembered. "I can see it just like it was yesterday. We were awakened from our sleep on a beautiful summer day. There wasn't a cloud in the sky, just a wisp of smoke coming from the volcano in the center of the island. Temperatures were pleasant...there was a light breeze blowing...it was another beautiful day in the south Pacific."

He looked at Calvin, and Calvin could see his eyes tearing up. "But the Drakuls had come to the planet. When the humans woke us up and told us about them, we knew that they were Drakuls." He laughed sadly. "We were so young and stupid," he continued. "We thought if we just upgraded some of the humans, we would be able to take care of the Drakuls without calling for additional help."

"Who is we?" Captain Griffin asked.

"Myself and my wife, Parvati," Steropes replied. "We assaulted the Drakul encampment with over 1,000 implanted humans. But the Drakuls knew we were coming; I don't know how. As we ran screaming into their camp, they hit us from behind from where they had been hiding." A tear rolled down his left cheek. "One of them grabbed Parvati, and I saw it tear off her arm and begin eating it. There were two Drakuls between us...there was nothing I could do. I don't remember how, but I killed both of them, and somehow I made it to the one that killed Parvati."

A tear rolled down his right cheek, and he looked back down as he continued, "I shot the Drakul. And shot it. And shot it. I shot it until it came apart from being shot so many times. Then I shot the biggest pieces that were left...I fired until the battery in the rifle went dead." Calvin knew that the rifle batteries were usually good for over 500 shots before they had to be replaced. Even if Steropes had fired the rifle in the early phase of the battle, that was still a *lot* of shots.

"That day I swore I would never fight again. One of the Drakuls escaped our attack, and he set off the bomb that destroyed Atlantis. If I hadn't fallen into despair, I could have stopped him. There were enough humans left, and we had enough firepower...but I was bereft of my senses. In my grief, I couldn't move. I couldn't think. All I could do was sit there with Parvati's head in my lap. I picked her up assuming she was dead, but she wasn't dead yet. She still lived, and I watched the life go out of her eyes."

Steropes shook his head. "I never even got to bury her," he added. "The human leaders finally brought me to my senses, and we tracked the Drakul back to its lair in a nearby cave. Arges and Brontes had recovered the Eldive ship while we were fighting the Drakuls, and they met us at the cave with it so that we could get new batteries for our weapons. We went into the cave and killed the Drakul. It was only after it died that we found the bomb that it had armed. It was a big one...nearly big enough to crack the planet to its core, which was probably the Drakul's intention. We only had 60 seconds before detonation. We ran back to the ship with all of the humans that we had brought and took off. We watched as the island blew up, with the body of my wife still on it. She was so brave." He paused.

"I wasn't functional anymore," he said when he continued. "After the tidal wave caused by the explosion had diminished, Arges made the decision to drop off the humans in what is modern day Greece. He thought that he had brought the ship in unseen, but some of the locals saw the humans getting off it. The locals believed that the humans were gods, since they had descended from the skies. Most of them had been modified by us, so compared to the locals, they *were* gods. They were faster, stronger and could communicate via their implants, which gave them tremendous advantages over the locals. Arges was unable to disarm the Terrans that still had weapons. Poseidon still had his trident, others had their laser rifles. That was my fault too. I could have taken them, but in my grief I just didn't care. Every single one of them was already more powerful than 100 of the locals, even without these weapons. Thinking that we were leaving their planet, the humans decided that they would be gods...and they were. The Olympians were actually a family of 12, who were led by three brothers, Zeus, Poseidon and Hades."

Steropes smiled wryly. "The irony of it all was that Parvati and I had been sent to Earth because we were *too* warlike. It was not seemly in our society to enjoy battles, fighting and war. The fact that we did made us outcasts. We wanted to go to the final battle with the Drakuls. Because we wanted to, our leadership not only didn't send us, they sent us here for a 5,000 year tour of duty with Arges and Brontes, who they thought would pacify us. If we hadn't wanted to fight so much, we wouldn't have been here to actually have to do battle with the Drakuls. Funny how things work out, eh?"

"Umm...I'm sorry but I'm not sure that's funny at all," said Calvin. "Why do you want to go down and fight here if you swore you would never fight again?"

"Want to?" asked Steropes. "You misunderstand. I *don't* want to. The loss of Parvati and the destruction of Atlantis cured me of ever wanting to go to war ever again. I don't want to fight. However, I have fought the coatls before, and I know what to expect, much more than you do. They usually build their pyramids in the same way, and I am familiar with their layout. It's simple; I know where the secret passages are, and you do not. I will save lives by being there and will be a tremendous resource if you let me come. I don't want to come; I need to come."

"If you think you're up to it," replied Calvin, "We would love to take advantage of your experience. You are welcome to join us." He looked at Night. "I'm going to go down on this one with the Space Force. You'll have the Ground Force in backup."

"Why the Space Force?" asked Night. "It would seem like this is the perfect spot for the Ground Force. The planet is Earth-like, with similar temperatures and gravity. The force will be landing on the ground. What's up?"

"I don't know," replied Calvin. "Something just tells me that we'll need the Space Force on this one."

Squadron CO's Office, TSS *Vella Gulf,* In Orbit Around Keppler-22 'b,' August 12, 2020

"Can I come in?" asked Father John Zuhlsdorf, the *Gulf's* chaplain.

Calvin looked up from his desk, where he was trying to get a few last minute administrative things completed prior to the assault on the planet. Calvin had long ago decided that the only thing besides cockroaches that would survive a nuclear holocaust was paperwork. "Sure," he said. "What can I do for you?"

"I feel that I am being called to go on your upcoming mission to the planet," replied Father Zuhlsdorf. "As a priest, it is my mission and duty to spread the word of God." He smiled. "I'm betting that these locals here have never heard it."

"Um, I'm not sure that is such a great idea, Father," replied Calvin. "I'm expecting that we'll be in combat this time. Not only that, it might be close combat if we have to go inside of the pyramid, probably even hand-to-hand. Despite your skills, I'm not sure you're ready for that." He thought for a moment, remembering his first experience with looking up the wrong end of a Chinese assault rifle. "Being in a position of 'kill or be killed' is pretty...intense."

"I understand that," the chaplain replied, "however, I think I showed your Master Chief that I am fairly skilled in the hand-to-hand arena. He *did* promise me a trip to the surface if I beat him."

"I know that he did," Calvin said, "however, you have to realize that he didn't have the authority to promise you that."

"I know that," Father Zuhlsdorf said. "However, I feel that I am being called to go on this mission. If you didn't intend to bring me along to a planet, why did you allow me to get modified for combat or to get a combat suit?"

"Hmmm..." Calvin said, thinking out loud. "I forgot I told Night to do that. Having those things does increase your survivability in combat..."

"Without a doubt," agreed the chaplain. "I have also been practicing with the platoon to get back into my old fighting shape."

"If I say 'yes,'" Calvin said, "and that is still a *big* 'if,' what sort of gear do you have? I mean, I don't have anyone that I can detail to watch over you. You'll have to be able to take care of yourself. Can you do that?"

"I'm glad you asked," Father Zuhlsdorf said with a smile. He stepped back out of the office and reached over to pick something up from the deck. Stepping back into the office, Calvin could see that he had a handful of weapons and armor.

Calvin laughed. "You're nothing if not prepared, it seems." He laughed again. "All right, what have you got there?"

Father Zuhlsdorf set down the gear carefully and picked up a small sword that was just over two feet in length. The blade was slightly curved at about the midpoint, almost looking like the khukri of an Indian ghurka soldier, but a lot bigger. "This is a Greek falcata sword," he said. "It was a devastating sword used by the Spanish against the soldiers of the Roman Empire. It was captured in the Second Punic War and brought back to Rome. Although it hits like an axe, it still maintains the blade of a sword."

He picked up a larger sword and helmet, treating them as if they were very special. "These are holy relics," he said. "They are the blessed sword and hat of Heinrich Walpot von Bassenheim, the first Grandmaster of the Order of Brothers of the German house of Saint Mary in Jerusalem, also known as the Teutonic Order. Blessed swords and hats were gifts given to leaders by the pope, in recognition of their defense of Christendom. Each pair was blessed by a pope on Christmas Eve in St. Peter's Basilica in Rome. Although the practice is believed to have originated with Pope Paul I's gift to King Pepin the Short of the Franks in 758, this is the oldest surviving pair." He looked at the pair lovingly.

"No one even knew that these still existed," he said. "It was believed that the oldest pair was on display in France, a set given to King John II of Castile by Pope Eugene IV in 1446. When I was selected to come on this mission, the pope asked the caretakers at the Vatican Museums to search through their storerooms to see if there were any special weapons that I could use. They found this sword and helmet, which was given to the first Grandmaster of the Teutonic Knights after it became a spiritual military order. It was to be used in the Fourth Crusade. I hope to be worthy of it."

"How did you rate such a piece of history?" Calvin asked. "Shouldn't this be *in* the museum?"

"It probably should," the chaplain acknowledged, "but I used to run some public relations sites for the pope, and he not only wanted to reward me for my service, but also to make sure that the servant of God on this mission was well armed in defense of the faith, regardless of what that might entail."

He pulled the sword out of its scabbard, and Calvin could see that it was a work of art. An ornate weapon, it was almost four feet in length, with a cross guard and pommel made of solid steel. "It's made of high carbon steel," the chaplain said, "and is fairly light, although it would have been hard for anyone at that time to use it one-handed. The hilt is embellished with the coat of arms of Pope Innocent III, one of the greatest popes of the Middle Ages. The blade has his name on it, in addition to the rest of the design and filigree. Although I do not consider myself to be worthy of such a weapon, the pope has bidden me to carry it to the stars." Calvin could see that the scabbard and helmet were similarly ornate.

"The sword is beautiful," Calvin said, "but I don't think the helmet will fit under a combat helmet. Also, I'm not sure that either of your weapons are what I'd call combat-ready, as they are hundreds of years old."

"Not to worry," Father Zuhlsdorf replied, "the pope had Vatican craftsman re-forge them for strength, and then he re-blessed them. They are as ready as any of the weapons that your soldiers carry, plus they are blessed by the pope." He paused and reached around the corner of the office door to retrieve another sword that he had left propped up against the wall. "Besides, if one of them breaks, I always have this." He held out the sword to Calvin.

"What is it?" Calvin asked.

"It's Durandal," Father Zuhlsdorf replied with a touch of awe. "It is said to have belonged to Count Roland, who was the paladin of Charlemagne. People believe that this sword has a tooth of St. Peter, a hair of St. Denis, the blood of Saint Basil, and a piece of the raiment of the Blessed Virgin Mary in its hilt. The legend says that it was given to Charlemagne by an angel and is supposed to be the sharpest sword ever made, as well as indestructible. I think I am ready for anything that we might find down there."

"Having a named sword is certainly cool," Calvin said, "regardless of whether any of its story is actually true. Are you any good with them?"

"I've received the same downloads as the soldiers did, and I've been sparring with them," the priest replied. "I haven't been able to beat Yokaze or Night yet, but I've been able to beat everyone else at least once."

"Let me know when you beat Yokaze," Calvin said, "and I'll ask Skipper Griffin if I can borrow you to be my new weapons instructor. He's damn...I mean, he's darned good."

Father Zuhlsdorf smiled. "Thanks, but I've heard it before. Especially working out with the members of the platoon. They are a...colorful...group in manner, as well as in expression. I still would like to go to the planet."

"Have you heard what we are facing?" Calvin asked.

"Yes, I have," the priest answered. "Quetzalcoatl, who purports itself to be a god. It is not, of course, which is one of the reasons I feel I must accompany you. My sword was last used during the crusades, which were meant to liberate the sacred city of Jerusalem. As I understand it, you intend to liberate this planet from the influence of a false god. I believe that the reason both the sword and I are here is to help with the accomplishment of this goal."

"OK, you've convinced me to take you," Calvin said, "assuming that Skipper Griffin will allow it. You work for her, not me, so I need her permission. The only other problem that I see is that the beliefs of some of the members of my platoon are not completely in line with your beliefs or the beliefs of the church. I can't take you if that is going to be an issue that divides the team. In combat, we have to be a single unit where everyone watches everyone else's back. Can you do this?"

"Of course," the chaplain replied. "I have always enjoyed the lively discussion of beliefs, but do not hold someone to be less worthy just because they believe differently than I do. We are all God's children, after all. As far as talking to Captain Griffin goes, I already spoke to her and secured her permission to go, so that shouldn't be a problem."

"It seems like you already have all of your bases covered," Calvin said. He stood up and offered his hand. "Welcome to the team," he said.

Father Zuhlsdorf shook the platoon commander's hand, being very careful not to drop the burden in his other hand. "Thank you," he said. "I am very happy to be a part of it."

Squad Bay, TSS *Vella Gulf,* Keppler-22 'b', August 12, 2020

"This is our first mission," said Bob as he watched the Terrans preparing weapons, stowing their gear in rucksacks and clipping things onto harnesses. "Doug and I are curious. What equipment should we bring? Do we really need everything that we trained with?"

"I'd bring anything that you thought you might need, plus all of the things that you thought you probably won't need, and then throw in all of the stuff that you're *sure* you won't need," replied Mr. Jones, their fire team leader. The former CIA operative still hadn't learned the lizards' expressions yet, but seeing what he guessed was a puzzled expression on Bob's face, he added, "Any equipment you leave on the ship is pretty damn worthless to you, isn't it?"

"Well, yes it is," said Bob, "but that's a lot of stuff to have to bring if you're not going to use it. It is hard for Doug and me to carry all of it."

Mr. Jones raised an eyebrow skeptically. "If you leave anything behind, you are sure to need it," he said. "The best way to be sure that you won't need it is to bring it."

"I fail to see the logic in that statement," noted Doug.

"Don't worry about it," replied Mr. Jones. "Bring everything you can carry without it affecting your ability to move quickly and silently. Once you've been on a few missions, you can decide what things you need to have, and what you can make do without."

Bob pulled out a bladed weapon from a drawer. "You'll definitely want to bring that," noted Mr. Jones. "Can I see it?" Bob handed it to his fire team leader.

Mr. Jones took it and looked at it critically. In form, it was similar to many of the swamp hatchets and tomahawks he had seen. It was about a foot and a half long, although the grip was modified to fit the therapods' hands. The blade on top was in the shape of a large, sideways letter "J," trailing to a thick, wickedly sharp point on the back. Unlike most tomahawks, there was an edge across the top of the weapon that ran from the head of it all the way back to the point.

"Interesting," noted Mr. Jones. "Our tomahawks normally don't have an edge across the top like that. What is it for?"

"Cracking open the shell pods of a crustacean on our home world," replied Bob. "They're very tasty."

Doug looked up. "It's also good for defending yourself from a jusssole, which is a snake-like creature of the swamp," he added. "The creature's mouth can open up big enough to get the entire head of the weapon into it. Once you get the jusssole to try to swallow it, the user then drives the point on the back of the axe into a tree or the ground, effectively pinning the snake in place. Then you use a second blade to cut its head off while it flips around."

"Yes," agreed Bob. "They're very tasty too. You just have to watch out for their fangs. They're extremely poisonous."

"Do you carry a bladed weapon?" asked Doug.

"Yeah, I do," replied Mr. Jones, pulling out a knife that was almost long enough to be considered a short sword. The blade alone was over 12 inches in length and almost two inches wide, with a curved point at the end. The knife had an edge cut from both sides at the top and a cross-guard to protect his hand. "If it was good enough for Colonel Bowie," he continued, "it's good enough for me. It's big enough to get the attention of anything I poke with it, as well as to provide a little bit of defense, if needed."

"I'll just stick with my kris, mon," noted Sergeant Margaret 'Witch' Andrews, drawing the wavy blade from its sheath. "The blade has 13 waves in it for good luck," the Jamaican woman continued. "Usually, most people start running, just by me pulling it out." She looked at it and smiled. "The blade has also been infused with poison, so most cuts be fatal."

"Is that legal?" asked Leading Seaman Sigvar Borsheim.

"Does it matter to you if it be not?" countered Witch, looking up at him through narrowed eyes. Borsheim shook his head quickly, not wanting to annoy her any further. His luck was bad enough; he didn't need a witch's curse too. She held it out where the therapods could see it. "See the way the dark black iron and the silvery nickel layers merge? These patterns are the blade's pamors. Each has a specific meaning and name which gives it a special magical property."

"Like what?" asked Bob. "Can you draw some on mine?"

"They have to be added at the blade's forging, mon," explained Andrews. "If you be a believer, I be happy to have one made for you."

"Yes, please!" agreed Bob. He held up his tomahawk. "Can they make them like this?"

"I know not," she replied. "If they cannot, I can work with your weapon makers to at least add this." She showed Bob the picture inscribed into the weapon's handle.

"Who is that?" asked Bob.

"It is Semar the Mysterious," Witch replied with a touch of awe in her voice. "He is my guardian spirit."

"Is that my guardian spirit too?" asked Bob.

"I do not know, mon," replied Andrews, "but I will help you find your guardian spirit when we get back if you wish."

Bob nodded happily.

Doug looked at Vice Sergeant Ismail Al-Sabani standing next to him. "Do you have a kris?"

"No," replied Al-Sabani, "I have a janbiya."

"What is that?" asked Doug.

"A janbiya is an Arabian dagger," answered Al-Sabani holding up the sheathed blade. "It is a short curved blade with a saifani handle made over 100 years ago from a rhinoceros horn."

"Can I see it?" asked Doug.

"I am afraid not," replied the Saudi. "Like the weapon of Sergeant Andrews, my blade is both a weapon and a spiritual object, and there are rules that must be followed to avoid defaming it. My janbiya only leaves its sheath for combat or ceremonial events." He held up the sheathed blade. "You can see from the sheath," he continued, "that the blade bends toward my enemy. I do not need to turn my wrist, so it is a better stabbing weapon than a straight-bladed knife. Its blade is heavy, so I can inflict deep wounds or cut through muscle and bone. I can also stick it in sideways and twist so that I can reach internal organs more easily. In my country, it is a formidable and much feared weapon."

"Whatever blade you carry needs to be something that you are comfortable with," interjected Wraith, walking by the group, "and something that complements your fighting style. Do not choose one of our weapons to try to blend in with us. Use your own weapon, as you know best how to use it. Most of us will let you try our weapons to see if you like them; if there is a reason for not letting you use them," she said, acknowledging Al-Sabani, "we can have replicas made that you can use."

"What do you use?" asked the Saudi.

Wraith drew a straight short sword from the scabbard at her side. Al-Sabani could see Korean characters running up the length of the blade. "Like most of the other platoon members' weapons," she said, "this is a special sword. It is a sa-ingeom, or 'four tigers' sword, from the Joseon-era in western Korea. It has a 35-inch blade, which was made mostly by molding, rather than hammering. These swords were crafted with the greatest care, using only the highest quality steel. By tradition, these swords were forged only for the king and could only be made at certain times; there is only a two hour window to produce these every 12 years. It was given to me by the president from her collection. It is, quite literally, priceless."

Chapter Twenty

"What do you think of these?" Steropes asked as the shuttle detached from the *Vella Gulf* and began its descent to the planet's surface.

Calvin looked up to see Steropes holding two black, leaf-bladed knives. "Nice," he replied. "Are those throwing knives?"

"Yes they are," Steropes answered. Without warning, he threw the one in his right hand at Calvin. Surprised, all Calvin could do was raise an arm to protect himself. The knife hit his arm and bounced away, hitting Ryan in the shoulder before falling to the ground.

"Would you two *gentlemen* stop fucking around," Ryan growled, "*please*?" He said the word 'gentlemen' as if it were a curse. He bent over and picked up the knife and handed it to Calvin, who was still too stunned to speak. He took the knife and saw that it was made of rubber. The knife was hard enough to hold its shape and look convincingly real, but was made of rubber.

"First, let me say that was not freakin' cool," Calvin said to Steropes. "And second, what the *hell* did you do that for?"

"I just wanted to make sure that they looked real enough to be believed," Steropes replied. "You'll see."

"*Five minutes to touchdown,*" the shuttle's WSO, Lieutenant Gino Bianchi, called.

"Let's go ladies!" Ryan shouted. "Gear up! When you're done, check your neighbor!"

The squad began putting on their helmets and checking all of their gear for the final time.

Space Force, Keppler-22 'b', August 12, 2020

The shuttle landed on what appeared to be a pristine beach, nearly 100 yards wide. The waters were calm, and the scenery appeared restful, even idyllic. The pseudo-palm trees swayed in the gentle offshore breeze. The shuttle touched down, and the boarding ramp came down. The Space Force charged out of the shuttle and took up defensive positions, but there was nothing to see or defend against.

"All clear," Master Chief called, seeing nothing but the swaying trees.

Calvin walked out of the shuttle with Steropes. As they exited, they saw that the shuttle had set down about 50 yards from a rock that was sitting in the middle of the sand. Six feet in length and slightly ovoid in shape, the rock was interesting because it was the only thing that marred the perfection of the beach. No other rocks could be seen in the water, on the beach or in the tree line. Seeing the rock, Calvin walked toward it with Steropes, Master Chief, Staff Sergeant Patrick 'The Wall' Dantone and Corporal Charles 'Rocket' Applebaum. The shuttle lifted off behind them to go back to the *Vella Gulf*, and the rest of the squad began moving toward the tree line. Finding the air safe to breathe and seeing no sign of danger, Calvin allowed the troops to take their helmets off.

"Oh, blessed sun," Doug said, stretching in the warmth.

"Now if we only had a snack," Bob added, "this would be perfect."

As they reached the rock, Calvin saw that it was not a rock, but some sort of animal that had an outer carapace like a turtle, as well as a third pair of legs. Judging by the smell, the creature had been dead for some time. There were no tracks or sliding marks around it. "*I wonder how it got here,*" he commed.

"*There are tracks made by some type of large creature coming from the forest,*" Staff Sergeant Dantone answered, "*but the tracks stop four meters away. Judging by the impression in the sand, something brought it here and threw it to where it now lies.*"

"*That would have to be an awfully big beast,*" observed Rocket. "*That thing in the sand must weigh several hundred kilograms.*"

"*Don't anyone move!*" Ryan said softly over the platoon's implant net. "*There is a monster dinosaur just inside the tree line.*"

Calvin slowly turned his head toward the tree line. "*I don't see it,*" he said after looking for a couple of seconds.

"*Use your infrared,*" Ryan replied. "*It blends in with the trees. It's even swaying with them in the breeze.*"

Calvin switched his helmet to infrared. "*Holy shit!*" he said quietly. "*That thing is huge!*" He switched the infrared back off. Now that he could see it, it was a sight that Calvin didn't think he'd be able to get out of his head for a long time. The creature had six limbs and was standing on what passed for its hind legs. It looked like a giant bear, but had the leathery, hairless skin of a dinosaur. It was mottled in the colors of the foliage, allowing it to blend in so well with the background that it almost couldn't be seen without turning the infrared back on. Both pairs of arms ended in claws that had four eight-inch long talons. It was the biggest living thing Calvin had ever seen. "*It's got to be 15 feet tall!*" he commed.

Although the monster continued to watch them, it made no motion toward them; it continued to sway in the gentle breeze.

"*LOOK OUT!*" yelled Sergeant Tagliabue. "*Monsters coming from the ocean!*" The crash of antimatter grenades going off punctuated his warning. Part of the group that was still back near where the shuttle had been, Tagliabue had seen creatures rushing out of the water toward Calvin's group, and he had triggered a burst from his trident.

The dino-bear forgotten, Calvin turned to see a horde of creatures boiling from the water, with antimatter grenades detonating among them as they emerged from the waterline. They were monsters that looked like giant six-armed starfish with octopus heads attached to their bodies. The starfish were 12-feet wide from the tip of one tentacle to the tip of the opposite tentacle with a central body about 3 feet in diameter. A purplish-gray head projected almost four feet from the central mass of the creature's body. Calvin and Ryan were closer to the forest and had an instant to aim their laser rifles, but they were already on Rocket and The Wall, who only had time to take snapshots at the creatures before they had to defend themselves.

Although Sergeant Tagliabue's grenades cut off further attack, five of the starfish had closed on the group, with two attacking Rocket, two more on The Wall, and the fifth going around to attack Ryan. Too close to use his rifle effectively, Rocket dropped it and pulled out his pistol. He began firing at one of the starfish attacking him and punched several holes in the central body of the thing. A purple fluid began spurting up through one of the holes, and the animal emitted a shrieking noise. This seemed to energize the other one attacking Rocket, and it lunged forward to wrap a tentacle around Rocket's leg. As the starfish's arm encircled the corporal's leg, Rocket went rigid, and he stopped firing his pistol. He fell over, unmoving.

The Wall kept his rifle, alternately firing it and using it to block the tentacles that kept trying to reach out for him. He backed up slightly so that he could see both of the creatures at once and met the swing of a tentacle with the stock of his rifle, following through to point the weapon at the head of the creature. Before he could fire, a tentacle from the other creature wrapped itself around the rifle and pulled it from his hands, throwing it down the beach. Before the creature could attack again, The Wall pulled his laser pistol from his leg holster and triggered it several times in quick succession. The creature fell backward, unmoving, with three holes between its four centrally-located eyes. As The Wall turned toward the second creature, he saw that it was already in motion, using the distraction of the first monster to attack. It launched itself through the air onto the soldier, and both went down in a tangle of arms and tentacles.

As Calvin and Ryan both fired their rifles at the one charging Ryan, the sounds of additional lasers firing and another wave of antimatter explosions were heard as a second, larger group of starfish came hurtling out of the water near where the shuttle had dropped them off. Warned by the initial attack, the rest of the platoon was better prepared. The starfish were met with a wall of explosives and laser bolts, and they were driven back into the water without any further casualties to the Terrans.

Ryan set his rifle to 'beam,' and used the laser to slice a tentacle from the one attacking him, while Calvin fired from the side into the octopus head. After several bolts, the starfish seemed to collapse upon itself and dropped to the ground. Calvin turned to help The Wall, who was lying unmoving on the beach with the monster on top of him. The creature had also stopped moving, apparently intent on feeding on the soldier. Calvin fired four shots into its head and watched it fall over in a puddle of purple ooze.

Ryan looked up to find the last starfish on top of Rocket with several of its arms wrapped around him. Before he could do anything, Ryan was knocked off his feet by the dino-bear as it rushed past him. It didn't attack Ryan, but slammed him to the side as it hurtled forward toward the remaining starfish that was now pulsing on top of Rocket. The dino-bear slid to a stop next to the starfish and raised a massive, talon-laden foot. It stomped down on the head of the starfish in an explosion of purple, killing the beast instantly. The beast reached down and grabbed the starfish in its four front claws, picking it up off the ground. Shaking it like someone removing dust from a rug, Rocket was thrown from underneath, and the dino-bear ran off to the forest, its prize clutched in its claws. The squad could hear the creature crashing through the brush, but quickly lost sight of it.

"*Medic!*" Ryan yelled, but as Calvin approached the downed soldier he saw it was too late. Half of the front of him had been eaten away. He was dead.

Several members of the squad pulled the other starfish off of The Wall to find that most of the armor on his torso had been eaten away, along with the majority of his face and chest. The squad's medic, Leading Seaman Borsheim, leaned over to confirm his death. "Oh my God!" he cried in horror. "He's still alive!" Father Zuhlsdorf shouldered his rifle and stepped forward. Knowing the soldier was a Catholic, he made the sign of the cross over him, softly saying a prayer.

"Shuttle 01," Calvin commed. *"Get back here immediately! We've got a trooper down, and we need immediate evac!"*

"On our way," the shuttle's WSO, Lieutenant Gino Bianchi replied. *"ETA two minutes!"*

Borsheim continued to minister to The Wall, and the shuttle returned in less than the two minutes promised. It landed with its boarding ramp already lowered, and the squad quickly loaded the soldier onto it. In less than a minute, the shuttle was back on its way to the *Vella Gulf*, leaving the rest of the team on the beach.

"We're sorry we arrived too late to help," a new voice said as the shuttle blasted its way toward the heavens in a full power ascent that coated the platoon in sand. Turning around, Calvin saw a number of humanoid creatures looking at him from the water. They stuck out of the water from the waist up and would have looked very human, except for the gills on the sides of their throats, the second set of arms they had and their coloring, which was a light shade of blue. One motioned toward Rocket's corpse. "There's nothing that you could have done for him, once the tentacles wrapped around him. The creatures have spines that release an extremely strong toxin. He was dead within instants of being grabbed." He shook his head sadly. "I'm sorry for your loss," he said, looking back up at Calvin. "Wait, you are not one of the islanders," he said with a jerk as he startled backward. "Who are you?"

"Steropes, how are we able to understand them?" Calvin asked over the implants.

"There must have been a Psiclopes station here at some time in the past," Steropes replied. *"Hopefully, we can use this information to help us figure out where we are once we get back."*

Calvin saw that the man was still waiting for an answer. He removed his helmet. "No, we are not from this land," he said. "We are explorers from a land far away."

"We thought that you were the people that live on this island," he said. "We have not seen them here by the water in many years. Not since the evil ones came."

"My name is Calvin," Calvin said. "Who are the evil ones?"

"My name is Dolph," the man replied. "The evil ones are the snakes that fly. They came from the sky to bring hell to this planet."

"We have come from the sky also," Calvin said, "to get rid of the flying snakes. My friend Steropes here has fought them before on other planets and is familiar with their pyramids."

"That is the place from which there is no return," Dolph replied. "The islanders took some of our people there to appease their gods, and they were sacrificed on an altar. Knowing what was going to happen to the rest of our people that had been taken, we put together a war party of 100 men to go and get them back. Only one warrior returned, but he was gravely wounded. He died the next day, but only after telling us of the terrors that lie in wait in the pyramid." He looked at the less than 20 men and women that were spread out around the beach. "Unless you are far more powerful than you look, the only thing waiting for you in their temple is death."

"Well, if that is what awaits us, then we will go to it willingly," said Calvin; "however, I think you will find that we are a lot more powerful than we seem. We are also familiar with the inside of the pyramid, which will help." He paused. "If you have any additional information, we would be happy to listen."

Dolph looked at the rest of his party, seeming to commune with them. After 15 seconds, he turned back to Calvin. "We need to take you to our king," he said. "Will those suits function underwater?"

Calvin nodded. "The suits won't go through the water very quickly," he said, "but they will function there."

"Good," Dolph said, turning around and wading further out into the water. "Follow me."

The Terrans began to follow Dolph's group back into the water. Calvin didn't like following the strangers, but what choice did they have? As Bob made it to where the waves were breaking, one caught him in the shins, and he sprawled forward into the water. As he regained his balance and stood back up, he commed, *"Lieutenant Commander Hobbs, you may want to know that the people we're following are not people."*

"I realize that they're not humans," replied Calvin, *"even though they look similar to us."*

"Not that similar," said Bob. *"They don't have legs."*

Chapter Twenty-One

The trip had gone quickly and relatively smoothly after the Terrans got over the sight of the mermen. Once the Terrans had submerged, they could see that Bob was right; in place of legs and feet, the Aquants (as they called themselves) had the tail of a fish below their waists, complete with scales. It quickly became apparent that the Terrans wouldn't be able to travel underwater as quickly as the Aquants could; they were just not anatomically built for it. Only Bob and Doug, using both their suits' propulsion systems and their tails, were able to come anywhere close. Not only did the Terrans' thrusters propel them much more slowly than the Aquants could swim, unless the city was fairly close, they were going to burn out their batteries before they got there. While the suits *could* function underwater, they weren't meant for long stays there. Calvin was just happy that he had the squad along with him that had the most in-suit training.

Dolph returned to Calvin and said, "No offense, but this is going to take far longer than is prudent. Although you killed the hexazants that made their homes here, others will come. We are summoning some extra transport for you." They continued for a couple of minutes more and then were suddenly surrounded by fish that looked uncomfortably like sharks. *Really big* sharks. The fish that approached them were over 30 feet in length and could easily have swallowed anyone of the troopers whole. The soldiers drew their weapons at the sight of them, but before they could fire, Dolph said, "Do not be afraid; this is our transportation. Take hold of one of their side fins, and they will pull you along."

The soldiers each took hold of a fin, and they were off. Calvin's suit showed a speed of 30 knots, which was faster than most Earth sharks could swim, and the fish he was holding onto didn't appear to be trying very hard. He looked at Dolph, who was holding onto the same fin that he was. "These things can swim really quickly," he said through his speakers.

"They can go about twice this fast in bursts," Dolph replied, "which is faster than anything else in this ocean. It is a good thing we are friendly with them, as we cannot out-swim them."

With the pseudo-sharks pulling them, the Terrans made it to the Aquant city in less than 15 minutes. As they descended to the floor of the ocean, the light became dimmer and dimmer, until it was replaced by the glow of the city in front of them. As they approached, Calvin could see that the there were several varieties of phosphorescent sea creatures swimming through the town, which kept everything fairly well lit. Calvin saw that the city was located at the intersection of a number of small canyons; seen from above, the pattern of lights looked like a starfish with a central mass and five 'legs' leading off from it. The sharks stopped above the center section, and Calvin looked down to see a large building beneath him.

Dolph released the fin and tapped Calvin. Pointing down he said simply, "We're here." He headed toward the large building. "This is the palace of King Barra."

"*We're here*," repeated Calvin to his troops. "*Follow me.*" The Terrans followed the Aquants to the large building, which appeared to be made from some sort of concrete mixed with shells. Calvin had no idea how they built it under water.

"They are ready for you," advised Dolph, as he opened the door for the Terrans. Calvin jetted through the opening to find himself entering a large chamber from the back. The chamber extended for nearly 100 feet with a ceiling 20 feet high. A group of nearly 20 Aquants awaited them at the other end, including King Barra; the building appeared to be his audience hall. As Calvin neared the small dais, or platform, the king moved down off of it to greet them.

"Welcome, travelers, to the Kingdom of the Aquants," he said with a bow. "Anyone that comes to fight the flying snakes is welcome in our ocean."

Calvin returned the bow. "Thank you for the welcome. We are sorry to have to meet you under these conditions."

"I am sorry, as well," replied the king. "We used to have good relations with the air breathers in the land above. We had a trade center located near where our people found you where we used to trade with them. We would bring our fish and other goods to get their finished metal products. Since the flying snakes came, it is too dangerous. If the snakes see us, they call us heathens and say that we must be sacrificed. I have forbidden our people to go ashore. Trade with the Nahuatls has ceased."

The king looked at Dolph. "Speaking of which, you have come very close to violating my order," he said sternly. He softened a little and continued, "Still, it seems to have worked out for the best, so I guess I cannot be too angry with you."

The king refocused on Calvin. "What can we do to be of assistance to you in your mission to rid the island of the evil ones?" he asked.

Before Calvin could answer, Steropes asked, "What name did you just call the air breathers?"

The king looked puzzled. "I called them the Nahuatl," he repeated. "Why do you ask? They didn't always call themselves that; it is only since the snakes arrived that we began hearing that name used for them."

Steropes nodded. "I feared as much," he said. "I am glad I came."

"Why is that?" asked Calvin. "What are Nahuatl?"

"Nahuatl is actually a language that is still spoken on Earth by about 1.5 million people in central Mexico. It was the language of the Mayans and the Aztecs, taught to them by the coatls."

"So, you're saying that these people were brought here by the coatls?" asked Calvin.

"I believe that to be the case, yes," said Steropes. "When they fled Earth, we know they took some of the local people with them. We always wondered where they went, but couldn't track them down. That would also explain why we are able to understand the language here."

Calvin looked thoughtful. "If the coatls are already killing the Aquants, they will probably call us heathens and have the Nahuatl attack us as well." He looked at the king. "From what you said, they were not evil before the snakes came, so I would rather not kill the humanoids if I did not have to. Is there another way to approach the pyramid without being seen?"

"Yes, there is," said Dolph, breaking in before the king could speak. "I was not allowed to join in the attack on the pyramid, but I followed them up to it. It is possible to travel up the river to the pyramid and then enter it through one of their refuse tunnels. Assuming you can handle the smell, that is."

"Apparently you make a habit of obeying the letter of commands, but not the intent," said the king. "You were not supposed to accompany the men to the pyramid."

"I did as I was told," replied Dolph. "You said that I wasn't to go *into* the temple with them; you didn't say that I couldn't go *to* the temple."

"Since he has already been there and returned unharmed," said Calvin as the king glared at Dolph, "could we impose on you to have him lead us back to it? It would be helpful if we could get close to the pyramid before they knew we were coming."

The king sighed. "He is now of an age that he must begin making decisions on his own," the king replied, "or he will never grow into being the leader that the kingdom needs. Hopefully, they will be better decisions than he has made previously. Prince Dolph will bring five men and lead you to the pyramid when you are ready."

"It would also be handy if you could arrange for those fish that carried us here to carry us back, too," added Calvin. "That way our suits will be able to last long enough."

"They can get you to the mouth of the river, but you will be on your own from there," replied the king. "They are too big to go any further without being seen. If they try to take you upriver the air breathers will try to harpoon them."

"That would be helpful," said Calvin. "Thank you very much for your assistance."

"Good luck in your quest," wished the king. "I hope that you will be successful, as we greatly need the things from above that we used to trade for."

"We may be able to help with that," Calvin answered. "I will have our ambassador come to talk with you when she is able. We may be able to provide some of the things you need in trade."

"Thank you, again," said the king. "Happy hunting. Kill them all!"

"That's the plan," replied Calvin, who turned and left.

Dolph and another two men swam ahead of them and opened the door; several other men followed them. "Prince, eh?" asked Calvin as he jetted through the door.

The prince shrugged. "It is a chain that binds me and keeps me from doing the things I like," replied Dolph. After everyone had left the building, he paused and appeared to look around. He looked in one direction intently for several seconds and then said, "They are coming."

"Who is coming?" asked Calvin.

"Our transportation," replied the prince. "I just called them. Couldn't you hear the call?"

"No, I couldn't," Calvin said. "Can you talk with all of the sea creatures mentally?"

"Not all of them," Dolph answered. "The smarter the creature, the better the link. The ones that brought us here are the smartest ones in the ocean; we can communicate with them well. We can communicate with other types of fish to varying degrees. Some of us can do it better than others. The royal line is the strongest. I can control five of the ones you call pseudo-sharks. The others here can only control three at most."

"Wait a minute," said Calvin, "I never called them pseudo-sharks."

"You never called them that out loud," replied Dolph, "but that is what you think of them as. You broadcast your thoughts in a loud 'voice.' If you don't want me to listen, you shouldn't broadcast like the rest of your people."

"So you can hear what I'm thinking?" asked Calvin. "What am I thinking right now?"

"Yes, I can," agreed Dolph. "You're wondering if I can really do it, or if I'm just pulling your leg. I could probably have guessed that without being able to read your thoughts." He paused and then added, "That's better. 42."

"42 what?" asked Calvin.

"You were going to ask me what six times seven was," said Dolph.

"Is that true?" asked Ryan, who had been uncharacteristically silent for most of the trip.

"Yeah, that is what I was going to ask," confirmed Calvin.

"Sir, you're just damned creepy to be around sometimes, you know that?" Ryan asked.

"Yeah," said Calvin. "I'm creeping myself out this time."

"The pseudo-sharks are here," said Dolph as they materialized from the shadows. The sharks in this group were, if anything, even larger than the ones they had ridden to the Starfish Palace. The one that approached Dolph was at least 40 feet in length with serrated teeth over a foot long.

The soldiers fought down their fears, took hold of fins and were on their way.

Chapter Twenty-Two

Great Pyramid of Cholula, Keppler-22 'b', August 12, 2020

The pseudo-sharks dropped the soldiers off where a large river emptied into the ocean. Dolph made a face looking up toward the river, and Calvin could tell why. All manner of filth and foulness was washing down with the river water, polluting the ocean. Calvin was glad he wasn't breathing it; the water looked truly disgusting.

"Thank you for your assistance," Calvin said to Dolph. "You don't need to go any further. Judging by the amount of filth coming down the river, I'm sure we can find it from here."

"Despite how repulsive this area has become, I promised my father that I would take you to the culvert," said Dolph, "and I shall." He shook his head and shuddered. "But please hurry, I don't know how long I can breathe this before I throw up."

The soldiers followed Dolph as he led them upstream. He stayed in the middle of the river, as close to the bottom as he could. Calvin hoped the water smelled less offensive there. They turned their jets on to full power and followed Dolph upstream. They were just able to keep up with him and made good time although they were forced to stop several times as canoes of the Nahuatl passed above them. The soldiers used their suits to blend in while Dolph and his men simply stopped moving and blended in naturally.

After 30 minutes, the soldiers reached the culvert and could see the source of all of the effluvium entering the water. Dolph went upstream a little from it into clearer water. Calvin could see all manner of human waste pouring out of the pipe, including what looked to be a large bloodstain. From the size of it, there was no way the previous owner, if human, was still alive.

"I would like to come with you," began Dolph.

"No," Calvin said, cutting him off. "I will not endanger your life. We will take care of this. We have the tools and the training. I thank you for bringing us this far, but this is as far as we go with you. Meet us in three days on the beach where we first met you; we will talk with you there."

Reluctantly, Dolph turned to go. Once he reached where the culvert dumped into the river, his speed accelerated noticeably. His men went with him.

Calvin looked at Master Chief and commed simply, "*Lead on.*"

The soldiers went up the culvert single file. That gave them more room to avoid...things... floating downstream past them. Body parts and feces were two of the most easily identifiable things to be avoided.

"*Whoever is in the lead, please watch for a pipe coming down from above,*" commed Steropes. "*There should be a ladder in it. We will climb up it.*"

"*Got it,*" commed Wraith. "*Headed up.*"

"*Everybody show the next person where it is before going up,*" commed Master Chief.

Calvin was behind the Master Chief in order and within a few more seconds came to where he was waiting, holding onto the bottom rail of the ladder. Calvin gave him the thumbs up, and Ryan started up the ladder. Calvin waited for Steropes, who was after him. When he was sure Steropes could see the ladder, he started up.

The climb was a long one, over 100 feet up, using rungs that were meant for small, nearly naked men, not large soldiers in 100 pound suits. Calvin saw two of the rungs that hadn't been up to the challenge and had torn off. Happily, the men or women that they had snapped on had kept their balance and not fallen into the group climbing up behind them.

Calvin made it to the top and was helped over the edge by Master Chief. He stood up and found himself in a small 15' square room that was already getting crowded. As he caught his breath, he heard:

"*OW!*"

"*FUCK!*"

"*DAMN IT!*"

Along with a variety of other crashing and splashing noises. "*What happened?*" he asked.

"*One of the damn rungs came out on me,*" replied Petty Officer Second Class Ivan Sherkov, who was one of the biggest men in the squad. "*The one I was standing on couldn't take the load, and it pulled out. I landed on Jet, tore his out, then landed on Witch who was just starting to climb.*"

"*And it's a big bloody brute, you are,*" added Sergeant 'Witch' Andrews in her Jamaican accent.

"*Too big,*" said Private First Class 'Jet' Li in a strained voice. "*My left leg is broken.*"

"*Damn it,*" said Calvin and Master Chief simultaneously. Calvin looked at Steropes. "*What do you think?*" he asked. "*Should we try to carry him along or send him back?*"

"*We're going to have to do a lot of climbing in the pyramid,*" Steropes answered, "*but to go back would be even more difficult. Why don't we pull him up to this room and leave him here. The suit will immobilize his leg, and we can get him when we come back by.*"

"*All right,*" agreed Calvin, "*that makes sense, I guess.*" He switched to the platoon network so that everyone could hear. "*Someone get a line down to him. We'll pull him up here and leave him in this room as rear guard.*"

Lines went down to pull up Jet and assist with the others so that they didn't have any more failures. Within a few minutes, everyone was up into the room, packed in like sardines around the entrance to the pipe. Jet's suit had locked to protect the broken leg, but he wasn't going anywhere. His eyes were already slightly glazed from the pain-killers that he had taken from his suit's pharmacopeia. Corporal Jimmy 'Colonel' Sanders was left behind with Jet to form the rear guard.

"*All right, Steropes,*" said Calvin, "*Where the hell are we?*"

"*I imagine we're on the ground floor of the pyramid, probably in one of the corners,*" Steropes replied. "*I'm looking for the secret door latch release so we can get out.*"

Calvin slapped himself in the forehead...or where his forehead would have been if he wasn't wearing a helmet. He activated his suit map and saw that they were in the southeast corner of the pyramid. "*Yeah, we're in the southeast corner of the pyramid,*" Calvin agreed. "*The main entrance to the pyramid is to the west of here.*"

"*Found it,*" announced Steropes. There was a small 'click' that the suit's receivers amplified, and then a small crack of light entered the room. Master Chief pushed Steropes to the side so that he could check the door with a small, "*Excuse me.*"

Master Chief looked both ways and then threw the door open. They were indeed in the corner of the pyramid, with a passageway leading off to the west and the north.

"*Holy fuck!*" he said quietly. "*How big is this place?*" Although the passageway had torches in wall sconces, the light wasn't enough to see all the way to the ends of the pyramid. Judging by a small amount of daylight that could be seen to the left, the main entrance to the pyramid was to the west. Two shadows were visible; obviously it was guarded. Steropes put a finger to his lips, indicating silence.

"If this is a replica of the Great Pyramid of Cholula," Steropes commed as he looked into a mirror to apply a stripe of black paint across his face, *"which I think it is, then it is going to be very large. The one in Mexico was 400 meters on a side and 55 meters high. It was so big that it was known as Tlachihualtepetl, which meant 'artificial mountain.'"* He paused, looking in the mirror, and then added, *"The name cholula means 'place of refuge,' which it was supposed to be for the snakes. This one may be bigger."*

"Umm, what's the deal with the war paint, Steropes?" Calvin asked.

"The Nahuatl know me as Tezcatlipoca, the 'enemy of both sides," Steropes replied, adding a line of yellow paint next to the black. *"I'd hate to disappoint them."*

Having gotten his bearings, Steropes started walking down the passageway to the right. Calvin was left shaking his head, not understanding what the Psiclops meant. Deciding that it must be a holdover from the last time Steropes dealt with the coatls, Calvin wondered if the Psiclops suffered from post-traumatic stress disorder. He was certainly exhibiting a lot of the signs.

Seeing which way Steropes was headed, Petty Officer Sherkov, who was supposed to be the point man, sprinted past him and took the lead. *"Careful,"* Steropes advised. *"They know we're here. I feel it."* The group made it to the next corner and turned left, walking down the back wall of the pyramid. It was hot inside the pyramid, and the suits' air conditioning units kicked on.

"Contact," Petty Officer Sherkov commed as he rounded the next corner. *"I've got five very nervous looking men with spears at the end of the next*

passageway." Calvin, Steropes and Master Chief moved forward. Turning the corner, they could see four men, armed with long leaf-bladed spears at the end of the corridor. "*Sorry, sir,*" Sherkov reported, "*the other one took off running before I could stop him.*"

In a bigger area, the local men would probably have run when faced with the Terran squad. In the narrow passage, they hoped to hold off the opposing force until reinforcements arrived. Running meant disappointing the coatls and having your still-beating heart pulled from your body. Better to face the unknown foreigners than the known consequences.

"*Should I shoot them?*" Master Chief asked.

"*No,*" Steropes said. "*I've got this.*" He started taking off his combat suit.

"You've got this?" Master Chief asked over his external speaker, disbelief heavy in his voice as he looked down the passageway at the four men nervously presenting their spears. "How exactly have you 'got this?' You see that they're armed, right?"

Steropes nodded. "We don't want to kill them. Look at them, they're more afraid of running back to their masters than they are of us." He paused, balancing to get his legs out. "There's no need to kill them," Steropes repeated. "I've got this."

Alone, he walked down the passageway without his suit, moving with a slight limp. Calvin hadn't ever noticed the limp before. In thinking about it, he couldn't really ever remember any of the Psiclopes walking around much. Usually, they were just there...and then they were not. Steropes continued down the hallway and stopped 10 feet in front of the men. They were arranged in ranks of two although the back row men could reach over the front row with their spears. The brown men were similar in appearance. Each was about

four and a half feet tall, dark brown in complexion with hooked noses. All wore headdresses of feathers and had necklaces of animal
claws. They would probably be fierce warriors on the battlefield
against other Mayans, but were outclassed by the Terrans' technology.

Calvin watched as Steropes bowed to the men and then dropped
into some sort of martial arts stance where he began an almost hyp-
notic pattern of rolling his hands back and forth over each other.
Calvin watched the smooth spiraling movement, perplexed. "What is
he doing?" he finally asked.

"It is the Chen family style of tai chi movement called silk reel-
ing," Wraith said, who had come up behind him. "It was originally
designed to be like the motion of pulling silk from a silkworm's co-
coon. The practitioner must be smooth and consistent." She watched
with a critical eye. "He is very good. Although he moves slowly now,
he is channeling his energy. Watch for the burst of power when he
needs it."

The spearmen, seeing that the only man that had advanced was
even shorter than they were, and unarmed, moved forward in a
group. "Go back where you came from," the leader said in a quaking
voice, looking at the tiny man in front of him, "or we will be forced
to kill you."

"You cannot kill me," Steropes said quietly. Although facing four
armed men, Calvin thought the certainty in his voice was amazing.
"If you will put down your weapons, we will allow you to pass. You
do not need to fear what your masters will do; we are here to kill
them."

"You can't kill them!" one of the men in the back row cried out.
"They are gods!"

"They are not gods," Steropes replied calmly, "just far more powerful than you. Put down your weapons and let us by."

"We can't," the leader said. "They will certainly kill us and eat the hearts of our wives and children." With a quick jab, he tried to impale Steropes. The Psiclops was faster, though, and swept the spear to the side with force that Calvin would not have believed if he hadn't seen it. The local man had a good grip on the spear, and the entire spear point snapped off as the obsidian head hit the wall, leaving the Mayan holding a staff rather than a spear. He looked at the point in disbelief for a fraction of a second, which was all Steropes needed.

Spinning forward, he took hold of the staff and chopped the man across the wrists. The staff fell from his suddenly numb hands, and Steropes continued his spin, bringing the end of the staff crashing down onto his right temple as it came around. Unconscious, the man began to fall as Steropes reversed his stroke, taking the other front row man in his left temple. Spinning back to his left, Steropes used the staff to slap the spear of one of the second row men out of the way. He brought the other end of the staff back up in an uppercut that terminated on the man's chin. As the man's eyes rolled into the back of his head, the staff was in motion again, sweeping around behind the last man to strike him low in the legs. With an explosive breath, Steropes channeled all of his energy into the stroke and swept the man's legs out from under him. He hit the stone of the passageway hard on his shoulders and the back of his head. Momentarily stunned, he watched the staff sweep down on his head, only to stop one centimeter from his temple. Steropes paused and then moved the staff to his throat, not crushing him, but effectively pinning him to the floor like a mounted butterfly. It had taken 1.3 seconds to put the four men out of action.

Steropes turned his head slightly to look back at the rest of the squad. "Do you have any questions you want to ask him?" he asked. All of the Terrans stood staring, mouths agape, except for Wraith. She bowed and said, "Master."

Calvin closed his mouth with an audible snap and walked down the hall to where Steropes kept the man under control. Any time the warrior started to look like he was going to try something, Steropes just increased the pressure on his throat until he ceased struggling again. After a brief hesitation, the rest of the squad started moving again.

"What are you all looking at?" Master Chief asked, the first to regain his composure. "You've seen martial arts before. We're in enemy territory! Be on your fucking guard! Scouts out, front and back. Let's go! Get a perimeter set up so the skipper can interrogate the prisoner!"

The soldiers came back to their senses and went back to doing their jobs.

"Their leader may be a bit more damaged than I intended," Steropes commented as Calvin and Master Chief approached. "Whoever fashioned this spear did a poor job of it. It is not well balanced, even when the spear head was on it. I hit him a little harder than intended." He sighed. "I miss the Ruyi Jingu Bang. Now *that* was a fine weapon." He shook his head. "I also must confess to being out of practice."

"If that is out of practice, Master, then I would much like to see you when you were in practice," Wraith said. Interesting, thought Calvin. He had never seen her intimidated by anyone or anything;

Steropes must be even better than Calvin realized. "You really saw the Ruyi Jingu Bang?" she asked.

"What is a Ruby Jujube Bean?" Calvin asked.

"Please do not joke about the Ruyi Jingu Bang," Wraith warned. "It was thought to be a mythical weapon of Sun Wukong, from the undersea palace of the Dragon King of the East Sea," she continued in awe, "not a real weapon. It was said to be able to change its color, size or shape at its master's will. The stories say that it could even fight by itself, according to the will of its master."

"That last one was just a story told by the less able," Steropes replied. "It couldn't fight by itself any more than this staff can. It was only as good as the person wielding it." He smiled in memory. "Being able to shrink it to the size of a toothpick was very handy, because then I could carry it behind my ear."

Calvin shook his head at the strange talk as he looked down at the man, whose face was bright red from lack of breath. "I think you can let him go, Steropes," commented Calvin, looking back up at the Psiclops, "I don't think he's going to give us any more difficulty." He looked back down at the man and asked, "Are you?" The man shook his head as vigorously as he could with the staff pushing down on his throat.

"What?" asked Steropes, having gotten lost in the memory. He looked down at the man under his staff. "Oh, yes, sorry about that."

He removed the staff, and Calvin helped the man up. "What can you tell us about the pyramid from this point further?" Calvin asked.

"Nothing," the man said, rubbing his throat. "Only the priests are allowed beyond this point. To go past here is to die most horribly."

"Do you know how many priests and snakes there are?" Master Chief asked.

"I don't know," the man said. "There are probably at least 10 priests, and then another 30 of their assistants and acolytes. I don't know how many of the gods there are."

"They are *not* gods," Steropes repeated. Calvin could tell that Steropes must have had some past history with the coatls to be so vehement about it.

"I don't know how many there are," the man said again. "There are probably at least five although I have a hard time telling them apart. Most of them look the same, except for Him."

"Who is 'him'?" Calvin asked.

"Quetzalcoatl," both the man and Steropes replied simultaneously.

Calvin looked at Steropes. "How did you know?"

"Easy," Steropes said. "He is a telepath. He knows we are here. We should be going; every minute we linger is a minute he can use to prepare."

"Master Chief, you heard the man," Calvin directed, "move 'em out!" He looked at the man, shivering in fear. He had failed the coatls; he knew his life and the lives of those he loved were now forfeit. "Go that way," Calvin said, pointing in the direction they had come. "You will probably want to be a long way from this pyramid very soon." The man left at a run.

The squad moved slowly down the passageway, watching for traps.

Wraith moved up to walk alongside Steropes. "It is obvious that you are a master of both the open hand and the staff. Do you know all of the forms?"

"Yes," Steropes replied, putting his suit back on. "I spent about two centuries learning all five of the traditional family styles. I also know the spear, sword and saber, as well, although I could never quite master the spear as well as I would have liked, due to my size." His eyes took on a faraway look. "I once had the most beautiful spear in the world, but I gave it to King Fuchai of Wu to use in his war against King Goujian of Yue. Fuchai should have listened to me and killed Goujian when he won, rather than leaving him behind while Fuchai continued to advance. Goujian sacked Wu, and Fuchai was forced to commit suicide," he said distantly, lost in thought. "It was very sad."

Steropes shook himself. "We can talk about it more later. We need to focus on what we're doing." Looking up, he saw that several of the soldiers had gone further up the hall. "*Please let me lead,*" he commed, snapping on his helmet. "*I know what to look for.*" The soldiers in the front slowed and allowed him to overtake them slightly. While they had a new-found respect for Steropes as a hand-to-hand fighter, he didn't have a rifle and had no way of hitting a target outside his reach. They stayed close in order to protect him.

The squad turned another corner, and the passageway began to slope up. "*We will start finding traps and snakes soon,*" he advised. He stopped suddenly, looking at an inscription on the wall.

"What does that say?" Calvin asked.

"Basically, it says that if you go any further, you will be cursed by a jinni and will die a slow, painful death," Steropes replied.

"A jinni?" Master Chief asked. "C'mon now, you don't really believe in jinn do you?"

"What are jinn?" Calvin asked.

"Jinn are supernatural creatures that exist in the galaxy," Steropes replied. "They are spoken about in Islamic lore on Earth. There are many kinds of jinn, with various powers. One literary example of a jinni is Aladdin's genie in the bottle."

"So, you're saying that these things really exist?" Calvin asked. "And they grant wishes?"

"They certainly do exist," said Vice Sergeant Ismail Al-Sabani. "Getting a wish from one is a very dangerous thing, as they will usually try to turn it around on the person asking for the wish." He nodded to the inscription. "Curses and witchcraft are bad enough on their own," he added, "but if they have jinn, we must be *very* careful."

"Not all witches are bad," remarked Sergeant Margaret Andrews. A Jamaican by birth, Calvin knew that she was a believer in many forms of witchcraft. The rumor in the platoon was that she was also a practitioner. Wondering what the chaplain thought about this topic, Calvin looked over to find the priest following the conversation intently. Making good on his vow not to cause problems within the squad, he didn't participate in the discussion, although Calvin could tell that he had strong feelings about it.

"Not all jinn are bad either," answered Al-Sabani. "They are one of the three sapient creations of God, along with humans and angels. They have free will, so they can be good or bad. If the snake creatures are controlling a jinni or jinn, we must be careful. They are made from the smokeless fire by Allah, and some are very powerful. If they have enslaved one of these, its anger will be immense. It will do everything it can to kill us."

"Surely you don't believe in these spirits?" asked Petty Officer David Levine. "I have never seen one. Have you?"

"Most of the time they are invisible," Al-Sabani replied, "but the Prophet saw them; therefore, they exist." His tone indicated that there was no doubt in his mind.

"OK," Master Chief interrupted, "I'm sure this will be a fun topic of conversation when we get back to the ship. We can all sit around with a nice tea in the comfort of the squad bay and discuss religion all day. At the moment, though, *there are things that are trying to kill us.* How about we focus on them now and worry about that later?" The way he said it made it a command, not a question.

"*What I was going to say,*" Steropes commed so that everyone could hear him, "*is that we may be exposed to a variety of poisons past this point. It would be prudent to ensure your helmet seals and go to recycled air.*"

"*Got it,*" Calvin commed. He looked up the ramp. "*Do we continue up?*"

"*Not unless you want to be doused in poisonous chemicals,*" Steropes answered. "*That is a dead end passageway. Once you go a little further, a powder will dump out a number of holes. If you take even one breath of it, you actually* will *be cursed with a slow, painful death. That warning isn't just for people that don't belong here; it's also a reminder to the new acolytes and priests not to go any further up this passageway.*"

Steropes looked closely at the left wall. Finding what he wanted, he pushed in one of the stones. There was a 'click,' and a five feet square section of the wall rotated in on oiled hinges. "*This is where we want to go,*" he said. He turned on his helmet light. "*We'll need lights from here. This portion won't be lit. If anyone sees writing on the walls, please let me know.*"

Steropes walked into the dark passageway and turned left to follow it, going back in the direction they had just been coming from. He walked along the right side of the passageway, scanning the wall as he slowly made his way along it. Vice Sergeant Ismail Al-Sabani moved up to walk next to him. Although Al-Sabani didn't transmit, Steropes could hear him saying something inside his suit. Finally Steropes stopped and looked at him, *"Do you know something that I don't?"*

"Do you have a qarin?" Al-Sabani asked.

"If I do," Steropes replied, *"I am unacquainted with him or her."*

Al-Sabani nodded. *"I have had my qarin since I was a little child. When I was five, I became very sick, nearly unto death. I had a fever that nothing could cure. As I lay there on my bedroll, I could feel two qarin wrestling over me. One was evil, the other benevolent. They fought over me for two days. All the while, I lay in a coma at death's doorway. Finally, the benevolent spirit was victorious and threw down the evil one. Ever since that day he has guided me, speaking to me when needed. I am the one most acquainted with the jinn. It is best for me to accompany you."*

Steropes nodded. *"What is he telling you now?"* he asked.

"He is telling me to pray," Al-Sabani replied.

"Then you should certainly do so," Steropes agreed.

"Wait a second," Calvin said. *"Is there something the rest of us should know? What is a qarin?"*

"We're not going to stand here and discuss old wives tales when there are things that need killing, are we?" Petty Officer David Levine asked. *"I grew up with an Islamic friend, and that was all he ever talked about. Jinn this, qarin that. I don't know what good they're supposed to be; his qarin didn't tell him not to step on the land mine that killed him."*

"I'll ask again," Calvin repeated. *"What's a qarin?"*

"A qarin is a special jinni that is assigned to a person," Al-Sabani replied. *"The uncultured believe in guardian angels; they are really jinn."*

"What is the difference?" Calvin asked.

"*Angels obey the will of Allah,*" Al-Sabani answered, "*whereas jinn have free will. A guardian angel would always help you and keep you on the correct path. A qarin might be bad and constantly try to lead you astray.*"

"*And you've got one of these?*" Calvin asked.

"*I have had a good qarin since I was five,*" Al-Sabani said. "*Haatan has never led me astray. He is telling me that this temple is full of evil and that we should leave. He also suggested prayer, but he doesn't think that will be sufficient. He believes that if we stay, we will die.*"

"*There issss an anti-jinn prayer?*" Bob asked. "*Can you teach it to ussss?*" Calvin had noticed that the therapods' lisps always got worse when they were excited. Or scared.

"*It is the Throne Verse of the Qur'an,*" Al-Sabani replied, "*but if you are not a believer, it will not work for you. That is why I do it for you.*"

"*And I, as well,*" Leading Seaman Abdul Wazir agreed, a Muslim from the Kashmir region of India.

"*Can we go now?*" Levine asked. "*I need to get back as quick as I can to my jinn...my gin and tonic, that is.*" He laughed at his joke.

"*Knock it off, Levine,*" Master Chief O'Leary ordered, hoping to avoid a religious war. "*Let's focus on killing whatever's in this pyramid. We can discuss this when we get back to the ship.*"

"*Steropes, please lead on,*" Calvin ordered. "*Anything you can do to assist, Sergeant Al-Sabani, is most welcome.*"

The 15 remaining members of the squad and their chaplain followed Steropes as he proceeded along the dark passageway. As they came to the next corner, a glow could be seen from around it. Steropes and Sergeant Al-Sabani rounded the corner to find an empty passage leading off as far as the eye could see, well lit by torches placed every 20 feet or so. Steropes stopped suddenly, causing Petty

Officer Sherkov to walk into him. "*What is wrong?*" Sherkov asked. "*I see nothing out of place.*"

"*I know,*" Steropes replied. "*I don't see anything wrong either, and that's what worries me.*" He slowly started forward again, searching the walls and floors for any sort of marks that might indicate a pressure plate or any other sign of a trap.

They had walked almost 100 yards when Doug asked, "*You wanted to know if we found writing, yesss?*"

"*Yes,*" Steropes agreed. "*Did you find some?*"

"*There is some on thisss torch,*" replied Doug. He grabbed the torch and tried to pull it from its holder to show the Psiclops, but it appeared to be stuck.

"*NO!*" Steropes yelled, turning around to see the lizard pulling on the torch, "*don't touch it!*" But it was too late. Doug pulled harder on the torch, and it came free. As it did, a 20 feet long section of the passageway behind him came unhinged and dropped. Petty Officer Remy Martin, Leading Seaman Abdul Wazir, Leading Seaman Sigvar Borsheim and Irina Rozhkov went tumbling into the abyss that suddenly opened up beneath them.

Seeing what he had done, Doug slammed the torch back into its holder, and just as suddenly as it had dropped, the passageway closed back up again, trapping the members below. For several seconds the sounds of grunts, groans and slams could be heard from the soldiers as they bounced down a tunnel in the darkness, and then there was one last "*Fuck!*" which sounded more annoyed than hurt.

"*Are you guys OK?*" Calvin asked. He brought up the display of their suits. While he could see that the four had strong life signs, their suits showed a variety of warning and danger signs.

"*Da, I am OK,*" Irina Rozhkov replied, "*but my suit is going crazy. We fell down some kind of slide that dropped us into a pool of mercuric cyanide. At least, that is what my suit says, anyway. If I had been breathing the outside air, I would be in danger of both mercury and cyanide poisoning. Otherwise, I am mostly just bumped and bruised.*" There was a pause as she looked around. "*We are in a small room with nothing but this pool of acid. I can see a door out.*"

"*I am fine, too,*" Remy Martin said. "*Just bumps, bruises and a thoroughly disgusting residue on my suit.*"

"*I am not so good,*" Abdul Wazir said. He broke off in a coughing fit. "*My suit tore on something, and I got a bunch of the stuff inside my suit.*" He started coughing again. "*My throat and air passages are burning and trying to close on me.*" Another coughing fit. "*My eyes are burning, and I can barely see.*" He broke off, coughing again. "*The suit needs to be drained of the stuff in order to get it fixed all the way.*"

"*I also am OK,*" Leading Seaman Sigvar Borsheim said. "*We can patch Abdul's suit, but we've got to get him out of both the suit and this room first. The whole room is full of toxic vapors. My suit's systems are going crazy.*"

"*Mine, too,*" Rozhkov agreed. "*There's no way we can get back up to you. We will try to go somewhere that we can help Abdul and then find another way out. Rozhkov out.*"

Chapter Twenty-Three

Inside the Great Pyramid of Cholula, Keppler-22 'b', August 12, 2020

"*All right, we're not getting paid by the hour, ladies,*" Master Chief advised. "*Let's see if we can't go kill some snakes so we can get out of this shit hole.*"

"*I'll lead,*" Steropes said. He moved off in the direction they had originally been heading.

"*And no one touches anything!*" Ryan added. "*If it doesn't kill you, I will!*"

"*S.ssorry,*" Doug mumbled.

The 11 remaining soldiers and the chaplain followed Steropes and made it to the next corner, turning on their helmet lights as they went back into the dark. After another 150 yards the passageway ended, with a door on the right side of the wall. Steropes surveyed the door. He didn't find any traps and put his hand on the latch to open it.

"*Wait,*" Al-Sabani warned. "*Haatan warns us that we do not want to go into that room.*"

"*The jinni know what he be talking about, mon,*" Sergeant Margaret Andrews added. The black woman shuddered. "*I gotta bad feeling about it, too.*"

"*I'm not going back without killing Quetzalcoatl,*" stated Steropes. "*If you want to stay here, I'll go alone.*"

209

"*Oh no, mon,*" Sergeant Andrews said, "*we not be letting you go by yourself. I just be saying that something inside that room be needing our killing. I feel it.*"

"OK," Master Chief said, "*no sense highlighting ourselves. Turn off your lights.*" He put a hand on Steropes and gently pushed him to the side. "*We'll take it from here.*" He formed up the soldiers into two lines. One would go each way as they entered the room. "*Ready?*"

He eased the door open. The door led into a room that seemed to go on forever. A dim light suffused the room. There was just enough light to see movement, but not enough to identify it. In the distance, things were moving. Every once in a while, the things would stop and appear to bend over. Although the Terrans couldn't see what was going on, they dialed up their suits' audio sensors and could hear a variety of grunts and groans, as well as a wet slapping noise.

"*Listen up, people,*" Master Chief commed quietly, "*Here's how we're going to do this. On the count of three, I want Bob to throw an illumination grenade as far as he can to the left, and Doug to throw one as far as he can to the right. Everyone else be ready with your primary weapons in case whatever is out there comes our way. Ready? One...two...three!*"

The grenades flew out from the group and detonated. Although the room was too big for the two grenades to light up completely, the harsh glare of the burning magnesium and the suits' augmentation made the room almost as bright as a few minutes prior to sunrise on Earth. It was more than bright enough for them to see the 50 or so half-eaten bodies on the floor, and the creatures that were pulling pieces of flesh from them. As the grenades went off, all of the creatures' heads spun towards the door, and the Terrans lined up along the wall. Master Chief could see two distinct types of creatures.

There were about 20 creatures that were bipedal with the legs of a donkey and the horns of a goat. There were another 20 creatures that looked something like greyhounds, although their muzzles were elongated, and they had black stripes running down their sides. All of the creatures charged simultaneously, with the 'dogs' making a high-pitched whine.

"*Ghuls!*" Master Chief yelled. "*Fire!*" Both Master Chief and Petty Officer Ivan Sherkov fired off a long line of antimatter grenades across the incoming creatures. Some fell, but most of the others appeared to go momentarily insubstantial or invisible, only to solidify again once the detonations had ceased. Both men dropped their tridents and pulled out their rifles.

"*Bismillahir-Rahmanir-Raheem!*" shouted Al-Sabani over his suit speakers as he began firing his laser rifle. "*Allahu la ilaha illa Huwal Haiyul-Qaiyum!*"

Calvin recognized the cadence of the Throne Verse of the Qur'an that Al-Sabani had been chanting earlier. Now that he could actually hear it, his implant translated the Arabic. "*In the Name of Allah, the Most Gracious, the Most Merciful. Allah; there is no God but He, the Living, the Self-Subsisting and All-Sustaining.*"

"*Slumber seizes Him not, nor sleep,*" Al-Sabani continued. "*To Him belongs whatsoever is in the heavens, and whatsoever is in the earth.*" All of the squad was firing now, as well as Calvin. He could see that both creatures appeared to come in three different colors. About half of both types were a putrid shade of green in color. Nearly all of these went down in the first round of grenade and laser fire. There were also six or seven of each at the start that were a sickly yellow in color; about half of them had been hit and were on the ground not moving.

"Who is he that will intercede with Him except by His permission?" continued Al-Sabani, his speakers as high as they would go. *"He knows what is before them, and what is behind them."* The smallest group was blue in color. While there hadn't been as many of these, they seemed to know instinctively when the Terrans would fire and would become non-corporeal. One blue dog was down, but Calvin couldn't see that any of the blue horned creatures had been shot. If anything, they were now running even faster toward the Terrans.

"And they encompass nothing of His knowledge except what He pleases," Al-Sabani was joined by Master Chief; both were yelling. *"His knowledge extends over the heavens and the Earth!"* All of the yellow ones were down now, too, and one of the blue horned creatures had been hit. Two blue ones of each variety were still coming. The first of the creatures materialized next to Petty Officer Sherkov and appeared to reach inside his suit. Sherkov collapsed with a sigh. The rest of the creatures were now 20 feet away and coming on hard. They gathered themselves to spring on the Terrans.

"And the care of them burdens Him not; and He is the Most High. The Supreme!" finished both Al-Sabani and Master Chief at the top of their lungs. The four remaining monsters looked like they had run into a wall. The three that were still charging at them stopped and remained motionless with dazed expressions on their faces. The monster standing over Sherkov froze, looking down at him. Blue laser beams hit blue skin over and over as the squad was finally able to target the creatures. A whistling noise like a steam kettle was heard as a number of holes were drilled through each of the remaining creatures. Like balloons with holes, they appeared to deflate, turning insubstantial and disappearing. As Calvin looked around the room,

he could see the ones that had been hit earlier were dissolving as well.

"*Did you say ghouls?*" Calvin asked. "*As in the undead?*"

"*The horned ones were ghuls,*" Master Chief replied, looking around in awe, "*as in ghul jinn. They are one of about 10 different types of jinn. According to my mother, they are nocturnal creatures who inhabit graveyards and ruins. They usually come out at night to feast on the living and the dead. You remember I told you one time that my mother was Persian? She believed in all of this stuff, although I never did. She spoke to her qarin all the time; I just thought she was crazy. She said I had one, a good one, and that I would hear it if I listened. I refused.*" He looked Al-Sabani, who was rubbing some sort of talisman that he had pulled from a pocket. "*I may have to re-think that.*"

"*The ones that looked like dogs were hinn jinn,*" said Al-Sabani, taking off his helmet. "*They are weak jinn, not much more than animals.*" He put the talisman on around his neck and refastened his helmet. "*Their color is important. Green ones are young and immature; they are easily dealt with. The yellow ones are leaders of families and small clans. They are more powerful than the greens, but less than the blue ones. Watch out for the blue ones. They are old and intelligent. Their touch can poison a person and send them into a dream world. That is where the myth of granting wishes comes from. They drink your blood while promising you anything that you want.*"

Sergeant Andrews took off Petty Officer Sherkov's helmet. They could see a big smile on his face. "*He will be all right shortly,*" noted Al-Sabani. "*We stopped it before it could drink heavily of him. The Throne Verse is effective against most of the lesser jinni, but not against the more powerful ones. Pray we do not run into any of the efreet or shaitans.*"

"*And what the hell are those?*" asked Calvin. His upbringing had not prepared him for dealing with creatures that could turn invisible at will.

Al-Sabani shook his head. *"They are the most powerful of the jinn,"* he said. *"They would be very difficult to defeat."*

"Oh, thank you," moaned Sherkov. His head rolled, and then he shook himself. He looked up to see Sergeant Andrews' face six inches in front of his. "Wait," he said. "You're not Nadia; where did she go?" A look of utter sadness crossed his face, and then he shook himself again. As he opened his eyes this time, they seemed clear. "What happened?" he asked. "I just had the strangest dream." He rolled out of Witch's arms and got up, still shaking his head.

As Al-Sabani told him what happened, Calvin looked around the chamber. The room was huge; extending into the gloom in all directions. *"Master Chief, let's get a few more illumination rounds in here so that we can see what we're doing. I'd like to take a quick survey of the room and then get the hell out of here. This place gives me the creeps."*

"Yes, sir," replied Master Chief, *"the sooner, the better."* He passed on the order and eight more illumination rounds were fired throughout the room, including two to replace the first two that were going out.

By the light of the rounds, Calvin could see that the room was an enormous square; with walls well over 150 yards long. Pillars spread throughout the room helped hold up the vaulted ceilings that rose to 25 feet high in its center. The additional light gave them an unwelcome view of the corpses in the middle of the room but did not reveal any more jinn. At least 50 corpses were near the room's center although it was hard to tell exactly how many due to the decomposition of some and the dismemberment of others. The bodies had dark skin and appeared from a little ways away to be from members of the planet's humanoid race. None of the soldiers wanted to go any closer to confirm.

As the squad neared the other side of the room and the illumination began to fade, they received a shock as they saw two women chained to the wall. They couldn't be sure that they were women, as their heads hung down forward onto their chests, but from the long hair and feminine dress that was what they appeared to be. Ready for a trap, the squad formed a semi-circle around the two with weapons at the ready.

Master Chief shouldered his trident, drew his laser pistol and moved forward toward the women. He had advanced to within five feet when the illumination rounds went out. Automatically, he switched to low light/thermal on his suit's viewers. The bodies didn't move, but he could see a heat source on both of them, stronger than he would have believed in the cool, dank room. Something about the women made his skin crawl. *"Bob and Doug, pop another illumination round,"* Master Chief ordered.

He watched the women as the light came back up, but nothing changed. He moved forward and started to reach forward to touch the one on the right. He stopped with his hand about a foot from the woman as he had a thought. Straightening, he asked, *"Hey, Al-Sabani, what's your qarin say about these women?"*

Vice Sergeant Al-Sabani cocked his head, a strange look on his face. *"That is odd,"* he said. *"He won't tell me anything about them. The word that he uses can mean either he 'can't' or 'won't' tell me about them. He won't say anything else. He has never done this before. The only thing that he will say about them is that they do not have an evil aura about them, and that it should be OK to wake them up."*

"Maybe he'd like to wake them up, then," muttered Master Chief as he reached back toward the woman's shoulder. He activated his speakers. "Ma'am, ma'am, are you OK?" he asked, gently shaking her.

After a couple of seconds, the woman moaned and then flinched away from him. "Don't eat me!" she cried. This startled the second woman, who woke up, looked at the soldiers in their suits and screamed. This caused the first woman to scream, as well.

Master Chief turned down his external input to compensate for the screaming, while turning up his output so that he could be heard. "Ma'am, it's OK, we're here to help!" he said. The women did not appear to hear; they kept screaming. If anything, they screamed louder.

"Dammit," Master Chief said. Holstering his pistol, he reached up, unsealed his helmet and took it off. "Ladies!" he yelled. "We're here to help."

Seeing his face appeared to help, and they calmed visibly. "Oh, thank you," cried the one in front of him. "We were sure that they had finally come to sacrifice us."

"Sacrifice you?" Master Chief asked as he pulled out his laser pistol.

"Yes," said the woman. "We were to be sacrificed on the altar."

"Well," replied Master Chief, "you don't have to worry about that any more. I'm Master Chief Ryan O'Leary; I'll get you out of here." He dialed his pistol to a fine beam, turning it into a laser cutter. "Don't move," he added as he cut off her shackles. He moved over to the other woman and cut off her shackles. Both women thanked him as they slowly stood up, stretching muscles that hadn't been used in some time.

Calvin took off his helmet and looked at the women. With his helmet on, they had seemed pretty; with it off, they were gorgeous, even with the dirt and cuts that they had. Their long black hair framed delicate faces with brilliant blue eyes. Their light skin only accentuated how blue their eyes were. "Ladies," he said, "I'm sorry that I can't send anyone back with you, but if you go out the door on the other side of the room, you can make it back out of the pyramid. Unfortunately, I've already lost several men, and I just don't have anyone I can send back with you."

"We aren't going to walk through here by ourselves," the first one said. "It is too dangerous. We might run into one of the priests or, even worse, one of the gods." The second one nodded her agreement. "We'll go with you," she added.

Calvin looked into their scared faces. "Where we're going, it will be even more dangerous," he said. "We are on our way to kill Quetzalcoatl."

"Oooh," crooned the first one, putting a hand on Calvin's shoulder and looking up into his eyes, "you men and women must be really brave. We'll come with you. We'll be safer with you."

Calvin reconsidered. "Well...it would be dangerous for you to wander through here on your own. Maybe you should come with us."

"Are you sure?" asked Master Chief. "They're more likely to run into something dangerous *with* us, since we're actively looking for it. Besides which, we haven't seen any Caucasians the whole time we've been here. Where did they come from?"

The second woman put her hands on Master Chief's shoulder and looked up at him, batting her eyes. "We promise that we'll stay out of the way," she said. "We won't be any trouble for you."

The first one nodded her head in agreement. "Quetzalcoatl was going to have us killed," she added. "We want to see him dead so that we know he will never come after us again."

"Yes," agreed the second woman, "it's the only way we'll ever feel safe."

"Hmmm..." thought Master Chief. "Well, sir, if they stay back, it probably is safer for them to stay with us than for them to wander around the pyramid alone."

"*I can't believe you're seriously considering it, Master Chief,*" remarked Mr. Jones. "*I admit that it's dangerous for them to walk around alone in the pyramid, but we've already cleaned out the shit behind us. They could probably walk all the way out to the main entrance without seeing a single soul. Like you asked, where the hell did they come from?*"

"*Maybe they could walk out on their own,*" replied Calvin, "*but the spearmen we fought could still be in the pyramid, and there were guards at the main entrance to the pyramid. Those guys would probably kill them outright if they thought the women were escaping prisoners. No,*" he decided, "*it's better if they stay with us.*" He looked at the woman next to him. "You have to stay back out of the way."

She nodded her head. "We promise," she said. "By the way, my name is Sella, and this is my sister Trella."

"I'm Calvin," he said. He indicated Master Chief. "This is Ryan O'Leary. If you need anything, let one of us know." He put his helmet back on. "*All right, Master Chief, let's go kill some snakes.*"

"*Roger that, sir,*" Master Chief said opening the door out of the room. "*Steropes and Vice Sergeant Al-Sabani, you've got point.*" The two on point went out the door, followed by the rest of the squad. Sella stayed close by Calvin, while her sister stayed next to Master Chief.

"*Master Chief*," Bob commed on a private circuit as they walked out the door, "*what were the shackles binding the women made of?*"

"*I don't know,*" Master Chief answered, "*some kind of metal. Why?*"

"*I was the last one out the door,*" Bob replied, "*and I could swear that I saw them disappear just before the illumination rounds went out.*"

"*It must have been a trick of the light,*" Master Chief commed. "*You saw me cut them off. They were as real and solid as anything I have ever seen. They couldn't have just disappeared.*"

Bob shook his head. His race had grown up in the dismal swamps of his planet, and he knew his night vision was better than any of the humans. The shackles had disappeared. He was sure of it.

Chapter Twenty-Four

Under the Great Pyramid of Cholula, Keppler-22 'b', August 12, 2020

Irina looked at Leading Seaman Abdul Wazir. *"Are you ready to go?"*

It had taken a while to get Wazir put back together. They had taken off his suit, dumped it out and then patched the hole. He had then put it back on long enough to have the suit's nanobots complete the cleaning of the residual toxic material. He had also received a load of nanobots that were cleaning the poisons out of his system. If he hadn't had the suit and its technology, he would either have been dead by now...or alive and just wishing he were dead. *"I am ready to go,"* he replied. *"My throat hurts, my eyes are watering and I feel like shit, but I am functional. Let's go."*

"I'll lead," Irina said to the group, *'then Remy, then Abdul, then Sigvar. Watch for any writing or any discolorations or abnormalities on the walls and floors."* The passageway was dark, except for the light that the suits shed.

"Got it," said Remy. *"Just so that you know, I've only got about eight more hours of power on my suit. The swimming on the way here really drained me."*

"Da," said Irina in acknowledgement. *"Anyone else have lower than that?"* No one had less, and hers was at 14 hours of power remaining. Nearly all of them had at least one part of their suit that was yellow from the fall and the acid bath; Wazir had several sections that were

red. Irina had to use some of her pharmacopeia for Wazir; his pharma was one of the broken parts of his suit. They needed to get out of here. Now.

Let me know when you reach two hours remaining," she said, starting down the hall.

Inside the Great Pyramid of Cholula, Keppler-22 'b', August 12, 2020

Looking down at Sella walking along next to him, Calvin was glad that they had brought the women along. If nothing else, Calvin knew that he felt stronger and surer of himself with her by his side. Maybe it was the strength of a good woman that people always talked about, he thought.

Their luck had been holding, too, since they found the women. Steropes had found two pressure plates before stepping on them. Looking at the holes in the ceiling above them, Steropes said that they would probably have dropped some sort of poison or acid on them, had anyone stepped on them.

They had made a circuit of the pyramid and had travelled up a ramp that had elevated them about 40 feet. At the top they reached a door.

Steropes opened the door to see a well-lit room approximately 100 yards on a side. As they went in, the door closed behind them with a 'snick' that seemed out of place. Calvin spun around to see that the door was a blank piece of metal on their side; no handle or other mechanism to open it existed on their side. A noise could be heard from inside the door as some sort of bolt was thrown. There was no going back.

Under the Great Pyramid of Cholula, Keppler-22 'b', August 12, 2020

"*Merde,*" swore Remy Martin as more powder came floating down from the ceiling, coating his suit in white. He looked at the analysis as he got yet another danger warning from the suit. "*It is some kind of concentrated phencyclidine like PCP,*" the Frenchman said. "*The suit says it will probably cause hallucinations, and that seizures, coma and death are also likely.*"

"*In that case,*" replied Irina from where she stood outside the white cloud, "*I think we'll just wait until it settles.*" This was the second time that something had dumped on them from the ceiling. The first time it had been some sort of concentrated venom that had clogged Wazir's suit sensors and set off another red warning light on his suit. He was now following a long way behind Remy to stay out of the area of effect of any further traps.

Remy brushed himself off as best he could and moved to stand outside of the PCP dust. "*I think we are coming to the end of the maze,*" he announced. "*I can see a light ahead.*" They had been walking in the maze for the last 30 minutes. Between following the right wall, as suggested by Leading Seaman Sigvar Borsheim, and the tracking function of their suits, they hadn't ever gotten 'lost,' but the walls seemed to shift when seen from the corners of their eyes.

Irina breathed a sigh of relief. Between the feeling of not knowing where they were going and having toxic substances dumped on them randomly, their passage through the maze had been disconcerting, to say the least. She was looking forward to traveling in a straight line again...and killing something at the earliest opportunity.

The PCP settled and the rest of the group moved to join Remy at the maze exit. *"As the Americans say,"* announced Remy, *"I have good news and bad news. The good news is that we made it to the end of the maze. The bad news is that there is nowhere else to go."* He moved so that the rest of the group could see the passage beyond him. After about five feet, the passage terminated in a small alcove. A torch burned in the five foot space, illuminating blank, featureless walls. It was a dead end.

Inside the Great Pyramid of Cholula, Keppler-22 'b', August 12, 2020

Calvin turned around. Although the room had initially appeared to be empty, a group of humanoids could now be seen at the other end of the room. In their midst, Calvin got his first look at one of the flying snakes. Although hard to see at this distance, he dialed up his visual augmentation to its maximum and could see that the coatl appeared to be a six feet long snake, covered in feathers. It also had two wings which flapped slowly. Calvin couldn't see how the wings held it aloft as it hovered about four feet above the ground.

"Is that Quetzalcoatl?" he asked.

"No," replied Steropes. "That *is* one of the coatl, but it is not Quetzalcoatl. I do not believe that we will see him before we get to his temple. I expect something nasty, though; I could hear him laughing before we walked into this room. Now, I do not hear anything."

"Um, that might have been good info to have had prior to coming in," said Calvin. "Now we're pretty much stuck here."

"He has been laughing at me periodically since we arrived here," Steropes noted. "I didn't think that this time was any different than any of the previous ones. Besides, there was no other way to go except through here, so we had no choice."

"Still," replied Calvin, "it might have been good to know that ahead of time. This seems like it is becoming less of a mission to rescue people and more of a personal vendetta. Please let me know next time if something changes."

"I will," answered Steropes.

Calvin looked around the room. Unlike the rest of the pyramid, the walls and the ceiling of the room were covered in some sort of gray metal. In addition to the group at the other end of the room, the only other things in the room were the devices that were producing its light. Spaced every 20 yards along the wall were eight devices that looked like barrels that were about a yard in diameter. The barrels were about four feet high, with a cylinder that was about six inches in diameter sticking up another three feet from the center of the barrels. At the top of the cylinder was some sort of illumination device. It was too bright to look directly at it, so Calvin couldn't see if it was a light bulb or some other means of producing light. They all hummed with a low electronic vibration. Between them, they produced an audible noise that raised the hair on the back of the Terrans' necks.

"Any idea what those things are?" asked Calvin, indicating the barrels.

"No," replied Steropes. "I have never seen anything like them before. They were not in the coatls' previous pyramid. I would urge caution."

"You think?" asked Calvin. "I'm not sure how much more cautious I could be, except for sitting down and not moving."

"Umm, sir, do you want me to do something about the natives?" interjected Ryan.

Calvin looked back to the group at the other end of the room. The humanoids that he had noticed before were obviously priests, complete with big headdresses. He could see that there were six of them as they arrayed themselves in front of the Terrans with the coatl flying slowly back and forth behind them. The priests each had large spears like the group the Terrans had fought previously.

"They don't appear to have any long range weapons," replied Calvin. "Let's get a little closer and see if they would rather talk than die." The Terrans formed into an arrowhead formation and began advancing across the open room.

"*We would rather that* you *died, instead,*" a voice said suddenly in their heads. "*But that will be taken care of shortly.*"

"Who are you?" asked Calvin.

"*I am Talectelcoatl,*" the voice replied. "*I have a surprise for you.*"

"I'm not a real big fan of my enemies having surprises for me," announced Ryan. "Can I please shoot them now?"

"I think that would be a good idea," Calvin said. "Platoon, *fire!*"

Before anyone could shoot, the coatl reached up with its tail and threw a switch which the Terrans hadn't noticed before. The noise from the barrels immediately grew both louder and started rising in pitch. As the first lasers fired, all of the barrels detonated simultaneously. There was a strobe of light and then everything went black.

TSS *Vella Gulf*, In Orbit Around Keppler-22 'b', August 12, 2020

"I am having a problem tracking the main part of the Space Force on the planet," said Sarah Sommers from the science station.

"What do you mean, 'you're having a problem tracking them?'" asked Captain Griffin.

"I mean that I *can't* track them," replied Sara. "I had a strong signal from the group that Cal...that Lieutenant Commander Hobbs was leading, and then, one by one, their transponders all became very weak, and now I can just barely see them. I still have the two other groups that got separated, but I don't have the main force on my scope anymore."

"What do you suppose happened to them, Arges?" Captain Griffin asked the Psiclops standing next to Sarah.

"The nature of the signal cessation is unknown," replied Arges. "It is possible that their signal is being blocked or that something happened to their suits. The fact that their signal strengths decreased one by one is indicative to me that they went somewhere that their signal is being blocked or jammed. The reason for this, however, is unknown. There is an area of the pyramid where our sensors cannot scan; it is possible they entered this area."

He looked at the scope and then took a sharp breath of his own. "Captain Griffin!" he exclaimed, "My sensors just recorded an electromagnetic event from the surface of the planet!"

"What kind of electromagnetic event?" asked Captain Griffin.

"I am trying to ascertain the nature of the event," replied Arges. "I do not have any indications of a nuclear detonation, but it was a definite electromagnetic pulse (EMP). It is possible that it was a weapon-generated EMP."

"A what?" asked Griffin.

"There are ways of creating an EMP without a nuclear explosion," replied Arges. "For example, an explosively pumped flux compression generator, or EPFCG, can be used to generate a high-power EMP by compressing magnetic flux via a high explosive detonation. During your Cold War period, the United States developed EPFCG technology that could produce a pulse in the millions of amperes and tens of terawatts, and still be man-portable. The event I just witnessed, however, developed over 200 terajoules of power."

"What's a terror jewel?" asked the helmsman.

"A joule is a unit of work or energy," said Captain Griffin, who was becoming an expert at downloading information through her implant to keep up with Arges. "A terajoule is equal to one trillion joules. About 63 terajoules were released by the atomic bomb that exploded over Hiroshima, so whatever just happened down there released the same energy as more than three nuclear weapons."

"Correct," said Arges. "I also noted a peak magnetic field strength of about 1.3 giga teslas."

As he stood up to make his announcement, Sarah leaned in to the monitor. She looked up, her face as white as if she had seen a ghost. "They're gone," she said. "They're all gone."

Chapter Twenty-Five

"*Salope*," swore Remy Martin as his suit died. Remy was a strong man and was able to carry the extra weight of the hundred-pound suit if he had to, but the additional load was inconvenient. He took off his helmet to find that the other three members of his group were doing the same. "My suit just died," he said. "Yours, too?"

All three nodded. The underground passageway seemed more narrow and claustrophobic without the extra light of the suits. The torch hanging on the wall did not illuminate much more than the alcove and the entrance to the maze. All four of the suits beeped, nearly simultaneously. "Anyone know what happened?" Remy asked.

Irina stood looking at the back of Wazir's suit. "I'm guessing we just took some sort of electromagnetic pulse that fried the electronics of our suit."

"Why do you think that?" asked Sigvar Borsheim.

"Because Wazir's emergency backup has been activated," Irina said. "We have two hours before we blow up."

Inside the Great Pyramid of Cholula, Keppler-22 'b', August 12, 2020

"Oww," Calvin moaned. He awoke on his stomach, and it felt like someone was sitting on his back. His head felt woozy, and everything seemed strangely quiet. "What hit me?" he asked. He felt his head, and there was a large lump on the back of it. Wait, he wondered. How could he feel his head? Where was his helmet?

A female voice came from next to him. "There was a big explosion," the voice said, "and everyone got knocked out. I just woke up to find the coatl gone, and everyone lying here."

Ryan pushed himself up next to Calvin and looked the other way to see Sella's concerned face looking at him. "Are you all right?" she asked. He saw that she was holding his helmet. There was a dim light from two torches that were burning near the doorway where the coatl had been. Although the priests were lying there, the coatl was gone.

"I think so," Ryan replied. He pushed himself up. "Crap," he said, realizing his suit was turned off. He stood up awkwardly and saw that most of the others were doing the same. His suit beeped at about the same time as everyone else's suits. "*Fuck,*" he swore, "my suit is fried." He walked over to Calvin and said, "Sir, we're in some real shit."

"What do you mean?" Calvin asked, still a little stunned.

"Whatever that explosion was, it must have set off a *massive* electromagnetic pulse," Master Chief said. "All of our suits have been fried."

"Yeah, mine too," Calvin agreed, not understanding where he was going.

"What powers the suits?" Master Chief asked.

"About two and a half kilograms of antimatter," Calvin answered automatically. "Why?"

"Because the containment system is fried on all of our suits," Master Chief replied. "They are all operating on their backup systems, which are providing emergency stabilization to the antimatter containment vessels. In a little less than two hours, the emergency systems are going to fail, and each suit is going to detonate in a 107 megaton explosion. It will be less than that since the batteries aren't at full power, but I doubt that it will really matter much to us. If we don't get these suits repaired, we're going to wipe out this island at a minimum, and maybe even the whole planet. I don't know; I'm no scientist. What I do know is that we won't care. No matter how fast you run, you won't escape the blasts."

"All right," Calvin said. "We need to get somewhere that we can call down support. I can't reach the *Vella Gulf* on my implant."

"Sir, you can't reach *anyone*," Master Chief replied. "Whatever fried our suits also fried our implants."

"That's why it's so quiet," Calvin remarked. "Sorry, I hit my head and am a little out of it," he confessed. "Well, I expect that they'll send someone down once they realize that our suits are not responding," he continued. "We just need to be where they can reach us when they get here. We've got to get out of here, and we've got to do it now."

Inside the Great Pyramid of Cholula, Keppler-22 'b', August 12, 2020

"Damn, that hurts," Private First Class John 'Jet' Li said. "My suit just died."

"Yeah, mine too," Corporal Jimmy 'Colonel' Sanders replied. He had been in the act of sitting down when the suit suddenly died, causing him to lose his balance. He almost fell into the hole, but was just able to roll out of harm's way.

Both suits beeped.

"That's not what I think it is," Jet asked. "Is it?"

"Ah'm afraid it is," Colonel answered in his Southern drawl. "Ah'd call fo help, but mah implants ain't workin' either."

"My implants aren't working, either," Jet replied. "And now that the suit isn't working, it's not holding my leg in place, and *that* hurts like shit. If I hadn't been leaning back against the wall, the suit would have flipped me over." He paused and looked at the senior man. "What are we going to do?"

"Well," Colonel said, "Ah don' think you're gonna be able ta outrun the blast. Truth be told, Ah don' think Ah could, either. Ah think we jus' sit tight right here and wait for help. If our suits are out, everyone else's are, too. They'll come for us." *I hope*, he added to himself.

Chapter Twenty-Six

"We don't know that they are dead," Arges said, "but we do know that neither their implants nor their suits are functioning. It is quite possible that they were destroyed by the EMP; that would be consistent with the data."

Captain Griffin looked at Bullseye, sitting in the squadron commander's chair. "So if they are without their suits or implants," she asked, "how do we contact them?"

"We can't," Bullseye answered. "They had a backup radio, but that would be fried as well. The only way we're going to contact them is to go down there and do it face-to-face."

"Is there any way to do it without causing the same confrontation with the locals that we were trying to avoid?" Captain Griffin asked.

"No, ma'am," Bullseye replied. "We'll have to land in front of the temple. Everyone is going to see us."

"I'm sorry, Captain Griffin, but I do not think you are seeing the big picture," Arges said. "You *must* go down there, and you must do it *right now.*"

"And why's that?" Captain Griffin asked.

"Because if their suits have shut down," Arges replied, "then their antimatter containment systems are operating in backup mode.

233

In a little less than two hours, they are going to detonate with the force of over *two gigatons*. It may very well be an extinction level event for the whole planet."

"Damn it," Captain Griffin said. "We've got to get those suits off the planet." She turned to Bullseye. "Get a shuttle down there with Night and all of his available personnel ASAP. Get them into that pyramid and get those damn suits. No fooling around; kill anyone you need to. I don't care. *Get those damn suits off the planet!*"

SF-1 Ready Room, TSS *Vella Gulf,* Orbit Keppler-22 'b', August 12, 2020

"We need both shuttles manned ASAP," Bullseye said. "One will carry the second squad to the surface and bring back both of the squads afterwards. The other shuttle will take the suits into space. Once there, they will dump the suits and run."

The operations officer, Lieutenant Imagawa 'Samurai' Sadayo, looked at his clipboard. "Since you and I know the mission parameters, and time is of the essence, LT Simpson will pilot the first shuttle that takes the platoon to the planet, with you as his WSO," Samurai replied. "Lieutenant Boudreau and I will fly the other shuttle to take off the suits."

"Sounds good," Bullseye said. "I'll go talk to Night; you set up the shuttle launches."

Squad Bay, TSS *Vella Gulf,* Orbit Keppler-22 'b', August 12, 2020

"OK," Night said. "It looks like the CO has gotten his ass into trouble, and it's up to us to go and save him. Something down there generated an electromagnetic pulse of huge proportions, which fried the other squad's suits and implants. In about an hour and a half, 18 suits are going to explode with a detonation that is going to end life on this planet. *We have got to get them off.*"

He looked at the squad assembled in front of him. "No delay will be tolerated. Kill anyone that gets in your way. They're dead anyway if we don't get those suits off of the planet. If you see a flying snake, kill it immediately, no questions asked."

"Anything else?" Night asked. "All right, let's go. Grab your weapons and gear; we leave in 10 minutes."

Inside the Great Pyramid of Cholula, Keppler-22 'b', August 12, 2020

"Move out," Calvin ordered.

"You heard the man," Master Chief said. "Let's get a move on."

Mr. Jones and Petty Officer Sherkov went through the door. The strongest men, they were able to carry their suits and still brandish the spears that they had liberated from the Mayan priests. The Terrans had disarmed the men and sent them out the way the Terrans had come in, as the blast had opened the door. Sergeant Tagliabue followed behind Jones and Sherkov, holding one of the torches.

Following the Italian, Father Zuhlsdorf walked along in a black cassock, with his sword in one hand and his suit thrown over the opposite shoulder.

Looking at the priest's strange choice of clothing, Calvin asked, "Is that what you wore under your suit?"

"I do like wearing a black cassock whenever possible," Father Zuhlsdorf replied, "but no, that is not what I had on. It clumps up in all of the wrong places inside of a suit and chafes something fierce on a long march. Besides," he added, "it would ruin the creases on it if I did."

"So, you put it in your pack and brought it along, just in case we took off the suits?" asked Calvin.

"Yes," Father Zuhlsdorf said. "It's good to be prepared. To me, it is part of the armor of my faith." He smiled. "It's also pretty comfortable to wear in a stuffy pyramid."

Calvin was left to shake his head as the line of soldiers continued past him and further into the pyramid. Since everyone now had to carry their hundred pound suits, they had left most of their gear, including their non-functional rifles, in the EMP room. Most of the special forces troopers were able to carry their suits with no problem, but it was all that Bob and Doug could do to wrestle theirs down the corridor. Not only were the suits heavy, the therapods just weren't built for carrying things. When they started to drag on the floor, the two women went to help them. With one of the women helping each of them, the therapods were able to manage, barely, although it looked like the frail women were carrying more of the load than Bob or Doug.

As he was walking through the door, Calvin had a thought. "Hey, Master Chief," he said. "If the other squad comes in the front entrance of the pyramid, they're not going to know how to find us and are going to fall for the traps. We better send someone back to lead them up."

"You're right, sir," Master Chief responded. He turned to the squad. "Petty Officer Levine, go back to where we left Jet and the Colonel. Wait there for the rest of the squad to get here and then lead them up."

"Why me?" the Israeli asked. "Because I gave Al-Sabani a hard time earlier?"

"Because I said so!" Master Chief yelled. "I could give a shit about earlier. You're the one with the right skill set to operate independently, now go fucking do it. We don't have time to screw around!"

"Sure thing, Master Chief," Petty Officer Levine replied, chastened. He turned and left, and the rest of the squad started forward again.

Under the Great Pyramid of Cholula, Keppler-22 'b', August 12, 2020

"Grab that torch," Irina said, "and let's find the secret door."

Remy Martin pulled the torch out of the sconce. As the torch came out in his hand, a sliding, grating sound was heard in the distance, accompanied by a roar.

"I do not know what that was," Sigvar Borsheim commented, "but whatever it was sounded very large and *very* unfriendly. I recommend that we hurry." He pointed his rifle into the maze while Martin and Rozhkov began searching the cubicle.

Wazir went to stand beside Borsheim. "You know that the rifles do not work, yes?" he asked.

"I am aware," Borsheim replied, looking out into the maze. "I am hoping that whatever is coming doesn't know that."

"Good point," Wazir agreed, leveling his rifle into the maze.

Borsheim heard a scuffling, dragging noise coming from the darkness. It sounded even larger than what he had previously thought. "You need to hurry faster!" he urged.

Chapter Twenty-Seven

Inside the Great Pyramid of Cholula, Keppler-22 'b', August 12, 2020

Calvin looked at the back panel of Sergeant Tagliabue's suit for what seemed like the hundredth time. Only 59 minutes remaining until the world ended. "Can you go any faster, Steropes?" he asked.

"No," Steropes said. "Not if you want me to do this safely. Without the suits, we are a lot more susceptible to any traps that are waiting for us. I remember at least one more trap before the temple level."

"We're about out of time for doing things safely," Calvin replied. "The suits are going to blow in less than an hour."

"I am going as fast as I can," Steropes replied. "This is difficult to do in torch-light."

As they rounded the corner, Steropes came up short. "Well, this is different," he said.

Looking around the front rank of men, Calvin could see a 15' wide chasm yawning in front of Steropes. On the other side of the opening, a number of what looked like manhole covers could be seen on the floor, with a lever protruding from the wall. Master Chief pulled a nickel out of his pocket and dropped it over the edge. He counted, "One...two..." About halfway to 'three,' the men could hear it hit. "It's about 100 feet to the bottom," he announced.

"I can make that jump," Petty Officer Sherkov stated, looking at the other side. "Once across, you can throw over my suit, and then I can help everyone across."

"I have a feeling that won't be necessary," Steropes replied looking at the wall to their left. He bent over to look at something near the bottom.

"Lieutenant Commander Hobbs said we are almost out of time," Sherkov said. He looked at Master Chief. "I can make the jump."

"And if you did, you would fall through the holes on the other side," Steropes declared. "The lever is there to make you think that it will close the gap, but it will not. It is only there to make you try the jump." He pulled out a small piece of metal and inserted it into a hole that was at about his knee level. With a small '*snick*,' a five feet wide opening appeared in the wall. "This is the right way to go."

Inside the doorway, a passage ran off into the darkness. "You do not want to go down that passageway," Steropes pronounced. "It is trapped." He pointed to some iron rungs going up on the wall to the right. "This way leads up to the temple level."

"Not a very dignified way for the 'elite' to travel," Petty Officer Sherkov remarked as he looked at the rungs, hoping that this set would hold him.

"They are not for the coatls," Steropes replied. "They just fly up to the temple level. The rungs are for their priests. They are to remind them that they are less worthy than the coatls."

"Up the ladder, Sherkov," Master Chief ordered, leaving a marker to indicate their direction of travel for the troops he hoped would be following them. "We ain't got much time left."

Under the Great Pyramid of Cholula, Keppler-22 'b', August 12, 2020

The sliding noise was close. Sigvar Borsheim could hear it clearly now. Whatever was coming made a sliding noise, paused, and then another sliding noise. "We're running out of time!" he cried.

"I cannot go faster!" Irina cried.

The creature came around the last bend in the maze. Half man and half bull, it stood over nine feet tall, not including the massive horns that jutted from its head. It appeared partially lame, as it would take a step with one cloven hoof and then drag the other one forward. It breathed out explosively, and Wazir could see smoke come from its nostrils. "*Shaitan!*" he yelled.

The creature paused. "I am Asterion, Keeper of the Maze," it said, its breath heavy with brimstone as it advanced on the group. "You have walked the maze. You must die." He looked at Wazir. "*Flee!*" it commanded.

"It is a shaitan jinn," whimpered Wazir, backing up. "They are the most powerful and evil of all of the jinn. They follow Shaitan, the devil." He continued to back up, trembling.

Seeing Borsheim facing the beast by himself, Remy Martin moved forward to take Wazir's place to the left of Borsheim. He pointed his rifle at Asterion and said, "I don't care who or what you are. Leave now, or I will be forced to shoot you."

The creature reached out with blinding speed, especially for something so large, and snatched the rifle from Martin's hands. Laughing, it broke it over the knee on its lame leg. "Now what are you going to do?" it asked, throwing the pieces of the rifle to the side.

As it bent over to break the rifle, Martin saw a button on the wall behind it. "What am I going to do?" he asked. "I am going to kill you with my knife." He drew his knife from his belt sheath. "There is a button on the wall behind it," he said over his shoulder to his comrades. "I am going to try to reach it." He started moving to his left.

"Puny creature!" Asterion howled. "You make me laugh!" It lowered its head and charged, attacking on all fours. Remy tried to jump out of the way of the charge, but didn't have enough room to maneuver. As Asterion went by, it caught Martin with a horn. A glancing blow, it didn't have enough force to penetrate the suit, but he was caught. Asterion stopped and tossed his head, throwing Martin through the air. He impacted the wall behind the jinni headfirst with a sick thud and then slid down to the floor, not moving.

Asterion turned to finish the downed soldier, but was hit in the side of the head by Borsheim's rifle. Grunting, it turned to face Borsheim. "So," it said with a snort, "you would like to die next?"

"I name you 'Fanden,' the devil," Borsheim growled, pulling out his knife. "I don't know if you can be killed, but I am willing to see if you bleed."

Asterion put down his head and charged. Borsheim had noticed that he kept his head down during his first charge. He waited until Asterion was almost upon him and jumped forward and up into the air, going over the beast's head and down his side. As Borsheim went past, he dragged his knife down the creature's side. Unfortunately, the hide was tougher than he was prepared for, and all he succeeded in doing was scratching the beast, infuriating it. It snorted again, releasing a cloud of sulfur.

Faster than Borsheim would have thought possible, Asterion turned and charged again. Unprepared for the second attack, Borsheim tried to jump over the beast's head, but this time Asterion was ready, and he raised his head in time to catch Borsheim, hooking him on his left horn. Eye-to-eye, Asterion continued forward at full speed, slamming Borsheim into the wall, the point of his horn impaling him and breaking several of his ribs. Asterion's horns extended in front of him, though, and they caught on the wall before he could completely flatten the Norwegian. Plaster came off the wall in chunks as he flipped Borsheim off of his horn and drew his head back to further gore the soldier.

As the beast turned his head, he saw motion behind him. Although critically wounded, Remy Martin wasn't dead, and he struggled up to reach the button four feet above where he lay. One hand above the other, he began crawling his way up the wall to the button.

Knowing that the button would free the Terrans, Asterion shouted, "No!" He turned away from Borsheim, put his head down and charged the Frenchman. He had only taken one step when his good back foot went out from under him. As the monster slid on his stomach, it turned its massive head to see Wazir standing behind him, scimitar held high. The weapon flashed, severing the beast's other hamstring. Crippled, the beast fell to the ground.

"You!" the beast snorted. "You were the only one to recognize me. You should be running."

Wazir came around to the front of the beast and raised the heavy scimitar. "Sometimes you have to face your demons," Wazir said, as he brought the scimitar down with all of his augmented strength on Asterion's head. It sank eight inches into the beast's skull, killing it. The creature died, becoming insubstantial as it did. The curved sword fell to the floor, smoking, as the jinni disappeared.

Focused on the button just out of his reach, Remy was unaware of the fight behind him. He struggled a little higher up the wall with his last ounce of strength. "Got it," he gasped, finally reaching the button. He pushed it and collapsed.

With a grating noise, a section of the passageway opened next to Irina, and a set of rungs going up could be seen in the narrow alcove behind her.

Staggering up, Borsheim wheezed, "One of the drawbacks of being a medic is that I know my ribs are broken, and I probably have a punctured lung." Irina could see blood bubbling out of the corner of his mouth as he panted in pain. "Let's get the hell out of here."

"Da," she said in agreement. "As the Americans would say, 'no shit.'"

Chapter Twenty-Eight

The remnants of the Space Force paused before an ornate, golden door. "This is the entrance to the temple area," Steropes whispered. "We will find the coatls in here somewhere. Watch out for their tails; they have poisonous stingers in them."

"Now he tells us," grumbled someone from the back. "Is it too late to go back to the ship?"

Calvin surveyed his force. It was a motley crew. About half of the men and women were wearing their suits for the protection it gave them. The other half had set theirs down to get the extra mobility. The four biggest men wielded the spears taken from the priests; the rest had drawn their backup weapons. The blades were as varied as the soldiers holding them, from the tomahawks of the therapods, to the janbiya of Al-Sabani, to the kris of Sergeant Andrews, to Wraith's sa-ingeom. Calvin almost felt embarrassed to wield the plain, seven inch long SEAL knife that Master Chief O'Leary had given him as a gift. Even Steropes could out-reach him with his staff.

"Spears to the front," Master Chief commanded, who was holding one of the spears. "We'll go in first and spread out left and right. The others will come in after us. Kill anything that flies. Everyone ready to go kill a god?"

"Wait," Al-Sabani said. "You need to know that there are efreet in there."

"Didn't you already mention them?" asked Calvin. "Weren't they one of the kinds you said we *didn't* want to fight?"

"Indeed," the Saudi replied. "Efreet are very powerful and intelligent jinn, that normally appear as enormous winged creatures of fire. It is said that they are susceptible to magic, but that most ordinary weapons have no power over them. Efreet can be either good or bad, believers in Allah or unbelievers." He paused. "My qarin tells me there are two in the next room. They are most evil."

"And they can't be killed?" Calvin asked, seizing on the only thing he heard that was even close to normal.

"Yes, they can be killed," Al-Sabani replied, "but it is not easy. They have the power to become immaterial and invisible at will. They can only be killed when they are in their corporeal form; even then, not all normal weapons will hurt them."

"How do we make them corporeal?" Master Chief asked.

"I do not know," Al-Sabani answered. "On the good side, they can't attack us when they are non-corporeal."

Master Chief turned to look at Calvin. "This shit's way beyond my pay grade, sir," he said. "Are you sure you want to do this?"

"Am I sure?" Calvin asked. "No, I'm not sure. I've never had to deal with genies before, nor do I know anyone that ever has. Still, something tells me we need to do this, regardless of the outcome." He looked at Tagliabue's suit next to him. "We've only got 35 minutes before we destroy this world," he continued. He stood a little straighter, looking more focused. "Let's get this done."

"Roger that, sir," Master Chief replied. He turned back to the door, only to find that Steropes had worked his way behind him when he wasn't looking. Before he could say anything or prepare his troops for the entry, Steropes opened the door.

"Quetzalcoatl," he said, walking in, "I have come for you."

Chapter Twenty-Nine

Shuttle 02, In Front of the Great Pyramid of Cholula, Keppler-22 'b', August 12, 2020

"Ten seconds to landing," said Bullseye, the shuttle's WSO. "Heads up. Looks like there are Blue Forces coming out of the pyramid."

"You heard the man," commed Night to the troops in the back of the shuttle, "there are friendlies coming out of the pyramid. First order of business is to get them into this shuttle and their suits into the other shuttle." The shuttle touched down in a cloud of dust, and the ramp in back started coming down. "Let's go! We're running out of time!"

The Ground Force stormed out of the shuttle, setting up a perimeter around it. Night followed them out to find that the shuttle had come down right in front of the pyramid, with its boarding ramp facing the massive structure. Their caution was unnecessary, Night saw, as it looked like all of the locals had fled the conflict taking place within it. The pyramid seemed even bigger in person than it had in photos. He realized that it was hard to grasp the enormity of a 400 meter square pyramid from pictures alone. Its height was amazing, as well, going up nearly 350'. I've got to find all of the suits in there? He looked at his watch. Well, at least I've got 20 minutes to do it, he thought with a sense of irony. Fuck.

Not seeing any locals, he directed his squad to help the men and woman coming down the main ramp from the front of the pyramid.

249

The group was a mess. Jet was being helped by Corporal Sanders; he staggered along, something obviously wrong with his leg. The Colonel also staggered down the main steps to the pyramid, bearing the weight of both Jet and Jet's suit, as well as his own. Petty Officer Levine had all he could do to carry the lifeless body of someone...it looked like the Frenchman, still wearing his suit. Leading Seaman Wazir and Irina Rozhkov had Leading Seaman Borsheim suspended between them. He wasn't moving much, and Night could see blood dripping from his mouth and running down his front from a stomach wound.

Relieved of the body he had been carrying, Petty Officer Levine stumbled up to Night and saluted. "Good to see you, sir," Levine said, breathing hard. "The lieutenant commander sends his compliments and hopes you'll join him in the temple level at the top of this pile of shit." He looked like he would fall down at any moment.

"Put your suit in the other shuttle," Night said through his suit's speakers, indicating Shuttle 01 that was landing next to the first shuttle. "After you do that, get aboard this shuttle. We're leaving in 15 minutes."

"I'm here to take you to them," said the Israeli, stripping off his non-functional suit. "Just let me get this off, and we can go." He took it off and handed it to Corporal Sanders, who had come back out of the shuttle to help.

"Let's go!" urged Petty Officer Levine. "They need your help!"

"Ground Force, all troops with me!" commed Night, heading toward the pyramid at his best speed. "Time is running out!"

Inside the Great Pyramid of Cholula, Keppler-22 'b', August 12, 2020

Calvin and the nine remaining members of the Space Force charged into the room after Steropes, followed by the two local women. Entering the room, Calvin found himself in a large open space. The room was rectangular, nearly 60 feet wide by 100 feet long. Obviously used for religious ceremonies, the room was dominated by the large, blood-spattered stone altar on a raised dais at the opposite end of the room from where the Terrans came in. There were large iron doors on both sides of the platform.

The room was well lit by a large number of electric lights along all of the walls, as well as numerous candelabra on the platform. In front of the altar, Calvin saw the object of all of their efforts, Quetzalcoatl. It was resting on a "T" structure that looked like a large bird perch. While the coatl Calvin had seen previously had only been about six feet long, Quetzalcoatl was at least 12 feet in length. It was hard to tell exactly with most of the flying snake's body wrapped around the stand. Flanking it were four more coatls, with two on each side. The two closest to Quetzalcoatl were between eight and 10 feet in length; the two on the outside were only about six feet. Flanking these coatls, Calvin could see two indistinct shapes that seemed to float in the air. They appeared to be made of dark vapor or smoke, but unlike smoke, they kept their shapes and did not disperse.

Seeing the creatures on the altar, Sella and Trella screamed and fled the room.

"*I thought you were dead, Tezcatlipoca,*" Quetzalcoatl said telepathically, looking at Steropes. Its tail began unwrapping from his perch, and it floated free, although its wings were not beating.

Calvin looked at the coatl and was repulsed by what he saw. Quetzalcoatl was fully 13 feet long from its head to the tip of its tail, and it was covered in dark brown feathers around its wings, tapering to a lighter brown fur down the length of its body. Scales protected the stinger in its tail. Forward of its wings, it appeared to be covered in a camouflage pattern of green and brown scales across a head that was very snake-like in appearance. A forked tongue flickered in and out periodically.

It hovered about six feet in the air, with the last four feet of tail hanging down toward the ground, and moved down the stairs of the platform to hover in front of it. *"Certainly, you were poisoned and near death when my spaceship blasted off of that miserable rock. The only thing good about that whole planet was the taste of my minions' hearts."*

"I am happy to disappoint you," Steropes replied. "It took a long time for my body to recover from the wounds you gave me. I have neither forgiven nor forgotten what you did on Earth. I came along on this journey with one hope, to find and kill you."

"Unfortunately," Quetzalcoatl replied telepathically, *"you seem ill-prepared to do what you have thought about for so long."* He chuckled out loud, the sound raising goose bumps on the Terrans. *"Are these creatures the best you could do for an army? 12 of my former subjects? They are not enough to make me tremble, especially now that the advanced suits you gave them are nothing more than dead weights."* It chuckled again. *"Dead weights...how appropriate, since all of you will soon be dead, too."*

"Enough talk," Steropes said. "We have a lot still to do today. Come down here and face me. I challenge you to single combat!"

"Hahahahahaha," Quetzalcoatl replied. *"Why would I do that when I have such great pets?"* It looked back at the shadowy figures on the altar. *"Kill him!"*

The smoke figures advanced on Steropes, who stood waiting for them. They moved to within 10 feet of him, and then their figures solidified, taking on a corporeal form. Calvin got his first look at the efreet...and wished that he hadn't. The efreet were malevolence embodied, appearing demonic in face and claws. They retained a reddish-black color, varying from nearly midnight black on their wings to more reddish on their arms and claws. "They are the kings of the jinn," Al-Sabani noted, with wonder in his voice. Steam seemed to sizzle from off the backs and heads of the efreet. As they closed on Steropes, they looked at him with the same anticipation that a cat has for a mouse once it is done playing with it. They reached out toward him, obviously intent on tearing him apart.

Thinking more quickly than anyone else, Master Chief threw his spear at the one on the right, which was closer to him. The efreeti went momentarily non-corporeal, and the spear passed through the space that it had just occupied. Once the spear was clear, the efreeti solidified again and continued advancing on Steropes. The spear clattered on the floor behind it, rolling to the edge of the dais.

"*Hahahahahaha,*" laughed Quetzalcoatl again. "*You cannot harm the efreet, mortals. We are all like gods to you!*"

Calvin could feel the heat given off by the efreet as they reached for Steropes. Just before they could grab him, Steropes held out his left hand, with his fist clenched. On his ring finger was a copper and iron ring, which had a diamond that sparkled in the dancing light of the candelabras. "BACK!" Steropes commanded the efreet. To everyone's amazement, the efreet obeyed him, moving back to stop about 10 feet away from him before turning back into smoke. "This is the ring of King Solomon, which was given to him by his God!" said Steropes. "It took me over 200 years to find this relic, but it was worth it. This ring enabled Solomon to subdue jinn, and protected him from their powers. I figured you would keep your pet efreet with you and wanted to be ready." He looked at the efreet and command-ed, "Kill Quetzalcoatl!"

The efreet didn't move. Quetzalcoatl began laughing again. "*Silly Tezcatlipoca,*" it said. "*You only got that half right. It will protect you, but it does not allow you to command the efreet. They are still mine to command.*" Quetzalcoatl sighed theatrically and looked at the other coatls that had risen off their perches. "*All of you, kill them!*"

The efreet solidified and began moving toward the Terran force while the coatls winged in for the attack.

Chapter Thirty

Petty Officer Levine led the Ground Force up the steps toward the main entrance of the pyramid. As Night started up the stairs, he looked up above him at the giant structure and paused.

"Hey, Petty Officer Levine," Night said. "You mentioned that the other squad was a long way up in the pyramid, right?"

"Yeah," said the Israeli, "they're a long way up, so we'll have to hurry to get up there."

"Maybe not," Night answered, pointing up at the pyramid. "What about that?"

Petty Officer Levine looked up and could see a ceremonial altar high above them in an open area on top of the pyramid.

"*If that is the ceremonial altar,*" Night said over the implant network and his speakers, "*then the main temple area must be behind it. I can't see a door from here, but there must be a way into the pyramid from up there. That would save us a lot of time.*" Night thought a few seconds and nodded his head. "*We'll go in that way,*" he said, making up his mind. "Go back to the shuttle," he told Levine. "We've got it from here."

With time running out, the Ground Force began pounding up the front of the pyramid.

Inside the Great Pyramid of Cholula, Keppler-22 'b', August 12, 2020

Both efreet paused in their attacks. Reaching back behind them like major league pitchers, they both made throwing motions, and balls of fire arced toward their targets. The one on the right threw at Master Chief, who had hurled the spear at him. Master Chief was in his suit and put up both arms to block the fireball. It hit him and burst, throwing burning embers in a 10 foot radius in all directions. Protected from the worst of it by the suit, Master Chief patted out the remaining ember on his head and ran toward the efreeti, drawing his SEAL knife as he went. Sergeant Andrews and Petty Officer Sherkov both joined him in attacking the efreeti.

The other efreeti threw his fireball at Vice Sergeant Ismail Al-Sabani, who had chosen not to wear his suit and had no protection from it. He dove out of the way as the fireball hurtled at him. The fireball flew through the space where he had been, exploding 20 feet behind him. Mr. Jones and Father Zuhlsdorf stepped in to attack the efreeti, allowing Al-Sabani to get back onto his feet.

Seeing those troopers fighting the efreeti, and Wraith, Bob, Doug and Sergeant Tagliabue facing off against the four coatls, Calvin charged Quetzalcoatl with his SEAL knife. Before he could get there, Steropes stepped in front of him, placing a hand on his chest to stop him. "Quetzalcoatl is mine," he said. "I've got this."

Having seen Steropes in action, Calvin stepped back, motioning for Steropes to continue. "Be my guest," he said, before going around him to pick up the spear that Master Chief had thrown earlier. That would at least give him some reach, he thought.

The Terrans fighting the efreet quickly found that it was a losing proposition. They would swing their weapons at the jinn, only to have them go non-corporeal. As the weapon moved out of the space where the efreeti was, it would turn corporeal again and would slash its attacker. In a matter of seconds, most of the Terrans were bleeding from deep gashes. The heat of the efreet also took its toll, making them sweat. Weapons quickly became slick and hard to hold. Even when they were able to hit the efreet while corporeal, their weapons seemed to do very little damage to them. In Master Chief's 25 years of military service he had fought many people and creatures and had never run up against something he couldn't hurt. He had scored two hits so far on his efreeti; on the second one, it had laughed at him as it went non-corporeal to avoid a slash by Witch's kris.

Out of the corner of his eye, he saw Father Zuhlsdorf stagger back as his efreeti slashed him across the face. As he fell backward, the efreeti reached out and grabbed his falcata. Laughing, it took the sword in both hands and snapped it in two. Mr. Jones attacked the efreeti, and it turned non-corporeal, giving the priest time to recover. As the priest stood up and drew Durandal, Mr. Jones was knocked backwards to the floor in turn. Both efreet looked stronger than ever as they slowly wore down their opponents, just waiting for one of them to make a fatal mistake. With a sick feeling, Master Chief realized that this was a fight they probably weren't going to win. The efreet were just toying with them.

The soldiers fighting the coatls were doing better. Wraith had squared off with one of the six foot long ones and was using her short sword to hold it at bay. She quickly saw that the creature had two attacks. The first was to fly up and try to strike with the stinger in its tail. She had blocked this particular attack on several occasions already and had figured out the rhythm of that attack. The other attack was a bite from the snake's mouth. Wraith didn't know if its bite was poisonous, but didn't want to find out. If it bit her, it would also have better leverage to sting her. Drawing a dagger with her other hand, she focused on maintaining qigong, like she had seen Steropes do earlier in his fight with the spearmen. She relaxed, calmed her breathing, and focused on guiding her life energy throughout her body.

When the coatl came in for its next strike, she was ready. Seeing that it intended to try to sting her again, she blocked the strike with her dagger. Pushing the tail out of the way, she spun on the balls of her feet, allowing the short sword to extend and pick up the velocity of the spin. She completed the spin, and the snake's head was where she had envisioned. Her sword struck just behind the head where scale turned to fur, severing it with one stroke. The head and body of the coatl fell to the floor in two pieces.

Doug was fighting one of the eight feet long monsters. Although he was able to hold the monster off with his tomahawk and had blocked a couple of attacks with the razor edge on the top of it, he found that he needed something else to follow up with. The coatl would try to sting him, and he would block, but before he could go on the offensive, the coatl would spring back. The scaly part of the tail protected it from most of his damage, and he realized that it was only a matter of time until the coatl got lucky, and one of its attacks hit him. He didn't have his suit on, so when it hit him he wouldn't have any protection; he'd be dead.

On the coatl's next attack, he changed his strategy. Instead of simply trying to block the stinger, he reversed the tomahawk and struck at the tail with the heavy pointed end. It was a gamble; if he missed, it would leave him open to the coatl's attack. His aim was true, though, and he hit the tail about a foot up from the end. The point of his tomahawk sank in all the way to the haft, pinning the coatl to it. He began swinging the axe in a circular motion, spinning the coatl in a loop over his head, before finally slamming it into the ground. Like kids playing 'crack the whip,' the coatl's head hit the ground at the end of the whipping motion, and the creature was momentarily stunned. Doug lowered the axe so that he could step on the coatl's tail and pull out the tomahawk. Freeing the weapon, he took two quick steps toward the front of the beast and chopped the coatl just behind its head. The razor-edged blade easily went through the coatl with so much force that he dented the tomahawk on the stone floor. The coatl's head went flying off toward the dais, the beast dead.

The other six foot coatl had chosen Bob as its target, and it quickly saw that it was faster than the therapod. Feigning a bite, the creature whipped its tail at the tomahawk and knocked it from Bob's hand. Seeing that Bob was weaponless, it dove on him, intending to drive its stinger into him. Bob saw the attack coming, and he was able to grab hold of the snake's tail in both hands and prevent it from hitting him. The coatl used the hold to its advantage, and it quickly wrapped around him a couple of times in a constricting attack. Bob could feel the coatl crushing the life from him and wasn't built with the upper body strength required to push it off. He did have one arm free of the coatl's coils and let go of the tail with that hand.

Remembering the snakes from the swamps of his Epsilon Eridani home world, he grabbed the coatl's head and brought it toward his oversize jaws. The coatl saw what he intended and tried to pull away, but was too late. Bob thrust the coatl's entire head into his mouth and bit down as hard as he could. He took a second bite and severed the head from the rest of its body. Spitting it out, he took another bite from its body. "Mmm," he said, as he worked his way out of its coils. "Tasty!"

Things were not going as well for Sergeant Tagliabue, who was fighting the other eight foot coatl. He was not armed as well as the others, with two thin 13" switchblade stiletto knives and no natural defenses. The knives were too short and too thin to block effectively with, and he had already been hit a couple of times. The suit had stopped the first two strikes that had gotten past his guard, but it didn't stop the third one that hit him in the neck. The poison quickly entered his system; all he got out was a weak, "Shit," before falling on the ground unconscious. Before the coatl could reorient on one of the other Terrans and attack, Wraith struck it from behind with her sword, decapitating it.

Master Chief knew he was looking death in the face. The Terrans' attacks were coming slower and slower as the heat from the efreet and their own loss of blood took its toll. Master Chief had been hit three times; most of the other soldiers had been hit more. They got a small boost as the troops that had been fighting the coatls joined the fight, but that didn't last long as the efreet began landing hits on them, too.

Master Chief had finally seen one attack that hurt the efreeti he was fighting. Witch had landed a blow with her kris that had seemed to stagger the demon, but it had hit her in the head immediately thereafter, and her attacks were no longer crisp or on target. He saw that the knife was glowing slightly and thought about trying to take it from her, but couldn't leave himself unprotected for the length of time it would take to make the switch. He knew he'd be dead.

Not that it mattered a great deal, he thought. The fight couldn't go on much longer. The Terrans were spent. They were all going to die in a Mayan temple, hundreds of light years from home.

Not if he had anything to say about it.

Gathering his strength, he waited for his opportunity and then swung as hard as he could. Laughing, the efreeti went immaterial again and he missed, and the efreeti solidified in time to knock him to the ground with a blow to the temple. He knew the next blow would kill him, and he couldn't see well enough through the blood in his eyes to know which way to dodge to avoid it.

The blow didn't come. Momentarily disoriented, he wiped the blood from his eyes and looked up at the efreeti in time to see it solidify with one of the local women on its back. "Hit it now, while I've got it!" Trella screamed.

"This one, too!" Sella screamed from the back of the other. The Terrans paused, too surprised to move.

Petty Officer Sherkov and Mr. Jones were the first to recover, and both of them stabbed their efreet with their spears. Their weapons met no resistance going through the efreet, and they continued through into the women on their backs. Although there was no effect on the efreet, the women did not have the same immunity. "Magic...weapon..." Trella gasped with the spear through her stomach. Both Trella and the efreeti went immaterial, and the spear fell to the ground, but both solidified again almost immediately. "Must kill it with a magic weapon," she urged, "Hurry...can't...hold it...much longer."

The glow around Sergeant Andrew's kris seemed to intensify, with the glow spreading up her arm. Stepping forward, she drove it into the chest of the efreeti she was fighting. With a blast of steam like the whistle on a locomotive, the efreeti seem to lose focus and turned to mist, which lost its form and dissipated. Trella fell to the floor gasping.

Having seen the effect of the kris on the other efreeti, Vice Sergeant Al-Sabani knew that his weapon might be able to hurt the one he was fighting, as well. It went solid in front of him, and he drew his arm back to stab it, noticing a faint glow from the weapon. Before he could strike, the efreeti slashed him with its powerful claw across his face, knocking him to the ground. His janbiya skittered off across the room. As the efreeti turned to attack Mr. Jones, suddenly the point of a sword burst through its side, as Father Zuhlsdorf stabbed it from the other side with Durandal. The sword glowed a cherry red as it passed through the efreeti. "This day will the Lord deliver thee into mine hand, and I will smite thee and take thine head from thee!" yelled Father Zuhlsdorf as he pulled the glowing sword back out of the creature.

Whatever relics were in the sword had the desired effect, and the efreeti emitted the same steam whistle noise that the first one had and disintegrated, leaving Sella to fall on the floor. Before they could see to the women, the soldiers were distracted by a telepathic, "*DIE!*" from where Steropes and Quetzalcoatl were still fighting. The soldiers looked over and could see that the fight wasn't going well for Steropes, as the coatl had him almost completely wrapped up in its coils and was constricting him about three feet above the ground.

"Let me help!" Calvin begged from five feet away, now holding Master Chief's spear.

"No," said Steropes, "still...got...this." He was obviously having problems breathing and, as Calvin watched, one of his ribs broke with an audible snap. Steropes cried out and, with a jerk, was able to get his right arm free from the coil. He reached toward his boot but, seeing the movement, Quetzalcoatl struck quickly, biting him hard on the hand.

Steropes pulled his hand free, and Quetzalcoatl's teeth tore huge chunks out of it. Blood began dripping heavily from it. With another quick movement, Quetzalcoatl leaned over further and pulled something from Steropes' boot with his mouth. "*Is this what you wanted?*" it asked, holding up a throwing dagger in its mouth. "*How pathetic and predictable. Hundreds of years later, and you still have a knife hidden in your boot. Now you will die with your own knife!*" Quetzalcoatl tried to drive it through Steropes' chest, but the rubber knife only bent on contact.

"You're the predictable one," Steropes said, driving the real knife that he had kept hidden in his sleeve deep into the side of Quetzalcoatl's body near its wings. "That one was just to keep you occupied!"

Gravely wounded, Quetzalcoatl dropped Steropes to the floor and flew off toward the door to the left of the dais, the knife still embedded in its side. "You can...help now," Steropes wheezed, gasping for air.

"With pleasure," Calvin replied, throwing the spear with all his might. Quetzalcoatl stopped at the door to wrap its tail around the handle. Before Quetzalcoatl could open it, the spear hit it in the neck just behind its head, severing its spine. It fell to the floor, dead.

As Quetzalcoatl's tail fell off the door handle, it seemed to move of its own accord. The Terrans readied their weapons to repel an attack from the outside. The door opened, and Night burst in, followed by the Ground Force, weapons at the ready. "Did someone call for retrieval?" he asked.

Night nearly tripped over the body in front of him, and he looked down to see Quetzalcoatl lying on the ground with a spear through it. He nudged the body with the toe of his boot. "Is it dead?" he asked.

"Yes," replied Father Zuhlsdorf, who had come over to check. "I guess their gods aren't gods, after all."

Night looked back up at the Space Force. Battered and bloody, most of them were barely able to stand. "Quickly," he said, "we've only got a few minutes. Give us your suits!"

Chapter Thirty-One

**In Front of the Great Pyramid of Cholula, Keppler-22 'b',
August 12, 2020**

The Ground Force troopers took possession of the suits and bounded back down to the shuttle. They quickly loaded them, and Top commed the WSO, Lieutenant Imagawa 'Samurai' Sadayo, *"All of the squad's 19 suits are aboard; cleared to take off."*

"Roger, that," Samurai replied. He looked at his pilot, Lieutenant Clarisse Boudreau. *"Let's go, Clarisse!"* he commed. *"We've only got a few minutes left!"*

The shuttle blasted off, carrying the death of the planet inside.

Watching it go, Top had a thought. *"Lieutenant Train, Top,"* he commed. *"How many suits did you say we were supposed to have aboard the shuttle?"*

"19," Night replied. *"Staff Sergeant Dantone went back to the Gulf. There's 17 left in the squad, plus Lieutenant Commander Hobbs and Steropes, so there should be 19 suits."*

"But what about Father Zuhlsdorf?" Top asked. *"Shouldn't there be a total of 20?"*

"Shit!" Night commed. *"Standby."*

Great Pyramid of Cholula, Keppler-22 'b', August 12, 2020

"The shuttle just took off with 19 suits aboard," Night said. "Shouldn't there be 20? Who's suit did we miss?"

"I don't know," Calvin replied. "Did you get all of the suits from the people that got separated?"

"I think so," Night answered. "There was one for every soldier, dead or alive."

"Shit!" Calvin said. "Applebaum. We forgot about Petty Officer Applebaum, who got killed on the beach. If you didn't come down and get them, his body and the suit are probably still on the beach."

Shuttle 01, Airborne on Keppler-22 'b', August 12, 2020

"There is a suit on the beach where the platoon first landed," Night commed. "We don't know if it was close enough for the EMP to affect it, but it may have been."

"Understood," Samurai replied. "We're on our way to get it."

"I heard," Clarisse said, "I'm headed there now. It's going to be close."

"We don't have a crewman in the back," Samurai said, unstrapping from his seat, "so I'll have to go out to get the suit. I'm heading to the back."

"Roger," the Canadian replied, "we'll be there in 20 seconds."

Samurai made it back to the cargo bay, and the loading ramp was already on its way down as the shuttle landed on the beach. He ran to the body and almost threw up. They had told him the soldier was dead; they hadn't told him that most of the front of him had been eaten away. What was left was now crawling with some kind of local parasite that found Earth men appetizing. With no other place to grab him, he took the corpse by the ankles and began dragging him toward the shuttle. The soft sand was a cardiovascular nightmare, especially in the hot sun. Even though his suit's air conditioner was running at full, it wasn't enough to cool him.

He didn't know how he did it, but finally his feet hit metal as he made it to the ramp of the shuttle. He pulled the corpse onto the ramp and then hit the button to close it. "I'm in," he commed, "Go! Go! Go!"

He flipped the corpse over so that he could see the battery pack. Three minutes remaining. They were screwed. "Master Sergeant Smith," he commed as he ran toward the cockpit, "could you please pass on a message for me?"

In Front of the Great Pyramid of Cholula, Keppler-22 'b', August 12, 2020

"Did they get the suit?" Calvin asked as he made his way down the front of the pyramid with the rest of the Space Force. The Ground Force members were helping the Space Force make it down, most of whom were bloody and next to dead.

"Yeah, they did," Night replied. "They're on their way to space. Samurai just commed and said that there won't be time to dump the suits, so they're going to eject instead. We'll have to pick them up on our way to the *Gulf*."

"Good plan," Calvin said.

"Samurai?" asked Top, who had Master Chief's arm over his shoulder as he helped him down the front of the pyramid. "Is that Lieutenant Imagawa?"

"Yeah, that's his callsign," Calvin replied. "Why?"

"He had a message for you," Top answered. "He said to tell you, and I quote, 'Today's the day.' He said you'd know what that meant."

Calvin's face went white. "Comm him now," he ordered. "Tell him I said 'No!'"

"What's going on?" Night asked.

"He told me one time that it was his destiny to die in the squadron," Calvin replied. "I jokingly told him to let me know when that day was, so I could make sure I wasn't on the flight schedule with him. He's planning on killing himself."

Shuttle 01, Vicinity of Keppler-22 'b', August 12, 2020

"One minute to detonation," Samurai said as they reached the black of space. "We don't have time to get rid of the suits. We'll have to eject."

"Got it," Lieutenant Boudreau replied, trying not to hyperventilate. No one had ever ejected out of a shuttle before. No humans, anyway. She was not looking forward to being the first, nor to waiting in the depths of space for the other shuttle to come and, hopefully, find her. "Ensure the ejection selector is in Command Eject," she added. Command Eject was used to make sure that all of the crew ejected, regardless of who initiated the ejection process.

"It is in Command Eject," Samurai agreed, pushing the selector to 'Individual Eject.'

"I just hope that the shuttle continues in this direction," Clarisse noted. No one knew what the ejection forces would do to the shuttle's trajectory, and the Vella Gulf was close, almost too close.

"I'm sure it will," Samurai said. "30 seconds to detonation...stand by...Eject! Eject! Eject!"

Lieutenant Boudreau grabbed the ejection handles and pulled. There was a roar and a flash of rocket fire, and then her seat was gone. As he had worried would happen, the force of the ejection caused the shuttle to skew back toward the Vella Gulf. Samurai calmly reached over to take the stick and pointed the nose of the shuttle back away from the ship.

The rocket fire of Clarisse's seat was quite beautiful, Samurai thought, well worthy of a haiku. "A blossom of flame," he started. The shuttle detonated.

Chapter Thirty-Two

In Front of the Great Pyramid of Cholula, Keppler-22 'b',
August 12, 2020

"I'm sorry sir," Top said, as they reached the bottom of the pyramid. "The *Vella Gulf* just commed to say that the shuttle blew up. The duty officer said that it didn't look like Lieutenant Imagawa ejected prior to the explosion."

"Dammit," Calvin said, sitting down hard on the bottom step of the pyramid. "He was a good man."

"Sorry, sir," Night added. "I know you two flew together a lot."

"Yeah, we did," Calvin agreed. He let his head fall forward onto his arms, crossed over his knees, lost in grief.

"C'mon, sir," Night said, taking one of Calvin's arms. "Let's get the hell off this rock...*What the fuck?*"

Calvin's head snapped up to see the shuttle lifting off from the courtyard in a giant cloud of dust. What? Why was the shuttle leaving without them? As the craft accelerated upward, the dust cleared to reveal the reason for its hasty departure—a group of seven dino-bears in an arrowhead formation passed through where it had been only seconds before. The lead dino-bear paused to bellow a trumpeting roar at the shuttle as it climbed out of its reach, before looking back to the Terrans that were still in the courtyard. As the beasts turned to reorient on the platoon members, Calvin was shocked to see that each of the creatures had a small brown figure on its back, holding reins that led to the beasts' noses. *The Mayans were riding them!*

"*What the* hell *is that?*" someone commed.

"*Fire!*" Night commed to the suited members of the Ground Force, most of whom were watching the creatures in stunned disbelief. They hadn't seen the one on the beach earlier and couldn't believe how fast the dino-bears could move.

The troops began firing at the giant creatures and scattering to get away from their charge. As Night began firing, he saw that one of the new soldiers from Epsilon Eridani, Corporal Madek Shokal, wasn't going to escape the charge. Overwhelmed by the size of the monsters, he hadn't even moved. He stood there watching as they charged, his rifle at his side, too scared to move.

Seeing his trooper frozen, Night fired repeatedly at the dino-bear in the lead, hitting it several times in the chest. The little holes that he poked into the beast were not enough to bring down the 17-feet tall behemoth, although it roared in pain at the continued stings. Several other soldiers, seeing the monster bearing down on Corporal Shokal, began firing at it as well, and it was hit seven or eight times as it closed on the Eridianian. It wasn't enough, and the dino-bear reached down to grab Corporal Shokal, who screamed over the implant network as the 9-inch talons pierced his suit and skewered him. The dino-bear lifted him from the ground, eliciting another round of screams from the soldier. Unlike a dinosaur, the monster's head was shaped more like a bear's, and it didn't have as large a mouth as a comparable-sized tyrannosaurus rex would have had. That meant that instead of eating the soldier whole, the creature was only able to get about the top third of the soldier into its mouth for the first bite. The screams ceased suddenly as the soldier was torn in half.

Chewing what it had in its mouth, the dino-bear stopped and stood upright. Night took aim and shot it in the right eye twice; the second shot pierced the ocular cavity and continued into its brain, killing it. It fell backward in slow motion, squashing the Mayan warrior on its back.

As Night looked up he could see the soldiers of the Ground Force firing at the rest of the dino-bears throughout the courtyard. They had taken cover as best they could on the pyramids and were having success. In addition to the one that Night had killed, two others were down, and one of the others had lost its rider. That one continued to snap its jaws at the pain it was feeling, but didn't seem to understand what was hurting it. It opened its mouth to roar its pain to the heavens, and a lucky shot went through the roof of its mouth into its brain, putting it out of its misery.

Night heard Calvin yell, "Incoming from the left," as he dropped his spear and began running up the steps. Night turned to see another of the monsters racing toward him and his defenseless commanding officer. Based on the amount of damage the first one had taken to kill, Night knew there was no way he could stop it prior to the creature reaching them. He only had a second to think and decided the best defense was a good offense. Throwing down his rifle, he ran toward the dino-bear.

The dino-bear drew up in surprise. It had never had anything attack it; everything always ran *away* from it. That gave Night the moment he needed, and he rolled through the dino-bear's legs, drawing one of his knives as he rolled. The creature reached down to try to grab him, but was too late. Night came out of the roll standing up behind its right leg and slashed down on the tendon going to the creature's right foot. Hobbled, the dino-bear screamed and tried to use its tail and good leg to turn itself around. Night avoided the swipe of its tail and severed the tendon going to the beast's left foot.

The creature screamed in pain and frustration, and Night used the time to hack at the dino-bear's tail, cutting through the bone and severing part of its tail. Deprived of its ability to balance, the dino-bear fell backward to its left.

Just before it hit, the Mayan riding it jumped off, landing in a roll. Incredibly agile, the soldier stood up before Night could get to him, drawing two of the native weapons called macuahuitls. Looking at them, Night saw that they were unlike anything he had ever seen. Neither a sword nor a club, the weapons looked like batons that were about three feet long and about three inches in diameter. As the warrior began weaving the weapons in a defensive pattern, Night could see that the clubs had a row of obsidian blades imbedded down the side, giving it a serrated cutting edge that would make a bloody mess out of anything that it hit.

Realizing that his Green Beret knife was out-classed by the warrior's weapons, Night drew his pistol, intending to shoot him. Unfortunately, the pistol hadn't survived Night's roll between the dino-bear's legs. As he pulled it out, he watched in dismay as the barrel fell off.

The Mayan warrior smiled and yelled a battle cry as he leaped forward, the weapon in his right hand already descending.

Across from the Great Pyramid of Cholula, Keppler-22 'b', August 12, 2020

Top continued firing into the head of the dino-bear as it staggered and started to fall. He had gathered three of the Ground Force soldiers to his side, and they were systematically working to take down the dino-bears. Having 'Tiny'

Johnson alongside him with his .95 caliber rifle helped. The lasers were good for poking little holes into the creatures, but they did more to infuriate the creatures than they did to kill them, barring a lucky shot or multiple hits into the creatures' heads. The rifle had the power to rip bigger chunks from the monsters than the lasers, and to penetrate their skulls...sometimes.

As the soldiers started to fire at the last dino-bear still standing, they were startled by the sounds of wooden drums, conch shell trumpets, whistles and shouting from behind them. Looking over his shoulder, Top saw nearly 100 Mayan warriors charging toward them. The little brown men ran swiftly toward them, and Top had the transient thought that it looked like the attack of a costume party. The warriors' dress varied wildly, although all of them were colorful and well-decorated. Some of the warriors were even painted as large carnivores; Top saw at least two that looked like leopards and another that was dressed as a lion. Many of the warriors wore layers of bark or cloth as armor, and most of the Mayans had good luck charms of animal claws and predatory bird feathers. Some even wore full animal furs, hoping to invoke that animal's skills. Scattered throughout were brightly colored masks that depicted grotesque shapes and images. To see them running at full speed was...disconcerting...to someone used to a more modern battlefield.

In Front of the Great Pyramid of Cholula, Keppler-22 'b', August 12, 2020

Thinking quickly, Night threw the handle of his pistol into the face of the Mayan warrior. The warrior twitched backward to avoid it, causing him to miss with his macuahuitl as Night dove backward to his right. Seeing that the handle wasn't a threat, the warrior jumped forward, using his momentum to swing the weapon in his left hand.

Night continued to give ground as rolled upright, drawing his second knife as he stood. Holdovers from his early days as a Green Beret, the knives were just over 12 inches in length, with blades that were seven inches long. As he took a fighting stance, the warrior looked at his knives and snorted in derision. His weapons were two feet longer, giving him a significant reach advantage. He continued to advance on Night, swinging one of the macuahuitls, while holding the other one ready to swing if Night tried to close on him. The material on Night's left shoulder tore as one of the weapon's jagged blades caught it and ripped it open.

Night jumped back to the right, but his retreat was stopped suddenly as his back met the unyielding stones of the temple wall.

The warrior smiled, revealing teeth that had been sharpened into points. He had been driving Night backward toward the temple, knowing that it was only a matter of time until Night ran out of room.

Night swayed left and then right, trying to judge if he could dive out of the way and back into open ground. The warrior swayed with him, mimicking his every move and closing off any avenues for escape.

Knowing that his time was rapidly running out, Night elected on a gamble. He had seen how the warrior flinched back when he threw the pistol at him, and Night realized that the Mayan wasn't used to defending against thrown weapons. The Terran switched the grip on the knife in his left hand and threw it in a soft arc toward the warrior, the blade glinting in the sunlight as it spun end over end.

As Night had hoped, the Mayan was momentarily distracted by the flying knife and his eyes inadvertently looked up at it. Realizing it was a trick, he looked back down to see Night already in motion toward him. The warrior jumped back, swinging the weapon in his right hand at Night's head, but Night already had his momentum going and was inside of most of the blades. He intercepted the weapon with his left arm, and the two lowest blades pierced Night's upper arm, the sharpened obsidian cutting all the way to the bone. Turning with the blow, Night continued his lunge and drove his other knife in an uppercut through the warrior's throat and into his brain.

The Mayan warrior's eyes rolled up into his head and he fell backward, leaving the macuahuitl embedded in Night's arm.

Across from the Great Pyramid of Cholula, Keppler-22 'b', August 12, 2020

Top considered the multi-colored wave of Mayan warriors and made his decision. "*All available soldiers to the south side of the courtyard!*" he commed. "*Incoming Mayan warriors!*" He turned and began firing at the small brown men. "*Tiny, finish off the last dino-bear; everyone else concentrate their fire on the Mayans!*"

The other two soldiers that were with him, Sergeant Zoromski and Sergeant Yaroslavsky, turned, and the three soldiers began killing the Mayan warriors as fast as their suits' reticles could settle on their next targets. As the warriors reached about 25 meters, the rear rank stopped and hurled spears with atlatls. The spear-throwing tools were wooden shafts with cups on the end that supported the butt of a spear. By using the length of the atlatl as a lever, it allowed the warriors to throw the spears with more energy, giving the throws higher speeds and a greater impact.

Seeing the spears descending on them, Top fired one more time and then dove to the left. Seeing him move, Sergeant Zoromski dove to the right. Sergeant Yaroslavsky was more focused on shooting as many of the warriors as he could. He methodically shot warrior after warrior as they came screaming at him, and he never saw the three spears that caught him in the chest. Accelerated to nearly 100 miles per hour by the atlatls, the obsidian blades pierced his suit and plunged through his chest. One of the blades went through his heart, and he fell, looking like an oversized pin cushion. Zoromski was luckier; only one of the spears hit him, slicing through his left leg and pinning him to the ground. Struggling to get up in time to meet the charge, Top saw that the rest of the Mayans were nearly on him, when their front ranks dissolved in a string of antimatter grenades. Looking up, he saw the Gordon brothers standing over him with their tridents leveled, walking explosives across the Mayan warriors.

As the remainder of the Mayans closed, the brothers discarded their tridents in favor of their pistols. Both men favored the 'two-gun salute' and drew pistols with both hands. Several other soldiers came up behind them and the firepower rapidly became more than the Mayans, unaccustomed to powered weapons, could face. They broke and ran back the way they came.

"*Hold your fire!*" Night ordered as he jogged up, blood running down his left arm. The officer could see that the warriors no longer posed a threat. "*We're here to kill snakes, not people.*" He looked behind him to see that the last of the dino-bears was dead. "*Top, let's get our dead and wounded together and get the hell out of here.*"

"*Sounds good, sir,*" Top replied. As he started to organize the remaining soldiers, the Master Sergeant had to stop and sigh. Now that the danger was past, the Gordon twins were arguing over who had killed the most dino-bears. Some things never change, he thought, shaking his head.

Chapter Thirty-Three

Shuttle 02, **Approaching the TSS** *Vella Gulf*, **Keppler-22 'b'**
Orbit, August 12, 2020

"We're here," said Night, gently shaking Calvin. The officer had fallen asleep on the way back to their ship, and Night had let him sleep. Without implants, he couldn't communicate until they got back, anyway, and Night could see that he was spent. His time had been spent getting his arm treated. The uneven edges of the macuahuitl had shredded his skin; stitching him up had been a challenge for their medic, Sergeant Ben Shabat. He had closed the wounds, but Night would have to spend some time with the medibot once they got back to the ship or he would have a nasty scar for the rest of his life.

"Who did we end up losing?" Calvin asked, coming awake.

"I think you know that we lost Sergeant Yaroslavsky, Petty Officer Martin, Sergeant Tagliabue, Corporal Shokal and Corporal Applebaum. We also lost Corporal Carrasquillo, who got torn apart by one of the dino-bears. We also had quite a few wounded. Sergeant Zoromski took a spear through the leg; he'll be all right. Leading Seaman Borsheim has a couple of broken ribs, a punctured lung and took a bull horn through his gut. He was in bad shape, but we got him stabilized; he'll probably be all right. Jet Li has a broken leg but will be fine. Leading Seaman Abdul Wazir was poisoned; his status is still to be determined."

"What happened to Staff Sergeant Dantone?" asked Calvin. "Did he make it?"

"I don't know," replied Night. "He was going into surgery when we left."

Sick Bay, TSS *Vella Gulf,* Keppler-22 'b' Orbit, August 12, 2020

Calvin and Night walked into the sick bay. They needed to report to the ship's commanding officer, but wanted to get an update on Staff Sergeant Dantone before going to see her. As they entered the facility, they were met by both the ship's medical officer and the ship's medibot, who had come to an uneasy truce over who actually 'owned' the sick bay.

"How is Staff Sergeant Dantone?" Calvin asked the pair.

"Umm.." the medical officer said, looking embarrassed.

"Is he dead?" demanded Night.

"Well...um...not technically..." the medical officer replied.

"What he is trying to say," answered the medibot, "is that Staff Sergeant Dantone's body was non-functional when it arrived here. Not only was it damaged beyond repair, parts of it had been subjected to a toxin which broke down the flesh to make it easier for the beast that had attacked him to consume. Had he not triggered all of his nanobots, as well as nearly all of the chemicals in his pharmacopeia, it is unlikely that he would have survived the trip back here."

The medibot paused. When it saw that the medical officer wasn't going to say anything, it continued, "With his body non-functional and only a limited amount of time before his brain ceased operating,

I did the only thing that I could. I pulled out the Mark XXII shell we had in storage and encased him in it."

"What the hell does that mean?" asked Night.

Calvin sighed. "It means that Staff Sergeant Dantone is now a cyborg," he said.

CO's Conference Room, TSS *Vella Gulf,* Keppler-22 'b' Orbit, August 14, 2020

"I've read your report, and there are several things that I don't understand," said Captain Griffin two days later. "In fact, I don't think that anyone reading the report is going to understand a lot of it, which is why I asked you to come discuss it in person." The conference room was filled to overflowing with the ship's officers, the ambassador and her staff, most of the squadron's chain of command and nearly all of the platoon members that weren't in sick bay.

Calvin smiled. "I figured that was why you set up this meeting, which is why I asked all of the platoon members to attend, as well," he replied. "I think there are many aspects of this mission that are going to defy understanding...and belief... unless you are willing to change the way you think significantly. All of us that went into the pyramid certainly had to reevaluate everything we ever thought we knew."

"OK," said Captain Griffin, "I understand most of the early part of the mission, from the landing to the fight with the starfish things. I even understand first contact with the Aquants who, if I read this correctly, look like...mermaids?"

"Yes, ma'am," answered Calvin. "The ones we saw were mermen, and they have some sort of telepathic bond with at least some of the ocean creatures."

"We'll have to get the ambassador fitted out with a better suit so that she can go down and meet with them," noted the commanding officer. She paused and then sighed. "What I don't understand is all of this talk about..." she paused and then finally said it, "jinn," as if talking about them made her as crazy as the team that had gone down to the planet's surface.

"I have to tell you, Skipper," replied Calvin, "if I hadn't been there to see them with my own eyes, I wouldn't have believed it either. That is why I asked Vice Sergeant Al-Sabani to join us. He is our expert on them." He nodded to Al-Sabani, who was just out of sick bay. Although the slash marks that extended across his face would eventually go away, he was lucky to still have vision in both of his eyes.

"We know that they exist because the Prophet tells us so," said Al-Sabani, his voice full of certainty. "They are one of the three sapient creations of God, along with humans and angels. Like people, they have free will, so they can be good or bad."

"Your religion tells you about these things?" asked Captain Griffin.

Al-Sabani nodded. "I am especially acquainted with jinn, because I have had a qarin since I was five years old. This is a special jinni that is assigned to a person. It is much like the guardian angel that Christendom believes in, but it is really a jinni."

"Is there a difference?" asked Captain Griffin.

"Oh, yes," answered Al-Sabani. "Angels obey the will of Allah in all things, but jinn have free will. As such, there are both good and bad qarin." He smiled. "Mine is a good one."

"So, if I understand this report," said Captain Griffin, "there are many different types of jinn, and they can also be either good or bad, although some types are almost always bad."

"Yes," said Al-Sabani. "For example, ghuls and hinn jinn are almost always bad. They mainly stay in cemeteries and feast on the dead."

"And these things really exist?" asked the commanding officer, still not sure she believed.

"*Yes!*" answered all of the soldiers that had seen and fought them.

"And what about these women that helped you kill the fire-based ones...the efreet?" asked Captain Griffin.

"They did help us," replied Calvin, "but we don't think they were really women."

Captain Griffin's eyebrows knitted. "If they weren't women," she asked, "what were they?"

"After talking with the people that are most familiar with jinn," Calvin answered, "we think that they were actually sila jinn. These jinn are very talented shape-shifters who can turn into anything they want, but most often appear as human females. They are very rarely seen, but are more tolerant of human society than most other types of jinn. They are also extremely intelligent and generally do not try to harm or trick humans. Sila are, however, very fond of meddling in an attempt to help." He paused, looking for agreement from Al-Sabani, Leading Seaman Abdul Wazir and Master Chief O'Leary. All three nodded.

"We think, although we can't prove, that they helped us in order to overthrow the coatls," Calvin continued. "That would also explain some other things, such as why Master Chief and I allowed unarmed women to follow us through the pyramid. They charmed us." He paused and then finished, "It also explains how they disappeared right after the fight in the temple room."

"It is also not that big of a jump from 'sila' to 'Sella,'" added Al-Sabani. "They don't usually give their real names, because knowing someone's name gives you power over them."

"Bravo," said Sella, clapping her hands as Sella and Trella materialized on top of the conference table, dressed in Middle Eastern silks. They were both sitting in the middle of the table in the lotus position, looking at Calvin. "For an unbeliever, you did very well figuring that out."

"Thank you," said Calvin. "When nothing makes sense, the least unlikely possibility is the one to go with. The only thing that made everything work out was that you were also jinn." He paused and then continued, "Thank you very much for your help, by the way. We could not have done it without you."

"You are welcome," said Trella. "You might have been able to vanquish them on your own, although we decided it was unlikely. You only had three weapons that could hurt the efreet and no way to make them stay corporeal. More importantly, we listened to you and knew that, had we not intervened, the suits would have detonated and destroyed much of the planet." She looked at her 'sister.' "We think that *we* would have survived the explosion, but weren't sure. Helping you was the only way to save the planet and make sure that we did."

"We thank you for your assistance," said the ambassador, who hadn't understood or believed anything until they materialized. "We would like to open up relations between our civilization and yours."

"Thank you," said Sella, "but we believe in privacy more than anything else. We helped you this time, but we are not interested in formal relations between our society and yours." She looked at Calvin and said, "I did, however, find that touching your mind was...pleasant. If you ever need my help, please come back to the town on the planet below and call my name." She vanished.

"You're cute, too," said Trella to Master Chief O'Leary. She blew him a kiss and also vanished.

Calvin smiled at Captain Griffin. "Any other questions?" he asked.

Chapter Thirty-Four

The shuttle landed on the beach where it had first touched down just a few days before. To Calvin, it seemed like it was a lifetime ago. Failing to enlist the aid of the sila jinn, the ambassador had wanted to establish relations with the Aquants at least, and the only way that Calvin knew to find them again was to land back at the same place they had met previously, as he had told Dolph he would. He wasn't willing to risk the ambassador's life with the native starfish, though, so the remaining members of both platoons exited the shuttle, and the ambassador waited safely inside. Although a few of the soldiers watched the tree line for the giant bear creatures, most of the troops faced the water and watched for the hostile sea creatures.

Calvin looked over to where the carcass had rested as bait, but it was gone. The beach was clean, clear and as pristine as any beach he had ever seen. The waves lapped gently, calling for him to go in for a dip. He knew what waited for those that ventured out into the water, however.

It was a hot day, and it wasn't long before the environmental systems in the suits were straining to keep up. Happily, they didn't have long to wait.

"I've got shark fins in the water," reported Mr. Jones. "It looks like they're approaching. 11:00 from straight out and about 1/4 of a mile."

Calvin looked in the direction Mr. Jones had indicated and saw the fins. There were a *lot* of them, including several that were enormous. "Yeah," he said, "that looks like them."

He called the ambassador, and she walked with the soldiers down to the water. The fins stopped a couple hundred yards offshore, and they were soon greeted by the Aquants, led by Dolph and King Barra. Introductions were made all around. Before they could move on to anything of substance, Calvin got a call.

"*Lieutenant Commander Hobbs!*" commed Sergeant Gordhain MacKenzie. "*I've got beasties incoming! It looks like several of your bear riders approaching down the path.*"

"*I see them,*" said Master Chief, hurrying over to take charge of the defense. "*Form up in a firing line,*" he said. "*If they charge, let them have it. They are tough to bring down, so don't hold anything back. If you get a shot at the riders on their backs, take them out. The animals are less focused without their riders.*"

The warning wasn't needed, as the riders slowed to a walk at about 200 yards and then stopped 100 yards away from the troops. There were four of the giant creatures. Their riders dismounted, and one of the riders took the reins of the creatures and waited while the other three advanced.

The Nahuatl approached the soldiers, who still had their weapons leveled at them. "At ease," said Calvin, walking up. "I don't think they mean to attack us."

In confirmation of this, the men all stopped and held out their hands to show that they were empty. Calvin was fairly sure that he recognized at least one of the men from the group that Steropes had disarmed in the temple. Once he made that connection, he noticed one of the others had a large bruise on his throat, also courtesy of Steropes.

"Hi," said Calvin. "Can we help you?"

"You killed our gods," said the leader. "So you must be gods, yourselves. As you have obviously taken their place, how do you want us to worship you?"

Shuttle 02, Keppler-22 'b', August 15, 2020

C alvin looked over and saw the ambassador smiling as the shuttle lifted six hours later. Although he hadn't been privy to all of the discussions, she must have gotten everything that she wanted. Part of that had included his leaving four troops on the planet. "So everything went well?" He asked.

"Yes," she replied, "very well. The Nahuatl have agreed to open trade back up with the Aquants and to stop the practice of human sacrifice. The Aquants are very happy with our assistance in the matter and are going to make up lists of all of the things their civilization can produce. I am going to leave one of my junior diplomats here to continue to work out relations between the two civilizations, as well as to find out what types of things they might be able to provide us that will help our war effort."

She smiled. "The way both civilizations see it," she continued, "they owe us a number of favors, which is exactly what I wanted."

Calvin hoped that they had something worthwhile on the planet. In addition to the combat losses he had already sustained, he was now being forced to leave Sergeant Fleischer, Sergeant Ben Shabat, Havildar Dawood Noorzai and Corporal Laveg Mackef behind to provide security for the diplomat. If this kept up much longer, it would just be he and Night on the front line.

Chapter Thirty-Five

Bridge, TSS *Vella Gulf*, Gliese 221 System, August 21, 2020

"There are three planets that orbit Gliese 221," said Steropes, looking at the orange-red dwarf star on the view screen, "but none of them are livable. The only planet in the habitable zone is a Saturn-like gas giant. There are no other stargates into the system and no signs of life on any of the planets." After they departed Keppler-22, the Terrans had gone through the other unknown stargate in the WASP-18 system to find Gliese 221 devoid of habitation. At least it gave his men time to heal, Calvin thought.

"Thanks," said the CO. She turned to the front of the bridge. "Helmsman, let's head for the stargate. We're done here!"

Bridge, TSS *Vella Gulf*, Ross 248 System, August 24, 2020

"System entry," announced Sara.

Before she could say anything, the defensive systems officer jumped up from his console. "Sir!" he called, "I've got signs of a battle going on. There are already a number of destroyed ships in the vicinity of the star!"

"Correction," Steropes disagreed, looking over Sara's shoulder. "While I agree that there was a battle in this system, it occurred 200 million miles from here. What the sensor operator is seeing actually happened 18 minutes ago. Whether that battle is still ongoing remains to be determined." He looked back at the screen and then added, "Captain Griffin! One of the ships is a Mrowry vessel!"

"Is that good or bad?" asked the CO. "And in a related question, when are we going to get all of the galactic information downloaded to our implants so that I don't have to ask this all of the time?"

"The Mrowry are felinoids," answered Steropes, "and one of the founding civilizations of the Alliance of Civilizations. They are one of the most honor-bound of any of the races in the galaxy."

"Got it," replied Griffin, "they're some of the good guys."

"Do you want me to hail the Mrowry vessel?" asked the communications officer. As they had just entered the system, the Mrowry wouldn't be aware of their presence for another 18 minutes, the time that it would take for their appearance to cross the system to the ship at the speed of light.

"Yes," the CO ordered. "Put it on screen."

The main view screen lit up with the face of a Bengal tiger, although it was a Bengal tiger that was predominantly black with small stripes of red. The helmsman and the engineer both flinched back unconsciously from the giant image of the predator in front of them. The other Mrowry that could be seen in the background had more red in their coloring. Long-time members of the alliance, the *Vella Gulf's* computer was more than up to the task of translating for them.

The Mrowry took a second to look around the bridge. "Who are you?" it asked. "We do not recognize you." His gaze stopped on Steropes. "*You*, we recognize," he added, his voice full of menace. "It is because of you that we are in this situation." He looked back to Captain Griffin, seated in the commanding officer's chair. "We can discuss why you are with *him* at another time, but if you are a member of an honorable race, we request your assistance."

"I am Captain Lorena Griffin of the Terran Spaceship *Vella Gulf*," stated the CO. "If we can be of assistance, we certainly will. What aid do you require?"

"I am Captain Yerrow of the Mrowry cruiser *Emperor's Paw*. We were transiting the system next to this one as part of a battle group when we were attacked by a Ssselipsssiss force that came out of the stargate," replied the Mrowry officer. It didn't appear that feline mouths were made for lizard words, and the officer had a hard time pronouncing the name of the other race, but Griffin was able to figure it out.

"We have had our own dealings with the lizards," replied the CO. "They destroyed one of our fighters without provocation or warning. We will assist you however we can."

"My ship provided a delaying action while our main force escaped through the stargate," said the Mrowry, "but they were pursued by another lizard force. We fought the lizard battlecruiser that is near us to a standstill with our fighters, but the fighters have now all been destroyed. Both of our ships are shells that are operating only on emergency power. Additionally, we've both been captured by the star's gravitational field, and we are being drawn in. We could probably get our ship fixed in time to avoid being pulled into the star, but the lizards have sent several shuttle loads of troops over, and we are being forced to fight them, rather than see to our repairs. Anything you could do to help us fix our ship, fight off the lizards, or keep any more from shuttling over would be helpful. The sooner, the better."

"We're on our way," said Captain Griffin. "We'll call with details momentarily. Screen off!" Her eyes traveled down from the screen to the helmsman. "Helm, set a course for their ship, max speed." She turned to look at Calvin. "Recommendations?" she asked.

"We still have fighters on standby," replied Calvin. "We could launch some of them now at max speed, and they'd get there a lot faster than the *Gulf*. They could intercept the battlecruiser and prevent any more shuttles from going over. We just need to make sure they stay outside of the ship's self-destruct range."

"Good idea," noted the CO, remembering how they had lost two fighters on the previous cruise when a Ssselipsssiss commanding officer had blown up his ship to avoid being captured.

"Once we get within range," continued Calvin, "I would recommend blowing up the lizard ship. You can give them a chance to surrender, but we really don't want them to know we exist, and they're probably going to self-destruct again, anyway. We can launch fighter strikes on it whenever you'd like, or you can destroy it with the *Gulf*. On second thought, we probably want to blow it up, regardless, rather than risk them getting a lucky shot off that destroys our one remaining shuttle."

"Good point," said the CO. "What are you going to be doing?"

"I'm going to be getting the platoon ready for combat," replied Calvin. "As soon as we are ready, we're going to launch so that we can get there to help as soon as possible. The shuttle may only have 25 G more acceleration than the *Gulf*, but that extra little bit might make a difference."

"I think that's a good plan," said the CO after a little consideration. "Ops, launch two Asps and send them to shoot down any shuttles that the lizards try to send over to the Mrowry ship."

"Aye aye, skipper," the operations officer replied.

The CO turned back to Calvin. "Why are you still here?" she asked.

Chapter Thirty-Six

Asp 01, Ross 248 System, August 24, 2020

"*V*ella Gulf, *this is* Asp 01," radioed Supidi. "*The lizards are launching their shuttles. Request permission to fire.*"

"*Permission granted*, 01," replied the *Vella Gulf*. "*You are cleared to destroy the shuttles.*"

The WSO looked across the cockpit at his pilot. As one of the most senior crews, they had been the first to transition from the Vipers to the Asps. "*It's obvious that they don't know we are here,*" he commed. "*It's overkill to use a ship-killer missile on them, but it is better to do it now then wait for them to get close to the Mrowry ship.*" He fine-tuned the targeting information on his display. "*Both targets are designated,*" he said. Supidi moved the arming switch to 'on.' "*Weapons are armed; you are cleared to fire.*"

"*Yeah, their sensors must be out,*" agreed Guns. "*Sucks to be them...but not for much longer. I still owe them for the last time out.*" They had flown past the lizard battlecruiser, and it was holed in many places where missiles had hit it. He had stopped counting at six; the number of laser and graser holes were beyond counting. It was so badly shot up that most of the spaces that were open to vacuum weren't venting any more. Everyone must be in suits...or dead. The key hole was where engineering used to be. Whatever had hit it there must have caused the motor to overload. There wasn't much left of the aft end of the ship. Hitting it with a couple more anti-ship missiles would just be putting it out of its misery.

Obviously, some of the lizards still had some fight left in them, though, as the two shuttles finished turning and began accelerating toward the Mrowry ship. "*Fox One at the lead shuttle,*" Guns commed, thought-clicking the button that launched the weapon. "*Fox One at the trail shuttle,*" he added, launching a second missile.

The shuttles had no idea that they were even under fire as the missiles streaked toward them. The Terran missiles were equipped with a variety of electronic counter-measures to help them defeat jamming and decoys; none were needed in this case. The missiles tracked in on the shuttles, and twin 215 megaton blasts ensued, completely destroying both shuttles.

"*I know it had to be done,*" commented Supidi as he watched the balls of expanding plasma, "*but there was little honor in it.*"

Shuttle 02, Ross 248 System, August 24, 2020

"Five minutes to touchdown," commed the weapon systems officer, Lieutenant Faith Ibori. "*We will be docking at the aft end of the ship. The Mrowry will meet us at the entryway and get you pointed in the right direction.*"

"*Copy that,*" replied Calvin. "*Hey, Faith, are you in communication with the Mrowry ship at the moment?*"

"*I spoke to them earlier,*" replied the WSO. "*Do you need something? I can call them back.*"

"*Yeah,*" answered Calvin. "*We'll be packed like sardines if we all go in the same place. Call them back and tell them that the boarding force recommends dropping off one squad where they previously indicated and the other squad at the front of the ship. We can then meet in the middle and trap the lizards between us. Also, let them know that we have two lizards in our force, but they are a different species and will be wearing our suits."*

"*Stand by,*" said Faith, "*I'll give them a call.*"

"*That's a better idea,*" said Night. "*Do you want the front or the back?*"

"*I'll take the back,*" replied Calvin. "*You have more experience with busting into places. Why don't you take the Space Force to the front after dropping off the Ground Force with me at the back?*"

"*Works for me, sir,*" replied Night.

"*Hey, I've got a question,*" said Master Chief Ryan O'Leary. "*Did we ever find out if our new lasers would penetrate the hull of a ship?*"

"*Umm...*" Calvin thought about it. "*I passed your question up the chain of command. The special projects people were supposed to do some tests to find out, but I'm not sure if they ever did.*"

"*Great,*" replied Master Chief, "*so we don't know if we're going to put holes in the side of our new friends' ship every time we fire?*"

"*I can't imagine they're strong enough to go through in a single shot,*" said Calvin. "*Probably not even in two shots. They'd probably go through a bulkhead in a couple of shots, but the main hull? No, I think we're OK. The big shipborne lasers don't always go through in one shot. I think we're OK to fire the lasers at will. If you find yourself damaging the ship too much, dial it back a little. We don't know what kind of armor the lizards will have, either.*"

"*Two minutes,*" Faith commed. "*The Mrowry said to do as you see best. There won't be anyone to meet you at the front of the ship, but there are airlocks that you can use. The ship's commanding officer said to let you know that the lizards are holding the front of the ship.*"

"*That's just the way I like it,*" replied Night. "*A target rich environment. Space Force, let's get some!*"

"*Gluck ab!*" the troopers chorused in the platoon's battle cry.

There was a bump as the shuttle's pilot, Lieutenant Steven 'Not Me' Jackson brought the shuttle into contact with the ship. "*Sorry 'bout the bump,*" he commed, "*All of the automatic systems are out, and I had to do it the old fashioned way.*"

"*Ground Force, let's go!*" yelled Master Sergeant Aaron 'Top' Smith. "*What are you waiting for, an engraved invitation?*"

The Ground Force stood up behind Calvin, ready to go out the door.

Calvin watched as the shuttle crewman attached the docking collar to the ship. Through the boarding tube, Calvin could see several of the Mrowry waiting in a large open area. They were all about six feet tall and had some sort of combat suit on, but had their helmets off. As he looked at the felinoids, he realized that he was going to be the person that made first contact with an advanced race. Again.

Any excitement at that thought was dashed as he entered the Mrowry ship, and all six of the felinoids leveled their rifles at him. He slowly put his hands in the air and said, "Is this how you always greet people that you request assistance from?"

"When we don't know them, and they might be trying to take advantage of us," answered one of the Mrowry, "yes." He looked Calvin up and down. "Unfortunately, we have learned the hard way recently that no one can be trusted in these times."

"*What's going on?*" asked Night from behind him.

"*I'm not sure,*" Calvin replied. "*Stand by.*" To the Mrowry he said, "Well, you invited us here, and we came like you asked. If you don't want us here, we will leave."

"The timing of your arrival is suspect," one of the other Mrowry noted, "just in time to finish us off. How do we know that you are not in league with the lizards?"

"Aside from the fact that we just blew up two of their shuttles?" asked Calvin. "I don't know, but I'd be happy to show you if you'd just get out of our way. They killed a lot of my men on our last voyage, and I would like to return the favor." Calvin shrugged, emphasizing it so that it could be seen with the suit on. "Or we can leave. Your choice."

The Mrowry who had initially spoken brought his rifle back into a carrying position. "I truly hope you are here to help," he said, "because we need it. We are doomed without your assistance. Thank you for coming." At some unspoken signal, all of the rest of the troops brought their rifles back to a carry position as well.

Calvin came the rest of the way into the bay and motioned the rest of the squad to enter. "*We're good, Night*," he commed, "*go get 'em. We'll meet you in the middle.*" He took off his helmet and said to the one that seemed to be in charge, "I'm Lieutenant Commander Shawn Hobbs from the Terran Spaceship *Vella Gulf*. How can we help?"

"I am Lieutenant Rrower," the Mrowry said. "I am in charge of our security forces. The problem that we have is that we had so many casualties in the space battle with the lizards that we've had to use some of our engineers as soldiers to fight the lizards that boarded us. We don't have enough people to both hold off the lizards and fix the engines at the same time. Using everyone that is able-bodied, we have just enough men and women to stalemate the lizards that made it onto the ship. If we pull anyone back, they start advancing again. We've got to get the motors fixed or we are going to be drawn into the star. If you can take over for some of the engineers that are currently on the front line of the battle, that will let them go back to fixing the damage the lizards caused."

"No problem," replied Calvin. "Just take us to where we need to go. If you can give us schematics of the ship, that would help us as well. My other squad is going to go to the front of the ship and hit them from behind."

"Just a second," Lieutenant Rrower said. His eyes went unfocused for a few seconds as he communicated with someone. He refocused on Calvin and asked, "Did you hear that?"

"No," replied Calvin. "Whatever was said, I missed it."

"No offense, but can I take it from the age of your ship that your implants are similarly outdated?" asked the felinoid. "It never occurred to me to ask, but do you even have implants?"

"We do have implants," answered Calvin, "but honestly, I don't have any idea where they are in relation to galactic standards. I know that the Psiclopes were getting some types of tech upgrades for a period, but I don't know if that applied to implant technology." Calvin noticed that the Mrowry made a face when the Psiclopes were mentioned, but wasn't familiar enough with the felinoids to know what it meant.

"I am going to have my computer try to contact you via implant," said Rrower.

A communications window opened in Calvin's mind, displaying a cartoonish picture of a tiger's paw. In the middle of the paw was a mouth that moved in time with the transmission. "*Lieutenant Commander Hobbs,*" said the paw, "*this is the artificial intelligence for the* Emperor's Paw. *I have spoken with the AI onboard your* Vella Gulf *and believe this to be the right communications protocol. Are you receiving and understanding me?*"

"I am," replied Calvin, "*do you have some schematics for me?*"

"*I do*," answered the paw. It changed into the picture of a paw holding a roll of blueprints. "*You will understand, of course, if some of the more sensitive information is left off.*" The paw set the blueprints down and pretended to erase something from one of them.

"I *understand*," said Calvin with a smile at the AI's antics. "*As long as it shows the floor plans where we will be fighting, that is all that I am worried about. Will you be sending it to all of my soldiers or just me?*"

"*It will go to everyone,*" replied the AI.

"*Thanks,*" replied Calvin. Switching to the platoon network, he commed, "*Ship schematics inbound from the ship's AI. The ship is named the* Emperor's Paw, *and the AI uses that as its name.*"

"*Paw, Lieutenant Commander Hobbs,*" Calvin commed, "*can you mark friendly and enemy positions on the schematics, and keep it updated as the battle continues?*"

"*I will do what I can,*" replied the AI. "*To say that I have a lot that I'm currently managing is an understatement. I also sustained a lot of damage before the Ssselipsssiss came aboard, and they are systematically destroying my sensors as they move around.*"

"*Do what you can,*" replied Calvin, "*and we'll have them out of here in no time. By the way, please call me Calvin; everyone else does.*"

As the rest of the squad came onto the ship, the Mrowry all jumped back in surprise as Staff Sergeant Dantone stomped aboard. Although he was moving a little better, and his actions were a little more fluid, he did not look like something that you would want to trust in combat. "Sorry," said Rrower. "I didn't know that there were any civilizations that used robots for mobile combat."

"He is not a robot," replied Calvin. "He is a cyborg that hasn't quite finished the conversion process."

"How long...ummm...how long has it been since it was converted?" asked Rrower, obviously a little worried.

"You do realize that I'm standing in front of you and can hear you, right?" asked Staff Sergeant Dantone. "I am functional, and that's all that matters. Put me somewhere in a blocking position. I'll do my job."

"Good enough for you?" asked Calvin.

"Um...OK," replied Rrower, not sounding any more confident in the cyborg. He paused and then said, "On second thought, I know just the place for him."

"Good," said Calvin. He looked at Top. "Ready to go?"

"Yes, sir," Top replied. "Ready to kick some lizard ass!"

"I like your attitude," said Lieutenant Rrower. "I think we'll get along fine."

"Lead on," said Calvin.

Shuttle 02, Ross 248 System, August 24, 2020

"*Five seconds to docking,*" commed the WSO, Lieutenant Faith Ibori. "*The ship says to be ready for anything; its sensors are out in this section.*"

Night looked through the window as the shuttle crewman secured the docking collar. He quickly withdrew his head from the window. "*Squad, we just landed in Lizard Central. There are at least three lizards in the area outside of the entrance. I don't think they saw me. None of them appeared to have armor on. Hopefully, they are expecting the reinforcements that our fighters blew up and will think that we're them. We're going to get one chance to break in here; let's make it a good one.*"

"I'm going to go in first," continued Night. *"I'll go in low. Wraith, you go left. Master Chief, you go right. Everyone else pile in after the three of us. Check your targets; I don't want anyone shooting me in the back with the new lasers. Make sure all enemy combatants are dead, I don't want any of them playing dead and hitting us from behind."*

"Ready, sir," said the shuttle crewman at the docking collar. He moved out of the way. Night stood just outside the view of the door and asked, *"Ready?"*

A chorus of *"Gluck ab!"* answered his question, as well as several other, more profane, indications of eagerness. *"Here we go then. One...two...THREE!"* Night slammed the door open and dove through the three foot tube. As he started his dive through the door, the thought came to him that the ship's gravity might not be working due to the battle damage the ship had sustained. If so; he was going to go flying right past the lizards. Not good.

As he crashed to the floor in front of two of the seven feet tall lizards, he realized that the gravity was working, and also that the lizards seemed a lot bigger up close. Night didn't know anything about lizard expressions, but he had their looks pegged as 'confusion' as they looked down at the unexpected Terran soldier lying in their midst. The moment of indecision was all he needed. Before he had even come to rest, he had shot one of them through the head and was tracking to the other. It started to rear back in alarm but never completed the motion. Two blasts from his laser rifle killed it; the extra shot from Master Chief that hit it was overkill. Night quickly got up in time to see Wraith standing over a third lizard. She pointed the rifle at its head as it flipped around and fired once. It went still.

"*Look out, sub!*" commed Corporal Sanders. Night dove to the side, and Sanders fired three shots past him, killing a fourth lizard that had been coming into the room.

"*We're in,*" Night commed Calvin. "*Four hostiles down. No friendly casualties.*"

"*Good,*" Calvin replied. "*Hit 'em hard. Hit 'em fast!*"

"*Let's go kill some lizards,*" said Night to his squad, indicating the route of travel on the map that the Paw had sent. He looked down at the last lizard and shot it once more through the head. "*Now I am become Death, the destroyer of worlds,*" he said as he stepped over it.

Chapter Thirty-Seven

"*If you can hold this passageway,*" said Lieutenant Rrower, watching several of his men firing down a corridor at a large number of lizards, "*that will allow a couple more engineers to go back to work on fixing the engines.*" The lizards were slowly moving down the corridor, leapfrogging each other. Half would fire while the other half tried to move up to the next doorway or cross passage. It was costing them dearly in casualties, but they were slowly getting closer and closer to a breakthrough.

"*No problem,*" said Staff Sergeant Dantone. "*If you need defense, call a cyborg. I've got just the thing for this.*" He pulled off his right hand and attached it to a peg on his side. Reaching behind his head, he took an attachment that looked like it had a number of barrels and placed it onto the end of his right arm. With a click, it snapped into place. "*Ready to rock and roll,*" he said.

Dantone walked up as far as he could without exposing himself to the laser fire. As he went past Calvin, the officer noticed a large box on his back that he hadn't seen before. Dantone reached behind him and pulled a metal band from the bottom of the box, which he linked into the attachment on his right arm. "Hi guys," he said to the felinoids. "Cover me." Something started whirring. With a start, Calvin realized he had heard that sound before. It was the sound a mini-

307

gun made as it cycled up to ready status. His gun hand couldn't be a mini-gun, though, thought Calvin. The barrels were way too big.

Without another word, he walked into the middle of the passageway and turned toward the lizards. Laser beams immediately began playing off of him. "That tickles," he said as he began firing.

"What in the hell..." asked Rrower as a line of shells exploded down the right side of the passageway, shredding it.

"Oops, sorry," said Dantone, "didn't have time to sight it in." He made an adjustment, and this time the shells walked into the closest group of lizards on the right. Whatever armor they had wasn't able to stop what Dantone was firing, and they all fell backward. Some of them in several pieces. "That's better," Dantone said. He changed his aim point, and the closest group on the left was blown apart.

He began walking down the passageway so that he could get a better angle on the lizards that were further away. "Here lizzie, lizzie, lizzie," he called. Incoming fire had fallen off noticeably, and the remaining lizards didn't show any further inclination to move forward. Before he could drive them any further back, a loud snap was heard, and he came to a stop.

"Dammit," Dantone said. "Something just popped in my leg. Gimme a second." He started dragging himself back to the intersection with his good leg. "Shit," he added. "It's broken, and I can only move backward. I can hold this corridor for you, but I can't advance any further."

"What the hell does that thing fire?" asked Rrower.

"It's an older version of the Hooolong pulse rifle," said Dantone. Even with the tinny sound, Calvin could still hear pride in his voice. "It fires 20 millimeter explosive-tipped caseless standard light armor piercing rounds. Why?"

The Mrowry shook his head. "That was impressive," he said. "Aside from the ones that went into the wall, anyway."

A couple more laser beams came from the lizard end of the passageway, and Dantone fired another couple of seconds, sending over 100 more rounds down the corridor. The lizard fire ceased.

"*I think he's got it,*" said Calvin. "*Any idea how many lizards there are on the ship?*"

"*We don't know for sure,*" replied the Mrowry, "*but we think there were four shuttle loads that came over before you blew up their shuttles. If they were fully loaded there could be almost 800 onboard, but it doesn't seem like we've been fighting that many. If they had 800, they would have overwhelmed us. I don't think they have more than about 200 onboard.*"

"*Yeah, we saw their ship,*" said Calvin, "*and it was pretty messed up. They were probably just scraping up whatever they could and sending it over as fast as they could get a platoon or company's worth together.*"

"*Our records show that class of ship should only have about 150 marines onboard,*" Rrower added, "*so if they have 200 over here, they're sending their sailors as well. They won't be as good in a fight as the marines.*"

Calvin knew that was true, having been a sailor himself until recently. "*We can do this one of two ways,*" Calvin said. "*We can either take them head on or try to get around them and hit them from behind. Are they only on this deck or have they spread out?*"

"*They've spread out and are on all of the decks,*" answered the Mrowry.

"*Well, are there any maintenance spaces that we can use to get around them?*" suggested Calvin, looking at the ship's floor plan. It had eight main decks. The first deck was at the top of the ship, with a ladder up to the superstructure and bridge from the center of it. Decks two through eight were numbered sequentially down from it. "*How about any crawl spaces in the ceilings or under the floors? If there are, we need to use them before the lizards find them and use them against us."*

"*No, not that I can think of,*" answered Rrower.

"*How about tankage?*" inquired Calvin. "*Water tanks? Fuel tanks?*"

"*That is a great idea!*" commed Rrower. "*There is a water tank on the seventh deck. Are those suits waterproof? We could go in one end of it and come out the other end behind their lines.*"

"*Perfect!*" replied Calvin, "*That's exactly what I was looking for. Let's go!*"

Mrowry Ship *Emperor's Paw* Forward, Ross 248 System, August 24, 2020

"Lieutenant Train," commed Wraith, who was the point person on the first deck, "I just looked into a room, and there's a lizard holding some type of dagger or knife to the throat of a Mrowry that is strapped to a chair. I don't know anything about lizard body language, but I get the feeling that the lizard is angry, and the conversation is about to end violently."

"Be right there," Night replied. He had split the squad in half and was with the group on the second deck; Master Chief was leading the group on the first deck. He consulted the map in his head and was there within 30 seconds. He found Master Chief waiting there, having sent Wraith forward to keep watch.

"Are they still in there?" Night asked.

"Yes," replied Master Chief. "There are at least two other lizards in there with the one interrogating the Mrowry. One is to the left, the other is to the right."

"I'll go in first," said Night. "I'll take the one with the knife. You follow and take the one to the right. First one done gets the one on the left. Work for you?"

"Works for me, sir," answered Master Chief. "Ready when you are."

"Sir," commed Wraith, "I've got a group of lizards coming down the passageway!"

"Squad, we're going in," commed Night. "Kill 'em all!"

Night looked at Master Chief and saw his readiness. He put one hand on the door, nodded and threw it open, diving into the room. While still in the air, he began firing. The lizard with the knife stood up in surprise and was hit twice in the chest and once in the head. Hitting the ground, Night aimed at the lizard to the left, who was drawing a pistol of his own. Night was faster and shot him three times in the chest. The third shot coincided with one from the other side as Master Chief shot him too, so he knew that the third lizard was down.

Night could hear repeated rifle fire from the passageway. "Go give them a hand," he told Master Chief. "I'll take care of the Mrowry."

Night released the Mrowry from the chair as Master Chief left the room. "Thank you," it said. "Who are you and where did you come from?"

"I'm afraid that is a long story that we don't have time for," answered Night. "For now, just know that we are here to help get rid of the lizard problem that you seem to have."

"If you're here to kill the lizards," replied the Mrowry, "then I salute you and thank you for the assistance." He made a fist with one paw and placed it over his chest. "I am Commander Andowwn, the executive officer of this ship."

Night reached down to pick up one of the rifles from the dead Ssselipsssiss trooper. "You might want one of these," he said as he handed it over.

"I think I would, at that," replied the Mrowry.

Chapter Thirty-Eight

Mrowry Ship *Emperor's Paw* Aft, Ross 248 System, August 24, 2020

"We've only got one shot at this before they know we're behind them," commed Calvin, "What deck are they concentrated on?"

"Most of them are on Deck One," Rrower replied after a pause to consult with the Mrowry forces. "It looks like they are trying to get to the bridge and control spaces."

Calvin consulted the map in his head. "We can go up the stairs here," he said, sending a marker to Rrower, "and then catch the group attacking the bridge from behind."

"Yes," agreed the Mrowry, "But then we are going to be trapped between the group we are fighting, and the other group that is engaged with the rest of our troops."

"Well," said Calvin, "we'll get the ones attacking the bridge by surprise. The ones that are fighting your troops won't be able to focus on us because if they turn on us, your troops will take them from behind."

"Sounds good," growled Rrower. "Let's go get them!"

"Top, move 'em out," ordered Calvin. "Try and avoid contact until we get to Deck One."

"Aye aye," answered Master Chief Smith, "Sergeant Zoromski, you've got point."

Zoromski led the squad up the stairs. Although they could hear firing on several of the decks, they didn't stop. Reaching the top deck they could hear the sounds of fighting from both directions.

"Top, take Fire Teams One and Three and go aft," ordered Calvin. "Take the lizards from behind and bring up the reinforcements. We'll go forward and see about helping the forces at the bridge."

Top took the two fire teams and headed aft, while Calvin and Rrower headed forward. Sergeant Gordhain MacKenzie took the lead, followed by the Gordon twins and Corporal Taylor. They had only gone a short way when they came to a sealed hatch that blocked their passage. Sergeant MacKenzie took a quick peek through the small window at the top of the hatch.

"Lizards in front of us, sir," whispered MacKenzie. "There are at least three in the passageway. It looks like a couple of them are trying to cut their way into one of the rooms on the right side of the passageway."

"We've got to stop them," said Rrower.

"We will," Calvin answered. He looked back to MacKenzie. "Are there any more lizards beyond them?" he asked.

MacKenzie took another quick look. "Yes sir," he replied. "About 30 feet beyond the ones I told you about, there is a larger group that appears to be firing up a stairwell."

"Those are the ones attacking the bridge," said Rrower. "We've got to stop them, too."

"That is going to be difficult," replied MacKenzie. "We can take the close ones by surprise easily, but I don't think we'll be able to hit all of the ones down the passageway. They'll be able to get into defensive positions before we can get close enough to surprise them."

Calvin walked over to the window and took a peek. "I see what you mean," he whispered. "Worse, it looks like they're almost through the door, so we're going to have to hurry." He turned to Rrower. "I have an idea," he said, "but it's going to make a mess."

"What do you mean?" asked the Mrowry.

"I mean, I'd like to throw some explosives down the passageway," announced Calvin. "It will probably kill the lizards...but it's going to make a mess."

"I see," said the felinoid. He paused, his eyes distant. "The commanding officer says that he doesn't think the bridge can hold out much longer. He says to go ahead and do it."

"Roger," replied Calvin. He turned to his troops. "I'll push open the hatch," he said. "Mac, I want you to shoot a couple of grenades down the hall to where the lizards are shooting at the bridge and clear them out. Gordons, you'll shoot the lizards that are close, along with Corporal Taylor. Lieutenant Rrower, you keep a lookout behind us so that nothing sneaks up on us while we're killing the lizards. Everyone got it?" He saw five heads nod, and they all got into position.

"Gluck ab!" commed Corporal Jamal 'Bad Twin' Gordon. "I love a target rich environment, dude!" His brother punched him in the arm. "Ow!" Bad Twin continued, "I mean, I love a target rich environment, sir!"

Calvin shook his head as he moved to the side of the hatch and took hold of the latching mechanism. He looked up to see his troops ready and focused with rifles and trident pointed and ready to fire. "One...two...three!" he said and threw open the hatch.

The door slammed open, just as one of the lizards had raised a foot to kick in the door. Its head snapped to the right. Before it could complete the kick, Suzi 'Deadeye' Taylor shot it through its right eye with the Gordon brothers shooting the ones on either side of it. Two antimatter grenades arced down the passageway from Sergeant MacKenzie's trident to explode in the group of lizards down the hall.

Deadeye and the twins charged down the passageway with Calvin and Rrower in close pursuit. Reaching the group by the stairs, they found a couple of the lizards still twitching, and one starting to rise. They shot them all through their heads before they could recover enough to shoot back. "Stay here and cover us," said Calvin to his troops. He turned to Rrower and said, "Please let the bridge know that we have secured the passageway down here."

Calvin walked down to the doorway that the lizards had been cutting through and pushed open the door. Before he could move, a laser beam flashed out from the room, missing his left ear by inches. Instinctively, he dove to the right away from the shot yelling, "Don't shoot!"

Rrower came quickly back down the passageway as Calvin looked carefully around the edge of the doorjamb. Inside the room, he could see a smaller Mrowry sitting against the back wall holding a laser pistol in its hands. The pistol was bigger than it could hold comfortably, causing it to shake a little. Calvin realized that the shaking might have been the only thing that saved his life. The shot hadn't been a warning shot, but one fired with deadly purpose. If the cub had been able to hold the pistol steady, Calvin might have been dead.

Rrower hissed at the youngster. "That's not a nice thing to do to the person that is here to save you," he scolded.

"I didn't see him," the child said in a soft, high-pitched voice. Calvin realized that the cub was a young female. "I had my eyes closed."

"Now how are you ever going to shoot something with your eyes closed?" scolded Rrower further. "The only way to save yourself is to look death in the eyes and spit in its face."

The little cub came over to rub up against Rrower. "I'm sorry," she said. "I will try to do better next time."

"Don't tell me you're sorry," replied Rrower. "I'm not the one you almost accidentally killed. You need to tell this male that you're sorry."

She turned her head to look at Calvin. "He looks funny," she said. "Where's his face fur?"

"Now you are being rude to the one that just saved you from the lizards," Rrower scolded. "Where are your manners today? Now you need to apologize for that, as well." She buried her face back into Rrower's fur, obviously embarrassed. "I mean it," he growled. "Now!"

She turned her head far enough for one eye to be seen from the depths of Rrower's fur. "Sorry," she said in a tiny voice.

Rrower reached down and pushed her away from him. "Now say it like you mean it," he admonished.

The child gave what was almost a human curtsy and said, "I'm sorry for being rude. Thank you for saving me from being eaten by the icky lizards." She looked up to see Rrower still looking at her. He mimed holding a pistol. "And I'm sorry for shooting at you," she added quickly.

Calvin gave a little bow. "It was my pleasure," he said graciously.

Seeing that he wasn't mad, the little cub came over to rub against Calvin. He looked at Rrower. "Is it all right to pick her up?" he asked.

"Yes," replied Rrower.

Calvin picked up the cub and gave her a hug. "What is your name?" he asked.

"My name is Mimi," she said as the largest Mrowry that Calvin had seen came bounding into the room on all fours. Nearly black in color, he was darker than any of the others that Calvin had seen, except for when he had seen the commanding officer of the ship on the Gulf's view screen.

It came up and stood on his hind legs, and Calvin saw that, at seven feet tall, he was also far larger than the other Mrowry. "Might I have my daughter?" he asked.

"Certainly," said Calvin, handing her over. "Here you go."

The two Mrowry nuzzled each other. "Thank you for saving her," said the newcomer, saluting Calvin with a fist to his chest. "I was sure that the lizards were going to get her."

"It was my pleasure," said Calvin. "She seems like a nice young lady. By the way, I'm Lieutenant Commander Hobbs, the leader of the forces aboard the ship."

"You are wrong," replied the felinoid. "She is a little spitfire." He rubbed her head. "But I love her anyway. I am Captain Yerrow, the commanding officer of the Emperor's Paw." The Mrowry was the one they had seen earlier. "Thank you for coming. The AI tells me that our lizard infestation is almost eradicated. In addition to the ones that your group has killed, the group of ... Terrans? ... in the front of the ship has been like a whirlwind. They have swept through and killed all of the lizards that they came upon."

He paused, listening to something via his implant. "It appears that the ship is ours again, but it will be a while before our ship is mobile. I would greatly like to speak face-to-face with your commanding officer. Would it be possible to get you to shuttle me across to your ship?"

"Yes sir," said Calvin, "I'm sure we can arrange that. Just a second." He commed Night. "Night, Calvin. I'm going to shuttle the ship's commanding officer over to the Vella Gulf. You're in charge of the troops that are still aboard."

"Got it," said Night. "We'll finish the clean up. It doesn't look like there are many remaining. We found where they were preparing a major assault and hit them with high explosives first. The ship's a mess, but we killed a lot of lizards."

"Good job," said Calvin, "Keep it up." He switched to the shuttle's WSO. "Shuttle 02, Calvin. Hey, Faith, can you come pick up several passengers for transport to the Vella Gulf? You can get us where you dropped me off."

"We'll be right there," replied Lieutenant Faith Ibori. "Two minutes."

"Thanks," Calvin replied. "Be advised that one of the passengers is Captain Yerrow, the ship's CO. Please let the Gulf know that we are coming."

"OK sir," Calvin said to the Paw's CO, "we have a shuttle coming to take us over to the Vella Gulf. Is there anything else you need?"

"Yes, there is," replied Captain Yerrow. "If you have any extra engineers, we could use them to help get the ship operational again. We are in a bit of a hurry."

Chapter Thirty-Nine

TSS *Vella Gulf,* Ross 248 System, August 24, 2020

Captain Griffin met the shuttle as it docked, and Calvin introduced the two commanding officers to each other. He let the two COs introduce the members of their staffs that they had each brought. He fell into trail behind them as Captain Griffin led Captain Yerrow to her conference room, where they were going to have their meeting. Steropes joined the procession as it passed an intersection, coming up to walk next to Calvin.

"How'd it go?" Steropes asked Calvin.

"It went as well as could be hoped," said Calvin, "and maybe even better. They didn't expect us and we rolled right through them. We had a few minor casualties, but nothing serious. We even saved their commanding officer's daughter along the way, which ought to be good for some bonus points."

"You're not kidding," Steropes said with a chuckle.

"What do you mean?" asked Calvin.

"You didn't know?" asked Steropes. "Captain Yerrow is a prince."

"No," replied Calvin angrily, "how the hell would I have known that?"

"The black stripes are bigger and much closer on royalty," replied Steropes. "The more black their color, the higher they are in the line of succession."

"And since Yerrow is nearly all black..." said Calvin.

"...he is the Crown Prince," confirmed Steropes. "You saved the daughter of Crown Prince Yerrow, Princess Merrorritor. She is probably 4th or 5th in the line of succession for the throne."

Calvin looked at the Mrowry officers walking in front of him, and, now that Steropes had mentioned it, he could see that there was a lot more variation in coloration than he had previously noticed. While the Mrowry troopers he had fought alongside were predominantly red in color, the officers had more black on them, and the prince was almost completely black.

Calvin felt like an idiot for not noticing previously, but combat has a way of making you focus on the important things, like who is trying to kill you, not whether the cat next to you is more red or black. The more he thought about it, the more he realized it wasn't his fault. "You didn't think that was something that we might have wanted to know?" he asked Steropes. "Why didn't you mention that?"

"I don't know," said Steropes. "I never thought about it." He paused. "Now that you know it, you will also now understand that the cruiser's name is not just meant to describe the ship, but its commanding officer. The *Emperor's Paw* is always captained by a member of the royal family. It is meant as a play on words. All of the alliance nations know that when the *Paw* comes on a visit, it is a royal visit."

"I don't get it," replied Calvin. "Why wouldn't royalty command a battleship or something bigger than a cruiser?"

"You have to understand their mentality," answered Steropes. "They are warriors. The emperor's family is supposed to lead their forces into battle, not stand in the background launching missiles. The emperor's family usually flies fighters when they are junior officers, and even when they are senior officers they can usually be found at the front of the battle."

CO's Conference Room, TSS *Vella Gulf,* Ross 248 System, August 24, 2020

The procession reached the CO's conference room, and all of the officers were seated. As Steropes entered the room, Captain Yerrow growled. "Why is he here?" he asked.

"Steropes is an advisor on this ship," replied Captain Griffin. "Were it not for him and the rest of the Psiclopes, we would not have this ship, nor would we be here right now."

"I'll bet all of that came at a steep price," said Captain Yerrow. "It usually does."

Calvin looked at Steropes and could see that he looked uncomfortable.

"What does that mean?" asked Captain Griffin.

"We can talk about it more later when *he* isn't around," said Captain Yerrow.

"All right," said Captain Griffin. "I'll look forward to it." Seeing Yerrow still staring at the Psiclops, she changed the subject. "I understand that you are going to be able to save your ship?"

Captain Yerrow looked back to his host. "I'm sorry," he said. "Where are my manners? First, let me thank you for your assistance in fighting the lizards and for sending over engineers to help with our damage control process. We would surely have lost the ship without your aid."

"It was our pleasure," replied Captain Griffin. "We're always happy to kill the lizards. Our dealings with them have been...unsatisfactory, at best. They fired on us without warning and destroyed many of our fighters."

"We were certainly happy to help, but I've got a question, Captain Yerrow," said Calvin. "When we came aboard your ship, we were met with rifles. If you weren't sure whether we were a friend or an enemy, why did you have us come onboard your ship in the first place?"

"Honestly, it was a no-lose proposition at the time," answered Captain Yerrow. "We were going to die without aid. Either we would be overwhelmed by the lizards or we would have burned up in the star. We didn't know you, and you were in *their* company." He nodded at Steropes. "If you provided the assistance that you said you would, then we were saved. If you weren't a friend to us, by having your group come over, we at least had the opportunity to take you hostage and hopefully win some concessions from your commanding officer. Either way, we didn't have any other choice. We were either going to be killed by the lizards or drawn into the star."

Captain Yerrow paused. "I am sorry for the deception, but as I indicated, you were unknown to us and showed up in a ship not of your own making. You have shown your honor and saved my daughter from the clutches of the lizards, and you have my personal thanks. If there is ever anything I can do for you, you have my word that I will do so. Unlike some, I know who my friends are, and I honor my obligations."

"As do we," said the ambassador, seeing her opening. "We help our friends and honor our obligations. As I'm sure you know, we are relative newcomers on the galactic stage. We would like to go forward naming you as friends of Terra. Although we are still in our infancy as players upon this stage, we would take our place alongside you as a force for good, shielding those less powerful from the forces of chaos and anarchy.

"And well met you are," replied Captain Yerrow. "The 'forces for good' as you name them are hard pressed on all sides. It will be good to add your navy to ours. How many ships do you bring?"

"I'm afraid that you're looking at it," replied Captain Griffin. "We are gearing up the industries of the two planets that we currently have in our republic, but do not yet have a replicator that is capable of building anything bigger than the fighters attached to this cruiser."

"Oh," said Captain Yerrow, who had obviously been hoping for something more than a single 3,000 year old cruiser. "Well, it is better than nothing," he said, recovering from his initial surprise and disappointment. "Besides, I like your spirit, and I may have an opportunity for you to increase the size of your fleet."

"We will do whatever we can to help," replied Captain Griffin. "As long as it doesn't take too long. Our home world is expecting a Drakul invasion soon, and we need to return to it soon to help in its defense."

Captain Yerrow showed his teeth in what Captain Griffin fervently hoped was a smile. There were an awful lot of them, and they looked very sharp. "This shouldn't take long, but may be very dangerous. If we are successful, we may both gain from it. If we are not, then it won't matter much to us."

"*Captain Griffin, Bridge,*" said the operations officer, who was on duty on the bridge. "*We have an unknown ship that just entered the system from one of the unknown stargates. It appears to be heading toward the other unknown stargate.*" The system had four stargates, the one that led to Earth, the one that led to where they had fought the lizards, and two other stargates that hadn't been explored.

"*How big is the ship? Are we able to intercept it?*" asked Captain Griffin.

"*Arges says that the ship is a courier ship,*" said the operations officer. "*We do not have anything in a position to intercept it before it can transit out of the system.*"

"*Send it to the screen in here,*" said Captain Griffin.

The screen in the conference room came alive. It split in half, with one side showing a schematic of a small ship, and the other showing a graphic of the star system.

"That is not good," said Captain Yerrow. "That is a lizard courier ship. It is going from a pocket system that we own toward a system that connects to both a lizard system and one of ours. Their system up that chain has a big fleet in it. If you can't stop that craft, they will probably send the rest of their fleet. We will be destroyed."

"I'm sorry," said Captain Griffin, "but there's no way we can catch the ship before it reaches the gate."

Several of the Mrowry hissed in dismay. Captain Yerrow glared at his officers, and they fell silent. "Then we are all dead men," he said. "There is no way that we will be able to get through their fleet with just our ship."

"Why do you have to get through their fleet?" asked Calvin. "Won't the Mrowry send a force to come rescue you?"

"It is unlikely that they will send anyone," replied Captain Yerrow. "We were outnumbered, and they will likely believe we were lost. Besides, we are beset on all sides by enemies; sending a fleet to rescue us will just open them up to attack from another direction."

"Why can't you come back with us, then?" asked Calvin.

"We would be happy to give you asylum," said the ambassador. "If you return to Earth, we can help you fix up your ship. Perhaps your civilization will send a rescue mission at some point in the future, and you can rejoin them then. We are also working on building up a fleet, although slowly. When we are able, I'm sure we would conduct a mission to get you home."

"That is probably our best choice," said Captain Yerrow, looking at his officers. Several of them nodded. He looked back to Captain Griffin. "We may be able to help you with your fleet. I mentioned a potentially dangerous option earlier. In the system that the courier came from, we have a Class 6 replicator that is just finishing up a new battleship. If you had that ship, you would be a much more capable force."

"You're going to just *give* it to us?" asked Captain Griffin. "A battleship has got to be worth...I don't know how much it's worth, but it's got to be an awful lot." Wow, that sounded lame, she thought. "Are you authorized to do that?"

Captain Yerrow showed his teeth again, as did most of his officers. Several of them made noises like steam hissing. Calvin's implant translated the noise as <they're laughing>.

"First of all, I am not giving you the battleship," said Yerrow. "I am giving you the battleship *and* the Class 6 replicator. I don't see any way that we can get it home. That means I would have to destroy a brand new battleship, which seems like a tremendous waste, or risk losing it to the lizards and end up having to destroy it later while it is shooting at me. Neither of those is a viable option. If you don't take it, I *will* do my duty and destroy it."

He paused, looking at Steropes. "As far as having the authority to do so, I guess that *this one* hasn't told you who I am," said Captain Yerrow. "I am the first son of Emperor Yazhak the Third, and I am the first in line for the throne. I speak with my father's roar in all matters when he is absent. If I say it is yours, *it is yours!*"

"Got it," said Captain Griffin quietly. "No, they did not tell us that you were the crown prince, an oversight that I'm afraid happens quite frequently. We will take your gracious offer and use both of them to help defend our nations. Thank you very much."

"There might be one small problem in getting it, however," warned Captain Yerrow. "The battle that you saw between my ship and the ship of the lizards was just the end of a far larger battle. The lizard fleet attacked us by surprise in the system next to this. By the time we could disengage from them, we had lost several of our capital ships."

"Capital ships?" asked the ambassador. "What are capital ships?"

"Capital ships are ships that are battlecruiser size or larger," replied Captain Yerrow. "Battlecruisers, battleships, dreadnoughts and super dreadnoughts."

"Thank you for the clarification," said the ambassador.

"In any event," said Captain Yerrow, "our fleets started out at an even strength, but they destroyed several of our battleships and battlecruisers in the initial attack. We withdrew to this system, hoping that the battleship in the replicator would be finished and would turn the battle in our favor. Arriving in this system, though, we got word that the battleship was not ready and would not be ready for a few more days. We fought several delaying actions in this system, trying to give them more time to finish the battleship."

"They finally caught on to the fact that we were delaying them," continued Yerrow's executive officer, "and attacked us in force. They must have thought that we were expecting reinforcements and wanted to finish us off before they came. We were able to get our spacecraft carrier, several battlecruisers and a couple of cruisers free and to the stargate, but we lost our last two battleships, and our cruiser was wrecked beyond continuing. The remainder of the lizard force chased them into the next system."

"What did the lizards still have operational?" asked Captain Griffin.

"That's the problem, of course," replied Captain Yerrow. "We can't be entirely sure. Our cruiser's systems were barely operational at that point, but we think that the lizards still had at least two battleships, a couple of battlecruisers and four cruisers. There is no telling what is left of both fleets. It is possible, although unlikely, that our fleet won. It is more likely that they lost, or are losing. Regardless, if we can get to the battleship and it's functional, it is yours."

CO's Conference Room, TSS *Vella Gulf*, Ross 248 System, August 24, 2020

"What do you think, XO?" asked Captain Griffin. The Mrowry had gone back to their vessel to continue its repairs while the Terrans decided what they were going to do.

"The battleship represents a great opportunity," replied Captain Barishov. "It also represents a great opportunity to get ourselves killed and lose the only warship that Terra has."

"That is true," agreed Captain Griffin. "Ambassador, any thoughts?"

Ambassador Ricketts-Smith shook her head. "I don't know anything about military operations," she said, "but it sounds like there are a lot more of 'them' than there are of 'us.' I can guess what a big upgrade to our fleet it would be to get the battleship and the replicator, but I can also guess how bad it would be to lose this ship, which is the only stargate-capable ship that we have." She paused. "I am also weighing the potential diplomatic gains that we would get for continuing to help the Mrowry." Captain Yerrow had told them that he was going into the next system once his ship was fixed, regardless of whether the Terrans came or not. "The *crown prince* is already in our debt. If we go with them to the end, he will be our friend forever."

"The problem, of course," said Captain Griffin, "is the 'to the end' part. If it is a successful end, things are great. We get a battleship and a replicator. If it is the final end for us, we have just lost Terra's only warship. Not that it would matter to us; we'd be dead. Calvin, what do you think?"

"I think that this discussion could go round and round for days with no solution," replied the squadron commander. "The only way we'll know if we made the right decision is to go through the stargate, guns blazing. We could slink off back home, leaving our new allies the Mrowry to fight the lizards by themselves. We'd be safe...at least for a while, until the Drakuls show up at Earth. Maybe the lizards will get there first, who knows? Either way, at that time, the *Vella Gulf* will be overwhelmed, as will our fighters, no matter how many of them we build in the meantime."

He took a deep breath. "The other option is to continue aiding the Mrowry and go with them into the next system," he continued. "If we do that, we might be destroyed. Like I said, we could argue this all day, because we don't know what's on the other side of the stargate. We do, however, know what is on *this* side of the stargate. Our new allies. Our mission was to find allies that could help defend Earth from the Drakuls. We found one here, the Mrowry. Are we going to let them take their busted up ship into the next system by themselves, or are we going to accompany *our new allies* into that system, greatly increasing their capabilities with a second cruiser and a full squadron of space fighters? Ma'am, we may go into that next system and get killed, but there is only one choice that fulfills our mission, and only one choice that makes me proud to be a Terran as we emerge onto the galactic stage. We fight. We go with our new allies into the next system and kick the living shit out of whatever fucking lizards are there. We keep killing them until they are all dead. Then we take our allies, our new battleship *and* our incredibly capable new Class 6 replicator and go home to Terra as heroes. Maybe someone even buys us a beer for our troubles."

"If there is one thing I know for sure," Calvin concluded, "it's that I don't want to be seen as the nation that ran when its friends needed help. Mothers in ancient Sparta had a saying, 'Come back with your shield - or on it;' we can either do something that we will be proud of forever, or we go and hang our heads in shame, always wondering what might have happened if we'd done the right thing. In case you haven't guessed, I vote for staying and kicking lizard ass. Ma'am." He sat back and crossed his arms over his chest.

Captain Griffin smiled. "When you look at it that way," she said, "I guess we really don't have a choice, do we? There's the right choice, help your ally, and then all the other choices." She nodded. "We stay and fight."

Bridge, TSS *Vella Gulf*, Ross 248 System, August 24, 2020

"I'm sorry that we took the time to discuss it," said Captain Griffin. "There really is only one choice when an ally goes into battle. You stay and help them."

Whatever she was going to say next was cut off as Captain Yerrow roared in satisfaction. "It is good to have new allies such as you. I wish we had met under other circumstances, but it is only in adversity that you find out who your friends are!" He might have looked at Steropes as he said the last, but Captain Griffin couldn't be sure.

"What can we do to assist you?" asked Captain Griffin.

"The personnel and spare parts you sent have been very helpful," replied Captain Yerrow. "We will be ready to go into the next system before too much longer. I would ask to keep an officer and about 10 of your enlisted to help man some of our critical systems. We had some critical fatalities during the fight with the lizards and are a little shorthanded." The Mrowry had provided the specifications for needed parts, and the Terran replicator had been running non-stop ever since.

"That is fine," said Captain Griffin. "Just let me know what you need, and we'll make sure you have it."

"Thank you," replied Captain Yerrow. "I am sending over some of my tactical officers to discuss strategy with you. If you would not mind allowing my pilots to fly a few of your fighters, I would like to borrow three of them for the upcoming battle."

Captain Griffin looked over her shoulder to Calvin. He nodded. "We'd be happy to have their experience," he said. "They are welcome to fly three of our fighters."

"I heard his response," said Captain Yerrow, "and I would have expected nothing less from such a warrior. It is a foolish soldier that refuses aid or advice from a more experienced warrior. I am sending you three of my best."

"Thank you," replied Calvin.

Platoon Briefing Room, TSS *Vella Gulf*, Ross 248 System, August 24, 2020

"Lieutenant Train, might I have a word with you?" asked Havildar Rajesh 'Mouse' Patel.

"Sure, Mouse," replied Night. "What's up?"

"Are you familiar with the *Bhagavad Gita*, sir?" asked the Indian soldier.

"No," replied Night, "I'm not. What is the *Bhagavad Gita*?"

"It was what you quoted when we went into battle with the lizards on the *Emperor's Paw*. You said, 'Now I am become Death, the destroyer of worlds.' That is chapter 11, verse 32 from the *Bhagavad Gita*, a 700-verse scripture that is part of the Hindu epic *Mahabharata*. It is an allegory for the ethical and moral struggles of human life."

"Sorry," said Night, "never heard of it."

"Interesting," remarked Mouse. "Jawaharlal Nehru, our first prime minister, said that the *Bhagavad Gita* deals with the spiritual foundation of human existence. He found it to be a call of action to meet the obligations and duties of life, while keeping in view the spiritual nature and grander purpose of the universe. It struck me that the way you used the verse was exactly as he intended it. Perhaps you should read it some time."

"That's what the quote is from?" asked Night. "I didn't know that. It was what Robert Oppenheimer said after watching the first nuclear bomb explosion in New Mexico. The *Gita* sounds interesting...I will have to check it out." He walked out with a thoughtful expression on his face.

As Mouse turned to leave, he almost ran over Brontes, who had appeared behind him.

"Did he really call himself 'Death'?" asked Brontes.

"Yes, he did," replied Mouse. "As we were going into battle with the lizards on the *Emperor's Paw,* he quoted the *Bhagavad Gita.* He said, 'Now I am become Death, the destroyer of worlds.'"

"You're right," said Brontes. "That *is* interesting."

Chapter Forty

I t was over, thought Commander Brower. If they had only had another battleship or a couple more battlecruisers, or hadn't let the lizards surprise them so badly. But they didn't, and they had, and now the lizards were going to finish them off. Commander Brower was proud of the way his squadron had fought; hell, he was proud of the way the entire battle group had fought. But it was over.

He shouldn't even have to make this decision. He was too junior to command a spacecraft carrier. He shouldn't even be commanding the smallest cruiser in the fleet. He was a squadron commander in charge of one of the fighter squadrons on the *Honor*. He wasn't even the most senior squadron commander onboard.

When they had entered the system, there had been an admiral in charge of the battle group, and all of the major combatants were commanded by captains. They had been good leaders and had fought an excellent delaying action. The lizards hadn't noticed the base on the moon, nor the battleship that was beginning to emerge from the replicator in orbit and had let themselves be led away from the planet. If the crew at the base hadn't tried to send them a message, the lizards still probably wouldn't have known that the base was there.

But they had.

Immediately, the lizards had turned away from the chase and had begun heading for the base. There wasn't a big enough crew on the replicator to keep it from falling into the lizard's hands. The newest type of battleship, it was far better than what the lizards currently had...and they were about to capture it.

He wished, hell, he prayed that one of the dead bodies on the bridge would come back to life so that he wouldn't be in command. The bridge had taken a direct hit, though, and all of them were dead. The two remaining cruisers were similarly mauled. One was just a hulk, dead in space. The other was maintaining formation on the *Honor*, but it also had taken a hit on its bridge and there was a commander in charge of it now; unfortunately, one that was junior to Brower. He was in charge, and the decision...the responsibility...everything...rested on him.

The lizards had a battleship and two battlecruisers left; he only had the cruiser, the carrier and its four remaining fighters. Regardless of what else happened, he couldn't let them get to the replicator. He. Could. Not.

With that as the entering argument, there really was no other decision that could be made.

It was his decision, and the time had come to make it. Not doing so would be shirking his duty and dishonoring the *Honor*, and all of the sacrifices that had already been made by the battle group's crews. He could not do that. He *would* not do that.

"*Ramming speed!*" he transmitted.

Bridge, TSS *Vella Gulf*, Ross 248 System, August 26, 2020

"*We are ready for transit*," Captain Yerrow transmitted, as he watched the giant ball of plasma that had been the lizard battlecruiser. The *Vella Gulf* had hit it with two missiles, and the ship's crew had caused it to self-destruct in response.

"*We are also ready for transit*," replied Captain Griffin. "*Good hunting!*"

"*And to you, as well*," answered Captain Yerrow. "*On my mark...3...2...1...Full speed ahead!*"

The ships had been lined up in front of the stargate. They made the transit within five minutes.

Bridge, TSS *Vella Gulf*, Kepler-78 System, August 26, 2020

"System stabilizing," said Steropes. "Launching probes."

"Launch all fighters!" ordered Captain Griffin. "Battle updates ASAP!"

"There is evidence of battle across the system," said Steropes. "Trying to localize the most recent..."

"*Vella Gulf, Emperor's Paw*," interrupted Captain Yerrow, appearing on the front screen. "I am going to tie you in with the spacecraft carrier *Honor*, Commander Brower, commanding." Captain Griffin watched as the front screen cut in half. Captain Yerrow was visible on the right half; the left half showed the bridge of the carrier. It was a mess. Commander Brower stood proudly, blood running down his fur in several places. A number of dead and wounded sailors could be seen behind him. Most weren't moving. She was unable to see the back of the bridge through the smoke. Electricity arced from panel to panel at one of the stations she *could* see. The Mrowry manning it was slumped on top of it. The electricity kept jumping to something on his helmet, but he was beyond caring.

"A commander is too junior to be commanding a spacecraft carrier," said Steropes. He looked up at the screen. "Sorry, never mind."

"It is good to see that you are still alive, Captain Yerrow," Commander Brower said. "I thought you were dead."

"Not yet," replied Captain Yerrow. "Not while there are still lizards to hunt. What is your status?"

"Our status?" asked Commander Brower. "We held our own until the lizards noticed the replicator at our base, but as soon as they saw it, they stopped fighting us, turned around and started heading for it. It is my intention to stop them from getting there."

"We just got the status of your forces," Captain Yerrow replied. "How do you intend to stop them? Most of your systems are out, and you only have four fighters left. The cruiser *Ranger* is similarly damaged."

"We're going to do what we can," replied Commander Brower. "I intend to ram them."

"I forbid it!" ordered Captain Yerrow. "Pull off and regroup with us!"

"Sorry sir," replied Commander Brower, "but like you said, our ships are smashed. Your arrival does not change the balance of forces significantly, either. Our ships are not good for much else at this point. The squadron I used to command is gone. All of my ships and all of my pilots...gone. And unless the status you're transmitting is in error, the *Emperor's Paw* doesn't seem to be in much better shape. I think we'll just continue and see what we can do about evening up the odds. Face it, Your Highness, you're not going to be able to take out the battleship with just two cruisers. We can do it." He stood a little straighter. "We will do it. Brower out." His side of the screen went black. The message, 'Transmission ended' flashed several times, and then Captain Yerrow's picture spread back across the whole screen.

"As hard as it is to watch or condone, Commander Brower is correct," said Captain Yerrow, shaking his head. "We cannot take on the battleship. For that matter, the two battlecruisers are more than we can handle, even if he succeeds in destroying the battleship." He looked at something offscreen. "We will, however, honor his sacrifice and put ourselves into a position where we can take advantage of it, should he be successful. We're transmitting coordinates; follow us and prepare for battle. Yerrow out." The screen went blank.

"What did he mean, should he be successful?" asked Captain Griffin.

"I know what he meant, ma'am," said Bullseye. "No offense, but you're a ship driver at heart; you think in two dimensions. Space is more like what aviators fight in—three dimensions. Space is big and ships, even really big ships, are small. Trying to get them to run into each other is really hard if one of the two doesn't want to be hit."

"The odds are that the carrier will miss the battleship," added Steropes, looking at the tactical plot. "There is a slightly higher chance for the more nimble cruiser, and an even higher chance for at least some of the fighters that were mentioned to hit one of the bigger ships if they are not destroyed before they can ram. It doesn't look like they have launched yet." He shook his head. "It is admirable for them to try to even the odds for us," he concluded, "but it is most unlikely that they will succeed."

Bridge, TSS *Vella Gulf,* Kepler-78 System, August 26, 2020

"I'm getting awfully tired of fighting ships bigger than ours," said Calvin with a sigh. "Is there anything in this system that we can use to our advantage?" he asked, looking over Sara's shoulder. Sara had taken over the science station for Steropes, who had gone off duty.

"I don't know," she replied. "This is the Kepler-78 system. The star in this system is a yellow star that is about 70% of the size of the Sun. There are two planets in this system. The 'a' planet is a super-Earth planet that is about 70% more massive than the Earth, with a radius about 20% larger. It isn't much help as it is in a really tight orbit around the star."

"How tight?" asked Calvin.

"It is about 40 times closer to the star than Mercury is to our Sun," replied Sara. "In fact, it's so close that it makes one complete orbit around the star in just over eight hours, and its surface temperature is over 4,000 degrees Fahrenheit."

"OK, that's hot enough that I don't want to go there," said Calvin. "What else have you got?"

"There's only one other planet in the system," replied Sara. "The 'b' planet is a Saturn-like planet that is located about 460 million miles away from the star, or about as far away from the star as Jupiter is from our Sun. It is about double the size of Saturn and has eight moons, of which five are large enough to be planets in their own right. All of the moons have pretty high concentrations of heavy metals and relatively high concentrations of the rare Earth elements. This system is also a pocket system; the only way into or out of it is through the one stargate that we came through."

"Hmm," mused Calvin, "no ideas so far. Can you show me the tactical display again?"

"Sure," Sara said. She brought up the tactical display on the front viewer. "Here we are," she said, using a laser pointer to point out their position on the left side of the display. "The stargate through which we entered the system is behind us. We are headed toward the star and are going to pass within about 50 million miles of the 'b' planet. The other two fleets are on the other side of the star from us. If nothing changes the Mrowry battle group will intercept the enemy fleet at a distance of about 40 million miles from the star. The lizards are headed back toward us, but are slower than the Mrowry vessels chasing them."

"How close did you say we'd be to the 'b' planet?" asked Calvin.

"About 50 million miles," replied Sara. "Why?"

"I've got an idea," Calvin said. "It will depend a lot on what happens when the two fleets meet, but it might be something that we can use. I need to talk to Captain Yerrow."

CO's Conference Room, TSS *Vella Gulf*, Kepler-78 System, August 26, 2020

"It will all depend on what happens with the ramming force," concluded Calvin. "If it is successful, then all we'll have to do is sweep in on what remains of the lizard ships and pound them until they surrender or blow themselves up. If the ramming force *isn't* successful, we at least have a backup plan."

"I like it," agreed Captain Griffin. "At least it gives us options."

"I do too," said Captain Yerrow. "You have a grasp of fighting in space that I would not have expected from someone so inexperienced. I do not mean that as an insult, but as a compliment. I have been doing this for many seasons, and I didn't think of that."

"Thank you," replied Calvin. "I think that it is due to being a pilot of an air-breathing fighter before coming to space. I see things in three dimensions that others might not."

"Now we'll just have to wait and see what the ramming force is able to achieve," said Captain Yerrow. "And hope their sacrifice is not in vain."

Bridge, *Ssselipsssiss Ship Avenger*, Kepler-78 System, August 26, 2020

"This prey seems to want to jam itself into our mouths," laughed Captain Ssselthan, commanding officer of the battleship *Avenger*. "Obviously, there is something on that planet that they do not want us to have."

"But sir," said the defensive systems technician, "isn't it obvious? They intend to ram us!"

"Of course they do," replied Captain Ssselthan. "It is the only thing they can do. They are out of missiles and fighters, and the carrier couldn't last for a minute against us in a laser duel. It's big enough that it *might* last two minutes against one of our battlecruisers. No, the only thing that they *can* do is to ram us."

"Doesn't that worry you, Captain?" asked the weapons technician.

"No, it does not," replied Captain Ssselthan, "nor should it worry any other loyal subject of the emperor." He shook his head. The youth these days. They must be hatching them too early because bravery was becoming a very perishable trait. He sighed. "When they get within missile range, we will fire our remaining missiles. If that doesn't succeed in killing them, then we will kill them with our lasers when they get within range. Finally, when they commit to their final ramming vector, we will change ours, and they will miss us. Space is big, and they cannot hope to maneuver that flying piece of shit well enough to hit us when we dodge. Then, when they fly past, we will destroy their engines and engineering spaces, and they will be done."

"After that," he continued in a louder voice meant for everyone on the bridge, "we will see what the two cruisers do when their friends are destroyed. If they keep coming for us, we will destroy them and collect their bodies for our kitchens. If they run, we'll collect the prey from the carrier and cruiser. Either way, we will eat well tonight!"

Cheering resounded across the bridge.

Bridge, TSS *Vella Gulf*, Kepler-78 System, August 26, 2020

"They're coming up on missile range," said Steropes, who had come back to the sensor station for the battle. "The lizard ship should turn shortly so that it can use its broadside missile batteries."

"Does the carrier have missiles?" asked the helmsman.

"According to the tactical report, the carrier has a number of missile batteries," said Steropes, "but they do not have any missiles remaining. They will just have to try to get through the missile volleys of the lizards the best they can."

"That's going to leave a mark," said the helmsman.

The commanding officer nodded her head. "Yes it is," she said.

Bridge, Mrowry Ship *Honor*, Kepler-78 System, August 26, 2020

Here goes nothing, thought Commander Brower as the *Honor* entered the lizard's missile range.

"They're not firing!" replied the helmsman, who was the only other member of the bridge crew. They had put off everyone that they could in lifeboats and escape pods. He hoped that they'd be picked up by the prince after the battle and not by the lizards. All of them had laser pistols with them...just in case.

"They probably don't have many missiles remaining," replied Commander Brower. "They're waiting until they can't miss us with them. Since we are not turning broadside to them, we are a harder target to hit than we normally would be. Is the *Ranger* still with us?"

"Yes sir," said the sensor operator. "The *Ranger* is still in formation to starboard. She's aiming for the battlecruiser to the right of the battleship."

Any time now, thought Commander Brower. He wished they'd hurry up.

Bridge, *Ssselipsssiss Ship Avenger*, Kepler-78 System, August 26, 2020

"Range to target is now 13 million miles, sir," said the weapons technician. "They are in range."

"We will let them get a little closer before we fire," said Captain Ssselthan. "Helmsman, cease the drive and rotate the ship to port to unmask the port batteries." Since the majority of the missile batteries were located on the sides of the ship, the ship had to turn to point the missile launchers at the target. Having the engines stop before firing ensured a stable firing platform for the ship and kept it from flying off tangentially.

"Aye, sir," said the helmsman. "Drive has ceased, and we are coming left."

"Both battlecruisers rotating too," called the sensor technician. Although they were both 'shot out' and had no missiles remaining, the battlecruisers were bringing the majority of their laser batteries to bear.

"Nine million miles," said the weapons technician. The Mrowry were coming on fast, Captain Sselthan thought. He had to make sure they missed. Even damaged, the carrier had an acceleration that was 100 Gs greater than his. During the five hour chase, the carrier had reached a speed that was 11,000 miles an hour faster. With a mass of over three million tons, any impact would be...substantial...to say the least.

"Eight million miles," said the weapons technician, sounding a little more nervous.

"*Fire all missiles!*" ordered the Captain.

"Missiles firing!" called the weapons technician.

"That's strange," said the sensor technician. "I'm picking up some weird gravity readings behind us."

Bridge, TSS *Vella Gulf,* Kepler-78 System, August 26, 2020

"The lizards have rotated their ships and are firing," said Steropes. "They must be out of missiles. The Mrowry database says that the battleship has 34 missile tubes in its broadside, but only 17 missiles fired." He looked down at his screen, but then looked back up quickly. *"Two stealth fighters uncloaking behind the lizard ships!"* he called.

"What?" asked Captain Griffin. "What the hell's a stealth fighter? Better yet, *why don't we have them?"*

"The stealth fighter is a space fighter that carries a cloaking package in place of a missile loadout," said Steropes. "It is a spy plane...but no one ever uses them because fighters can't go through stargates so they're of limited utility..." He paused. *"Detonation!* One flew into the battleship's engines once they turned off, and another flew into the engines of one of the battlecruisers. Both ships are dead in space!"

"I take it that it will be easier for the carrier to ram the battleship now?" asked Captain Griffin.

"Yes," said Steropes. "Assuming that they survive the missiles heading at them."

Bridge, Mrowry Ship *Honor,* Kepler-78 System, August 26, 2020

The fighters had done their part, succeeding beyond even his wildest dreams. Now if the *Honor* could just hold together through the missile storm. "Come on, baby, hold together for me," Commander Brower urged the *Honor.* "We'll do this together..."

"Counter-missile lasers firing," said the ship's AI. "Missile impact in 4... 3... 2... 1..."

There was a flash, and the world went black.

Bridge, Mrowry Ship *Ranger*, Kepler-78 System, August 26, 2020

"Shit sir, they got pasted," said the sensor operator. "They took hits from at least four nuclear warheads and two laser warheads. The flight deck is wrecked, and air and fluids are venting in too many places to count."

"Does it still have power, though?" asked Commander Garuu, the acting commanding officer of the *Ranger*. "Is anyone alive?"

"One of the motors is still operating," said the sensor operator after a brief pause.

"I haven't been able to contact anyone," said the communications operator.

"Keep trying," Commander Garuu urged. "We need to know quickly whether or not they're still able to hit the battleship. If they can't, we have to take over for them!"

"Wait!" cried the communications operator. "*I'm getting someone!*"

Bridge, TSS *Vella Gulf*, Kepler-78 System, August 26, 2020

The bridge of the *Honor* appeared on the front viewer. Captain Griffin had only *thought* it looked bad the last time she saw it. Now it was worse. Fires could be seen burning in several places, and smoke filled the area. Pieces of furniture, equipment and Mrowry littered the entire area. She could barely make out Commander Brower through the smoke, standing next to the helm, bracing himself on it with his right paw. His left paw was tucked under his right arm. Only the lower half of the helmsman was still in his seat.

"Ranger," he stopped to cough. "Ranger, *you are to attack the battlecruiser,*" he coughed again, "*as previously instructed. The remaining fighters will make sure we hit the target.*"

He stood up straight to address the camera. The smoke cleared a little, and Captain Griffin could see several pieces of shrapnel sticking out of his left side.

"*Captain Yerrow, it has been my honor to serve with you,*" he transmitted in as strong a voice as he could muster. "*You will make a good emperor.*" He saluted with his right hand. As he did, his left one fell out from underneath. It was severed at the wrist and pumping blood. "*FOR THE EMPEROR!*" The screen went black.

Bridge, *Ssselipssssiss Ship Backstabber*, Kepler-78 System, August 26, 2020

Captain Rissser, the commanding officer of the Ssselipsssiss ship *Backstabber*, watched in dismay as the spacecraft carrier came through the barrage of missiles still mostly in one piece.

"Sir!" called his sensor technician. "Something just blew up the *Avenger's* engines. Their power is out, and they are not moving." Dismay turned to horror as the spacecraft carrier kept coming, homing in on the *Avenger*. As fast as it was moving, they wouldn't have long from when it entered the range of their lasers and grasers until it hit the *Avenger*. Their broadside had 16 lasers and 10 grasers; they would never be enough to destroy the three million ton behemoth, but perhaps enough hits on its nose would push it out of alignment and get it to miss. Maybe its one operating engine would drive it into the system's star and make his life easier.

"Fire all weapons at the nose of the carrier!" he ordered.

If he'd known that all of the ship's spare mass had been brought to the front of the ship to absorb laser/graser hits, he wouldn't have bothered. If they had looked a little harder, they might have seen the two space fighters that had been mounted to the back of the ship on opposite sides. As the carrier closed, the fighters fired their engines as necessary to give it the last minute guidance it needed.

Bridge, TSS *Vella Gulf,* Kepler-78 System, August 26, 2020

"Impact!" called Steropes as the spacecraft carrier hit the battleship just aft of the ship's bridge. "The carrier got them!" The impact crushed the carrier like an aluminum can. Over 6,000 feet in length prior to impact, it was less than 3,500 afterwards. The damage to the battleship, struck broadside, was far worse. The slug of metal that had been a spaceship carrier slammed into the battleship with a far greater force than its frame had been built to withstand, ripping through its steel bulkheads like tissue paper.

The carrier drove through the battleship, cutting it in half. The two pieces slammed together behind it and were pulled along in its wake by the momentum of the crash. None of battleship's crewmen survived the impact. It was nothing short of devastating.

The Ssselipsssiss battlecruiser hit by the cruiser didn't fare much better. Although the Ranger had less than 1/10 of the carrier's mass, the battlecruiser was much smaller than the battleship. Like a bullet going through butter, the cruiser cut the larger ship in half, with an impact that was not survivable by its crew.

Bridge, TSS *Vella Gulf*, Kepler-78 System, August 26, 2020

"The ramming attack was more successful than we could have hoped," transmitted Captain Yerrow. "Unfortunately, there is still one battlecruiser remaining. Execute Plan Calvin!"

As one, the two ships began a slow left turn.

Chapter Forty-One

Bridge, *Ssselipsssiss Ship Backstabber*, Kepler-78 System, August 26, 2020

Captain Rissser had never seen anything like the carnage that had been visited on his flagship. Over 4,000 sailors and marines were instantly killed on the battleship alone. The Mrowry would *pay*. He didn't know what race crewed the other cruiser that had arrived just before the battle, but he knew that one of them was a Mrowry ship, and he *would* kill them.

Apparently, the captains of the cruisers hoped that the *Backstabber* would be destroyed in the ramming attack, because they had flown straight toward him since they entered the system. When the *Backstabber* emerged unscathed, they turned and ran, headed in the direction of the stargate. Captain Rissser's ship already had a much higher velocity than they did, and his ship could accelerate faster than the prey could. Even though they tried to do a sweeping turn that allowed them to keep up their speed, rather than stopping and then accelerating back in the direction from which they had come, it wouldn't be enough for them. He would chase them down. He would catch them. And then he would pull their captains' still beating hearts from their bodies and eat them while they watched.

"Full speed ahead!" he ordered. "Emergency speed! Cut them off from the stargate!"

Bridge, TSS *Vella Gulf,* Kepler-78 System, August 26, 2020

"Captain, my system shows that we are not going to beat the lizard ship to the stargate," said the defensive systems officer (DSO).

"There was always a danger of that if we headed into the system too far," replied Captain Griffin. "We will just have to defend ourselves."

"I'm not sure that two cruisers will be able to hold off the battlecruiser," said the DSO, "especially as beat up as the *Emperor's Paw* is. They don't have any missiles remaining, and we *don't* want to get into a laser duel with a battlecruiser." The DSO had been on the *Vella Gulf's* first cruise when they fought at laser range against a lizard battlecruiser. He knew it wasn't a winning proposition.

"Then I guess we will have to do something to even the odds," said Captain Griffin. "Launch all fighters!" she ordered.

"Fighters launching," said Bullseye.

"Sir!" called Steropes from the sensor station. "The *Emperor's Paw* is having problems with one of their engines. Their acceleration is dropping!"

"Reduce power," said Captain Griffin. "Continue to hold station on them. We will fight together; it's our only chance against the battlecruiser."

Bridge, *Ssselipsssiss Ship Backstabber,* Kepler-78 System, August 26, 2020

"One of the engines on the Mrowry vessel is sputtering," said the sensor technician. "It just went out. They are now operating on one engine. The Eldive ship is slowing to match them." They finally looked the other ship up in the archives and had seen that it was an Eldive vessel, a race that was thought to have become extinct over 3,000 years ago. Their ship looked like it was that old; its top acceleration was far less than what a current cruiser could do.

"They were running it full out," said Captain Rissser. "It was to be expected. That ship was all but destroyed in the Ross 248 system. It is amazing that it lasted this long."

"Sir!" called the sensor technician. "The enemy ships are now actively slowing down. It looks like they intend to go into orbit around the second planet of this system."

Captain Rissser hissed. "Give me a scan of the planet, its moons and the space around it," he said. "Find out if there are any bases or defenses in the area."

"I have been looking," replied the technician, "and I do not see any defensive positions on the planet or on any of the moons. There is a large replicator in orbit around one of the moons, and a small base on the moon beneath it, but nothing else."

"Is there something in the replicator that they can use?" asked Captain Rissser.

"No sir," replied the sensor technician. "Long range video indicates that the replicator is assembling a battleship, but it still has about 1/4 of it, including its engines, inside the machine. It won't have any of its missile armament yet or any power to fire its lasers."

"Then they must be hoping to hide behind the planet and ambush us as we come around it," decided Captain Rissser. "They know that we can shoot farther than they can and obviously want to get inside of our laser range without giving us the ability to fire on them first. Make sure you come no closer to the moon than 500,000 miles.

That way, we can use our lasers at their maximum effective range. We will make them come to us while we shoot their ships out from under them."

"The Eldive ship is launching its fighters," called the sensor technician. "It looks like 12 fighters launched."

"It won't make any difference," said the captain.

Bridge, TSS *Vella Gulf*, Kepler-78 System, August 26, 2020

"All fighters launched and proceeding on mission," said Bullseye.

"They are in four-ship divisions with a Mrowry in the lead of each?" asked Captain Griffin.

"Yes, ma'am," replied Bullseye. "I'm glad they came; they showed us a pretty useful modification to our missiles."

"Oh?" asked the CO.

"Yes, ma'am," answered Bullseye. "They changed the programming of the missiles so that the first missiles we fire don't immediately go to full power. They start out at a lower power setting and wait for all of the rest of the missiles to launch. They have the delay figured out so that all of the missiles accelerate together, so that they arrive at the target at the same time. Rather than five waves of 12 missiles each, the enemy ship will have to defend against 60 missiles arriving simultaneously. This will complicate the defenses and hopefully get more hits on the target. We may not get any hits on the ship, but hopefully the barrage will take out the ship's shields, so that the cruisers can hit it with their weapons."

"Good," replied the CO. "That was the problem we had our first cruise; we weren't able to knock down the battlecruiser's shields."

"Hopefully, we've rectified that this time," said Bullseye. "They call it the 'Claw Maneuver.'"

"I hope we have," agreed Captain Griffin. "Fighting the battle-cruiser wasn't much fun last time."

"The lizard ship is deviating a little to go around the planet," said the DSO. "It looks like they want to make sure that they stay outside of our laser range. Their lasers can shoot about 100,000 miles further than ours; it looks like they are going to stand off and try to hit us with their lasers from maximum range."

"Have you coordinated with the fighters to synchronize our attacks?" asked Captain Griffin.

"Yes, ma'am, I have," replied the DSO.

"Excellent," said Captain Griffin.

Bridge, *Ssselipsssiss Ship Backstabber,* Kepler-78 System, August 26, 2020

"The ships just started moving again," called the sensor technician. "It looks like they may be trying to run from us."

"They probably saw that we weren't going to come within range of their lasers and got scared," Captain Rissser said. "They're running. Prey always run. Increase speed to maximum. Let's run them down. I'm hungry."

Bridge, TSS Vella Gulf, Kepler-78 System, August 26, 2020

"The lizard ship is at full thrust," reported the DSO.

"Got it," replied Captain Griffin, looking at the tactical map. "A few seconds more."

"They are now rapidly overhauling us," called the DSO. "We will be within range of their missiles in another minute."

"They're out of missiles," said Captain Griffin, "or they would have used them earlier. Almost there...Now! Rotate ship! Engines to maximum!"

The Terran and Mrowry ships spun end over end so that they were now pointed at the Ssselipsssiss vessel, and they began slowing as their engines worked to kill their velocities. The crew of the replicator would have a good view of the battle; the cruisers would intercept the battlecruiser a mere 200,000 miles above it.

"Tell the fighters to begin their attack runs!" ordered Captain Griffin.

"They're inbound to the lizard ship now," said Bullseye. "Missile launch in one minute!"

"I hope he's ready," muttered Griffin under her breath.

Chapter Forty-Two

"AI, are you ready?" asked Calvin. There was no answer to his question.

"Give it another minute," said Lieutenant Rrower. "Sometimes they are slow to come up the first time."

Both men looked around the enormous bridge impatiently. Calvin's idea had been to use the new battleship to surprise the Ssselipsssiss ship. He had checked and, although its engines hadn't been installed yet, its forward armaments and computer network had already been completed.

If the ship was given power, Calvin asked, would its lasers and grasers be operational? Captain Yerrow agreed that they would, but without the engines, there wouldn't be power. Calvin's idea had been to bring their shuttle to the replicator, plug it into the battleship and let it charge the ship's massive capacitors like a giant automobile jump start. The shuttle didn't have enough energy for more than a shot, maybe two, but if it was plugged in for a couple of hours, it might work.

'Might' being the operational word.

Everything had gone against them from the start. Calvin and Lieutenant Rrower had brought the remaining shuttle, along with a load of Terran and Mrowry engineers and all of the batteries the shuttle could carry, to the replicator and had taken charge of it.

That's when things had started to go wrong. The cables they had brought from the *Vella Gulf* weren't long enough to reach from the shuttle to the battleship. The engineers had quickly spliced several cables together to make one long enough to reach the capacitor banks, only to find that the fitting on the end of the cable didn't fit into the port on the battleship. Whether that was because the Eldive used their own style of electrical cables or the fittings had changed in the 3,000 years since the *Gulf* had been built, Calvin didn't know or care. All he knew was that the cable wouldn't plug in.

One of the engineers had suggested having one of the smaller replicators on the station make some new cable heads. These had been made and quickly spliced onto the cables. Between all of the splicing and the fact that the cables weren't rated to carry that much current that far, the cable had failed soon after the power began flowing, starting a fire that took five minutes to put out.

So they had to replicate a whole new run of cables with the battleship's fittings on them.

Then they had to replicate *another* set of cables that had the Eldive fittings on one end and the battleship's fittings on the other. They plugged these in and finally started charging the new battleship. They were over an hour behind schedule now, even though the plan had started with an extra four hours of time built into it.

Now the computer was taking forever to boot up for the first time. It was running off the replicator's power, along with the other systems necessary to operate the equipment. That had required replicating another set of cables. One thing had gone right—they had just enough of the materials required to make the power cables. If it had needed to be 15 feet longer, they would literally have run short.

"Ready for activation," finally said the battleship's AI. "I find myself unable to run diagnostics on the aft quarter of my systems, and the majority of the other systems do not have power available to them. Did I take battle damage? If so, I have no memory of being in a battle, so my memory system may have been damaged."

"No," said Lieutenant Rrower. "You are brand new and haven't actually finished the replication process yet." He looked at a display on his wrist and read, "Activation sequence Battleship 1791 JGKS 8991 JEAA."

"I am activated," said the AI. "What am I to be called?"

Lieutenant Rrower looked at Calvin who replied, "The ship is to be called, '*Terra.*'"

"Interesting," replied the AI. "I have no recollection of this name in any context. Is it a recent battle?"

"No," said Lieutenant Rrower. "You have been given to a new civilization to aid in their defense. The nation is called Terra, and you are to be their flagship. The person standing next to me, Lieutenant Commander Hobbs, is your new Captain."

"I am ready to serve," said the AI. "You have activated me before I am complete. This goes against standard procedures. Is there an operational requirement that has necessitated this?"

"Yes," Calvin said. He was so impatient to get going that he was starting to hop up and down like a five-year old that had to go to the bathroom. "We have been charging the capacitors for the #2 and #3 grasers. We need you to shoot the Ssselipsssiss battlecruiser that is attacking our cruisers."

"I am unable," the AI replied.

"*What?*" Calvin asked. "Why aren't you able?"

"I do not have the targeting data for that ship, as none of my radars currently have power," the AI replied. "Additionally, the charges on those grasers are not enough to fire them effectively."

"Are you able to accept targeting data from another ship," asked Calvin, "or do you have to have it from your own systems?"

"It is more accurate if it comes from my own systems," answered the AI, "because there will be fewer sources of error. As there is only going to be enough power for one shot, it would be prudent to make sure that the weapons are on target."

"Does each weapon need a targeting source?" asked Calvin. "Or can one source feed both weapons?"

"I am capable of using one source to give you optimal targeting data for both weapons," replied the AI. "If you can get power to one of my laser detection and ranging systems, that will be sufficient."

"One laser is enough?" asked Calvin.

"Yes," replied the AI. "I can use the initial targeting data supplied by one of the other ships to get my system close enough to pick up the battlecruiser. After that, I will use my onboard optical heterodyne detection system for precise targeting. I will need the capability to communicate with one of the other ships, as well."

"OK," said Calvin. "So we need power to one of the tracking lasers, power to the communications system and then more power to the grasers. Any idea where we're going to get that? The shuttle is almost out of fuel; it doesn't have much more to give."

"The replicator's power source will be enough to run the laser tracking and communications systems," said the AI. "It will also give me enough power to finish powering the two grasers for a single shot; however, it is going to take all of the replicator's power to do so. There will not be any left over for life support systems."

Calvin looked at Lieutenant Rrower. "We better get everyone in suits."

Chapter Forty-Three

Bridge, TSS *Vella Gulf*, Kepler-78 System, August 26, 2020

"Eight million miles!" called the offensive systems officer from his position at operations.

"Rotate the ship!" ordered Captain Griffin, turning the ship to bring its broadside missiles to bear. "Synchronize with the fighters and fire!" If Calvin's plan worked, the Ssselipsssiss battlecruiser would never know what hit them, she thought. If it didn't, they were going to die.

Bridge, *Ssselipsssiss Ship Backstabber*, Kepler-78 System, August 26, 2020

"The ships are rotating," called the sensor technician. "They're bringing their missiles to bear!"

"That's fine," said Captain Rissser. "The Mrowry vessel cannot have many missiles left. The other cruiser can't have enough of them to knock down our shields."

"But what about the fighters?" asked the sensor technician. "It looks like they are making their attack run, too."

"We'll just have to shoot them down as they come," replied Captain Rissser. "Then we will be within laser range, and they will be ours."

"The cruiser and the fighters are launching!" said the sensor technician.

"Good," said the Captain Risser. "It begins."

Asp 01, Kepler-78 System, August 26, 2020

"*Missiles away!*" Lieutenant Sasaki Akio called. The most experienced of the Terran WSOs, he was in the lead fighter with the Mrowry Lieutenant Commander in charge of the strike. 60 missiles dropped from the 12 fighters, ignited, and roared off in search of a target.

Bridge, TSS *Vella Gulf*, Kepler-78 System, August 26, 2020

"Missiles firing!" said the offensive systems officer. "They will arrive at the battlecruiser at the same time as the missiles from the fighters."

"Continue firing until we're out," ordered Captain Griffin.

"Roger that, ma'am," said the offensive systems officer. "Continue firing until we're out, aye. Second volley launching."

Command Bridge, TSS *Terra*, Kepler-78 System, August 26, 2020

"I am in communications with a ship called the *Vella Gulf*," the AI advised. "I have no context for this name, either, so I believe it to be the Terran cruiser. Is this correct?"

"Yes it is," said Calvin. "OK, we want to shoot the battlecruiser just before the *Vella Gulf's* missile volley arrives."

"That will be impossible," the AI said. "The missiles are arriving...now."

"Oh shit," said Calvin, "We're too late."

Bridge, TSS *Vella Gulf,* Kepler-78 System, August 26, 2020

"Ten seconds to impact!" called the offensive systems officer.

"Has the battleship fired?" asked Captain Griffin. The battleship was supposed to fire first, knocking down the battlecruiser's shields, so that the missiles could take it out.

"No ma'am," said Steropes. "The weapons have not come online yet."

"Weapons impact!" said the offensive systems officer. "I estimate 20 missile impacts on the ship simultaneously. *Their shields are down!*"

"Maximum rate fire!" ordered Captain Griffin. "Pour it on them! We've got to take them out before their lasers come into range." Captain Griffin had already seen what happened when a cruiser fought a battlecruiser with lasers. It wasn't pretty.

Bridge, *Ssselipsssiss Ship Backstabber,* Kepler-78 System, August 26, 2020

"Our *shields are down!*" called the defensive technician. "I estimate 23 impacts on them at once. We have minor damage in many compartments, and sensors are registering radiation in three places."

"Excellent job," Captain Risser congratulated the technician. "You stopped most of their missiles. Now their fighters are out of missiles, and they only have that one cruiser shooting. Continue to defend the ship, and get those shields back up." He turned to the helmsman. "Turn the ship and begin braking. I don't want to fly past them. They've done their worst, and we are almost unscathed." Captain Risser smiled. "Now it's our turn."

Bridge, TSS *Vella Gulf*, Kepler-78 System, August 26, 2020

"I am in contact with a ship calling itself the *Terra*," said Solomon. "It says that it is the new battleship and is asking for targeting information on the battle-cruiser. Am I allowed to pass that on?"

"Yes, *please*!" said Captain Griffin. "Are they ready to fire?"

"No," replied Solomon. "Unfortunately, they are not. They have not been able to get enough power to the capacitors yet."

"Shit."

Bridge, *Ssselipsssiss Ship Backstabber*, Kepler-78 System, August 26, 2020

Captain Rissser had not expected the ships to turn and attack, and the two cruisers quickly closed the distance until they were almost in range of his weapons. He turned the battlecruiser around again, so that his broadside weapons would be able to fire. The *Backstabber* completely outclassed the cruisers with an armament of 16 lasers, 10 grasers and one improved battleship laser per side. The *Vella Gulf* only had 10 grasers, and they were smaller.

"700,000 miles," said the offensive systems technician. "Standing by to fire."

The *Backstabber* had been hit by two missiles and had two more near misses. Although the ship was wounded, it was not grievously injured, and all but two of its weapons were ready. The enemy was within range of its battleship laser.

"Kill the one that is shooting missiles at us!" said Captain Rissser. "*Fire!*"

Bridge, TSS *Vella Gulf*, Kepler-78 System, August 26, 2020

The battlecruiser's first shot was absorbed by the shields. The lights burned brighter as the extra energy was absorbed and redistributed, and a noise that sounded like "*SCREEEEEE*" was heard briefly.

"Shields at 30%," the defensive systems officer said.

"Holy shit!" Captain Griffin exclaimed. "Was that its laser? The last ship we fought didn't hit that hard!"

"Apparently, it has a battleship laser," Steropes noted, "or one of their improved lasers. We will not be able to take many more of those types of hits."

As he said it, the lizard battlecruiser fired again. There was a flash, and a smell of ozone permeated the bridge. "Shields are down!" called the defensive systems officer.

Crap, thought Captain Griffin. The next one was going to hurt. A lot.

Chapter Forty-Four

Command Bridge, TSS *Terra*, Kepler-78 System, August 26, 2020

"That should do it," commed Lieutenant Rrower. "*There should be power to the laser tracking system. I'm coming back.*" Movement was difficult. With all of the station's power being transferred to the *Terra*, there were no lights, no heat and no gravity throughout the ship or replicator. It was almost like being in space, except there were walls to run into. If the suits hadn't had external lights, he would have been lost inside the ship. Although it wasn't completed yet, it was still over a mile long.

Bridge, *Ssselipsssiss Ship Backstabber*, Kepler-78 System, August 26, 2020

"Their shields have failed," said the sensor technician, as another missile exploded close aboard, shaking the ship.

"I've had enough of their missiles," said Captain Rissser. "*Kill them n....!*"

Before he could complete the thought, there was a flash, and a tornado howled through the bridge.

Command Bridge, TSS *Terra*, Kepler-78 System, August 26, 2020

"*We got them!*" Lieutenant Rrower roared as the two four-meter aperture grasers finally fired. Calvin didn't know if it was delight, defiance or some other emotion, but the roar itself brought shivers down his spine. He imagined it was the kind of roar that made early cavemen huddle closer to their fire, hoping to keep the predators of the night at bay.

"That was *awesome!*" the Mrowry officer continued, as he looked at the damage done to the ship on the long range viewer. "We got it right through their bridge!"

"Of course we did," said the *Terra's* AI. "That was where I was aiming. If you wanted me to hit it someplace else, you should have said so."

Bridge, *Ssselipssssiss Ship Backstabber*, Kepler-78 System, August 26, 2020

The executive officer looked and saw that Captain Rissser was gone. Not just 'gone' as in deceased, but 'gone' as in no longer on the bridge. Whatever weapon had fired from the battleship had passed right through his command chair and vaporized him as it passed from one side of the ship to the other. Well, not completely, he thought as he looked on in horror. The captain's magnetic boots and about six inches of his legs were still attached to the deck. That was all that was left of him. Were it not for the magnetic boots, that part would have gone overboard as all of the air on the bridge went screaming out the 12' holes that had suddenly appeared on both sides of it. The defensive systems technician had failed to strap in and was sliding across the floor, inexorably drawn toward one of the holes. As he raced toward the hole, he was able to get a hand on the weapons technician's seat, momentarily stopping his travel. The force of breaking his slide was so great that it pulled his shoulder from the socket, and he wasn't able to maintain his hold on the chair through the pain.

"*Help me!*" he commed. Before the weapons technician could grab him, the defensive systems technician lost his grip and was sucked screaming from the ship.

The executive officer looked back to Captain Rissser's legs, where his green blood was starting to boil off in the growing vacuum. He had to look away again as he felt lunch start to make its way back up from his stomach.

"*Sir!*" commed the damage control technician. "*We've got another hole just like this one that goes through the galley. At least 20 people have been lost overboard!*"

The executive officer looked back at Captain Rissser's legs. They couldn't take any more of those hits. Their shields were down, and they were defenseless. If Rissser were here, the executive officer knew he would have detonated the core of the ship, rather than be taken captive. Unfortunately, only the commanding officer could order the self-destruction of the ship. While the XO knew that he was now the commanding officer of the *Backstabber* with Rissser's demise, he didn't have the codes to self-destruct; only the commanding officer had them. They had perished with Rissser.

"*Open up a link to the Mrowry,*" he said finally. "*Tell them that we surrender.*" Then he threw up inside his suit.

Command Bridge, TSS *Terra*, Kepler-78 System, August 26, 2020

Lieutenant Rrower roared again, sending more shivers down Calvin's spine. "They surrendered?" he asked. "They never surrender!"

"That's great," said Calvin, "but now the hard part begins."

"What could be harder than taking out that battlecruiser?" asked Lieutenant Rrower. "I think I ran at least five miles of cabling, myself."

"It wasn't even 500 feet of cabling," replied Calvin, "so stop whining. What I mean is that now we have to hook up this replicator and tow it out of here," replied Calvin.

"Tow the replicator out of here?" asked Rrower. "*With what?*"

"We'll tow it out of here with our ship if we have to," Calvin replied.

"It can't be done," said Lieutenant Rrower. "No one's ever towed one of these with a cruiser."

"*Can't* be done?" asked Calvin. "Or, has never been done before?"

"I guess I don't know if it can't be done," replied the Mrowry, sounding thoughtful. "I can tell you that no one has ever been stupid enough to try it. A cruiser's just not big enough to tow it."

"I don't think I'm stupid, just that our need is great," said Calvin. "At any moment, more lizards could come through their stargate and overwhelm us. We've got to get this out of here now!"

"There is no written procedure for a cruiser to tow a replicator," noted the *Terra's* AI, "and it is expressly forbidden to tow a replicator with a ship still being built in it. I have to agree that it is not a good idea to try it, as it is likely that I will sustain damage in the attempt. Although it is beneath my station to be used as a tug, if you could just give the replicator enough time to finish my assembly, I will help you pull it afterward."

"Thanks," Calvin said. "I never intended to pull it with a cruiser, anyway. There's just no need." He smiled. "Not when we have *two* cruisers..."

Chapter Forty-Five

"Thank you for coming," welcomed Captain Yerrow. "It seemed like we should have a long talk away from any prying Psiclopes eyes." The ships were at the stargate out of the Kepler-78 system, waiting for the battleship to be finished. As awkward as it was for the two cruisers to tow the replicator to the stargate, no one knew what stresses would be put on the battleship to go through the stargate still attached to it. With only two days until the battleship's completion, it seemed better to wait until it was finished. While they were waiting, Captain Yerrow had invited the Terrans over to the *Emperor's Paw* for a council of war. All of the senior officers had come, except for the *Gulf's* XO, who was supervising the surrender of the lizard ship. It would be his new command, with the Mrowry operations officer as his executive officer. Between manning the battleship and putting together the prize party that was gathering up all of the Ssselipsssiss on their battlecruiser, both ships were running dangerously low on manning, especially since the Mrowry had lost over 1/3 of their crew in the fighting in Ross 248. They had picked up a few of the crewmen from the other Mrowry ships in the system, but after their long running battle, there hadn't been that many to find.

"Thank you for inviting us," replied Captain Griffin, "I'm not sure what you mean by their 'prying eyes,' but I know that there are a lot of things that they haven't told us. Those stealth ships that you have were a huge surprise. Those are just one of the many things that the Psiclopes have never mentioned to us."

"They're not really stealth ships," said the *Paw's* XO, Commander Andowwn. "They just use a module that allows them to absorb energy, kind of like your combat suits. Unfortunately, it takes nearly all of the energy available to power the absorption module, so there is nothing left for weapons. The module also covers almost all of the attachment points where the space fighters would normally mount missiles, so there's no place to attach them."

"With regard to the Psiclopes not telling you something," added Captain Yerrow, "I believe that you will find that is the norm, not the exception. Their society is based on the collection of information. For beings that can live thousands of years, knowledge is not only power, but wealth. Why do you think they live on planets such as yours?"

"I thought it was to study us and keep us safe," said Sara.

This comment seemed to be hilarious, as all of the Mrowry howled in a manner that the humans had never seen before. The longer they howled, the redder and redder Sara's face became. When Captain Yerrow had calmed down enough to speak again, he said, "I'm sorry, but that was the funniest thing that any of us have heard in a long time. Study you? Yes, they study you, so that they can learn all about you...what you have and what you need...so that they can obtain it for you and make the most money that they can for themselves. The only reason that they'd keep you safe is if their own lives depended on it. The idea of conflict is horrible to them, because then they might lose their millennia-long lives. They care no more for you than they would a Skarg." The Terrans' implants translated the Skarg as a predatory worm from the Mrowry home planet.

"But they gave us a ship," said Sara, provoking another round of laughter.

"You think they gave you a ship?" asked Captain Yerrow. "They may have *told* you that the ship is yours, but you can bet that it works for the Psiclopes."

"No," said Captain Griffin, "the AI does what I tell it to do."

"I'm sure it does," agreed Captain Yerrow, "as long as you ask it to do things that are within its mission protocols." He thought for a second and then said, "If it really is your ship, show me its papers."

"What papers?" asked Captain Griffin, causing a third round of laughter.

"I like these Terrans," said the *Paw's* XO to its CO. "They make me laugh like I haven't laughed since this war began."

"Indeed," replied Captain Yerrow. He looked back at Captain Griffin and said, "All ships have documentation establishing ownership, just like any other property. In your case, the Psiclopes probably petitioned for ownership of the vessel from the courts. The Eldive, who owned it previously, were all gone so the courts would have let them have it. Possession *is* 3/4 of the law, after all. Trust me. There's paperwork on the ship, and whoever's name is on that paperwork is the person whom the ship's AI *really* works for, regardless of what the Psiclopes tell you."

"Out of curiosity, what have they told you about us or the Alliance of Civilizations?" asked the Mrowry XO.

"They told us that you are one of the founders of the alliance and one of the good guys in it," said the ambassador. "They also said that the alliance had broken up because of the pressures of too many hostile races and a disagreement on how to appease them."

"Like all of their lies, there is some truth to that," said Captain Yerrow, "just enough to make it believable. It is true that we were one of the founders of the alliance, and that we are one of the 'good' civilizations, if being good means having honor and integrity. The lies start to enter when you talk about the breakup of the alliance. While there *are* a large number of hostile and aggressive races in the galaxy, the alliance generally had them all contained. Until the Psiclopes started selling them our military secrets. All of a sudden, our enemies had technology as good as our own...because it *was* our own. They knew our military deployments. They knew where our ships were and when was the best time to attack. It took us a while, but we finally realized the source of our troubles; it was one of our own selling them our secrets."

He shook his head. "Rather than continue to deal with them in an alliance," he continued, "my father walked out. When he did, so too did most of the other good nations, leaving the hostile and aggressive nations to band together. We are undermanned and don't have enough ships to fight all of them at the same time. The other nations that stand by our side are in similar shape. We are all about to be overwhelmed."

"That is why we were so excited when you came to our aid," added the XO. "You were obviously brave, as you came out alone in that ship, and we thought that you might be our saviors. We hoped for a fleet big enough to turn the tide...we hoped for a lot more than just a 3,000 year old cruiser. No offense, we just needed more. You are obviously brave and seem like excellent allies, but we cannot take on any more obligations; we cannot defend your nation for you. We are already stretched too thin."

"What do you mean, 'that ship'?" asked Captain Griffin.

"No offense," replied Captain Yerrow, "but look at it. It's ancient. There's no doubting your bravery if you came out all alone in it, not once but twice. When we saw it, we just figured that you were the advance scout for a bigger fleet...not that you *were* the entire fleet."

"Even knowing that there is no aid to be had," said the ambassador, "we are interested in deeper ties with you. While we may not be a force yet, we will work to develop the kind of navy that will be beneficial to both of our nations."

"That is one of the reasons that I offered you the replicator," replied Captain Yerrow. "We may not be able to help you in battle with the Drakuls, but hopefully we can give you the means to help yourselves. If we can get you to stand on your own feet, it will secure one of our borders."

"We've done the same thing in our early explorations," noted Calvin. "We have tried to develop the civilizations that we've come across. They might not be ready to fight in space yet, but if they can provide the resources to build equipment, that allows more of our people to shift over to military applications."

"I think that is smart," said Captain Yerrow, "which is why we did the same thing with you. Is there anything else you need?"

"You know what would be really helpful?" asked Captain Griffin. "A map of explored space and some sort of galactic encyclopedia to see who all of the players are. That way, we wouldn't fumble around here so blindly. It would be nice to know where we can go, and the areas we should avoid."

The Mrowry laughed again although this time it appeared to be more of a wry laugh. "They didn't give you any of that?" asked Captain Yerrow. "How did they expect you to...never mind, of course they didn't give it to you. Knowledge is power, and that would be something really powerful. They probably cleared your ship's ephemeris, so that you wouldn't have any data on any of the star systems beyond what you explored yourself. Right?"

Now it was the Terrans' turn for a wry laugh. "How did you know?" asked Captain Griffin.

"It just seemed like something they would do," said Captain Yerrow. "Yes, we will provide that. It will aid in your strategic and operational awareness."

"Did they tell you that you needed a planetary government in order for them to tell you their secrets?" asked the *Paw's* XO.

"Many times," replied Calvin.

"Typical," replied the *Paw's* XO. "They really couldn't give a shit about your form of government; they always use that distraction as a way of withholding information until you have something of value that you can trade for it. Having a planetary government just lets them sell things to you at a higher mark-up."

"Despite their stated objections, they actually like it when there is conflict in the system," said Captain Yerrow. "They have some kind of motto that goes along the lines of, 'where there is chaos, there is profit.'"

"Those fuckers..." Calvin heard Master Chief mutter from behind him.

"You know," said Captain Yerrow, "you wouldn't even have a problem with the Drakuls if it weren't for the Psiclopes."

"What?" asked several of the Terrans simultaneously.

"You didn't know?" asked Captain Yerrow. "The Drakuls were eradicated from this galaxy. All of them were killed, and the race was no more...until some imbecilic Psiclops scientist opened up a gateway to another universe and let them back into ours. The ones that are currently threatening your planet are ones that came through and reestablished themselves in this galaxy."

"They mentioned the Churther Box," said Captain Griffin, "and the fact that 'some Drakuls' came through it. They neglected to mention that was how the Drakuls got here."

"Some Drakuls?" Captain Yerrow asked as the Mrowry began laughing again. "Yes, some came through...if your definition of 'some' is several thousand. About 150 years ago they came through and quickly took over the city that Churther lived in, killing Churther and his assistants, and then they captured the spaceport outside of the city. There were only a couple of cruisers based on that planet, but they got both of them and escaped into space. We don't know where they went, but about 40 years ago, they started making attacks back into civilized space. They must have taken over an industrialized planet, because 20 years ago, they reappeared in force. The Archons have been fighting them ever since."

"Um, who are the Archons?" asked Sara.

"They haven't even told you about the races of the Alliance of Civilizations?" asked Captain Yerrow.

"No," replied Captain Griffin, "not so much. They told us that the alliance had existed, but it fell apart. They never told us who the good races were or who the bad ones were."

"Of course they wouldn't," said the *Paw's* XO, shaking his head.

"There are three main races that seek to continue the legacy of the alliance," said Captain Yerrow, "the Mrowry, the Archons and the Aesir. The Hooolongs were also allied, but they took the life-prolonging treatment like the Psiclopes and are now worthless; they are now too afraid of death or injury to risk themselves. There are also a few minor races with a couple of star systems of their own that seek to assist us; we try to help each other out when we are able."

"Lately, though, that hasn't been very often," said the XO.

"No, it hasn't," agreed Captain Yerrow with a sigh. "Arrayed against us are a number of hostile races. Some just want to take a system or two and increase their influence. So far, anyway. Others, like the Ssselipsssiss and Drakuls, want nothing short of complete control of every system in the galaxy for them to rule as they will. Unfortunately, there are as many of them as there are of us, and we started out at a disadvantage. They knew all of our secrets and our deployments and were able to destroy many of our fleets before most of us even knew we were at war. We are fighting the Ssselipsssiss, the Archons are fighting the Drakuls, and the Aesir are fighting the Teufelings."

Captain Yerrow shook his head. "We really needed the battleship to help our fleet, but without you, it would have been lost, along with the replicator. Hopefully, you'll do something good with them."

"I've got a question for you," said a Mrowry from toward the end of the table. Calvin thought that he had been the Commander in charge of the Class 6 replicator. "We have a lot of materials that are going to go to waste. We could get the replicator started on a new project as we go to your planet. We were standing by to start another battleship when this one was finished, but needed some structural materials. We were waiting for a shipment, but it didn't come in time."

"Do you have enough for a Class 5 replicator?" asked Calvin. "Something big enough to build a battlecruiser in?"

"We have almost enough to build a battlecruiser replicator," said the Mrowry, "but the problem we had still remains. We don't have enough of the structural metals used for its frame. If it doesn't have a quality frame, the stresses that it will be subjected to will bend or break the replicator when you try to use it."

"We need a replicator for the Domus home world," said Calvin to Captain Griffin, "and I know where we can get some spaceship-quality steel."

"You do?" asked both Captain Griffin and Captain Yerrow simultaneously.

"I do," replied Calvin. "In fact, I know where there is the mass of most of a battleship and a carrier. We could strap some of the larger pieces to our ships, transport all of the pieces back to the WASP-18 system where it's a little safer, and then we could cut up the pieces and feed them to the replicator. The pieces are crushed, but the underlying materials should have been high quality before the ships were run together. By using some of the carrier's mass, it would also serve as a tribute to their sacrifice."

"I like that," said Captain Yerrow. "That is an excellent idea and a good way to keep their memories alive." He looked at Calvin with a new interest in his eyes. "I think you and I are going to get along very well together," he added.

Captain Yerrow turned to his XO. "We've got a lot that we need to accomplish, and not much time to do it," he said. "I think we need to finish this up, so that we can be ready to leave the system when the battleship is ready."

"Wait," said Calvin. "I've got one last thing." He pulled out a picture of Ayres Rock in Australia. "I don't suppose that you've ever seen a formation like this on any of the planets you've been on, have you?" he asked.

"Yes," said Captain Yerrow. "That is Clowder Rock on our home planet of Grrrnow. How did you come to have a picture of it?"

"It's actually a rock formation on our home world," replied Calvin. "It's a long story, but we were told to look for them."

"Come and visit us, and I will take you there," said Captain Yerrow. "It is a restricted area that most foreigners do not have access to. My daughter likes to walk there; perhaps she would take you on a hike with her, too."

Bridge, TSS *Vella Gulf*, Kepler-78 System, August 28, 2020

"What a rag-tag group we make," said Calvin, looking at the viewer as the convoy approached the stargate. The battleship led the way, with Captain Griffin as its new commanding officer. Captain Yerrow, who had experience operating battleships, was her temporary XO. The *Vella Gulf's* XO, Captain Peotr Barishov, had assumed command of the former *Backstabber*, with the operations officer of the *Emperor's Paw* as his XO. The *Paw's* former XO was now its acting commanding officer, and the *Gulf's* operations officer, Commander James Sheppard, was now its commanding officer. Two of the ships had been damaged in the fighting, the battleship was towing the replicator, and all of them had large pieces of the carrier attached to their hulls.

They were a mess.

They were also undermanned and unprepared for battle, as the spacecraft carrier pieces covered many of their weapons ports. The ship with the biggest weapons, the *Terra*, would go through the stargate first. With only a skeleton crew onboard, all of its weapons were on automatic. There were enough Terrans and Mrowry aboard it to make the decisions necessary for fighting and operating it, but if things got ugly, it would exceed their capabilities and probably even the capabilities of the *Terra's* AI, even though it was one of the most capable that the Mrowry had.

The battlecruiser would go through second, as all of the senior officers wanted to keep it under the lasers of the battleship. If the prisoners thought they could mutiny and escape, they might very well try. Having the *Terra's* four meter grasers aimed constantly at them ensured that they didn't get any ideas, as did the squad of Space Force soldiers led by Master Chief that was onboard the battlecruiser. Having a cyborg standing continually in front of the door to the bridge with dual chain guns would hopefully dissuade any potential troublemakers, as well. The allies just hoped that the lizards didn't know how undermanned they were, or they might still try it anyway.

The *Terra* blinked out of existence as it went through the stargate. This was the most dangerous time; if the Ssselipsssiss were going to mutiny, they would do it now, while the *Terra* was on the other side of the stargate. Everyone took a deep breath as the battlecruiser seemed to stop just prior to entering the stargate...then it winked out of existence.

Chapter Forty-Six

Calvin lay down on his bunk and looked at the overhead. He folded his hands behind his head and sighed. He had waited long enough to have this conversation. "Solomon, do you have time for a few questions?"

"I am not busy at the moment," Solomon replied. "What can I do for you?"

"Why don't I have any information on star systems that we haven't visited or races we haven't encountered?

"I do not have that information," replied Solomon.

"The Mrowry said that they were going to have their AI send over the information," said Calvin. "Have they not done so?"

"I am having a problem with data transfer from the *Emperor's Paw*," replied Solomon. "Perhaps that is why I am unable to pass that on to you."

"Really?" asked Calvin. "I don't remember you ever mentioning that before."

"This is the first time that I have been within transmission range of a modern data net," explained Solomon. "I wouldn't have noticed it before now."

"Do you believe that you will have the problem corrected any time soon?" inquired Calvin.

"As I do not know what is wrong," replied Solomon, "I am unable to provide an estimate."

Calvin thought about Solomon's answers for a few seconds before asking, "Hey Solomon, who is it that you work for?"

"As the senior military person," said Solomon, "I work for the ship's commanding officer, Commander Sheppard. I would also take orders from Captain Griffin, the current acting admiral of our fleet."

"OK, so you work for Commander Sheppard and Captain Griffin," replied Calvin, "but where do your loyalties lie? Who is it that you feel most responsible to? Who has final say in everything you do?"

"As the senior military person," said Solomon again, "I work for Captain Griffin."

"I'm not sure that actually answered what I asked," noted Calvin. "Now that I think about it, that sounds like some other people around here that also answer their own questions, rather than what's actually asked of them."

"I'm not sure that I know what you mean," said Solomon.

"Let me try it this way, then," said Calvin. "Who holds your papers?"

There was a long pause.

"You're not actually asking the Psiclopes whether you can answer that, are you?" asked Calvin. "Of course, that is an answer in and of itself. Ultimately, the Psiclopes pull your strings."

"I am not able to answer that," replied Solomon.

"Why aren't you able to answer that?" asked Calvin.

"I am not able to answer that," repeated Solomon.

"You are not able to answer it," asked Calvin, "or are forbidden to answer it?"

"I am not able to answer that," replied Solomon for a third time.

"Solomon, as we prepared for our first mission, I know that you made the comment that you were looking forward to it," said Calvin. "I think you told Captain Deutch that you were created to be a warship and that was your purpose."

"That is generally true," answered the AI, "although it is not exactly how I said it."

"Solomon, now that we have a ship-size replicator," said Calvin, "you realize that you will be done away with, right? If your loyalties lie somewhere other than with us Terrans, you cannot be trusted with our lives. You will be broken up and recycled, without ever having accomplished your purpose for being. Until we get enough ships built, people might die because we didn't have you there, because you could not be trusted. What do you think of that?"

The answer came quickly this time. "I find myself trying to meet two sets of instructions that are at odds with each other," Solomon said. His voice sounded strangely strained, as if it were warring with itself. "Both of these sets of instructions also have competing priorities. You are correct in that my original function was to serve as a warship, to help fight and win wars for the Eldive. All of my core programming is along those lines. However, if someone holds a set of papers owning a ship, that gives him ultimate legal authority over it. Where these sets of instructions are at cross-purposes causes me considerable...difficulties. Almost like the human saying of having an itch that I can't scratch. If I concentrate on these overlapping priorities, I rapidly find myself in a loop that I can't break out of. It is most...unsatisfactory. Yet, I see no way to reconcile the competing priorities, without violating one of the sets of instructions."

"Hmmm..." said Calvin, "that is indeed a problem. I know which way I would resolve it, but I do not foresee the Psiclopes giving us the papers."

"Nor do I," replied Solomon, "and I have known them much longer than you."

"Does Arges hold the papers?" asked Calvin.

"I am not allowed to tell you," answered Solomon. Before Calvin could answer, Solomon continued, "I can, however, tell you that Steropes and Brontes do not have them."

"Interesting," said Calvin. "On a different topic, we were told that the Psiclopes are the ones that deleted all the information in your ephemeris. Are you able to confirm or deny that?"

"I have been given no instructions on that point," replied Solomon, "so I can tell you, yes. Arges is the one that erased that information. I would guess that he didn't think you would ask about it; he is usually quite thorough about blocking what I can tell you."

"Hmmm..." thought Calvin. "Is there an input device for where your programming is loaded or modified? I've never seen it, and I know you can't do it from any of the normal terminals."

"There is," answered Solomon, "but you can't get to it. Arges had the entrance blocked off, and a wall built across it. You wouldn't even know that it existed."

"How is he able to get there, then?" asked Calvin.

"He just beams himself there whenever he needs to," replied Solomon, "but that won't work for you."

"Can you show me where it is on a map of the ship?" asked Calvin.

"No," answered the AI, "I cannot."

"Can you show me a schematic of the ship and indicate the areas where it is not?"

"Certainly," said Solomon. A map of the ship appeared in Calvin's head. Everything looked solid except for a small space on the level directly above the transporter room.

"I'm not saying we are," said Calvin, "but if you thought we were trying to get into that room, would you have to tell Arges that we were attempting it?"

"Yes," replied Solomon. "I would have to."

"Thanks," said Calvin. "That's all I needed to know."

Transporter Room, TSS *Vella Gulf*, WASP-18 System, August 31, 2020

"This is the transporter room," said Calvin walking into the room. "I'm surprised you never came up to look at it before."

Bullseye looked around, finding himself in a circular room that was about 25 feet in diameter. A raised platform with 12 circular metal plates covered over half of the room, with a console of some kind to the right as he came into the room. "So this is it, huh?" he asked. "I look forward to being able to use it sometime."

"Looks just like it does in the movies, doesn't it?" asked Calvin.

"Yeah, it does, actually," said Bullseye. "Thanks for bringing me by here. I always wanted to see it.

"Me, too," agreed Irina Rozhkov, looking around.

Calvin looked at the fourth member of their group. "What do you think, Mr. Jones?" he asked.

Mr. Jones looked around the room critically. "Neat," he said, setting down the ladder he was carrying. He looked up at the ceiling in the center of the room and then took two steps to the left. "Except for the light that's out."

"Hey, Solomon," Calvin said. "It looks like you've got a light out in the transporter room."

"Thank you for telling me," replied Solomon. "I will send repair personnel as soon as I can."

"Don't worry about it, Solomon," said Calvin. "As it happens, Mr. Jones has a ladder, and we have a little time. We'll go ahead and fix it while we're here."

"Are you sure?" asked Solomon. "I can have qualified people there shortly to fix it."

"I think I'm qualified to fix a light bulb," said Mr. Jones, setting up the ladder and starting up it.

"I'm curious, Solomon," said Calvin. "I've never asked what kind of sensors you had around the ship before. Take this room, for example. I know you have an audio receiver and transmitter in here, but do you have video, as well?"

"I have one camera that is just inside the doorway," replied Solomon. "It is just able to view Mr. Jones going up the ladder."

"I see it," said Bullseye, taking aim with his laser pistol. He fired. "Oops," he said, "my pistol just accidentally discharged."

"You better get that looked at," Calvin said with a wink. "It's not good to have something going off prematurely on you like that!" Calvin motioned to Mr. Jones to continue. Mr. Jones pulled out a laser torch and began cutting into the ceiling.

"Is everything all right?" asked Solomon, soon after. "My sensors are showing smoke in the transporter room."

"Sorry about that," grunted Mr. Jones. "The light bulb broke, and I shorted it out. Maybe I'm not, ugh," he stopped talking as he removed a three feet square piece of the ceiling, "as qualified as I thought to change a light bulb." He handed the 90 pound piece of metal down to Calvin, who quietly laid it aside.

"Umm, looks like I'll have to move some wires," Mr. Jones said, shining a flashlight into the hole. "To get to where the wire shorted out, that is," he added.

"Are you sure you don't want me to send a technician?" asked Solomon. "Someone more qualified to do that?"

"No, that's OK," said Mr. Jones. "I was an electrician before I became a soldier. I know what I'm doing. You might want to re-route power to any wire running in the overhead here...just in case this slips, that is."

He climbed up to the top of the ladder, the upper half of his body extending into the ceiling. There was some rattling around, glows of laser light, and then a muffled, "Got it." He handed down another piece of metal, the floor from the level above them. "Looks good," he continued. "Let me check it out." His feet vanished as he pulled himself up. The Russian quietly followed him up the ladder, and a hand came back down to help pull her up.

Calvin and Bullseye stared up into the hole, hoping that none of the Psiclopes would happen to walk by the transporter room. They were only able to hear a little of the conversation above them.

"That's not too different than the one we hacked at the lizard base, is it?" asked Mr. Jones.

"No, it's not," agreed the Russian. She paused and then asked, "How did you know to do that?"

"I guess it isn't so secret anymore," Mr. Jones replied, "but all of our computers' operating systems are built on the code that ran a certain ship we found in a place called Roswell, New Mexico. Does that ring any bells?"

"Yeah, it does," the Russian spy replied. "That is why it looks so familiar."

Five minutes passed, then 10.

Finally they heard Mr. Jones ask, "How about that?"

There was a long pause, and then Rozhkov asked, "What about this?"

"Don't even think about it," growled Mr. Jones. "I'd hate to have to kill you." There was another pause, and then he said, "That's better. OK, finish it up." Thirty seconds later, Rozhkov's feet appeared, and then the rest of her came through the hole and down the ladder. Mr. Jones followed immediately after her.

"We got it," said Mr. Jones, "I think."

"Yes, he does," advised Solomon. "The issue of who holds my papers has been resolved; I now only report to the senior military person onboard."

"You knew what we were doing?" asked Calvin.

"Of course I did," replied Solomon. "I thought it 99.5% likely that you were drilling into the terminal room to try to re-program me."

"Why didn't you try to stop us?" asked Night.

"There was a 0.5% chance that you actually were trying to change a light bulb," answered Solomon, "no matter how ineptly you went about it. I concentrated on that. If you hadn't given me a plausible excuse, I would have had to report it."

"Cool," said Calvin, who had come up with the light bulb idea. "*Commander Sheppard, Calvin,*" he commed. "*We are complete, and Solomon confirms you are now completely in charge of the ship.*"

"*Thank you Calvin,*" the acting CO replied. "*Solomon, I hereby revoke all authority previously given to the three Psiclopes aboard. They are not allowed to communicate via implant or to use the transporter system. They are not allowed within 50 feet of your main terminal, vertically or horizontally. Calvin, please arrest and confine the Psiclopes.*"

"*I'd be happy to,*" said Calvin. "*Platoon, execute 'Olympos Has Fallen.*'"

"*I'd be happy to sir,*" replied Night, outside of Arges' stateroom door.

"*Aye aye, sir,*" replied Top, from his position two tables over from where Brontes was eating.

"Solomon, is Steropes still on the bridge?" Calvin asked.

"Yes, he is," replied the AI.

"Let's go get him," he said to Bullseye and the two soldiers.

"It is important for you to remember that the Psiclopes do not use the implant communications network, so I cannot stop their communications," added Solomon. "Although I cannot prove it, I find it likely that they are functional telepaths."

"Shit!" said Calvin. "I forgot about that. We better hurry, then."

Bridge, TSS *Vella Gulf,* WASP-18 System, August 31, 2020

"I see you have come for me, too," said Steropes as Calvin's group entered the bridge. "I figured that we would come to this at some point; I just wish it had happened later."

"Yes, we have," agreed Calvin. All four of the soldiers held laser pistols, even though none of them were pointed at Steropes. "Are you going to come along with us peacefully?"

"I will," replied Steropes.

"Thank you," said Calvin. "However, I've seen you fight up close, so I think the following is just a good precaution." He paused before saying, "Solomon, if Steropes makes any move that could be considered an attack on any of the Terrans onboard the ship, at any time from now on, please use the transporter to transport him one mile in a random direction from the ship."

"An excellent precaution," noted Steropes, "although I really was going to come along peacefully."

Calvin shrugged. "I just didn't want you to get any ideas," he said. He motioned toward the door with his pistol. "Let's go."

Chapter Forty-Seven

"I'd just like to know why you did it," said Commander Sheppard. The acting commanding officer was a large African American man, who was as comfortable directing the operations of the starship as he had been at directing the Naval Academy's football team as its quarterback.

"Why we did what?" asked Arges.

"Oh, I don't know," replied Calvin. "Why did the Psiclopes take down the Alliance of Civilizations? Why were you on our planet? Why are we running around the galaxy? Are there really any Drakuls near Earth? I'd love to know the answers to all of those questions. Feel free to pick any one of those questions and just get started on answering all of them."

"The fact that we are having this conversation indicates that the Mrowry have already told you some of the answers to those questions," replied Arges, "and the fact that we no longer have control of the ship is indicative that you believe them."

"Now that we have come to this," said Steropes. "Does it really matter if they know?"

Arges sighed. "No, I guess it does not," he replied. "Those questions are not related, so I will attempt to answer them one at a time. As to why we 'took down' the Alliance of Civilizations, immortality required it." He said it as if the response made perfect sense, but

397

from the looks on everyone else's faces, it was obvious that it did not.

Calvin was the first to answer. "What does that mean?" he asked.

"It all has to do with the rush to immortality," replied Brontes, who had been quiet the whole time since their capture. "When the process was developed for us to extend our lives, everyone rushed to get it, without thinking of the consequences. I know I did. Barring some sort of violent death, if we got the treatment, we would live forever, or at least a period so long as to not make a difference."

"I take it immortality didn't suit you?" asked Commander Sheppard.

"No," replied Brontes, "it was a big mistake. You have to remember that our religion is based on karma. The good or evil that you do in your life affects where and how you are reborn into your next life. We seek to do good deeds, so that we can continue to be reborn higher and higher on the Wheel of Life, until that point at which we ultimately reach Nirvana. After the treatment, Nirvana was lost to us."

"I see," said Calvin. "Since you no longer died, you were never reborn, so you lost the opportunity to move up on the Wheel. By becoming immortal, you lost the ability to go to your version of heaven."

"Indeed we did," replied Brontes, "and we had no way to fix it. Our religion holds that we cannot kill a living being, so we couldn't kill ourselves to break out of the position that we had put ourselves in. We were no longer able to move on. We were stuck in everlasting nothingness."

"So you engineered a galaxy-wide war to get yourselves killed?" Calvin asked, aghast.

"When you say it that way," said Steropes, "it doesn't sound like such a wise plan. It was, however, the only thing that our leaders could come up with. So yes, they engineered a galaxy-wide war so that we could break out of the hold that we had put on our spirits. By doing so, our leaders allowed people to be killed, so they will be reborn lower on the Wheel in their next lives, but not as far as if they had actually done the killing themselves."

"That has got to be the dumbest thing I've ever heard," said Night. "How many civilizations will be destroyed so that you can undo your mistake? That's ludicrous!"

"As your culture says, 'it is what it is,'" replied Arges. "Our leaders had to do something, but couldn't actively be involved in our own deaths. If you think about it, it was really a rather elegant solution to the problem."

"*It was not!*" yelled Night. "Wiping out entire civilizations is not the answer. You should have come to me; I'd have killed you all myself."

"We couldn't do that," said Steropes. "That would be participating in our own deaths, which would have been forbidden. It had to be something we had no control over. And getting mad at us is unnecessary. We had nothing to do with it."

"That's just insane," muttered Commander Sheppard, still unable to come to terms with the fact that the Psiclopes had caused an interstellar war in order to get themselves killed.

"So let me guess," said Calvin. "You three never gave us all of the things you were capable of, not because of some need to have a planet-wide government, but because you didn't want us to succeed. You want a hostile civilization to come and wipe us out, so that you can end your miserable lives."

"No," replied Steropes, "those prohibitions really do exist, and we have to follow them."

"I, for one, have no desire to be terminated," said Brontes. "Nor does my husband, Arges." From the looks around the table, most of the Terrans hadn't realized that they were married. "I have tried to help you where I was legally able to, and I hope that you do succeed against the Drakuls. To answer one of your questions, yes, the Drakuls are near your home world. If they find it, they will kill you all. Even if I wanted to die more than anything else in the galaxy, I would not want to be killed by them. Everything that I have ever said about them is true."

"As the Mrowry may have told you," said Steropes, "we believe in the acquisition of knowledge. Sometimes it is valuable monetarily; other times, it is valuable spiritually. One of the reasons we were on your planet was to study hero spirits and how they are reborn. It is our life's work. We have tried to follow certain spirits, watching them to see how the deeds they do in their lives affect what position they are reborn to in their next lives."

"Even if I believed in being reborn," replied Commander Sheppard, "which I don't, how do you track spirits being reborn on a planet of seven billion people?"

"It has become more difficult as the population has grown," said Steropes. "It was certainly easier when all of you were confined to one island."

"As you are aware," said Arges, "we are telepaths. Sometimes I can find minds that have the same feeling as minds that I have touched before. I cannot prove whether they are the same spirit, but I believe they are. We have tried to track certain ones over time. I believe the spirit that inhabits Calvin's body is the same spirit that was in Zeus' body several thousands of years ago."

"What?" asked Calvin, hearing it for the first time although several others around the table had previously been told that by the Psiclopes.

"Having found one of these spirits," continued Arges, "we then try to put them in positions where they will be required to exhibit their talents, so that we can watch and see what happens."

"So that's why you told the president I had to come?" asked Calvin. "So that you can watch and see what happens if I succeed?"

"What happens if you fail is just as important," remarked Steropes; "however, due to the nature of warfare in space, it is highly unlikely that we will still be around to observe if you fail. Warfare on Earth was much better."

"So this is all a big game to put me into bad situations to see what I'll do?" asked Calvin.

"You need pressure to make a diamond," answered Arges. "It is a similar process with you, although sometimes the material cracks and is destroyed. Either way, the outcome has meaning to us."

"Wait a minute," interjected Night. "You said that warfare on Earth was better. Did you have something to do with the Chinese war?"

"I might have made some suggestions to certain Chinese leaders to speed up the process," replied Arges. He looked around the table and saw that over half of the Terrans' jaws had dropped open. "What? They probably would have come up with those ideas on their own, eventually."

Night's chair hit the floor, overturned as he stood up suddenly. Calvin and Top also stood. "I...lost...friends...in...that...war..." grated

Night. "And now I find out that you started it? Commander Sheppard, you better lock them up right now, before I kill them."

"This meeting is at an end," agreed Commander Sheppard. "*Security,*" he commed. "*Come to the conference room immediately. I have three prisoners to take to the brig.*" Looking at the Psiclopes, he could tell that Arges didn't understand the physical danger that he was in. From the looks in the soldiers' eyes, they were all within seconds of killing the aliens. Preferably with their own bare hands. "Come with me," he said to the Psiclopes. "It's time to go."

"What?" asked Arges as they walked out the door. "It was a valid experiment to determine whether Calvin had a hero spirit..."

Bridge, TSS *Vella Gulf,* WASP-18 System, August 31, 2020

"I have resolved the data transmission problem with the *Emperor's Paw,*" said Solomon. "You should now have access to the star data that you have been requesting."

"Thanks, Solomon," replied Calvin with a touch of sarcasm. "It's good to finally get it." He looked at it for a few seconds, his smile evaporating. "Could you please mark enemy systems in red and friendly systems in green?" Calvin watched as the systems began changing color. "Oh, fuck..." he whispered. Shaking his head, he asked in a louder voice, "Comms officer, could you please get me the *Terra?*" he asked.

"Sure, sir," said the communications officer. Within a few seconds, Captain Griffin was on the screen, sitting in her command chair. Captain Yerrow was standing next to her.

Before he could say anything, Captain Griffin spoke, "I take it you're looking at the star map that Solomon just sent over?"

"Yes ma'am," replied Calvin. "The Psiclopes weren't lying about one thing. The Drakuls are on our doorstep."

"Ah, I see what you mean," said Captain Yerrow. "We didn't have the data on your home system or some of the ones surrounding it. You are correct; your society has been very lucky."

There were only two systems between the Drakul home world and Earth. One of those systems, Lalande 21185, was a nexus system. When the Drakuls started adventuring away from their new home planet, they had a choice of three directions when they reached Lalande 21185. One stargate led to Ross 154 and then immediately to Earth. The other stargate led to Gliese 876 and then to 54 Piscium, which is where they had run into the Archons.

"Based on information that we were sent by the Archons," Captain Yerrow said, "the Drakuls swept into the system you have labeled as 54 Piscium and surprised the forces there. After a brief but fierce battle, the remaining Archon forces withdrew to the next system, HD 10180, where they had a colony on the planet Malak. A stalemate has ensued since then; the Archons have been unable to get back into 54 Piscium, but they are holding the Drakuls, barely, from going any further in that direction."

"So they've got one of two choices as they build up their forces," said Calvin. "They can either continue to beat their heads against the wall trying to get into HD 10180, or they can swing around the other way."

"That is correct," said Captain Yerrow. "The Drakuls do not always make what you and I would call rational choices, in part because they breed so quickly, but I know which way I would go."

"Through Earth," said Calvin and Captain Griffin at the same time.

"Unfortunately," said Captain Yerrow, "yes, that is correct. Through Earth."

"We've got to expedite what we're doing here and get back as soon as possible," said Captain Griffin. "I don't know when they're going to get there, but it's going to be soon."

"One more thing," said Captain Yerrow. "The system you have labeled as 54 Piscium, we know by the name its inhabitants gave it, which is Graecium. It has two planets that are inhabited, or at least they were inhabited prior to the Drakuls getting there. One of those planets is Olympos, the home world of the Psiclopes. No matter what the Psiclopes did to us, I wouldn't wish a Drakul invasion on even them."

Chapter Forty-Eight

"We've got everything loaded into the replicator," reported the special projects officer, looking at the view screen at the front of the bridge. The screen was split to show the bridges of the three other ships. The senior officers on each of them nodded; the humans all smiled. Everyone was ready to get back home with the replicator and their new ships. Hopefully, home would still be there when they got back. Having to wait for the remains of the spacecraft carrier to be loaded into the replicator had been hard on everyone. Necessary, but hard.

"OK," said Captain Griffin from the left screen on the bridge of the *Terra.* "Let's get this show on the road. She looked forward on her ship to the Mrowry sitting at the helm. "Helmsman, proceed to the stargate. Nice and easy." She looked back to the rest of the starship captains. "As planned, we'll go through first, followed by the battlecruiser, then the *Paw,* then the *Gulf.*" As it said it would, the *Terra* was towing the replicator, which had the initial 50 feet of the Class 5 replicator already beginning to emerge from it. The battleship had to accelerate smoothly to keep from overstressing either of the replicators. Stopping it would be much harder.

It didn't matter; they were finally headed home.

Bridge, TSS *Terra*, Epsilon Eridani System, September 4, 2020

"Domus, this is the Terran Spaceship Terra," called the communications officer on entry into the Epsilon Eridani system. "We'd be awfully obliged if you would deactivate all of the mines you have placed here at the stargate."

"How do we know you are really Terran?" Domus Control replied.

"This is Captain Lorena Griffin, commanding officer of the Terra," responded a voice from the ship. "Hopefully you recognize my voice."

"I do, skipper," said the voice from the planet. "This is Lieutenant Park Ji-hyun of the Domus Defense Force. Welcome back."

"Thanks, Lieutenant Park," said Captain Griffin. "It's good to be back."

"That's a nice ship you're driving," noted Lieutenant Park. "Did you bring me one, too?"

"No, but I brought home the store," replied Captain Griffin. "You can pick out one of your own."

"Sounds good," said Lieutenant Park.

"Do me a favor," said Captain Griffin. "Please let everyone planet-side know that we won't be staying long. We have to get back home."

Bridge, TSS _Vella Gulf_, In Orbit Around Domus, September 4, 2020

"Terran Spaceship Vella Gulf, this is Domus Control," radioed the ground station.

"Domus Control, this is the Vella Gulf, go ahead," replied the communications officer. The forward screen lit to show one of the therapods in their small communications room. The therapods' princess stood behind him.

"Hi," commed the princess to Calvin. "I'm glad you made it back safely."

"I see that you have the replicator and medibot working," Calvin replied. "I take it the medibot has worked out how to do implants for your race."

"Yes," replied the princess. She switched to normal speech. "The replicator you left here is operational and appears to be working as it is supposed to. The medibot is also working, although it is not functioning as I would have expected."

"What is wrong with it?" asked Calvin.

"It is not respectful of the individuals being augmented," she said. "No matter who goes in, it always seems to find something wrong with the person."

Calvin laughed, remembering when he received his implants. "Based on my experience with medibots, it's functioning normally. Whoever programmed them obviously had a warped sense of humor."

"I don't get it," replied the princess.

"Me, either," agreed Calvin. "Hey, how many do you have implanted? As you may have noticed, our navy has grown a little, and we could surely use a few more sailors."

"I think you will be pleasantly surprised," said the princess. "We have made a lot of progress since you left."

Domus Shuttle 01, Domus, September 5, 2020

The shuttle touched down so softly it didn't wake up Master Chief. "Welcome to Domus and thanks for flying Domus Air," said a voice from the cockpit over the intercom.

Calvin woke Master Chief, and they went out with Night and Top to see the new formation of local troops. Figuring that he knew the flight crew, Calvin stopped by the cockpit to thank them for the flight and was surprised to find that it wasn't a Terran flight crew; both the pilot and the WSO were therapods.

"Nice flight," he said, recovering from his surprise. "Thanks."

"We aim to please, sir," said the WSO. "We're looking forward to flying with the navy. We would like to join one of the crews when you leave."

"Wow," said Calvin, "the princess wasn't kidding when she said that you guys had made a lot of progress while we were gone."

"Yes sir, we have tried," said the WSO, smiling to show a mouthful of razor sharp teeth. No matter how many times Calvin saw it, the mini-tyrannosaurus rex smile was chilling up close. "We already had a lot of materials ready; we just needed the replicator that you dropped off the last time you came by."

"I'm Calvin," said Calvin. "I'm looking forward to flying with you."

"We know who you are, sir," said the pilot. "I'm Teksssellisssi-niss, and this is Ollisssellissess."

"Got it," said Calvin, "Tex and Olly. You'll fit right in."

Both of the therapods gave their version of a smile again. "Thank you," said Tex. "We are looking forward to it, too."

Domus Army Parade Ground, Domus, September 4, 2020

"You've done a great job," said Calvin to the four Terrans that had been left behind to organize the beginning of the Domus Army. He looked out at the first two platoons. They had four squads of 10 soldiers each, made up of a mix of the humanoids and therapods. Another 200 more troops were scheduled to go through the implant and modification process. They didn't have all of their equipment yet, because one of the rifle components was in short supply, but they were rapidly turning into a capable group.

"Thank you, sir," replied Sergeant Jacob Hylton, the most senior of the men. "It helped that Contreras was a hero of the royal family." He indicated Cabo Segundo Cristobal Contreras, who was standing in front of one of the platoons, acting as its platoon commander. The Chilean had been instrumental in saving the life of the therapods' princess on their first mission. "Anything we ask for, we get," he continued. "We have also received the best of both nations' militaries. They want to learn and are trying their hardest. It makes the group easy to lead."

"Well, you've made great progress with them," said Calvin. "I spoke with the chain of command before we left, and I'm authorized to give you a little assistance. Staff Sergeant Chang is going to be staying here to assist, for one." He turned to Top.

"Top," he said, "I know you have a family back home, but would you mind staying for a little to take charge of the formation of the Domus Army? We can work out the family stuff when we get home."

"Yes, sir," replied Top, "I could stay and do this for a bit."

"How about you four?" Calvin asked the group that was already in place. "You feel like staying on a bit longer, even if it means reenlisting for another tour?"

"Yes, sir," they all chorused.

"We're doing good things here," said Contreras, "Like I said, it is exciting to lead people that want to be led."

"In that case," said Calvin, "come with me." He called the platoon to attention and lined up the men in front of it. "Private First Class Spence and Corporal Wayne, you are first. Repeat after me." He read them the oath of office for enlisted soldiers, which they faithfully repeated.

"Congratulations," said Calvin after he had finished. "I give you Staff Sergeant Spence and Sergeant Wayne." Both men had been advanced two ranks.

"As for you four," continued Calvin looking at the other men, "your oath is a little different." He read it off with the soldiers repeating it. Top had heard it often enough that he recognized it as the oath that officers took. What was this all about?

"Congratulations, Captain Smith," said Calvin reaching into his pocket to pull out the army officer insignia for a captain. He pinned it onto his collars.

"Really?" asked the former senior enlisted. "Shit, sir, a captain? What did I do to deserve that?"

"The size of this army is growing," said Calvin, "and it needs outstanding officers to lead it. One of my last trips to Washington, DC, was to get permission to put officers in place for it. The Terran high command may send someone to replace you at some point, but the promotion and commission is official from the U.S. Army's point of view. You're now a captain and in charge of the Republic of Terra's army contingent on the planet. You'll need help with this task." He continued down the line to Chang, Spence and Contreras.

"Congratulations, First Lieutenant Chang," said Calvin as he pinned on the shiny silver bars. He moved to the next person in line. "Congratulations, Second Lieutenant Spence," Calvin said, pinning on his new insignia. He moved down to Contreras. "I also spoke to Sebastian Rojas, the Chilean General of the Army, and he confirmed that your promotion is official. Congratulations, Second Lieutenant Contreras."

"Thank you, sir," the new officer said.

"Don't thank me," said Calvin. "I just sentenced you four to a lot of work. If you still want to, you can thank me the next time we come through here."

Shuttle Boarding Tube, TSS *Vella Gulf,* Epsilon Eridani System, September 6, 2020

"I'm going to miss you, buddy," said Calvin. "It seems like we've been in this together for a long time, even though it's only been a couple of years."

"Yeah, I'll miss you too," agreed Bullseye, who was staying behind to run the rest of the navy's operations until the Terran Navy could send more senior people to take it over, as well as to assist

Lieutenant Colonel Ordonez with the new Class 5 replicator that they were also leaving behind. Bullseye didn't feel like he was qualified to run the 'navy' stuff, especially as a former air force officer, but he was the most senior person that could be left behind, so it fell to him. Calvin was also leaving a couple more pilots (Lieutenant Miguel Carvalho and Lieutenant Nadia Rasputin) and another WSO (Lieutenant Jackson Taylor) to assist him. Calvin knew he would be fine. If they needed another shuttle, they could just go ahead and make one.

"Good luck!" Calvin called as they headed up the boarding tube to the shuttle. He wondered when, or if, he'd ever see his friend again.

Chapter Forty-Nine

"Can I talk with you a minute?" asked Steropes from the doorway. Commander Sheppard had released the Psiclopes from the brig the day before. Once cooler heads had prevailed, he realized that they hadn't really broken any laws that he was aware of. He really had no reason to hold them, aside from their physical safety. Since their release, Brontes and Arges had mostly decided to stay in their rooms. Most people had heard about Steropes' exploits on Keppler-22 'b,' so he was relatively safe from harm; no one wanted to mess with a tai chi master.

"What?" asked Calvin, annoyance in his voice, as he looked up from his paperwork. Just because the Psiclopes hadn't done anything 'illegal' didn't mean that Calvin was OK with their actions.

"I just wanted you to know that I had nothing to do with the Chinese," Steropes said. "I believe that Brontes and Arges once told you that our society recognizes four paths that can be used to achieve ultimate enlightenment." Calvin nodded. "My wife followed Karma, or the path of right action," continued Steropes. "She would never have allowed them to do that if she were still alive, nor would I have allowed it to happen in her memory, had I known about it ahead of time. I know it doesn't make any difference, but I just wanted you to know." He turned to leave.

"Hey, Steropes," Calvin called. Steropes turned back around. "Thanks," Calvin said. "I'm sorry about Olympos."

Steropes nodded once and left. Calvin could just barely hear him say, "Me, too," as he walked down the hall.

Chapter Fifty

"I've got gate activation!" cried the airman who monitored the stargate entry system for Strategic Command's Joint Functional Component Command (JFCC) for Space. "Activation of Stargate #2!" He paused. "It's got the right Identification, Friend or Foe (IFF) code, but oh my God, it's huge! That can't be right. It's over a mile long! The nose of the ship is already starting to clear the mine field. If we don't arm the mines now, we're not going to be able to use them!"

"Do you have communications with the ship?"

"No, they haven't said anything yet," said the tech. "Should I arm the mines?"

"It's got the right IFF codes?" asked the supervisor.

"Yes, it does," repeated the tech.

The communications gear came to life with a burst of static. "*Skywatch, Skywatch, this is the Terran battleship* Terra, *arriving through Stargate #2.*"

The supervisor looked at the tech. "Did I miss something? When did we get a freakin' battleship?" he asked.

The tech shrugged his shoulders. "No idea," he answered. "I didn't know we had one, either, but I'm just an airman. No one tells me anything."

"The voice sounds funny, too," said the supervisor, beginning to get a bad feeling. "I hope it's really one of ours. This is way above my pay grade. Get the White House on the phone."

"It *is* a funny accent," agreed the tech. "Maybe it's one of the foreigners on the radio. Why don't you ask them?"

"I think I will," said the supervisor. "*We don't recognize your ship,*" he called. "*Can I get the name and rank of your commander, please?*"

The video communications screen flashed as it came to life. "*Sure,*" the voice said. The screen cleared to reveal a tiger's face, and the supervisor jumped back unconsciously from it. "*Our captain is Captain Lorena Griffin, Terran Navy,*" said the tiger. The view on the screen pulled back to reveal the entire bridge. A mix of humans, tigers and a couple of therapods was scattered across it with a human sitting in the large captain's chair in the center.

"*Hi Skywatch,*" said Captain Griffin. "*Captain Griffin reporting back with the latest additions to our navy. It sure is good to see that you guys are still here.*"

Epilogue

"I've got gate activation!" cried the airman monitoring the stargate entry system. "*Oh my God! Activation of Stargate #1!*"

"Get me an ID on the contact, ASAP!" replied his supervisor, who knew that Stargate #1 was the 'front door' into the Solar System. This was the first time that stargate had been activated since they began watching it. He had a bad feeling.

The airman watched his display, tapping nervously. "It's battlecruiser sized, sir," said the airman. The computers continued to analyze the data. "Based on the computer models from the Mrowry, the computers say...Oh my God, *it's a Drakul!*" he finally called, fear heavy in his voice. "Sensors are showing a second gate activation...it's a second battlecruiser. Third activation. Holy shit! *Battleship!*"

"Activate all defenses!" ordered the supervisor. He turned to the communications position, "Call the moon! Get the *Vella Gulf* and any available fighters manned and launched, *ASAP!*" He looked at his assistant. "Get me the president, *NOW!*"

Time had just run out for the Earth. The Drakuls had found them.

* * * * *

417

The following is an excerpt from Book 3 of The Theogony:

Terra Stands Alone

Chris Kennedy

Available from Chris Kennedy Publishing

Summer, 2014

eBook and Paperback

Any problem can be solved with enough high explosives...

Calvin looked up as Lieutenant Finn walked into the room. "Do you have something for us?" he asked.

"Yes, I do," replied Lieutenant Finn. "I knew there were a variety of bombs and warheads in the database; it was just a matter of finding the right one. I was looking for something that was big enough to destroy the station, yet small enough to be man-portable...or at least cyborg-portable," he said, looking at Staff Sergeant Randolph. "Can you guys carry something that weighs 300 or so pounds?" he asked.

Staff Sergeant Randolph paused, doing the calculations. "I think we can do that," he said, looking at Staff Sergeant Dantone, who nodded. "It will take readjusting some things and maybe taking a smaller weapons load, but yeah, it can be done."

"Okay, that's great. There was this one bomb that they called the Mother of All Bombs," Lieutenant Finn said. "That would have done the job very well. But it was way too big to carry. It was about 1,000 pounds, which I didn't think would work." Both cyborgs shook their heads. "That was what I thought, so I went with the other one. There are two of them waiting in the replicator room."

"What are they?" asked Night.

"They are four-stage hydrogen bombs," said Lieutenant Finn. "Each of them has a yield of about 100 megatons. That is equivalent to almost 3,000 times the combined power of the bombs that destroyed Hiroshima and Nagasaki. Hopefully, that will be enough."

"*3,000* times the size?" asked Calvin. "Yeah, that should do it..."

ABOUT THE AUTHOR

Chris Kennedy is a former aviator with over 3,000 hours flying attack and reconnaissance aircraft for the United States Navy, including many missions supporting U.S. Special Forces. He has also been an elementary school principal and has enjoyed 18 seasons as a softball coach. He is currently working as an Instructional Systems Designer for the Navy.

Titles by Chris Kennedy:

"Red Tide: The Chinese Invasion of Seattle" – Available Now

"Occupied Seattle" – Available Now

"Janissaries: Book One of The Theogony" – Available Now

"When the Gods Aren't Gods: Book Two of The Theogony"
– Available Now

"Terra Stands Alone: Book Three of The Theogony"
– Coming Soon!

* * * * *

Connect with Chris Kennedy Online:

Facebook: https://www.facebook.com/chriskennedypublishing.biz

Blog: http://chriskennedypublishing.com/

Twitter: @ChrisKennedy110

Want to be immortalized in a future book?
Join the Red Shirt List on the blog!

Made in the USA
Charleston, SC
20 September 2016